I0524381

Ill Winds Blowing Across a Toubled Sea

- The Journey's End -

A NOVEL

By

Mark M. McMillin

Hephaestus Publishing

Praise for *The Butcher's Daughter*

"... [A] pleasurable and action-packed read ... a delicious spin to the otherwise tired clichés of male captains ... the joy of the open seas - as well as the danger churning below - pulses throughout this rip-roaring, hearty tale of the high seas." - *Kirkus Reviews*

"A wonderful novel in the best tradition of maritime literature ... authentic and rich with details, the characters are alive and passionate, and the plot is full of thrilling action, intense drama, and stunning surprises ... exhilarating adventure ... an unforgettable journey ..." - *The Columbia Review*

Praise for *Blood for Blood*

"McMillin's prose ... is as full of romance and swagger as one would expect in a tale of a pirate captain ... the novel upholds the fine tradition of old high-seas adventure stories with a pace that doesn't let up until the final cutlass clatters to the deck." - *Kirkus Reviews*

"McMillin skillfully recreates the time period with clever insertions of historical events interwoven with Mary's fictional tale ... the battle with Spanish forces in Panama is a nail-biting sequel to one of the most famous occurrence[s] in Drake's Caribbean escapades ..." - *Cindy Vallar, the Pirate Lady*

Praise for *Ill Winds Blowing Across a Troubled Sea*

"... [P]aced like an adventure movie, filled with sea battles, colorful bit players, and double crosses ... a rousing, sprawling yarn about two indefatigable pirate women." - *Kirkus Reviews*

Ill Winds Blowing Across a Troubled Sea
- *The Journey's End* -

Copyright © Mark McMillin 2022

Author's website: www.PrivateerLukeRyan.com

ISBN: 978-0-9838179-8-7
ISBN-10: 0-9838179-8-7

Hephaestus Publishing: www.hephaestuspublishing.com

Ill Winds is a work of historical fiction. Apart from well-known actual people, events and locales described herein, all names, characters, places and incidents are the product of the author's imagination. Any resemblance to current events or locales or to living persons is pure coincidence.

This book in its printed form is designed for the reading public only. All dramatic rights in it are fully protected by copyright, and no public or private performances, professional or amateur, and no public readings for profit may be given without the express written permission of the author and payment of a royalty. Those disregarding the author's rights expose themselves to prosecution.

This book has been printed in the United States of America. Without limiting the rights under copyright reserved above, no part of this publication (except for any artwork in the public domain used herein) may be reproduced, stored in or introduced into a retrieval system, or transmitted in any form or by any means (electronic, mechanical, photocopying, recording or otherwise), without the prior written permission of both the copyright owner and the publisher.

The pictures used in this book are faithful photographic reproductions of original works of art, which are in the public domain in the United States and in those countries with a copyright term of life of the artist plus one hundred years or fewer or were offered as free downloads on the internet

Books by the Author:

The Tales of Captain Luke Ryan, Ben Franklin's Most Dangerous Privateer Series:

Gather the Shadowmen (The Lords of the Ocean)
Prince of the Atlantic
Napoleon's Gold

The Tales of Captain Bloody Mary, The Queen's Privateer Series:

The Butcher's Daughter (A Journey Between Worlds)
Blood for Blood (The Uncertain Journey)
Ill Winds Blowing Across a Troubled Sea (The Journey's End)

The World

Orbis Terrarum by the Dutch astronomer, cartographer and clergyman
Petrus Plancius (published in 1590)

Foreword

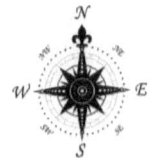

Cada mástil debe sostener su propia vela.
Each mast must hold its own sail.

- The wisdom of a Spanish mariner
from long ago...

BOOK I

Elizabeth & the Company
(The VOC)

Chapter One

Early Spring, 1603

Like a sudden, fleeting cloudburst on a warm summer day, or the grains of sand slipping through an hourglass when time is not your friend, seven years, two years and one year had slipped by with unsettling quickness. Anniversaries of moment.

Seven years had passed since I, barely more than a girl of fourteen, had fled from the Caribbean as a stowaway aboard Mary's swift battlecruiser *Phantom* to escape my intended betrothed. Mary at once loved me and I her and she agreed to keep me. In that same year Mary had also exacted her terrible revenge against the *Síol Faolcháin*, freeing us all from a vicious cycle of endless bloodletting, pain and sorrow.

For the next few years, I applied myself with maddening passion and boundless energy, learning everything I could about ships, sailing, navigation and the sea. Mary indulged my ravenous appetite. I worked hard to acquire the skills I needed to win her approval and once I had, she turned me over to her dark, mysterious Turk who began training me in the ways of deadly combat alongside his other young disciple, Robert Shaw. Day by day my skills improved until I was a match for most any man.

Two years had passed since Mary had summoned me to her great cabin one evening with all her officers present. She had asked me for my binding oath of loyalty, a blood oath, which I freely gave as I knelt before her. After she stabbed the dead fish lying on the table through the heart, after she anointed my head with seawater and spoke the sacred words of initiation I had longed to hear, I was accepted into the clan by one and all. I became one of Mary's officers.

And alas, one year had passed since the blackest of days shattered our lives, since a freakish storm in the dead of night off the eastern coast of Florida had overtaken us with little warning. I watched in horror as a part of *Phantom's* aft rail gave way. I watched helplessly as Mary tumbled overboard, as a surge of water from a cruel and pitiless sea dragged her off into oblivion. We searched and searched those waters for days but never found her or her body. Mary's tragic death was a terrible, heart wrenching blow to us all.

Within days after losing Mary my own father, his body riddled with the cancer, died too while resting peacefully in his bed at his hacienda near Havana. Rodriguez Miguel de Cortés y Ovando had been a wealthy man, an entrepreneur who had made his fortune over the years smuggling goods between the New World and the old one in partnership with Mary. Between the monies Mary had bequeathed to me in her last will and testament, and the inheritance my sister Isabella and I shared equally as my father had left no male heirs, I became a modestly wealthy woman.

For no particular reason I knew of, I solemnly reflected on these matters alone in the dark while sitting at the table of my new, spacious great cabin, as our ship peacefully rode anchor. Like Mary, I am susceptible to gloomier moods at times and relish my solitude. I missed her dearly. I missed her unfaltering love and friendship. I missed her wisdom, her clarity of thought and good counsel.

Prior to setting out on our last voyage to the West Indies, I had commissioned the same two maritime architects Mary had once hired to refurbish *Phantom* to find me a new ship suitable for war. One fellow, a Dutchman from Amsterdam went by the curious name of Mr. Ink and the other, a Frenchman from Boulogne, called himself Mr. Blot. Messrs. Ink & Blot, Esqs., both aliases of course. Mary had taught me never to be miserly when it came to investing in the business. She had always lavished money on the ships and had bought the best and so would I.

Upon our return to Westport the two men had been waiting for us with a masterpiece tied against the pier. Our new square-rigged frigate, a seven-hundred-ton beast with a rugged frame and graceful lines, was over two hundred feet long at the waterline. Her masts and spars could carry an impressive forty thousand square feet of canvas. Her hull was double planked for strength. Except for the great war galleons, she promised to be the equal of any ship and then some.

I promptly had our lads offload *Phantom*'s New World cargo. I promptly had them transfer *Phantom*'s guns - twenty-six twelve-pounders and four long-barreled chasers, two nine-pounders mounted at the bow and two at the stern - over to the new ship and then I took her out for her trials. We sailed past Clare Island and well into the Atlantic. I put her through her paces. She proved herself sound and eager and though not as fast or as nimble as *Phantom*, she was a larger, more formidable ship. I know not why but the crew chose the name *Ghostrunner* for her and I approved.

After returning to Westport, Jacob Atwood and I, as joint owners of the aging *Phantom*, sold her off to a local shipyard and then I gave my men two months' liberty. But our voyage to the West Indies had been dismal from beginning to end and sadly unprofitable and I was forced to send each man home with wages any fieldhand would scoff at. Following my father's death, and with Mary gone, our political clout, and many of our important merchantry connections in the West Indies, had quickly withered away and died with them. We could no longer compete smuggling goods in and out of the New World.

Neither could we supplement our wealth here and there by seizing Spanish ships for prize money as English privateers. While King Phillip II of Spain and Queen Elizabeth I of England had lived there could be no peace between the two kingdoms. But with the death of Phillip II in 1598, and the recent passing of England's Tudor Queen only days before our return to Ireland, King Phillip III of Spain and King James I - the newly-minted sovereign lord of England, Scotland, Wales and Ireland - had decided to make peace after nearly twenty years of exhausting, costly war. The world was changing and to survive we needed to change with it.

With the sounds of water slapping against the rudder below, a squeaky ceiling lantern swaying back and forth overhead and a lonely buoy bell tolling in the distance following me across the cabin, I went to open the ship's stern windows for fresh air. I paused to take in the street lanterns flickering along the harbor's sleepy waterfront, barely visible through a thick sea mist, before returning to my chair to reread a document the secretive John Martin had left with me earlier. Martin, once Mary's benefactor at the English Court, had remained a good and steadfast friend after her death. He had powerful friends in the Dutch government and had acquired, through some chicanery I suspect, a commission on our behalf to sail for the newly-formed *Vereenigde Oostindische Compagnie*, the United East India Company, or simply known as the VOC or the Company. The Dutch government had forced several Dutch trading companies, old rivals, to join as one to create the first corporation in the world to offer its stock to the public.

I spread the flag Martin had left behind with the commission across the table. The Company's standard, with the distinctive VOC monogram imprinted in the center of three horizontal stripes of red, white and blue - the colors of the seven Dutch provinces - caught the eye. And though the thought of working for others, especially foreigners, troubled me, Martin had been most persuasive about the new company's prospects and the potential riches we might find in the East.

When I heard a firm hand rapping at my cabin door, I told the man to enter. Atwood, a one-eyed bear of a man, bent down to step through the doorway, dragging my godson by the collar with him. Mary had named me guardian of her son James in her will. I loved and cared for the boy as if he were my own.

"What's this Jacob?" I asked.

"I caught someone fighting in town again," Atwood replied and grunted. "James broke another boy's nose."

I bit my lip to keep myself from smiling. "Sit yourself down Master James Hunter Ryan," I ordered sharply and pointed to a chair across the table from me. The boy, barely nine years of age, dutifully removed his woolen skullcap and took a seat.

"*Eso es un ojo morado impresionante que tienes señor,*" I said, reverting to my native tongue. "That's quite a shiner mister."

Silence.

"You bloodied another boy?" I asked. "Who threw the first punch?"

Silence.

I narrowed my eyes to show James that I meant business. "Well, what say you?"

James squirmed around in his chair for a bit and cleared his throat before answering. "The son-of-a-whore called me a liar Elizabeth; he said my grandfather was a filthy, street beggar, not Lord O'Malley."

Eoghan Dubhdara O'Malley had been a powerful Irish chieftain during his life. With men-at-arms and a fleet of well-armed ships, he had controlled County Mayo along with vast stretches of the Irish west coast. He was the last of the Kings of Umaill and Mary had been his bastard daughter. As far as James knew he was Mary's flesh and blood - though the truth was something different.

"And this trivial insult was worth a broken nose and your black eye?"

James sheepishly looked away and fell silent again. Mary's death had struck the boy particularly hard.

"Violence begets violence young man," I said with some disdain for my own hypocrisy. Ours was a world of blood, violence and vengeance.

Atwood laid a huge, gnarly hand upon the boy's shoulder. "With all that vigor you have Master James, I could use you up on deck with a bucket, a holystone and some soap. Start with the poop deck. You can work-off some of that pent-up anger you're carrying around by scrubbing the decks down clean."

"Aye, sir," the boy answered respectfully.

Atwood plucked the Company's flag off the table as James shuffled out of my cabin. "You intend to fly this pretty piece of cloth off the mizzen gaff darlin'?"

"Not without unanimous consent," I said. "But what choice do we have Jacob?"

"There always be choices Elizabeth. Mary never much fancied the notion of sailing to Asia. Too many unknowns. Too much risk."

When I answered Atwood with a disapproving frown, he sighed and nodded. "Auck, very well. Assemble the lads?"

"The hour is late but yes, please Jacob."

One-by-one the ships' officers - who liked to call themselves Mary's Men while in port to my great annoyance - filed into my great cabin. As was our custom my brothers stood by their chairs until I took my seat at the head of the table. Mary had not named a successor but, as her promising protégé and charged with the responsibility of raising her son, and by far the wealthiest amongst us, I more or less assumed the role. No one had objected.

I glanced around the table to consider each face just as Mary had once done. Next to me stood Jacob Atwood, an affable if feisty giant from Scotland with a wild mane of red hair and a patch over one eye. He was an exceptional seaman and a competent tactician in battle. For years he had been Mary's second-in-command. Next to Atwood stood Michael MacGyver, a serious, red-bearded Irishman from Rush who possessed a genius for things mechanical. And then there was Henry, a short, lean Carib Indian from Guadeloupe. The warlike Carib are the Vikings of the Caribbean and the Spanish had always stayed clear of them. Henry had pierced his ears with a dozen golden rings, each ring signifying some brave deed in battle. He had tattooed a sword over a battle axe across his chest. I felt my heart quicken when he flashed his sharp fangs at me. Some say the Carib are cannibals. An African Blackamoor as dark as night with rippling muscles named Kinkae stood like a rock next to Henry. Mary had rescued Kinkae and his men from Trinidad slavers many years ago. Being Spanish and accustomed to having slaves in my father's house as a child, I did not know what to make of Kinkae at first. Tattooed around his massive arms were a pair of matching barbed whips to remind him of his days in chains. Maurice, a handsome light-skinned mulatto with a physique like chiseled stone, a Cimarron from Panama, a man who never flustered and always had a ready smile, stood next to Kinkae. At one time Maurice had sailed with the pirate Guillaume Le Testu but was now the master of his own powerful battlecruiser, the eighteen-gun man-o'-war *Cerberus*, and sailed with us. Next to Maurice stood a dashing figure of a man from Westport, and my lover, Robert Shaw. He winked playfully at me when the others weren't looking. And then leaning against the wall in the shadows there was Mary's mysterious Turk from Istanbul, her dark assassin, Mustafa Agah Efendi, acknowledged by one and all to be the deadliest man alive. Following Mary's death, he kept his distance from the rest of us and never had much to say.

Except for Shaw, who was about my age, these were the men Mary had handpicked for her lieutenants years ago, long before Shaw or I had come along. Every man was a fierce fighter, a fine mariner, cunning and staunchly loyal.

As I took my seat, my brothers took theirs. "We have this very fine warship," I said while pouring each man a glass of wine just as Mary used to do. "Now we must decide how to best use her."

"With the death of Queen Elizabeth," Atwood said, "England and Spain will soon make peace. That doesn't bode well for us."

"That's the rumor floating about town," I replied. "I've also heard the Dutch are indifferent to any such peace treaty. They're looking for Englishmen willing to sail out as privateers against the Spanish whilst they continue their struggle for independence."

Maurice cleared his throat. "Won't be like the Caribbean, Liz," he said softly. "Iberian ships plying the waters between Spain and the Netherlands will sail in convoy and will be well-protected by some of Spain's best war galleons. High risk there if we sail as Dutch privateers."

"Yes, I quite agree."

"Without your father's friends Elizabeth," MacGyver interjected as he poured himself another glass of wine, "we'll go broke if we return to the West Indies."

"So," Atwood said, "tell us about this Dutch commission from Martin."

"The Dutch government," I said, "has empowered the Dutch East India Company with broad powers. The Company holds exclusive trading rights in India from Surat to Calcutta, in Java, the Spice Islands, Malacca, Siam, Canton, Formosa and beyond - as far as to Japan. The Company boasts it will someday have its own navy and its own army. Until that day comes the Company is hiring adventurers willing to make the journey east."

Atwood grunted. "I think Spain and Portugal might have something to say about these bold Dutch claims. To reach Indonesia I hear is a cruise of about eight months or more."

"For large fleets and slower ships making only a few modest knots per hour, yes. The other day, under very favorable conditions I admit, we squeezed almost twelve knots out of *Ghostrunner* as you know

Jacob."

"'Twas an exhilarating pace to be sure for such a big ship," Atwood agreed. "But how often do we sail in ideal conditions with a clean bottom, free from the worms and barnacles that slow ships down?"

I placed my hand over Atwood's hand. "I concede your point Jacob. Even if we can shave a month or two off the customary time, this voyage will be long and difficult, longer and harder than what we're accustomed to."

Atwood squeezed my hand reassuringly. "And more perilous."

"We are gathered around this table to discuss all options," I said.

"And Mary," Atwood replied with a nod, "would have approved, even encouraged this discussion."

"*Mucho gracias mi amigo*," I said. "I'm not advocating one particular course of action or another. I'm simply stating facts. We're losing money in the Caribbean. There is no profitable trade for us in Europe without risking war with one of the clans. Mustafa has many times warned us against dipping our toes into the Mediterranean or the Black Sea as those waters are infested with brigands of the worst kind. The profits in spices from Indonesia can be substantial. We've all heard about the astonishing success of Jacob van Neck's expedition to the Spice Islands. He left Texel in May of '98 with eight ships and returned in July of '99 - little more than a one-year journey - with a great fortune."

"They say," Maurice added, "Neck's financial backers made profits of four hundred percent."

"An enticing prospect, yes?" I asked no one in particular.

We drank and discussed the matter for some time before we voted. Our Ten Rules required a unanimous decision on any proposal to put the ships and the lives of our men at great risk. I had feared Atwood might vote against me but in the end, all agreed to sail for the VOC. Atwood reminded us that Mary had always sailed with three ships and with three ships she had always prevailed in battle and so we also agreed to purchase a third vessel for our grand adventure east to replace MacGyver's ship *Diablo*, which we had to abandon near one of the Caribbean islands, after she broke her back upon a jagged rock hidden just beneath the waves.

We went ashore to Shaw's splendid tavern *Banshee's Lament* after I adjourned our council of war to fill our bellies with wholesome food and to quench our thrust with good wine and new ale. Once we finished supper, I sent Atwood and MacGyver off to see their homes and families. The two men would share a coach as far as Dublin where Atwood would then catch a ship for Ayr across the Irish Sea while MacGyver continued on to Rush. Maurice and his French and Cimarron crew departed for France with *Cerberus* while Kinkae and his Blackamoors, along with Henry and his Carib warriors, remained in Westport with Efendi, Shaw, little James and me.

The following morning, I took the skiff and rowed ashore alone. I walked into town, borrowed a horse and rode to Cruach Phádraig, meaning Saint Patrick's Stack in Gaelic, or known as the Reek by the local town folk though I know not why. The mountain had been one of Mary's favorite spots to escape the world, to meditate in solitude.

I climbed to the top of the mountain on foot, spread a blanket across the ground and plopped myself down with a round of cheese and a bottle of wine as Mary had liked to do. The day was bright and clear and deliciously warm for early spring. I took in the startling beauty all around me. The sea below, the color of lapis lazuli and churning with white caps, stretched across the horizon for as far as the eye could see while tiny fishing trawlers off Clare Island lazily rose up and down on the swells, dragging their drift nets behind them. Then I closed my eyes, sat back and let the magic of the mountain seep into my bones and when I awoke from a deep and comforting sleep, I felt refreshed and full of energy and hurried back to Westport.

I stopped at Shaw's tavern to write letters to Messrs. Ink and Blot, the two men having already departed Westport on a ship bound for Ostend, and instructed them to make haste for Boulogne to find me a modest vessel of good quality, a ship to complement *Ghostrunner*. I wanted a French-built ship, the best, and included my specific requirements for speed, size and armament. The cost would just about break me, but I knew Atwood was right. Sailing with a small squadron of three ships would greatly improve our chances against any outlaws we might encounter along the way to the East Indies.

I gave my letters to the barkeep to mail and then went looking for Shaw. I longed to feel his touch, to feel his bare skin against mine and found my lover in a back storeroom looking for one thing or another. I snuck up behind him, wrapped my arms around his waist an began nibbling on his ear.

"*Señor*," I said in a low, lusty voice.

"Ah, *mi bella dama*," he replied cheerfully. "Where have you been hidding?"

"I was out riding," I answered as I slowly slipped my hand down inside his trousers. Mary had taught me about lovemaking, about all the carnal pleasures. She had taught me how to delight a man and how to be delighted by him. She had taught me things a young girl doesn't learn from her father and I found myself the richer or it.

His manhood instantly turned thick and hard in my hand as I stroked him. He turned to embrace me. He kissed me passionately on the mouth and quickly undid my trousers.

"Take me," I pleaded, aroused by what we were about to do with only a thin wall standing between us and the tavern's patrons on the other side.

Seized with raw, untamable lust, Shaw spun me around, pushed my face against the wall and took me from behind. He spread my legs, eased himself inside of me and started thrusting, slowly at first and then with increasing vigor. I cooed softly at first but then had to bite my lip to stifle my raucous moaning as Shaw drove himself deeper and harder into me. I savored every guilty moment as we reached that wonderful place of ecstasy together. I felt warm and fulfilled and I for one was well-satisfied.

"You're an amorous vixen this day," Shaw said and kissed me on the nose.

"And you are a wonderfully, wicked lover," I replied as I pulled my trousers up.

"Supper?"

"*Sí*. I'm famished..."

The rest of our days in port were tedious and dull. *Ghostrunner* needed very little maintenance and there wasn't much for my Blackamoors or Carib to do. I allowed small numbers of them to go ashore from time-to-time but constantly worried about trouble with the Irish, a people who did not care much for dark-skinned foreigners from strange lands. The Spanish are far more tolerant.

As most of the Blackamoors and Carib had families in Guadeloupe, I wrote letters on behalf of each man, forty-two letters in all, explaining to their loved ones that their men would be gone for a year or more as we intended to sail to the East Indies, though I didn't know if anyone on the island could read. Neither was I quite sure how to deliver my letters as the Spanish post service didn't stop in Guadeloupe and so I decided to entrust the letters with a dear friend in Santo Domingo named Esmeralda, who had been my father's able governess and my loving maidservant. Esmeralda, a cultured Castilian Negro Ladino, a clever, resourceful woman, would find a way to get my letters to Guadeloupe.

And, then I received my own letter from Mr. Blot in Boulogne informing me that he had found two ships meeting my requirements. I left Efendi in Westport to watch over our men and immediately caught a carriage to Dublin, bringing my lover with me, where we boarded an English packet ship bound for Boulogne.

Chapter Two

I was so very cold. My clothes were heavy. My limbs were numb. As towering swells lifted me up and down in the dark, I fought against an angry, frothy sea with everything I had to keep myself from drowning. But when my struggle became too hard, when all seemed lost, I made my peace with my God and stopped fighting.

Something struck me from behind as I sank. The mind of course always imagines the worst, especially at night in the water. I frantically clawed my way back to the surface and filled my lungs with air. I spun around in a circle expecting to see a shark's fin against the bolts of lightning flashing overhead but instead found a length of flotsam, a section of smooth, varnished wood with jagged edges at both ends bobbing up and down alongside me - a true Godsend. I grabbed ahold of *Phantom's* splintered railing and held on tight.

But when my imagination conjured up the worst again, I wanted to let go and die. Had I doomed us all with a miscalculation in navigation? Had my poor *Phantom* broken apart upon the rocks? Did I alone survive? I wept as I imagined a ravenous sea devouring my ship and crew.

When morning broke, in calmer waters, I watched the gale that had ravished *Phantom* with such terrible violence just hours before moving off to the northeast. I looked in every direction but saw no land or sails. I was alone, clinging to a piece of driftwood, floating aimlessly across a barren sea.

I refused to abandoned hope. We had been hugging the coast of Florida when the storm had smashed into us. We had been within sight of land. I covered my head with my vest to protect myself from the sun. I pointed my makeshift raft west and started paddling clumsily in my boots. To the west was my salvation.

One day slipped by and then two. Two days became three and then four. I survived on the *ch'arki*, meaning dried meat in the Quechuan language of the Incas, I had stuffed into my pockets before my tumble into the sea and drank the rainwater that fell briefly each afternoon. I grew weaker by the day. And when I became too exhausted to paddle, I took my belt, lashed myself to my makeshift raft and drifted with the currents. To where I had no inkling.

For days I floated in and out of consciousness and just when God seemed to have forsaken me, just when all seemed lost, I felt a strong pair of arms lift me from the water. Two Indians dressed in nothing more than buckskin breechcloth pulled me into their canoe. They gently laid me down next to a pile of flopping fish and gave me water before I closed my eyes and drifted off into a deep and dreamless sleep.

When I awoke, I found myself naked, wrapped in a blanket and lying next to a fire inside a mud hut with a squat, elderly woman wearing a frock of buckskin grinning at me. Her skin was as dry and as wrinkled as parched soil. She wore her long, grey hair parted down the middle with braided tails resting against her bosom. She handed me a wooden ladle of fresh water and after I took a few sips, she exchanged the ladle for a clay bowl filled with chunks of roasted fish mixed with slices of orange and blackberries. As I greedily stuffed the morsels into my mouth, I anxiously glanced around the hut looking for my clothes and breathed a sigh of relief when I saw them hanging on a line to dry - for hidden inside the heels of my boots, and sown into my trousers, were twenty gold doubloons, gold I'd need to survive.

The following day two young women came for me. They combed and braided my hair. They helped me into a buckskin frock, slipped leather sandals on my feet and led me by the hands through their village. Judging by the gawking eyes we passed, I'm fairly certain I was the first white woman any of the villagers had ever seen before. Most of the men went about bare-chested with only breechcloth to cover themselves though a few wore baggy trousers in the Spanish style. The women wore frocks like mine or skirts woven from Spanish moss or from blades of long grass. I saw no hostility in any face. I was allowed to walk through the village unbound.

The size of the village surprised me. I saw hundreds of round huts with thatched roofs and clay brick walls wrapped in plaited palmetto leaves sprawled across acres of flat land. I saw impressive five story wood-framed buildings too built on stilts to keep them off the ground. What surprised me most was the stone church we walked past, a church no bigger than a chapel, with a plain wooden cross rising from the center of a simple wooden dome.

When we reached a long rectangular building, encircled by a ring of black facemasks placed atop wooden spikes, masks expressing all the emotions like joy, love, anger, sadness, pain, confusion and so forth, a man with long, white hair and a deeply furrowed brow stepped outside to greet me. I noted the gold crucifix dangling from a strip of leather around his neck. He spoke to me in Spanish.

"Welcome," he said. "Do you speak Spanish?"

"I do."

"You mumbled strange words in your sleep."

"I come from a place called Ireland where folks speak English, Gaelic or even Latin."

"Is this Ireland near Spain?"

"No. Ireland is a large island far north of Spain. Ireland is a part of the English kingdom."

"English? England?"

"Yes, the same."

"Ah, I have heard of this England. Our fishermen found you floating on the water. You were on a ship?"

"Yes."

"The sea swallowed your ship?"

"I'm not sure. We were overtaken by a sudden storm and I was swept overboard when the ship's rail gave way. It was dark. The waves were high. I couldn't see what happened to my ship or crew."

"What is this rail?"

"'Tis like a fence."

"Ah. What lands were you sailing to?"

"To Ireland, to home."

"Home, good. God must favor you. When you are stronger, we will talk more. I am Tayhoot."

"I'm Mary."

"Oh, you share the name of our Lord's blessed mother. I am pleased to know you, Mary. We are the Tequesta, one of the great tribes."

"And I am honored make your acquintance Tayhoot. The Spanish have been to your village? Your Spanish is excellent."

"Yes. We know the Spanish well. Many years ago, they built a small fort near our village to keep the French out. They were good neighbors. Then one day they collected their things and left."

"The Spanish call this land Florida?"

"Yes. The name of our village is Chequescha."

"*Che-ques-cha...* The bay, does it have a name?"

"The Spanish call those waters Bahía Vizcaína."

I allowed myself a slight smile for now I knew where I was. The Indian village was not far from Cayo Hueso, Key West, and the Keys were not far from Cuba and from Cuba I could easily make my way back to Ireland.

"You are a chief?" I asked.

"I am a priest, a healer, a soothsayer," Tayhoot replied and held up his crucifix. "I can read bones and the entrails of birds. My people look to me for council, but I am no leader. Our chief died from the bite of a spider whilst on the hunt some time ago. He had no sons, no heirs to take his place. Soon I pray my people will choose a true chief for I grow weary of the burden."

"So, you are a holy man?"

"I am a holy man."

"You wear a crucifix."

"Yes. I learned about Jesus from Jesuit missionaries who came to Chequescha with the Spanish soldiers when I was a boy. The Jesuits built the small monastery nearby. When the soldiers left the monks, all but one or two, left with them. Those who remained behind have long since passed away."

"You are Christian?"

"I pray to many gods, the Christ child amongst them. For me, the story of our Savior is very powerful. But I pray to the deer as well."

"The deer are gods?"

"No, the deer are messengers to the sun god who speaks to us through the deer."

"I see. Well, I am most grateful to the men who rescued me."

"A charitable, good Christian deed - yes?"

"Aye. Am I a prisoner?"

"Prisoner? No, you are free to stay or leave as you please. You are our guest."

"What is to become of me?"

"What do you desire?"

"I wish to return home."

"You have no wish to search for the fabled Fountain of Youth?"

I laughed. "If the great Ponce de León couldn't find it, what chance have I? There is an island not far from here called Cuba. Do you know it?"

"I've heard of this island."

"Do your people ever sail to Cuba?"

"No, no. We have no tall ships. We Tequesta are the children of the land not the sea. The place the fishermen found you is as far from shore as any Tequesta will venture."

"Pity."

"Despair not my child. All is as it should be."

Chapter Three

Shaw and I arrived in Boulogne in a fine drizzle. The air had turned chilly for mid-spring. We walked straight for the *King's Arms*, a modest tavern along the waterfront where Mr. Blot, our French architect, kept a room. We warmed ourselves next the tavern's fireplace, had a quick drink with Blot, just one, and then hurried down to the shipyards in the rain to see what the Frenchman had found for us. Both vessels were in drydock having their bottoms graved in preparation for being sheathed in lead.

I was elated after we finished inspecting the ships. The vessels were nearly identical, I could barely tell them apart. Both ships were frigate-rigged, weighed nearly three-hundred-tons apiece and could each carry as many as twenty medium calibre great guns.

During his due diligence Blot had learned that the ships had originally been built as a matching pair of swift interceptors for the French navy but when the principal investor defaulted on his loans with the shipyard halfway through construction, the shipyard owner, a fellow named Jehan Maunoys, took possession of the frigates after he had the investor hauled off to debtors' prison. But precious time had been lost and the French navy cancelled the contracts, forcing Maunoys to finish building the ships with his own money. Unfortunately for Maunoys, there wasn't much of a market for selling or leasing war frigates and both ships sat idle in port. Folks around town said Maunoys was broke.

When Shaw, Blot and I returned to the tavern the next day to meet Maunoys to discuss purchasing one of his fine vessels, the ornery little fellow with greasy, unkept hair and bad teeth stubbornly insisted we buy the pair despite his desperate need for cash. After a bit of haggling, and a round or two of drinks, I finally agreed to take both frigates off his hands at a better than fair price and paid the man in full with a thick wad of bank notes. As luck would have it my Dutch architect Ink had already located thirty-two great guns of high quality for me sitting in a warehouse nearby in Ostend. Though eight less than I wanted, the guns were bronze, long-barreled nine-pounders forged in Sweden by some of Europe's finest blacksmiths.

After I paid Blot a handsome commission for his services and sent him on his way, I took Shaw to a hostel called *le Porc-épic* in the center of Boulogne where I knew our favorite Cimarron spent most of his days whenever he was in port. I led Shaw down a narrow, stone staircase and into a spacious cellar, a cellar that had been transformed into a refined establishment favored by gentlemen of substance known aptly as *la Grotte*. The walls and support columns were paneled in light, knotted wood. A dozen wrought iron chandeliers hanging from a fancy coffered ceiling provided ample light. In the middle of the cellar stood a circular brick bar surrounded by small tables for dining and larger tables for games of chance. We spotted Maurice playing dice at one of the tables.

"Are you winning or losing?" Shaw called out as we made our way towards Maurice while passing by a bevy of young beauties on the hunt floating in-between the great room and to various private rooms off to the side.

Maurice spun around on his heels and offered us a friendly grin. The Cimarron, the word means wild or untamed in Spanish, was a fine-looking man with broad shoulders and an easy-going manner, though there was a certain sorrow in his eyes that never seemed to fade, not even when he smiled.

"Winning of course!" he answered jovially as he tossed the dice across the table without looking. Another good throw judging by the hoots I heard around the room and the backslapping that followed.

"Good," I said. "You're buying."

"'Twould be my pleasure my lady," Maurice replied as he scooped-up his winnings and then led us to a quiet table against a far wall, stopping briefly to order a pitcher of ale and three buckets of oysters from a buxom tavern wench.

"What brings you both to France?" he asked as he slapped the woman playfully on the bottom before she sauntered off.

"Elizabeth purchased two frigates today," Shaw answered as we took our seats.

"*Deux? Excellente ma dame!* Three ships are better than two for the hard journey ahead and four ships are better than three."

We fell silent when a freckle-faced boy with an impish grin stopped at our table holding a pitcher in one hand and three pewter beakers in the other.

"Indeed," I said as I shooed the boy away and poured the drinks myself. "We need you to collect our new ships once your crew returns from leave-taking. Then you must put in at Ostend to take delivery of thirty-two nine-pounders. I've made all the necessary arrangements with our man Mr. Ink."

"Jacob will take command of one frigate and Michael the other?" Maurice asked.

"Yes."

"And you still intend to sail east?"

"Are you having misgivings about the plan?"

Maurice ran his fingers through his long, black hair before answering. "No, I simply respect the challenges such a voyage will bring."

I acknowledged Maurice's concern with a nod but my mind was firm. I would not reconsider. Mary had found renown and great riches during her lifetime by taking bold action and I was determined to do the same.

On the first day of May, on the day the Irish honor the ancient Gaelic festival of *Lá Bealtaine* to mark the beginning of summer, my brothers and I gathered at Shaw's tavern to drink, eat and celebrate. While the men of Westport lit the bonfires and slaughtered sheep, fair young maidens with garlands of primrose, gorse and hawthorn in their hair, with floral sashes wrapped around their waists, merrily danced up and down the streets as was their custom to hang wreaths made with flowers, ivy, berries and sprigs of holly on doors, in windows and along the fenceposts to ward off any evil. I did my part. I purchased four large wreaths - one for each of our ships anchored in the bay - and sent two men out in a boat with my purchases to place one wreath on the tip of each bowsprit for good luck.

"You are both satisfied?" I asked Atwood and MacGyver as we ate our supper in a private room Mary had built. The two men had returned earlier in the morning after taking their new frigates out into the bay to see what they could do.

"Aye, Elizabeth," Atwood replied flatly.

I knew the big Scot was disappointed as I was keeping *Ghostrunner* for myself with Shaw as my first officer. I pretended not to notice his disenchantment.

"Whilst sailing from Ostend to Westport," I said in a conciliatory tone, "Maurice drove both ships hard. He was impressed."

"I was indeed," Maurice agreed. "These frigates are fast and nimble and handled well in the moderately tricky seas we encountered."

I looked over at MacGyver. "Michael? What say you?"

"She's a beauty," he replied smiling, happy to have command of a ship again.

"What of the new men?" I asked no one in particular. Over the weeks, Efendi, Shaw and I had scoured the taverns, farms and brothels up and down Ireland's west coast hiring new men to crew our new ships. We signed on men who had never sailed with us before, men we didn't know. We hired fieldhands, farmers, merchants, bakers, common laborers, tradesmen and men who had fallen on hard times. We even took on boys.

"Unproven," MacGyver answered.

Atwood took a swig of ale. "Few have any military service. Many have never been to sea. I have no reason to have much confidence in any of them."

"We can," Efendi offered, "sprinkle our veterans amongst the new recruits. There'll be plenty of time during the long voyage ahead to break them in."

Atwood shook his head. "That's all fine and well Mustafa, all fine a well. But I still don't like taking on so many new men of questionable skills, of unknown mettle. Train them all you like. Training will only carry an inferior man so far. We'll be sailing through unfamiliar waters into unfamiliar lands ruled by heathens and barbarians where stout hearts will be needed, where experience can mean the difference between life or death for us all."

"Have you decided upon a name for your ship, Michael?" I asked, wishing to change the subject.

MacGyver, a lover of Greek godlore, grinned. "*Achilles*, I will name her *Achilles*."

"*Muy bien.* Jacob?"

"Haven't given the matter much thought."

"No Greek or Roman god or hero strikes your fancy?" I asked as I refilled Atwood's tankard. "*Hercules* perhaps? *Athena*, *Venus*, *Jupiter* or *Poseidon*?"

"God's wounds, no. I like plain. Hmmm. *Homeward Bound*, aye, I'll name her *Homeward Bound* for such will be my thoughts once we reach the far end of the world."

"*Homeward Bound* it is then," I said cheerfully and turned to Kinkae. "All your lads intend to sail with us?"

"Every man, Elizabeth," Kinkae replied. "And they are grateful for the letters you sent to Guadeloupe."

"Henry, do any of your men wish to catch a ship for home?" I asked.

"No," he said in his soft voice. "All stand with you Elizabeth."

I raised my glass of wine. "Excellent," I said. "To *Achilles* and *Homeward Bound*, to *Ghostrunner* and *Cerberus*, may Neptune be merciful and grant us safe passage to the East and back."

But before taking a sip I tipped my glass, spilling a few drops on the floor. My brothers - mariners, forever superstitious - joined me in my sacred offering.

With a mix of excitement and uneasiness in the air, we set out from Ireland the next morning under unsettled grey skies, plowing through heaving swells under full sail. Our four formidable warships must have made an inspiring sight to the spectators standing along the shore.

We sailed for Amsterdam first - a bustling seaport of clean, cobblestone streets, of grand new buildings and a dizzying array of church steeples and spires rising towards the heavens - for there in the great city we had pilgrims to collect. The Dutch government, led by the ambitious warrior prince Maurice of Nassau, had been encouraging Dutchmen to make the long and arduous journey east. The Dutch were on the march to colonize territories, to create a new Dutch empire, a grand empire of commerce to rival, nay eclipse, all others and thousands willing to risk everything for land and riches were flocking to Amsterdam to answer the government's call.

After we dropped anchor just outside the city walls, I took Atwood, MacGyver and Maurice ashore in a longboat with me to meet a man named Houtman. We walked to Dam Square and a little way beyond to an older, unremarkable building where the Company was leasing space out of an old warehouse.

"Welcome, I'm delighted to meet you at last Señorita de Cortés," the Dutchman said in excellent Spanish as we squeezed into his bland, neglected office with barely enough room to stand shoulder-to-shoulder. The piles of paper I saw strewn across a cheaply made desk, and the stacks of files littering a badly worn floor, did not inspire confidence. The man himself was an unremarkable, stocky little fellow with a red goatee and a shiny, bald head.

"I received your letter accepting the terms of our commission," he continued. "I am Jan de Houtman and I will be your agent. Please call me Jan. May I address you by your Christian name Elizabeth?"

"Of course," I replied with a pleasant smile. "Allow me to introduce Captains Jacob Atwood, Michael MacGyver and Maurice to you. I've sailed with these gentlemen for years. I can vouch for their quality. They are seamen of great skill and courage."

Houtman leaned forward from his desk to shake hands. "A genuine pleasure, gentlemen," Houtman said then turned to me while gleefully rubbing his hands together. "John Martin shares your opinion. He has only the highest praise for you all. Though our original agreement was for three ships, I'm informed you've entered our fine harbor with a flotilla of four ships of impressive stature. I'm informed you've brought over four hundred men and eighty pieces of artillery with you."

I nodded. "You are well-informed. Four heavily-armed ships yes, and you are at liberty to inspect our little squadron whenever you please."

"I intend to. I've heard outlandish talk here and there about fair maidens holding positions of power. Aside from nobility of course, I've never met one. Certainly, I've never encountered a ship's master of your gender before. Rather extraordinary."

"We live in extraordinary times," I replied. "How many Dutchmen will be sailing with us?"

"Three hundred souls, give or take, along with as many tons of arms, tools and supplies as your ships can transport."

"Conditions," Atwood said, "will be cramped aboard the ships but we'll make do."

"We Dutch are not afraid of hardship. Years of bloody conflict with Spain have forged us into a tough and hardy people."

"That is good to know," I said awkwardly.

Houtman reached for a roll of papers secured by a thin red, white and blue ribbon sitting on his desk. "Sea charts, routes, destinations and your instructions, along with letters of introduction should you need them," he explained and handed me the papers. "I will inspect your ships in the morning. Now I would be honored if you would all join me for supper as my guests. Martin informs me you have a few wild stories worth telling regarding your excursions to the West Indies. I look forward to hearing one or two."

After a long evening with Houtman, we rowed back to our ships just before dawn awakened the city. We rallied our men, weighed anchor and set the tops'ls. We raised the Company's flamboyant red, white and blue flags too as we gingerly eased our ships up against four open piers a short distance away where three hundred Dutchmen dressed in plain, black clothing stood waiting for us in the rain amidst hundreds of boxes, crates and barrels. From the main deck, I glanced down at the Dutchmen with displeasure for I could see apprehension in many a face and fearful men Mary had taught me cannot be trusted.

Then I spotted Houtman in the crowd. He stood out in his bold red and blue striped landsknecht trousers and his copotain hat, trimmed with an exceedingly long, red feather, cocked to one side. His black leather slashed doublet with capped sleeves and broad reticella lace collar appeared expensive.

I waved him up the gangway and poured him a tin of fresh coffee. "Jan, welcome aboard *Ghostrunner*," I said cheerfully as I handed him his coffee.

He raised his cup in thanks and took a sip. "Ahhh, delicious. A rather dreary day to launch an expedition. This dampness cuts right to the bone."

"Perhaps you should join us. We are off to warmer climes I hear."

"Ha! I like my soft, cozy bed too much. Shall we?"

I accompanied Houtman as he inspected our ships, beginning with *Ghostrunner*. The Dutchman knew his business and was thorough. He even stepped down into the bowels of each ship and waded into the bilge water, poking at timbers and planks here and there with an iron rod.

"Very fine, very fine," Houtman said as we crossed the gangway over to the pier. "Your ships are sturdy, in good repair and heavily armed. My compliments to you on the cleanliness I saw. Too many masters don't mind sluttery. Imbeciles. Sluttery invites sickness and sickness impacts profits. What may I ask is the quality of your men?"

"They're disciplined and good fighters. We do have a fair number of new recruits too, which is not uncommon as you must know. Ships' masters are forever scouring the land looking for able-bodied men to replenish the ranks. I cannot yet attest to the skills of these new men, but they'll learn what is expected of them from the veterans and they'll learn quickly too or else."

"Marvelous. You have delivered on your promises Elizabeth - which is exceedingly important to the Company - I implore you to remember that. I'm pleased to approve this expedition."

I leaned close to the Dutchman's ear. "Some of your people seem skittish today, Jan."

Houtman nodded while removing a sheet of paper from his doublet's breast pocket. "It is not given to us to know who will survive this voyage to see home again and who will not. I'm no seafaring man but I'm not oblivious to the hazards and sacrifices. The elements, disease, mishaps, rotten food and tainted water, killers lurking about the islands. The Company has carefully explained the risks and the potential rewards to each man. A handful of these fine fellows have made the journey before. I've written their names down and a word or two about their accomplishments on this paper. You may find their knowledge useful in the long days ahead. Koopman and Dijksma at the top of the list are the highest-ranking men. They are both officers of the Company. At sea the authority of the ship's master is absolute. This is maritime law. But whilst in port, you will defer to these two men. Understood?"

"Understood."

"Good. Stay well clear of the Islas Canarias, Cabo Verde and the Moroccan coast Elizabeth. Those waters are infested with ruthless Barbary rovers and other unsavory sorts who enjoy killing for sport. These godless heathens will show you no mercy. We Dutch have paid dearly learning this lesson."

"We shall heed your good advice."

Houtman doffed his fancy hat as we shook hands. "Very well, I'll let you get to it then. No doubt you are anxious to embark upon your new quest. I wish you safe journeys and pray we meet again sometime within the next year or two. Farewell my lady."

After Houtman left we started packing the Dutch and their supplies into the ships. We packed them in tight. And once all was ready, I gave the order to cast-off the mooring lines and drop sail and soon our ships started slowly drifting away from the piers. To reach

Banten, our primary destination, we needed to cross twelve thousand miles of water in ships filled to bursting from stem to stern. We faced a daunting task with so many miles ahead of us and so few safe havens for refuge.

To my chagrin I had to share my great cabin with Efendi, Shaw, my little man James and three crewmen. James bunked with me while the rest laid their bedrolls out across the deck and slept on hard wood.

With John Davis' new book *The Seaman's Secret* published in 1595 in hand, complete with sea charts, an hourglass, magnetic compass, an astrolabe or star-taker, a chip log and a back-staff, or as some like to call it a Davis Quadrant, I led our small fleet into the English Channel and then pointed us due south. We'd continue our southerly course until we reached the bottom of the world. At navigation, I excelled even Atwood and did what I could to snip off a few miles here and there.

Irksome squalls though plagued us down Channel and followed us well into the Atlantic. We cruised along in a close diamond formation under half sail for we dared not push our crowded ships too hard and made poor time tacking against the buffeting headwinds and contrary currents.

We endured the wet and the cold as best we could. We had no space to hang our wet things and suffered in our damp, smelly clothing. We lived on cold porridge and ate ch'arki, a favorite snack amongst my men but not very satisfying as a meal, as the cooks couldn't light the brick ovens in the heavy seas battering our poor ships about. Deprived of hot food, sleep and simple comforts, misery was our close companion in the early days.

When the sun at last broke through the clouds, accompanied by a lively north wind and drier air, we were some two hundred miles off the coast of Portugal by my reckoning. My crew and our passengers rejoiced with cheers and laughter as they took turns up on deck to enjoy the delightful weather. Mindful of Houtman's warning, I kept us well clear of the Spanish Islas Canarias and we passed the archipelago on the windward side. And though we saw many a sail in the distance, none ventured our way.

After thirty-five days of tedious sailing across three thousand miles of ocean, we slipped past Cabo Verde, looping around the southern shores of those islands, and then headed due east for Africa. I led our ships straight for the tiny island of Gorée where the Dutch maintain a well-garrisoned stronghold according to the instructions Houtman had given me.

"You are Ewoud Dijksma?" I asked in English when the Dutchman stepped up onto the quarterdeck to join me. I kept my gaze fixed on the African coast slowly taking form in the distance as the hotness of the great Sahara Desert brushed against my face like a blast of searing heat from a furnace.

The handsome, cleanshaven Dutchman, a sturdy fellow with intelligent, blue eyes and dressed in the black, flat-topped hat and unadorned black jacket, breeches and black buckled shoes favored by the Dutch Protestants on board, nodded. "I am madam."

I turned to face Dijksma and smiled. He kept his blonde, curly hair cut short. A prominent nose and a strong, square chin gave him an air of authority. I had watched him over the past few days strolling up and down the decks with swagger. I had seen how the other Dutchmen deferred to him.

"Before departing Amsterdam, Meneer Houtman gave me a list of names and descriptions of the men who have sailed to the East before," I said and handed the Dutchman a nipperkin of wine. "According to the information Houtman provided me, you speak, besides Dutch, English, Spanish, Portuguese, French, Italian and Javanese."

"I do, along with some Malay and a smattering of Japanese."

"Japanese? Impressive. You've made this voyage at least once before?"

"Yes, indeed I have. I sailed with Jacob van Neck's fleet in the spring of '98 to the *Oost Indië*."

"*Oost Indië*? East Indies?"

"Very good, madam. I have every confidence we'll be conversing in Dutch together before this voyage is over."

"We shall see. I have a good ear for languages but find Dutch difficult. People say van Neck's expedition was extraordinarily successful."

"Very. Van Neck returned to the United Provinces with over one million pounds of various spices worth a substantial fortune. Amsterdam's city fathers paraded him through the streets like a conquering hero to the sounds of fife and drum, to blaring trumpets and tolling church bells. The pageantry was grand."

"Much like how the English honored Sir Francis Drake after he circumnavigated the globe."

"Quite so."

"I trust you and your colleagues are not suffering too much discomfort below deck? These past few weeks have been rather unpleasant."

"We are making do, though I must confess I miss my wine. Our daily ration of flat ale is barely tolerable. I'm enjoying this tasty beverage very much, thank you. Most refreshing."

"Good, good. This happens to be a Spanish vintage. I was a bit concerned you might find Spanish *vino* too tart, too bold, perhaps altogether disagreeable."

Dijksma smiled as he held his glass out for more. "We Dutch do not find everything Spanish detestable. The wine is delicious and you, my dear lady, are delightful. I understand you were born in Barcelona but were raised in Santo Domingo?"

"True. You need not worry whether I'm a Spanish spy or not. I have no loyalties to Spain. I am a woman of the Caribbean. I am a child of the sea."

Dijksma started laughing. "*Wonderbaar!* I shall sleep much better tonight knowing this."

"I do believe you've found some amusement at my expense."

"Never!" the Dutchman declared with a wry smile.

"We are an easy sail away from Gorée. You've been to this island?"

"I have. And I've been to the Lebou village called Ndakaaru directly across the water from the island."

"What can you tell me about this place?"

"At one time the Portuguese used the island as a base for their slave trade. The Dutch seized Gorée from the Portuguese some years ago and then ran them out of Ndakaaru. We maintain a strong presence in this part of Africa. The spot is convenient for Dutch ships sailing to and from the East Indies to safely refit, resupply and rest. This land is known as Senegal and is ruled by the Kajoor. The Kajoor prosper handsomely trading with we Europeans and rest assured my lady, we'll be greeted warmly."

"Excellent. I intend to stay for a few days, give my men and you Dutch pilgrims a chance to stretch your legs on shore - unless you think this unwise."

"Two or three days on solid ground would be most welcome."

"I am curious, if I may ask, what is your position on this expedition?"

"I am, hmmm, how do I say this in English? Ah, I am a colonial administrator."

"That title has the ring of importance."

"Not nearly as important or as inspiring as a beautiful, young mistress with warships and men-at-arms under her sway."

"My, aren't you the rascal? I'll need to be on my guard around you. I'm easy prey to flattery."

"Aren't we all dear lady, aren't we all."

We spent three lazy days on Gorée, taking on food and water, repairing our ships, bathing, washing clothes and reposing. The Dutch island's commander, to my surprise a Swedish mercenary named Karlsson, was most hospitable towards my officers and me. Each evening he invited us into his modest quarters within the island's fort for supper along with Dijksma and Gerrit Koopman, whom I had not met before as he had been sailing with Atwood. Karlsson plied us with good food, good wine and quality cigars while we traded stories well into the night. The Swede was a wonderful host. Dijksma, a personable, jovial fellow, entertained us with his outrageous tales of adventure in the East Indies while Koopman, his shy colleague, was a better listener than talker. A serious and unkind world I supposed had left Koopman scarred with a serious and unkind demeanor.

For Kinkae and his Blackamoors, our brief stay on Gorée was bittersweet for this was the place some thirty years ago where Kinkae and his brothers had been dragged in chains aboard a Portuguese slaver bound for the New World. When it was time to weigh anchor, we left two of Kinkae's men behind as was their wish. Older than the rest, the two men decided to return to the village of their forefathers to live out the rest of their days.

We headed for Cabo das Tormentas next. The Portuguese explorer Bartolomeu Dias had named the rocky promontory the Cape of Storms for obvious reasons but King John II of Portugal, a practical man, renamed the headland the Cape of Good Hope to give we mariners traversing the waters between Europe and Asia a sense of optimism over portents of doom. We could sail close to land, hugging the western coast of Africa, or take our chances cutting across the South Atlantic in a straight line through deep water to save ourselves many miles and time. With Atwood's blessing, I chose the straight line.

I had brought an English copy of Jan Huygen van Linschoten's 1596 rutter with me, a handbook of sorts entitled the *Reys-gheschrift vande navigatien der Portugaloysers in Orienten*, the *Travel Accounts of Portuguese Navigation in the Orient*. While sailing with the Portuguese to the East Indies, Linschoten, an enterprising Dutchman, had learned everything he could about Portuguese secrets in navigation, secrets it had taken the Portuguese nearly a century to compile. Linchoten painstaking recorded detailed descriptions and invaluable information on shorelines, harbors, islands, channels, tides, landmarks, reefs, shoals and passageways to India, Indonesia, China and Japan. I found his instructions on how to determine position and plot routes with calendars, astronomical tables, mathematical tables and by using the rules of calculation, especially the rule of marteloio and triangulation, particularly useful.

Fair weather and cooler air blessed us for most of our journey across the South Atlantic. With playful winds and favorable currents, we made good speed. We passed no hostile sails or ships of any kind.

And then misfortune struck. One of Dijksma's men, the only

portly fellow onboard, died peacefully in his sleep from a bad heart. After Dijksma gave a fitting eulogy, as we lowered the body into the sea, the winds abruptly vanished. Not even a whiff of breeze brushed against our sails. We lost nearly a week becalmed within the Doldrums, languishing in those waters under a merciless sun.

When the winds did return, they returned with welcomed vigor and we laid on more canvas - as much as we dared - to make up lost time. After two months at sea, after plowing across four-five hundred miles of blue water, spirits soared when we came within sight of land.

We were surprised to find a handsome Portuguese man-o'-war, a twenty-four gunner, anchored close to shore when we reached Table Bay. Efendi had the gun crews prime and load our great guns as a precaution, but we did not run the guns out lest we unnecessarily provoke the Portuguese. Pursuant to the terms of our commission from the Company, we were free to seize any Portuguese or Spanish vessels we intercepted along our journey for the prize money the ships and their cargos would fetch at auction, except around the waters of the Cape of Good Hope as those waters are considered neutral ground, a district for free trade of sorts for ships of all nations. But for a few friendly smiles and the waving of hands the Portuguese ignored us and we ignored them as we floated past their vessel.

After we dropped anchor, I summoned Dijksma up to the quarterdeck to seek his good counsel. And after the Dutchman assured me it was safe to go ashore, I promptly led the first longboat in.

When Atwood stepped off his longboat and into a gentle surf lapping at his boots, I rushed to his side and threw my arms around his neck. "All is well Jacob?"

"Aye, and you?"

"Yes. So far, we've been most fortunate."

Atwood reached over to shake Dijksma's hand. "Good of you to make it Ewoud."

"'Tis good to see you too Captain," Dijksma replied. "Where is Koopman? I trust he's alive and well."

"Your associate is feeling poorly and has taken to his hammock.

He hopes to join us later. Gout perhaps is the cause of the fellow's misery."

"Pity, I hope he recovers soon," Dijksma said. "Gerrit possesses a wealth of experience we'll be glad to have in the days ahead."

Atwood pointed at the Portuguese ship. "Can we trust our Portuguese friends to play nice?"

"I should think so, though I'd keep a goodly number of men on the ships to keep the Portuguese honest if I were you. And be mindful of the weather here. The elements can turn quickly and Table Bay offers little protection as you can see."

"I understand," I said. "Rotate the men Jacob, bring half ashore?"

"Aye and let them step into Africa well-armed. What are the natives like Ewoud?"

"The Khoikhoi inhabit these lands. They are a nomadic, ordinarily friendly people - provided we come only to trade and rest. They'll gladly provide us with fresh meat, fruits and vegetables in exchange for the necessaries we Dutch brought along."

"When are they not friendly?" Atwood asked.

"One of the Khoikhoi tribes known as the Goringhaiqua, though rarely seen, despise foreigners. We must remain vigilant."

"Very well," Atwood said. "I see Maurice and Michael coming in. We have another six thousand miles of open water to cross by my calculations before we see land again. We should remain here Elizabeth for however long it takes to overhaul the ships proper. We'll need the ships in top condition for the long stretch ahead."

When I nodded my agreement, Atwood bellowed out orders to the waves of men coming ashore. They immediately went to work pitching tents, collecting firewood and securing a perimeter for our defense.

The Khoikhoi were quick to come down from the surrounding cliffs and hills to greet us. Khoi men and women, wearing little more than loincloth, walked towards us in a single file carrying large wicker baskets. Every Khoi carried a spear, a short sword and at least one knife. They keep their curly hair cropped short and like to wear bracelets of stones, beads or bones around their necks, arms and ankles. I was surprised to see several mixed-race Khoi. Unlike the Spanish and the Portuguese, who are meticulous in sorting mixed races into well-defined groups, the Dutch simply call all light-skinned Khoi *bastaards*.

The Khoi greeted us with friendly smiles as they set their baskets on the sand for our inspection. In exchange for fresh ostrich, kudu and wildebeest meat, for fruits like sour plums, sour figs and marulas and vegetables like marama beans, cowpeas and cassava, the Dutch paid the Khoi with tobacco, iron, copper and bolts of cotton dyed in various bright colors. We ate well around the campfires during our time on shore. One evening I invited the captain of the Portuguese warship and his officers to join my officers and me for supper though, except for Dijksma, our Dutch friends declined to partake. Our guests were most cordial and I for one enjoyed their good company.

We remained on African soil long enough to repair our ships and refresh ourselves. When the Portuguese broke camp a few days later and headed north for home, we returned to our own ships too and sailed east for Indonesia - and for the fabulous wealth awaiting us there.

Chapter Four

The Tequesta treated me well. They pampered me with kindnesses, compassion and a good dose of curiosity. A handful of Tequesta spoke tolerable Spanish and eagerly engaged me in long conversations as we sat around the campfires at night. They were captivated by my tales of adventure in the New World and fascinated by my descriptions of Europe. They seemed particularly fond of my stories about the Queen of England, who had once held me captive in the Tower of London but later called me sister. I gladly shared my stories of buried Aztec gold, of war, love and betrayal with the Tequesta and they in turn happily shared their history, their laws, traditions and customs with me and I found myself the richer for it.

The Tequesta are a docile, friendly people, not at all like my warlike Carib friends of Guadeloupe. Even the Spanish found no cause to be hostile towards the Tequesta when they first landed in the Bahía Vizcaína. The Tequesta live in peace and harmony with neighboring tribes to the north and west. They are protected by the sea to the east and by vast stretches of impenetrable swampland to the south the Spanish call Laguna del Espíritu Santo. Unlike their neighbors to the north and west, the Tequesta have no interest in tilling the soil. They are hunters, fishermen and gatherers. Wars are rare and food is plentiful.

I ate venison and bear with my Indian hosts and fowl like duck, goose and wild turkey. We dined on unleavened bread, fruits, a variety of vegetables and all manner of creatures from the sea. We ate sea turtles, snails, whale, sea-wolf, trunkfish, lobster, manatee - a delicious meat - shark, clams, oysters and conches. No one went hungry in

Chequescha.

The men are fond of a drink they call cassina, the black drink, brewed from yaupon leaves. The concoction is far more potent than the darkest coffee and I did not care for the strong, bitter taste. If the Tequesta had any fermented or distilled drinks, I never saw any of it.

I spent my days helping the women skin and clean the game and fish the men brought back to the village. I helped them cook, tan hides and sew. I learned the Tequesta language as best I could.

Though most held on to the old beliefs I was surprised by the number of Tequesta who had embraced Christianity, or some vague semblance of Christianity. Even those who professed to believe in Jesus still prayed and made daily offerings to a stuffed stag standing in the center of the village. The Tequesta believe we have three souls. One soul can be seen in the eyes, another is in our shadow and the third can be found within our own reflections. On occasion, or so I was told, the Tequesta offer human sacrifices to celebrate certain momentous events.

As the days turned into weeks and the weeks turned into months, I bided my time with my daily chores and made friends. I worked hard and caused no trouble. I did my best to earn the trust and respect of the Tequesta before I decided to approach Tayhoot again. And when I finally did stop by his hut, he stepped outside with open arms and a gracious smile to welcome me.

"A good day to you, sir," I offered cheerfully in my tortured Tequesta and clasped his hands in greeting. "I trust you are in fine spirits and in good health. I come to seek your good counsel. I wish to sit with you and speak as friends."

Tayhoot beamed with delight. "You wish to be my woman?" he asked in Spanish.

Annoyed with myself for my awful skills with languages, I repeated my words in Spanish.

Tayhoot waved me inside his hut with a chuckle. He laid out two Spanish blankets next to his campfire and invited me to sit.

"A good day to you, Mary. You appear fit. Your strength is back?"

"I am fully recovered, thank you."

"I am glad. I hear only good about you."

"I'm very grateful for the many kindnesses you and your people have shown me."

"You have earned our kindness."

"When we first met, you told me I was free to come and go as I pleased."

"I did."

"There is a Spanish settlement in Florida, though I am not sure how far it is from your village. The Spanish call their town San Augustín. Do you know it?"

"I do."

"With the help of the Tequesta, I'd like to go there. From San Augustín, I can catch a ship to return to my home in Ireland."

"As you can see, we Tequesta have few horses. Such a journey would take many days on foot and would not be without danger."

"I've trudged across many a mile through the jungles of Panama, a rugged, harsh land to the west. I have strong legs, a broad back and a will of iron."

Tayhoot nodded. "It is good you rejoin your own people. Perhaps it would be wise for the Tequesta to look in on our Spanish neighbors to the north, see what mischief they might be up to."

"Amongst my people, I'm considered a great warrior. I command many men. I have powerful warships with masts as tall as the tallest tree and armed with large cannon. If I survive the journey back to Ireland, I will return to the West Indies and when I do, I can find the Bahía Vizcaína. I'll return with gifts to repay your generosity."

"You are not a hostage. We require no payment, no ransom."

"Even so, I am indebted to you and I repay my debts."

"I have a nephew. He is a fine hunter. He is clever. He speaks good Spanish. His name is Nephetu and he will lead. But he cannot depart until after the Feast of the Sun, on the day when the sun slowly awakens from his long slumber and the days grow longer again."

Following the Feast of the Sun, I set my Tequesta clothes aside and slipped into my trousers, donned my shirt, my vest and pulled my boots on. After Tayhoot offered prayers to bless our journey north as we stood around a bonfire, I kissed the friends I had made farewell, took the straw hat and a cape of deerskin to use for bedding the women had made for me and headed out with eighteen stout warriors, lean, sinewy men led by Tayhoot's strapping, young nephew.

I'd never been to San Augustín and did not know how I'd be received by the Spanish there, but I had to try. San Augustín was the only way I knew out of Florida. The great Englishman Sir Francis Drake had sacked the town not long ago in 1586. As Catholic Spain and the Catholic Irish were on good terms, at times even allies, I'd need to make certain the Spanish understood that I was Irish and not English.

We covered nearly twenty miles a day by my reckoning, depending on the ground we traveled over. The days were brutally hot and we kept to the shade whenever we could. The nights were warm and sticky. We slept on grass and kept our capes wrapped around ourselves to keep the swarms of mosquitoes, chiggers and flies away. At first light each day we'd take up the march again, walking at a brisk pace, and didn't rest until the sun went down. Nephetu, a serious fellow with a high brow and a sharp nose, was always courteous around me as were his men. The others treated him with respect, though they had nicknamed him All Hearing because his ears were too big for his face.

On the fifth day we stepped into the lands of the warlike Jaega where many warriors - with hide-covered shields strapped against their backs and armed with spears, hatchets, knives, bows and arrows - intercepted us. They had decorated their hair with colorful feathers and had painted their faces with streaks of black, white and red. Two Jaega rode large stallions without saddles, blankets or stirrups. Armed only with their warclubs and short knives, without feathers or painted skin, the Tequesta seemed tame by comparison.

Nephetu and the two horsemen sat under the shade of a nearby palm tree. They traded small talk, shared a cigar and when they had finished, the Jaega let us pass through their lands unmolested. Ten days later the Ais welcomed us with open arms. We tarried in their village for two days, feasting and drinking Spanish beer. After we said our farewells the Ais sent us off with a guide who knew the shortest trail into San Augustín.

Twenty-two days after leaving Chequescha, we reached the wooden gates of the Spanish port. I bid my Tequesta friends Godspeed and embraced each man before I made my way towards the center of town.

The settlement was smaller than I had imagined and protected by nothing more than a flimsy, wooden palisade and a dozen light field pieces. The Spanish garrison though appeared large and well-equipped. I saw soldiers heavily armed with muskets, pikes and swords. I passed by soldiers wearing steel breastplates, morrión steel helmets, chainmail skirts and steel greaves - all at great cost to the king - and when I walked by the harbor, I saw several respectable Spanish warships at anchor. I couldn't help myself and started concocting schemes to take the city for plunder, just to amuse myself and pass the time. I had no wish to make war against the Spanish.

I stopped at a shop where I was able to purchase new clothes, including a stylish black cavalier hat with a long, blue feather, two serviceable pistols and a very fine sword forged from quality Nürnberg steel. And then I found an agreeable hostel where I could bathe, wash my old clothes and sleep on a feather bed, my first. The next day, after treating myself to a large breakfast of eggs, juice and strips of bacon, I took a stroll down to the waterfront, struggling against the cold, blustery winds of the Atlantic, to look for a ship bound for Europe, or to one of the islands where I had friends.

Chapter Five

I felt an ill wind at my back as we plowed across a crimson sea and into the fading light of a dying day. I could not shake off the uneasiness nagging at me. All was well. *Ghostrunner* was a marvelous ship, a fine sailor. She was sturdy, well-balanced and remarkably agile for a large ship. Morale amongst our Dutch passengers was astonishingly good. They accepted their hardships with quiet resolve and grace. My own lads went about their duties with light hearts and we had suffered no significant mishaps. Our luck was holding fast and still I felt on edge.

After departing Table Bay, with Linschoten's rutter never far from my side, we skirted around the tip of Africa, known as the Cabo das Agulhas, the Cape of Needles, where the cold waters of the Atlantic collide into the warm waters of the Eastern Ocean and the winds perpetually blow strong. I learned from Dijksma that the Portuguese had bestowed the odd name of Needles to the cape because true north and magnetic north, as determined by the needle of a compass, are the same in that region of the world. During the winter months rogue waves as big as mountains can rise up without warning in those waters and crush a ship in one breath. And though we were rounding the cape in late July in the midst of winter, we found ourselves cutting across the languid, green waters of a mild-tempered sea sailing with winds that were better than fair.

Corsairs. Two weeks out from Table Bay, using the fantastical spyglass Atwood had taken off a dead Spaniard in Panama years ago and presented to Mary as a gift, glass that makes objects in the distance appear closer, I was the first to spot the sails of nine vessels with black sails coming down from the north, whether Iberian raiders or pirates sailing down from Madagascar or even from India, I did not know. Efendi rushed across the main deck to join me at the helm after I gave the order to raise the red pennant up the main mast, the signal to come about and attack.

"Elizabeth," he said as he grabbed the line attached to the pennant to haul the signal back down. "We should keep to our present course. We can safely let out more canvas and give ourselves a little more speed if you like."

I looked at Efendi in disbelief. My blood was hot for action.

"You wish to run?" I asked. "Run from flimsy coasters?"

"We do not know the calibre or the skills of these men Elizabeth."

"I hardly think we are facing battle-hardened professionals, Mustafa."

"Why take the risk Elizabeth? Why endanger the lives of our men and the lives of our Dutch passengers?"

"The better question is why let these scoundrels shadow us? Why give them the chance of picking us off one-by-one during the night?"

Atwood leaned over his ship's rail after he eased his ship alongside us. "Whatcha thinkin' Elizabeth?" he shouted across the waves and shrugged his shoulders.

"I think we have trouble sailing our way, trouble we need to deal with Jacob," I shouted back.

Atwood pointed to the nine ships. "I pray you tell me why. Those men aren't sailing ocean-worthy vessels. They'll not venture far from land. We should ignore them. When mornin' comes, they'll be nowhere in sight."

"My thoughts precisely Jacob," Efendi interjected.

"Mary never ran away from a fight!" I replied defiantly.

Atwood stroked his beard as he shook his head. "Elizabeth, I assure you, she did. Mary fought only when she had no choice and then only when the odds were soundly in our favor."

I knew Atwood's words weren't quite true. Mary had shared many stories with me, some in confidence. She had shared her misgivings about some things she had done over the years and her doubts about some of the choices she had made. On occasion, she even expressed remorse. But she never regretted standing firm against an enemy bent on killing. Never.

I had proven myself to Mary and the others and they had accepted me as their sister. But I had yet to lead men into battle as Mary had done. Mindful of the Ten Rules, I couldn't ignore Atwood or Efendi. I knew I needed to bide my time - but I would not be denied my destiny forever.

"Very well," I said in a testy tone. "I hope you're right Jacob. Mustafa, you may lower the red pennant. We'll spread out more canvas and keep to our easterly course."

In the morning I climbed the main mast up to the masthead with my Spanish glass. Atwood's prediction proved true. I could find no trace of the ships with the black sails from the north - but I had not been wrong in raising the red pennant and wanting to fight.

The days passed by slowly as we glided across the vastness of the great Eastern Ocean. We made no better than seven knots, often less, and found ourselves becalmed twice for long stretches of time. The distance between Ireland and the West Indies across the Atlantic is nearly four thousand miles. Crossing the length of the Eastern Ocean, or the Indian Ocean as the English prefer calling it, is over six thousand miles, farther if one is blown off course and must double-back.

I spent my days schooling little James in all the customary disciplines, in the classic Seven Arts of Antiquity, when the lads weren't teaching him about ships and the sea or Efendi and Shaw weren't training him in the martial arts. Efendi and Shaw were students of Vadi, Fechtens and Monte and had trained me in koshti, ringen, and fencing. I was skilled with knives, muskets, cannon, reflex bows, crossbows, garrotes, hira-shurikens, manrika chains and a host of other exotic weapons. I was more than proficient at all of it and little James would be too. I kept his days full.

I also enjoyed intermingling with our Dutch passengers, particularly with Dijksma who happily began schooling me in Dutch. With his help and encouragement, I acquired the language quickly.

After a seven-month voyage - nearly eclipsing van Neck's time - we entered the narrow straights of Sunda, slipped between the islands of Sumatra and Java and coasted into a bay crowded with vessels from many nations. We had reached Banten. With our colorful Company banners flying high, with our decks awash in cheering men, we took in sail and dropped our anchors not far from shore while sailors from around the world stared at us in awe.

I was standing on the poop deck next to the ship's wheel when I spotted Dijksma on the gun deck below. I called the Dutchman to me. He doffed his hat and offered his hand as he approached.

"Congratulations, Elizabeth. You've brought us safely across two oceans and halfway around the world, in remarkable time I should add. Fine, fine seamanship."

"*Bedankt voor je compliment Ewoud,*" I said, practicing my Dutch. "We were most fortunate. That handsome vessel over there, Malaysian?"

"No, she's a Red Seal ship, an armed merchantman from Japan. I believe the white flag with the black circle flying off her mizzen gaff is the heraldry of the House of Araki, one of Japan's wealthiest trading families. The Japanese export mostly silver, diamonds, copper and their exquisitely crafted swords. And that ship sitting just beyond her flying the pennant with the blue dragon on a field of yellow is a Chinese junk, a ship of the Emperor of China. Most of the other vessels I see are Malaysian, though I see some Indian grabs and an Ottoman gallivant or two."

Atwood then climbed aboard using the rope ladder my lads had tossed over the side. He had brought Maurice, MacGyver and Koopman with him and had two other boats in tow, one filled with Dutchmen and the other loaded down with a number of large chests.

I hugged my three brothers in turn and then shook hands with Koopman. "Gerrit, welcome aboard. I'm glad to see you're alive and well. You've fully recovered from your ailment?"

Koopman had the leathery skin of a field serf and the squat, thickset physique of a common laborer. But I knew from Dijksma that he was a man of some importance back in Amsterdam.

"Madam, I'm happy to report I'm enjoying excellent health," Koopman replied flatly in fair English as he reached over to shake Dijksma's hand. "Ewoud, good to see you. This is a glorious day."

"Indeed, Gerrit," Dijksma replied. "I was just now expressing my gratitude to Elizabeth. She and her men have acquitted themselves brilliantly."

"I too offer you my compliments," Koopman said with a forced smile.

"Thank you," I replied proudly. "Banten is Java's most important pepper port I think?"

"It is," Dijksma said. "Banten is the jewel of Java, a great city. You'll find many Arabs, Turks, Greeks, Persians, Gujaratis, Tamils, Bengalis, Malaysians, Japanese, Chinese and of course Javanese merchants trading in spices, silks, jewels, exquisite porcelains, teas, carpets, drugs, jewelry, exotic foods, opium and other assorted goods at the Grand Bazaar within the city. Last year the Company established a modest trading post outside the city walls. Foreigners are welcome inside the city during the day to trade but must leave by nightfall before the gates are closed. Our English friends, who arrived in Java last year just as we were completing the construction of our trading post, have built their own post nearby. Ah, over there, you can just make out the colors of the English East India Company fluttering above the roof of the building next to that long godown, just to the left of the river delta. Do you see it?"

"I do," I said. "What is a *godown?*"

"Godown is Malay for warehouse."

"The city's defenses," Atwood observed, "appear rather meager, Ewoud. I see only a modest wooden wall and a dozen flimsy watchtowers. I see no harbor guns or sturdy stone ramparts, not even any earthworks. I see no fortifications of any kind worth a damn."

"This part of Java is ruled by the son of Sultan Maulana Muhammad, Pangeran, meaning prince, Ratu, a child of about nine years. He retains an impressive army of professionals and maintains a strong confederation with the other Saracen kingdoms throughout Indonesia. His army and his alliances are enough to keep the

Portuguese clear of Java. We fall under his protection and need not worry."

"Does this child prince," I asked, "favor the Dutch or the English?"

"He seems, or rather his uncle and regent, a conniving, odious, little fellow named Mandalika, to favor us equally - at least for the moment. Mandalika is certainly no friend of the Portuguese."

"Is it true," I asked, "the Portuguese have a stronghold not far from here in Malacca? I found some mention of it in the papers Houtman provided me."

"Yes. Nearly a hundred years ago the Portuguese landed a substantial force at Malacca. They easily overwhelmed the city's defenders. Once the city capitulated the slaughter began. The Portuguese rounded-up every Muslim, every man, woman and child, and thoughtlessly, barbarously, put them to the sword, sparing none. These abominable acts made the Portuguese many enemies in the East Indies. The Portuguese have fortified their city with high, stone walls and heavy cannon and have built Fortaleza de Malacca to protect the harbor, making Malacca a formidable fortress city."

"Well gentlemen," Atwood asked, "now that we're here, what's the plan?"

"Ewoud and I will go ashore," Koopman said, "to deliver our letters of introduction from our government to Prince Ratu. And we have gifts for the boy."

"Gifts?" I asked out of curiosity.

Koopman called down to his men sitting in the second longboat and had two of them carry a chest up to the poop deck. After the Dutchmen placed the chest at my feet, he bent down and opened the lid. Inside I saw glassware packed in-between layers of cotton and straw.

"We brought a dozen chests with us filled with gorgeous Venetian glass," Koopman said and handed me a beautiful, crystal goblet. "We have cristallo glass, enameled and gilded glass, filigrana glass made using these thin glass rods with inner threads of white, gold and other colors twisted into these marvelous shapes and we brought rare ice glass, glass which appears to have fine cracks. These fragile baubles are worth a small fortune. Venetian craftsmanship is stunning, yes?"

"Exquisite," I said nervously and quickly handed the goblet back to Koopman before I broke it.

"Once Prince Ratu accepts our letters, we can start bringing our men ashore."

"And what if this prince rejects your letters?" I asked.

I caught the subtle cruelness in Koopman's eyes. "He won't," he said coldly while carefully returning the goblet to the chest.

Atwood leaned over the rail to spit. "You need that many men in Banten to support a small trading post?"

"One can never be too careful," Koopman answered. "Not far from here to the east is a small village the Bantenese call Jayakarta. Jayakarta has an excellent deep-water bay, much superior to Banten's and worth surveying. If the prince is agreeable, we will establish a major trading post there and I'll need men to do it. Jayakarta is the key to Java."

Dijksma removed a hand mirror framed in sterling silver from the chest with the clearest, polished glass I'd ever seen and handed the mirror to me. "A gift from Murano for you, my lady."

"What about the English?" MacGyver asked as I admired my reflection in the nearly flawless glass.

"What of them, Michael?" Koopman said. "The English have a silly philosopher king to lead them. We have a warrior prince, Maurice of Nassau."

"And you, Ewoud?" I asked as I continued admiring my gift. "What do you plan to do?"

"Once we've rested the men and your ships are again in good repair, you will transport me and my lads to the Spice Islands."

Chapter Six

San Augustín. Little more than a remote military outpost with an unexceptional harbor and not much commercial trade, is nonetheless a key port for Spain. San Augustín is a safe haven, the last stop, for Spanish treasure ships destined for Europe needing shelter from killer storms or marauding pirates. The Spanish military was there in force to keep the French, who had shown interest in establishing settlements to the north and west, out of Florida.

I spent my days languishing in the dark, unsavory drinking holes along the waterfront waiting for a suitable merchantman to sail into port. My time in San Augustín passed by slowly, putting me in an exceptionally foul mood. And because I was a woman traveling alone, and not some tavern whore, an unmarried woman who spoke Spanish with a heavy Irish accent, I was an oddity and attracted attention, attention I did not want. More than one man tried to woo me into his bed. Happily, I escaped unscathed each time and had no need to bloody anyone.

Nearly a week slipped by before a heavy carrack, a freighter, coasted into San Augustín's quiet harbor. From the wharf she looked old, abused and worn. I had made discreet inquires around town about the ship and her crew and heard nothing to alarm me. The carrack coasted into San Augustín every few months to deliver supplies for the military.

Her master, a German fellow from one kingdom or another in the Hansetic League, was not hard to find once he came ashore. San Augustín didn't have many taverns and I knew them all.

I looked down on the two mariners from the freighter sitting at a table and offered them my finest, flirtatious smile. I put on my best demeanor too even though the men looked unwashed and reeked of foul odors. One fellow was little more than a runt with black teeth, oily skin and a badly pockmarked face. The other, a bigger man, wasn't much prettier but with his piercing blue eyes and a mane of bright red hair braided down the middle, he stood out. He crudely looked me up and down as he ran his fingers over his ears like a comb.

"Which one of you gentlemen is the master of that fine carrack anchored in the harbor?" I asked in Spanish.

"That would be me," the bigger fellow replied cautiously with a thick, German accent.

"May I sit?" I asked and took a seat without waiting for an answer. "My name is Mary."

"Name is Schmidt, Conrad Schmidt," the German answered. "And this handsome fellow sitting next to me is my first officer, Nuno Amrrique. How may we be of service dear lady?"

"I was a passenger aboard a ship bound for Havana when a terrible storm overtook us. Sadly, our ship foundered and everyone but me perished. Fishermen of the Tequesta found me floating on the water and when I was strong enough, my Indian friends helped me reach San Augustín. Now I'm looking for passage out of Florida."

Schmidt lazily scratched the red stubble on his chin. "A sad tale to be sure dear lady. You're lucky those savages didn't roast you alive over a pit of burning coal and serve you up for supper. But as for transportation from this place, my ship hauls cargo, not passengers."

"Surely you can accommodate one modest woman? I only need to reach one of the islands, say to Havana or Santo Domingo? Even better if Europe is your destination."

"We have no business in Havana or in Santo Domingo or across the Atlantic."

"What, pray tell good sir is your destination?" I asked in an alluring tone, batting my eyes for affect.

Schmidt's first officer leaned across the table. "We're not a charity for street beggars," he said unkindly. "We don't rescue shipwrecked souls - now fuckoff."

"I'm hardly a beggar," I replied gruffly, annoyed that the two men seemed immune to my feminine charms. "I can pay."

Schmidt reached out to take my hand. I could see the lust in his eyes as he caressed the top of my hand with his thumb.

"Oh, and how do you intend to compensate me for my troubles?" he asked with a lewd smile.

"I have gold and silver," I answered and plopped a leather pouch fat with coin down on the table.

Schmidt emptied the pouch and smiled at the coins rolling around and around. "Indeed you do my lady, indeed you do. Perhaps we were a bit too hasty with this one Nuno. What say you?"

"I think she's bought herself passage out of San Augustín, Conrad."

"Excellent!" I said and pushed the coins back into the pouch. "Havana?"

"Havana it is," Schmidt agreed.

"Wonderful. Allow me to buy supper. When might we sail?"

Another tiresome week slipped by before my new German friend was ready to depart San Augustín. I met Schmidt and Amrrique on the docks next to a small skiff. Amrrique took the center bench and grabbed the oars.

"Do you have the money?" Schmidt asked harshly as Amrrique rowed us out towards the freighter.

"I do."

"Half in advance as we agreed," he demanded and extended his hand.

I pulled ten gold ducats out of my trousers' pocket. The German grinned as I dropped the coins into the palm of his hand.

"How do I know," he asked, "you're good for the balance due?"

"I showed you I had enough gold and silver the first night we met."

"Perhaps bad luck followed you to the gambling tables these past few days. Perhaps thieves robbed you. Let me see the rest."

"How do I know you'll keep your end of the bargain and take me to Havana?"

"Ha! Very well. Fair warnin' though, Nuno here doesn't take

kindly to liars or cheats. Isn't that so Nuno?"

Amrrique glanced over his shoulder with a menacing look in his eye. When I answered him with nothing, showing no emotion at all, he snorted, turned away and resumed pulling on the oars.

"Nuno doesn't talk much. You best jump over the gunwale now and swim back to shore if you don't have the rest of what you owe me."

"I keep my promises," I said and looked away.

Had I not been in a pickle, I would never have remained aboard Schmidt's vessel. I keep a clean and orderly ship. I believe in the curative powers of soap. I only sail with a disciplined crew. As I stood on the main deck taking in my unwholesome surroundings, I felt an uneasiness bubbling up from the pit of my stomach. The carrack, an ungainly, fat Portuguese-built vessel, was neither clean nor orderly. Her men - slovenly, filthy creatures - sneered and gawked at me with crooked smiles. Schmidt did nothing to discourage them.

Once at sea, I spent my days up on deck with little to do. And though Schmidt had promised me a small cabin of my own, and my privacy, I was given a hammock and slept with the crew.

I was not surprised when early into our voyage I was tested. Two brutes gagged me while I was sleeping one night and dragged me up to the ship's rope locker near the bow where a third man stood waiting. The first two men pinned my arms against the bulkhead while the third man dropped his trousers.

I had no need to mull things over. I drove my knee into the groin of one of the men holding me and as he doubled over, I pulled the dagger hidden inside my boot and stabbed the other in the shoulder above his heart, a wound meant to maim, not kill. He stared at me in shock, released his grip and staggered backwards. The third man ran off, struggling to pull up his trousers.

I soon found myself up on the quarterdeck standing before Schmidt with my hands tied behind my back. Barefoot and dressed only in his nightshirt, Schmidt held a lantern close to my face as he looked me up and down with disgust. The air was warm and sticky with only a hint of a fading breeze. I could feel beads of sweat clinging to my skin.

"You've drawn blood," he said with a scowl. "We punish such wanton misbehavior. We punish such sordid transgressions harshly aboard this ship."

"Three of your brutes intended to violate me," I replied defiantly. "I only did what needed to be done to protect myself, no more. No one was badly injured. No one died."

"My lads only did what men do when looking for a bit of fun and you assaulted them, most viciously. The man whose balls you crushed won't be able to climb the rigging for days. The fellow you stabbed won't be able to pull his weight for even longer. You've crippled two of my crew and that's an insult against me."

"I pray you tell me what would you have had me do? Submit?"

Schmidt walked past me to stand against the quarterdeck rail. He cleared his throat as he glanced down at his men gathered on the main deck.

"I would have had you restrain your intemperate ways woman!" he bellowed for all to hear. "You bloodied good men. This is your trial. The lads assembled below are your jury. How do you plead to the charge of assault with the *mens rea* to murder?"

"You must be joking!"

"Do you see me laughing? Lads, from what our guest says, I believe she is pleading not guilty - though deny her actions she does not. What say you all?"

"*Guilty, guilty, guilty!*" the crew thundered with one voice.

"Guilty it is!" Schmidt roared and turned to face me. "An eye for an eye, a tooth for a tooth..."

"You intend kick me in my privates and stab me in the shoulder?"

"This is our law. But you do have a choice. You can demand single combat as an alternative. Not many do as such a duel is to the death. *Du verstehst, ja?* You understand?"

The choice for me was easy. The crew formed a circle around me on the main deck. They taunted me and insulted me with vulgar words. I ignored their silly attempts to goad and unnerve me.

Then the ship's champion stepped forward. He was not what I

expected. Instead of a large, brawny, clumsy fighter, I found myself face-to-face with a slight, wiry Asian, a man no taller than me.

He removed his boots and discarded his shirt, revealing a chest and back heavily tattooed with all manner of ungodly beasts. The fool grinned at me and wasted no time.

He crouched low, spun around and tried to land a foot in my stomach. He missed - just barely - as I deftly stepped aside. Then he snapped his forearm up at my nose. He was fast but I was just as fast and blocked the blow with my forearms. He spun around in the opposite direction, tried again to hit me in the face and failed. He was as quick and as agile as a cat. His attack was disciplined at first and I did not recognize his style. But his movements soon became predictable as we sparred. He had grossly underestimated his opponent as I held back and waited. His attack turned arrogant and rash. Then he made a mistake as he tried hooking his left leg around the back of my right knee to pull me off balance. My right fist caught him square in the Adam's apple and down he went clutching at his throat. I had spent grueling, monotonous hours over the years training in the martial arts with Efendi as my tutor and this was my reward. The contest hadn't even winded me.

I stood triumphantly over my opponent as I cast my eyes up to the quarterdeck where Schmidt was standing. His men fell silent as he stared down on me with contempt.

"A tooth for a tooth you say?" I shouted up to him. "I say let bygones be bygones. I'll not take this man's life."

"Then you forfeit the match and now I will take something from you..."

Those were the last words I heard before I felt a sharp blow to the back of my head, before my world turned black.

Chapter Seven

climbed down into the first longboat with Atwood, Koopman and Dijksma. I called over to Maurice and MacGyver to join us and left Efendi behind with Shaw, Kinkae and Henry to watch over the ships and men. With Atwood at the tiller, we headed into shore in smothering heat without a whiff of wind. It was only midmorning and I was already soaked in sweat and though we had arrived in Banten in the midst of the monsoon season, the sun had broken through the clouds and was baking everything around us. All along the beach I could see steam rising off the puddles.

I took in the city and surrounding countryside while the crew worked the oars, leastwise what I could see of the island from the bay. Banten is built on flat ground against the water. To the left of the city is a river and to the right is high ground. Dense rainforests of tropical evergreens, palms and banana trees blankets the land. Beyond the city to the south, I could see mountaintops and volcanoes. Java reminded me of the Caribbean.

We approached an impressive seawall of stone reinforced with wooden timbers just outside the city. Scores of piers and interlocking footbridges jutted out over the water to accommodate the smaller boats. After we docked our longboats, Atwood, Maurice, MacGyver and I accompanied our Dutch friends to the city gates and there we parted ways. Dijksma, Koopman and two dozen Dutchmen carrying a dozen chests between them made their way towards the royal palace while my brothers and I headed for the Grand Bazaar.

Banten is a practical city of unadorned brick buildings the color of sand with stone-paved streets running north and south and east and west in perfectly straight lines. The city is devoid of architecture. I saw no buildings of interest or parks, or trees, or gardens as we walked. And then a hot breeze rushing down from the mountains suddenly blew past us kicking up dust and debris, leaving the city dirtier than when we had entered.

The Grand Bazaar, dwarfing anything I'd ever seen, sprawled across several city blocks. The marketplace was awash in tents, tables, merchants and throngs of people from many faraway lands. We walked by countless baskets filled with a wonderful assortment of fresh, dried and pickled fruits and vegetables. We passed countless clay amphoras overflowing with spices and grains. We saw porcelain cups, plates, vases, pitchers, figurines and the like of remarkable beauty from Japan and bolts of the finest quality mulberry silk from China.

And when we came to a massive tent of red and white stripes enclosed by a high wrought-iron fence, a special place reserved for the gold, silver and jewelry merchants, a squad of heavily armed retainers, burly, scarred men who had seen war, stopped us at the only gate into the great pavilion and made us surrender our weapons before we entered. Inside the pavilion we saw dozens of tables set out in neat rows and I marveled at the stunning silver and gold rings, the exquisitely crafted necklaces, pendants, brooches, billiments and girdles on display. Precious and semi-precious gems like diamonds, rubies, emeralds, opals, topaz, sapphires, Turkey stones, carnelian, jasper, onyx, bloodstones, moss agates, sardonyx and pearls embellished many of the pieces. I saw jewelry any royalty would envy.

After the pavilion we strolled past countless apothecaries, shamelessly hawking their medicines. They tried selling us potions, elixirs, pills, powders, poultices and scented candles guaranteed to ease our pain or heal any ailment. They claimed to have drugs to increase strength, potions to induce enlightenment and magical elixirs to extend life or even to enhance sexual pleasure.

I put my hand to my mouth and gasped when I caught my first glimpse of a tiger pacing back and forth in a bamboo cage. The enormous beast kept his eyes fixed on me as we walked by. And then we heard a loud commotion and made our way to a circle of shouting men making wagers on a cobra and a mongoose maneuvering for position within a ring of dirt. The match was to the death. That day the mongoose won.

By late afternoon we were hot and thirsty and had grown weary of pressing against the multitudes of people. We made no purchases for our astute Dutch trading partners had told us that they could procure whatever we desired in bulk and at the very best prices.

"I need a cool drink to clear the dust out," Atwood said as we looked for a place to rest.

MacGyver chuckled. "If you want something with some bite to it in this land of Islam, we'll need to return to the ships I suspect."

"True," I said, "I doubt we'll find any taverns within the city. But just outside the city walls, or so Dijksma told me, there are a number of establishments that gladly cater to foreign infidels."

Atwood smacked his lips and smiled. "Excellent, by all means lead the way princess."

Dijksma had not misled us. After we passed back through the city gates we headed for the river along the city's east wall where we found rows of inns and taverns up and down the riverbank, mangy, unpleasant establishments offering food, drink and games of chance along with abundant amounts of opium and a variety of male and female harlots to choose from.

We chose a shithole for a tavern that wasn't too crowded and I ordered a pitcher of ale from a large, beefy fellow with thick jowls, fat arms and no neck. The barkeep gave me a hard look, unsure of what to make of me, and said nothing. I doubt he'd ever seen a white woman before, especially a woman dressed in men's clothing and armed with pistols, knives and a sword. I wore no hijab or burqa and wondered if this perhaps offended him. But when I overpaid the man in gold, all turned well between us. He flashed a toothless grin at me before hurrying off to fetch our drinks.

"The other lads are well?" Maurice asked as we took our seats around a small table.

"Kinkae, Henry and Rob are well enough," I replied. "Mustafa remains quiet and aloof."

"He has," Atwood said solemnly, "yet to come to terms with

Mary's death. His mood has been black ever since the day we lost her."

"Aye," MacGyver agreed while staring absently into the flame of a single candle on our table. "We've all been touched by the mulligrubs over Mary."

I took my handkerchief to wipe the sweat out of my eyes. "Her death was a terrible blow," I acknowledged. "The hurt is still fresh. I propose tomorrow we start allowing small numbers of men to come ashore."

"We'll be sending them into port," Atwood said, "with nothing but fiddler's pay."

"What is this fiddler's pay Jacob?" Maurice asked.

"As the Dutch have yet to pay us," Atwood replied, "we only have enough to send the lads ashore with our thanks and a few meager coins for a drink or two - fiddler's pay."

"Ah-ha. The French have a similar phrase: *salaire du mendicant*, beggar's pay."

Then Atwood turned to me. "Elizabeth, did Gerrit or Ewoud give you a specific day when we should be ready to sail?"

"I know not the day," I replied. "A week I suspect, perhaps two."

"We best get to it then and start overhauling the ships in the morning," Atwood said. "We'll need to find a good spot to grave their bottoms. I shudder to think what we'll find after all these months at sea in warm waters."

"Where away next, Elizabeth?" MacGyver asked. "The Spice Islands?"

I paused before answering when an ugly, arseworm of a man with a dirty face and dirtier hands appeared with a pitcher and four glasses. I dismissed the man with a flick of my hand and used my scarf to wipe the glasses clean.

"Yes, we must travel to the Spice Islands to fulfill our obligations to the Company. Ewoud mentioned Sumatra too. I only know what you know. The Dutch can be secretive folk."

Atwood winced after he took a sip of ale. "Jesus, tastes like watered-down piss."

"So, it's true you old swill-belly!" MacGyver said as he leaned forward in his chair and smiled. "You've tasted piss before! I've always heard you Scots enjoy a pint or two."

Atwood nodded. "Nothin' like warm Scottish piss up in the highlands on a cold winter's night to keep the blood flowing. 'Tis better leastwise than that godawful drink you Irish favor distilled from sheep dung."

MacGyver raised his glass to Atwood in salute. "And after the islands Liz, home?"

I smiled. The tales of Marco Polo had always fascinated me. As a young girl I loved to read about Polo's adventures in China, of his exploits on behalf of the mighty Kublai Khan as described in his book *The Travels of Marco Polo*.

"Perhaps before we return home, we should visit China." I blurted out.

Atwood raised an eyebrow. "China? What the devil for?"

"For trade of course."

"Beijing?" Atwood asked.

"Why not? Beijing is China's greatest city."

"Unless you intend to sell-off our Dutch passengers to the Javanese as slave labor, we have no money."

"Perhaps the Dutch will bankroll us. If not, I have a fistful of banknotes stashed away, notes that belong to all of us."

"I doubt the Chinese will accept paper."

"If I may," a stranger behind us asked, "what bank issued these notes you speak of?"

I swung around in my chair to face a shadowy figure sitting against a far wall in the dark watching us. "You speak English," I said.

"I speak many languages."

"A skill more befitting an ambassador than a tavern fly."

"Why do you," Atwood asked in a threatening tone, "skulk in the dark eavesdropping on the private conversations of others friend? 'Tis a bad habit, one that can lead to a bad end."

A ruggedly handsome, cleanshaven fellow with dark, alert eyes stepped out of the shadows with outstretched hands in a gesture of peace. He was dressed in a Chinese black *changshan*, though I wasn't quite certain whether the man was Chinese or something else. He had shaved his head except for a round patch of hair on one side braided in a tail running down the length of his back. The stranger piqued my curiosity.

"I am Arslan. I mean no harm. This a pub, public place. I overhear your words. If you wish pri, private con, conversation, perhaps you should retire to private place."

"You are Chinese?" I asked.

"*Posso continuar em português?*"

"Of course," I replied in Portuguese. "I can translate for my friends."

"My father was Mongolian, my mother Chinese. I am a half-breed."

"Why do you wish to know what bank issued the notes?"

"I have some experience with such matters."

"Oh? Well, I see no harm in telling you. The notes were issued by the House of Mendès."

"Excellent, a house with impeccable credentials. The Portuguese will accept such paper, but at a heavy discount. Chinese merchants will accept the notes at face value with a modest fee for administration, say four or five percent, possibly less if you know who to see."

"The Portuguese have a settlement in Beijing?"

"No, Macau. Macau is in southern China and 'tis but a two week journey from Banten. In Macau one can purchase the best quality porcelains, the rarest silks, exceptional wood furnishings, exquisitely crafted artwork, all manner of goods and abundant quantities of the finest teas, etcetera."

I blew the man off with a laugh. "Ha! We can save ourselves thousands of miles of sailing and purchase all those things here in Banten at the Grand Bazaar."

The half Mongolian, half Chinaman smiled confidently. "At retail prices, yes. In Macau one can purchase at wholesale prices. In Banten you are purchasing second quality goods. In Macau one can purchase first quality goods. Macau's Portuguese and Chinese merchants keep the best for themselves before shipping the rest across the ocean. And consider: it is unlikely you will find any merchant in Banten willing to take your banknotes but even if you do, you will be disappointed in the value offered. Your Dutch friends will confirm the truth of what I say."

"What is your business here?"

"I'm a man of many talents, some quite useful. I dabble in imports and exports here and there. I once served the emperor as a tax assessor in the Province of Guangzhou. At the moment I find myself without employment and far from home."

"How interesting. Come, sit with us Arslan and tell us your story. Tell us more about this place called Macau."

Chapter Eight

Schmidt was neither a forgiving nor a merciful man. He rewarded my chivalry following my duel against his hapless champion with a pair of shackles, a pisspot and confinement to the ship's cramped rope locker. He stripped me of my gold. Many a miserable day passed by while I wasted away below deck and it did not take me long to realize our destination was no longer Havana, if Schmidt's destination had in truth ever been Havana.

I've borne worse torments locked inside a rope locker. But I had been younger, stronger and angrier back then. And though the crew did not beat or abuse me, I still suffered. The air inside the locker was thick, oppressive and nearly unbearable at times. My clothes, damp with sweat, clung to me and chafed at my skin. I languished in filth. I survived on scraps discarded by the crew and was forced to drink the droplets of dirty rainwater that trickled through the seams of the deck above my head whenever the weather turned foul. I wasn't too proud to do what I needed to do to survive. The worst of it was my loss of hope. But for my life and my wits, Schmidt had taken everything from me.

The task was neither quick nor easy. Using my fingernails and a shard of sharp wood, I managed to pry a bent nail from one of the deck planks. After my attempts to pick the lock to my shackles failed, I used that nail to whittle away the hours scratching drawings into the walls to entertain myself. And though my days drifted by slowly, I kept my mind busy.

After I heard the splash of the anchor, Amrrique and two of his swine were quick to fetch me. They grabbed me roughly by the arms and pulled me up on deck. I immediately recognized my surroundings.

We had sailed into the arsehole of the Caribbean, into a festering canker on the face of the earth men call the Port of Spain. Under an unwritten, uneasy truce between Trinidad's Spanish governor and the ruling pirate clans the port was a safe haven for all comers. The Spanish turned a blind eye to a certain amount of lawlessness in exchange for a certain amount of peace. The ships of brigands, slavers, smugglers and other unsavory creatures of every kind filled the harbor's polluted waters. I flinched when I heard the sound of heavy bootsteps coming up behind me for fear of being struck over the head again.

"*Großer Gott!*" Schmidt cry out. "You have a fierce stink about you woman."

I turned on my heels to face the German. "The Port of Spain?"

"*Ja, ja*, you know the port?"

"Aye."

"*Wunderbar*. I'm I man of my word. I promised to transport you to one of the islands and *voilà*, Trinidad. I've brought you to the Caribbean's most notorious island where all manner of commerce is welcome. Why the sad face? I thought you'd be pleased."

I pursed my lips to show Schmidt my displeasure but in truth my heart sang with joy. I found hope again. I knew the Port of Spain and knew it well. From the Port of Spain, I could make my way back to Ireland with little difficulty, except for the gold I lacked. Not to worry I told myself. I'd find a way.

I raised my hands to be released from my shackles. "Our business is then concluded."

"*Oh nein, nein meine fraulein*, I fear you misunderstand," Schmidt offered playfully, pausing to remove a document from inside his jacket. "Our business is not yet finished."

"What is this?" I demanded.

"It would seem you're a fugitive from justice," Schmidt replied as he thrust the document in my face. "This is a warrant for your arrest."

"Murder and robbery?" I blurted out as I examined the warrant. "In San Augustín? Who did I murder? Who did I rob? What buffoonery is this?"

"Nuno is a gifted forger, an artist. The wax seal with the Spanish royal coat-of-arms is a nice touch don't you think? I've instructed Nuno to take you to the slave markets where you'll be sold off to the highest bidder. Between the gold I've taken from you and money I'll make at auction I'll see a tidy profit."

It was if someone had punched me in the gut. I felt the urge to fall to my knees and vomit. Then the greater urge to kill seized me. I considered wrapping my chains around the German's neck and jumping over the side. Either Schmidt's neck would break in the fall or he'd drown. But I was weak and unsure of myself. I didn't know if had the strength or the quickness to accomplish the grisly deed and even if I succeeded in killing Schmidt, and somehow escaped into the streets of the city, I'd still be in shackles, I still had no money. I had no friends or allies in Trinidad. No, killing Schmidt would mean my own death.

Still, I let my temper get the better of me. "You dickless, fucking coward," I hissed.

Schmidt smirked as if amused. "'Tis just smart business Mary. A beautiful, healthy, white woman like you is certain to fetch a handsome sum in the markets. I pray you are in fact healthy?"

"Why don't you take me below to your bed and find out for yourself?"

"Ha! And risk the great pox - or a sharp nail in my eye? No, I think not. Nuno, get our lovely strumpet ready. Have the lads clean her up some. She reeks of foul, displeasing odors."

I grabbed Schmidt by the wrist before Amrrique grabbed me. "You fool, Schmidt. You've made a terrible enemy, an enemy who delights in serving up vengeance. I will come for you."

Schmidt yanked his arm away. "Feeble words uttered by a feeble woman full of empty bombast. You're just a runaway now, just a lowly, loudmouthed outlaw whose luck has run out. No one will miss you. No one will come looking for you. The world thinks you dead. You'll live out the rest of your miserable days as a slave toiling in the fields alongside those wretched, black-skinned devils. The work is long and hard I hear. Most die young."

I set my jaw. I grit my teeth. I took a step forward to come nose-to-nose with the German.

"I belong to no man half-wit and I'm hardly feeble. I'm Captain Mary, known by many as Captain Bloody Mary. When we meet again my face will be the last one you ever see - I swear it."

Schmidt offered no reply but just before he turned to walk away, I saw the look I longed to see. I caught the unsettled mien in his eye. I caught the fear, like shadow, passing across his face.

Amrrique and his hairy baboons, with smiles all around, removed my shackles. They forced me to strip naked in front of them out on the open deck. One man handed me a bucket of seawater with a chunk of soap. Another handed me a soiled rag. Amrrique made me wash my clothes first and then myself. He kept my boots and my fashionable, capitano hat with the long, blue feather for himself.

After I finished dressing, Amrrique had his men lower away a boat. He rowed me to an open slip along the waterfront, tied a halter around my neck, shackled my wrists again and dragged me by the neck in my bare feet through the port's dirty streets, streets cluttered with trash and teaming with diseased, wretched beggars. He dragged me to the city square and led me over to the auction blocks just as dark clouds began settling over the island. But he did not take me to the place where the Irish - the victims of English Plantation - and other unfortunate Europeans were sold into servitude. No, I was to be sold off with the Africans.

Suddenly the heavens unloosed a deluge of water, turning the streets into liquid muck and the port into a cesspool. Amrrique exchanged a few quick words with one of the auctioneers, himself a Blackamoor, and handed the man the forged warrant. The man looked me up and down and nodded. He removed the halter around my neck and unlocked the shackles on my wrists. He pushed me to the front of a line of naked African men and women and forced me up a dozen wooden steps, steps worn smooth by thousands of bare feet before mine. I stepped out onto wooden platform where I stood alone in the rain with a crowd of vile men gawking up at me from the street below. I heard laughter, jeers and lewd entreaties of the worst kind.

Standing on platforms to my right and left were scores of men and women. Some wept. Some trembled. I saw one man standing like a rock staring defiantly straight ahead while a young girl next to him began swaying back and forth and fainted. Her limp body hit the plankboards hard.

I did not weep. I did not stare defiantly ahead or faint. I was too numb, too weak, too sick of heart to do or feel much of anything. Though my recollection of that godawful day is clouded, I still remember the spirited bidding to own me. There seemed no end to the humiliation.

One man, a wealthy merchant judging by his fine apparel the color of ivory and the manservant holding an umbrella over his head, an elderly Spaniard with a mane of long, silver hair and a matching goatee, had had enough of the bidding and doubled his own offer to quell all the rest. I have no recollection of the price paid but after the deed was done, I wanted to fall to my knees and die. Had I a knife, I think I could have slit my own throat.

A Blackamoor, because of his respectable clothing and good grooming I assumed was no fieldhand, stepped onto the platform holding a brass-tipped cane in his hand. He grabbed me by the arm, hustled me down to the street and led me behind the rows of auction blocks and into a back alley where two dozen African men dressed in rags stood barefoot in the mud chained to a wooden whipping post. The air reeked of shit, urine and vomit. After the man with the cane chained me with the others, he led us to the waterfront where the Spaniard who had purchased me was standing next to a younger, bronzed-skinned man on a pier with their backs against the sea.

With the rains tapering off and the heat returning, the older man removed his hat, a simple straw thing, and used a handkerchief to dab the beads of sweat off his brow. The creases around his eyes and mouth cut deep when he smiled.

"Raise your hand if you understand me," he commanded in Spanish with a raspy, tobacco voice and then repeated his words in Portuguese.

I raised my hand along with a handful of Africans.

"Good," the Spaniard said and turned to the man who had led us to the docks. "Felipe, make certain my words are translated for the benefit of the others later. For the rest of you, my name is Señor Esteban Francisco de Salamanca and I am your new lord and master. The man standing next to me is Señor Juan Carlos, my overseer. You will obey his words as if I had spoken them. Felipe, the man holding the cane, is a boss man too and you will obey him as you would Juan Carlos. We sail with the tide for Veracruz. Do what is asked of you by Señor Carlos and Felipe and you will be treated generously. Fail to heed their instructions, or try to run away - God forbid you fail to show me respect - I promise you there will be dire consequences for such disobedience, no matter how trifling the infraction. There now, I am glad we understand one another. I'm glad we have that ugliness behind us. Felipe, leave the woman with me. See the rest to the ship."

After the man named Felipe unchained me and led the others off with his cane resting across his shoulders, Salamanca motioned me to step closer. "I don't think you are Spanish. What is your name and who are your people?"

"My name is Mary. I come from Ireland."

"Ireland? Huh. Well Irish, I won't have a white woman confined with my blacks even if you are a convict. Many of these men are animals and have no souls. The freighter we sail with is a modest caravel but Juan will find some cranny where you can safely lay your head without fear."

"I'm most grateful Señor Salamanca," I said respectfully. "But sir, I am no convict. I was kidnapped by pirates after my ship went down. These brigands wrongly sold me off on false papers. I've murdered no one. I've robbed no one. I'm innocent."

Salamanca carefully placed his hat back on his head and smiled. "None of us are innocent my dear. The deed is done. I've paid a pretty penny for you and I have the papers to prove you now belong to me."

"But I know a man, a rich man with powerful friends in government who can vouch for me. His name is Rodriguez Miguel de Cortés y Ovando. He has homes in Santo Domingo and in Havana. He is my partner in trade. If you take me to the local magistrate I can prove -."

"But hush now Mary," the Spaniard commanded softly as he brushed my cheek with the back of his hand. "Any further protest by you could be construed as disrespectful. Nothing distresses me more than disrespect. It is too late in the day to be doling out punishments. Hmmm, what to do with you? Such lovely, unspoiled skin. You are much too pretty for the fields. Be not concerned. We shall find some task worthy of your talents at my hacienda. 'Tis a lovely tract of land not far from Veracruz. Juan, escort the Irishwoman to the ship and see to her needs. I have a bit more business yet in town but shall be along directly."

There was a foul stench of rot buried deep within the caravel's timbers. At night I slept on hard wood in my little nook next to the forecastle. During the day I was free to walk about the main deck. I ate breakfast and supper with the crew. The fare never varied much. We ate cold gruel and drank flat ale. Every few days the cook would add a bit of bacon or a chunk of fat to each man's bowl and hand us a thimble-full of a dark, sweet drink, a new drink, distilled from molasses the sailors call brum or rum. I did not care for the taste very much.

I often saw Salamanca standing up on the quarterdeck engaged in casual conversation with the ship's master while he sipped his wine. Kept chained below with the ship's cargo, I never saw the Africans up on deck, not once.

With little to do monotony filled my days though the voyage was not entirely unpleasant, leastwise I was better off than wasting away in a stuffy, cramped rope locker. We glided across calm seas with fair skies for most of the voyage and after twenty-nine days of easy sailing, the crew dropped anchor in the bustling harbor of Veracruz near the stronghold of San Juan de Ulúa, an impressive fortress of thick stone walls reinforced with concrete and iron, of high battlements with heavy cannon and sturdy watchtowers - the very place where the Spanish navy back in 1568 had trapped an English fleet led by Drake and his cousin John Hawkins.

Veracruz is where the powerful Casa de Contratación, which

oversees all trade throughout the New World, keeps a strong presence. The Spanish Crown assesses a twenty percent tax, the quinto, against all imports and exports - forty percent if the Spanish navy is asked to provide war galleons as escort.

Known as Chalchihuecan by the Totonac people before the destroyer of worlds, Hernán Cortés, landed there on Good Friday in 1519 and renamed the village Villa Rica de la Vera Cruz, the Rich Village of the True Cross, the small hamlet rose quickly in power and prestige under Spanish rule to become the most important port in New Spain. Immigrants from across Europe and slaves from across Africa pour into Veracruz by the tens of thousands each year while vast quantities of gold, silver, cochineal dye, chocolate, vanilla, chili peppers, hardwoods and much more are exported from Veracruz back to the mother country.

And Veracruz is unique among cities. I know of no other place in the New World where there are no laws against marriages between the races. Many of her citizens, rich and poor alike, perhaps the majority, are mulatto, Spanish blood mixed with black, or mestizo, Spanish blood mixed with Aztec, Totonac or Huastec blood. All stand equal under the laws and social morals of Veracruz.

Yes, I know Veracruz. Over the years I had smuggled quality manufactured goods into the port from time-to-time under the noses of the Casa. Avoiding Spain's obnoxious taxes on imports and exports is how I had made my fortune.

I went ashore with Carlos on a flat-bottomed river barge carrying Salamanca's baggage, along with a large assortment of boxes and parcels wrapped in oiled parchment containing the purchases Salamanca had made in Trinidad. When Carlos stepped onto the wharf, he waved for me to follow.

"No shackles?" I asked as we made our way through the city.

"I suspect," he answered in broken English, "you're the only Irishwoman in Veracruz. Where would you run?"

"You speak English," I said surprised as we walked past a row of small shops open for trade.

"Yes, English, French, Portuguese, Italian and a bit of Dutch.

Good languages to know in this part of the world, especially if you're in the employ of Salamanca."

"Is Salamanca's property far?" I asked as we walked by the construction of the city's new municipal palace.

"His hacienda is about eighty miles and then some to the northwest, up in wooded, hilly country," Carlos replied.

"Where," I asked as we skirted around the monastery of Nuestra Señora de la Merced founded by the Franciscans and then past the Hospital de Nuestra Señora de Loreto, a very fine hospital I had once had cause to visit a few years back to set a broken arm, "are we walking to?"

"Over yonder to that large warehouse there are wagons, carriages and drivers for hire. We'll need one carriage and several utility wagons, five should do I think."

I thought my prospects were improving until I realized Carlos was hiring the carriage for just Salamanca and himself. When we returned to the wharf with one carriage and five open wagons, we found Salamanca and the Africans waiting for us under the shade of a large storehouse. Dockmen had already brought the rest of the ship's cargo ashore and, with the help of the wagoneers Carlos had hired, promptly began loading Salamanca's baggage and packages into the first wagon and then the assorted goods Salamanca had purchased, tools, furnishings, furniture and the like, into the remaining four wagons. I rode in the back of the first wagon surrounded by Salamanca's baggage with Felipe at the reins. The Africans followed us in a single file chained to the last wagon.

Once our modest caravan reached the outskirts of the city, a dozen light cavalrymen, Spanish lancers, charged with protecting us from the marauding bandits and runaway slaves who roam the king's highways looking for travelers to rob joined us. The road we would take, the Camino Real, the Royal Road, running between Veracruz and la Ciudad de México, was particularly dangerous Felipe explained.

When we reached the foothills in the late afternoon, covered in dust, sweat and grime, cool, invigorating breezes sweeping down from the mountains to the west came to greet us. I took a moment to savor the pleasant change and then turned to take one last look at the city. Many refer to Veracruz as the City of Tables because from the surrounding highlands the square, flat-roofed houses of the city look like tables set-out in neat, checkered rows.

I reached over to tap Felipe on the shoulder. "May I ask how much farther Felipe?"

"Another four or five days on the road. After we roll through the village of Córdoba, we'll be close."

"Where do we sleep?"

"There are small coach inns along the way for folks like Señor Salamanca and Carlos. You, me and the drivers will sleep underneath the wagons."

"My bum hurts, may I sit up front with you?"

"I don't mind none."

I plopped myself down on the driver's board next to Felipe. "How long have you been with Señor Salamanca?" I asked.

"I was born on the master's property."

"I see. It would seem you've done well for yourself."

Felipe looked at me quizzically. "Ah, ha," he answered evasively and looked away.

"What is Salamanca's business?"

"You ask a lot of questions."

"I intended no disrespect. I'm simply curious to know what is produced on his lands."

"You have a curious mind."

"Aye, I suppose I do."

"Curiosity can be a blessing or a curse in this part of the world, depending upon how you use it. Fair warning: I'd be mighty careful if I were you."

"Fair enough."

"As for Señor Salamanca's business at the hacienda, we produce many things. The land is rich here. We have abundant rainfalls and fertile soil. We grow coffee, vanilla beans, sugarcane, tobacco, bananas and corn. Our forests are thick with hardwoods prized for their strength and quality. We harvest the earth's treasures below the ground too. We mine gold, silver, iron, coal, copper, sulfur and marble."

"This land you describe sounds like paradise."

"Ha! Ask those poor wretches trailing behind us if we are on our way to paradise."

"Indeed. Do you have a family?"

"Enough talk woman..."

"I mean no harm."

"You're trouble. I see it in your eyes. Show our master disrespect and I swear I'll crack your skull open with a hammer."

"Very well," I said, without showing my displeasure. "Should you wish it, you'll find me a very good friend to have."

Felipe merely grunted and ignored me for the rest of the journey.

Nestled in a valley surrounded by soft rolling hills, tall trees and fields of dark, rich soil that had been recently ploughed and seeded, Salamanca's estate appeared substantial, though without the obvious trappings of wealth. The main house, a large, three-story building of whitewashed clapboard and ugly brown shutters was surprisingly plain. The rows of military style barracas used to quarter Salamanca's slaves, the shacks for curing meats and tobacco and the storehouses used to hold the harvest, looked as rugged as the surrounding terrain. As Felipe had said, Salamanca's wealth was in the land.

To the west I could see the snowcapped peak of Pico de Orizaba, better known as Citlaltépetl by the villagers in their native, Nahuatl tongue, rising high above the surrounding hills. Magnificent Pico was the largest, grandest mountain I'd ever seen.

Filipe followed Salamanca's carriage down a gravel pathway to the front porch of the house while the other four wagons peeled-off towards the barracas in the back. The commanding officer of the lancers, a handsome fellow with the rank of a lieutenant, gave Salamanca a crisp salute, wheeled his stallion around and followed the other wagons.

After I stepped off the driver's board I paused to take in my surroundings. I removed my arming cap, a cheap, soiled scrap of felt I had pilfered off the caravel, to let the mountain air run through my hair.

I was an unwilling servant, a prisoner, in a strange, faraway land, a world away from home and friends. I found the despondency gnawing at me a heavy burden. *Day-by-day* I mumbled to myself. I would need to get through each day as best I could and think no more beyond that.

I brushed back a tear and held on to a simple truth: the sea, the rough and tumbly sea that had nurtured me, that was life to me, that had raised me as a free spirit, was a mere eighty miles away. I swore I'd gain my freedom back or die in the trying.

Chapter Nine

Arslan as best I could tell was a wanderer, a blithe adventurer far from home and short on funds. I know not why, but I was determined to see China and Macau would do just fine. Atwood was adamantly opposed to such a voyage and was hardly shy about expressing his disapproval.

"I say again Elizabeth, I say it plainly," Atwood declared curtly as we casually made our way back to the waterfront. "Risk verses reward. 'Tis a simple principal Mary lived by. The potential reward we might gain by sailing to China is far outweighed by the untold risks we'd face."

"We've come this far Jacob," I said. "Why not venture a little farther? Where's your sense of daring, your desire to explore new lands, to meet new people?"

"I've never had any sense of daring and I couldn't care less about exploring new lands. As for new people, ha, I'd be content if I never crossed paths with any of my neighbors back home again - old or new."

"Ugh! Why must you Scots always be so contrary! You heard what Arslan said. China offers many profitable possibilities."

"Gluttony Elizabeth. Gluttony can kill."

"No, not gluttony Jacob opportunity, opportunity to prosper," I said just as the skies unloosed a deluge of water, instantly soaking the world around us. Having brought no raingear, I buttoned up my shirt and raised the collar up around my neck for what little good it did me.

"What say you Michael, Maurice?" I asked. "You've both been painfully quiet."

"I have no opinion on the matter Liz," MacGyver answered as the ground beneath our feet rapidly turned to goo.

"As for me," Maurice said, "I share Jacob's concerns. This far side of the world is significantly larger than the Caribbean with people, laws and customs we don't understand."

I sighed and bit my tongue. Though I had more to say, and was eager to speak my mind, I decided to wait for a better moment. When we reached our longboat, we found three inches of water sitting over her keel. While Atwood and MacGyver quietly worked the oars, Maurice and I took turns scooping out rainwater with a bailing bucket.

Dijksma and Koopman returned to the ships not long after us. I invited both men to join my officers and me for supper in my great cabin. We feasted on slices of succulent ham, on a variety of fresh vegetables and fruits our ship's cook, a new man the crew had dubbed Tiny because of his smallish hands, had purchased from enterprising Javanese farmers who had rowed out to our ships earlier in their little boats to sell us their bounty. For dessert we ate hot biscuits with freshly churned butter and drank our fill of mellow wine. The audience with Prince Ratu had gone well the Dutchmen reported and the mood around the table was light. To my delight, neither Dijksma nor Koopman batted an eye when I floated the notion of making a trip to Macau.

We spent the next few days overhauling the ships in the rain. We replaced frayed lines, rusted iron fittings and the like. We patched torn sails, repaired rotted planking, scrubbed away smudges of mold and mildew as best we could and painted any bare wood. We cleaned, sharpened and oiled our swords, muskets and knives too. And while we readied ourselves for sea, we ferried half the Dutch and their supplies ashore with Koopman to lead them along with some of our own men, fifty or so at a time, with a few coins to spend.

A week after our arrival to Banten, with our ships restored to fighting trim, though we had yet to grave their bottoms, I called for another council of war. Despite the incessant rains I was in fine spirits. I had regained sole possession of my great cabin and had used my freedom for one night of delicious debauchery with my all too eager lover. I had not felt Shaw's wicked touch since leaving Ireland and had suffered for it. We joyfully spent the night teasing and pleasing one another in my bed and when morning came, I awoke refreshed and full of energy.

"That's it, that's my proposition," I said after I could see that everyone around the table had had enough of discussing a voyage to Macau. I leaned back on my chair and took a sip of good, fresh ale. I was confident I had won over Kinkae and Henry. I could not read Efendi and MacGyver truly seemed indifferent. Atwood, Maurice and Shaw - to my great displeasure Shaw - had all strenuously argued against sailing to China and I could see that Atwood was about to throw the Ten Rules in my face and insist I needed a unanimous vote to have my way.

But before Atwood could say more, we heard a knocking at my cabin door. When I told the man to enter, Dijksma and our ship's physician, a German fellow from the town of Munich named Joachim Stachel stepped inside. Despite his weakness for the gambling tables Stachel had proven himself a gifted healer and was well-liked by the men.

"Gentlemen, what vexes you?" I asked when the two men hesitated. "Why the glum faces? A man is missing, someone died?"

Stachel took a step forward while removing his hat. "Elizabeth, there's been an incident outside the city walls. Seven men have been arrested, four of ours and three Dutchmen."

"Arrested?" I asked. "How do you know this?"

"Because I was there."

"Where?"

"At a tavern along the river, a lowly, unsavory establishment, one that caters to foreigners."

"Let me guess," Atwood interjected. "A brawl broke out over a whore or someone was caught cheating at cards. Might do the lads some good to cool their heels locked inside a Banten birdcage for a day or two."

"I fear matters are much worse than that Jacob. There was indeed a scuffle at one of the tables. Heated words were exchanged followed by taunts and insults. The entire tavern erupted in chaos. Blows were struck. Stools, tables and all manner of things went flying through the air. Someone pulled a knife. A Javanese man was stabbed in the leg. I did what I could to save the fellow's life but the blade cut deep and severed an artery. Poor bastard bled to death on the dirt floor."

"Merciful God," I said. "Did you see who stabbed this man?"

"No, it could have been anyone. Just about everyone was splattered in someone's blood. I saw cuts and bruises and broken bones. I have strong doubts any of our men killed the man. I saw the blade used to stab him lying next to him. The knife was unlike the kind our lads carry. The blade was cheap and ordinary and not very sharp. The handle had no carved initials or markings to identify its owner."

"This is outrageous," I said, shaking my head in disgust, "We must secure the release of our lads at once."

"Who arrested our men?" Efendi asked in a low voice.

"Wardens armed with clubs patrol the streets up and down the river Mustafa. A handful of these ruffians entered the tavern and cracked a few skulls to stop the brawl. There was a lot of finger pointing and shouting around the dead man's body. Though I did not understand the words, it is not hard to guess what men were saying. One of the wardens recognized the dead man and sent a runner back to the city. No one was permitted to leave. When the warden's man returned with soldiers, the soldiers arrested our men and led them away. I followed them as far as to the city gates. It would seem this dead fellow was a person of rank, perhaps nobility."

"This," Dijksma said with a troubled voice, "is very grim news indeed. Justice in the East Indies under Islamic law is swift, often arbitrary and can be quite harsh by our standards."

"What do we do?" I asked.

"In the morning we go to the palace and petition Prince Ratu for the release our lads," Dijksma said soberly.

The next day I went ashore with Dijksma. Atwood, MacGyver, Maurice and Efendi all insisted on coming. Except for the Alcázar de Colón in Santo Domingo, a modest building of coraline stone blocks and elegant white arches fashioned in the Gothic Mudejar style, I'd never stepped foot inside a royal palace before. The Kraton of

Surosowan, the word kraton means palace in Javanese Dijksma explained as we made our way through the city, had been built some fifty years earlier by Sultan Maulana Hasanuddin on the designs of a Dutch architect.

A six-foot-high wall, made of red bricks and coral stone, a wall any determined foe with ladders could easily scale, surrounded the palace. I saw a few modest wooden watchtowers along the perimeter, but saw no cannon, no moat or sturdy battlements to repel an enemy. We approached a pair of arched doors, the main gate, where a clutch of sentries dressed in plain brown *thawbs*, black boots and dome-shaped leather helmets and armed with spears and round wicker shields, barred our entry. When Dijksma asked the captain of the guard for permission to see the prince the man led us over to a gatehouse, used to stable the guards' chase horses, and instructed us to wait.

While I passed the time breathing in the stench of horse dung and watching mice scurrying in and out of piles of hay in that awful place, Dijksma and my brothers were perfectly fine napping in the dirt. Several hours went by before a dozen soldiers, handsomely dressed in fitted black tunics, crimson trousers and tall black caps with silver tassels - these were the prince's elite palace guard Dijksma explained - came for us. The palace guard escorted us inside a royal compound of unremarkable redbrick and coral stone buildings spread across six acres of ground. We walked along a crooked stone path overgrown with weeds until we reached an inner courtyard of great beauty and serenity, a quiet place of shade trees, sculptured bushes, flowers, stone benches and a stream of clear water stocked with exotic fish.

After the prince's men confiscated our weapons, the senior man led us into a building grander than all the others just beyond the courtyard and left us standing inside a great hall on a black marble floor polished to a high gloss. Except for a magnificent white fountain standing in the center of the hall, the hall was empty, devoid of any chairs or tables or furnishings. An arcade of high arched columns cut from white marble, swathed in white gossamer curtains, supported a stunning vaulted ceiling paneled over in white squares decorated with hexagonal ornaments in gold leaf. Directly above the fountain at the center of the ceiling was a large sun medallion made of white plaster with casts of important people and events taken from the Quran, or so I supposed.

And then a man dressed in white flowing robes embroidered in gold with matching slippers, a tall, long-bearded fellow with a dark complexion and a hawk's beak for a nose, suddenly appeared from behind the fountain. He wore a long dagger with a jeweled scabbard strapped to his side. Rings of silver and gold studded with precious jewels adorned each of his fingers and his thumbs. He took a moment to consider each of us, scrutinizing me the longest.

"This is Agung," Dijksma explained as he bowed. "Most of the people across the East Indies do not have family names, so he is simply known as Agung, the son of Dahan. Agung is the Supreme General of the Army and also serves as the Captain of the Royal Household Guard, a very high position of honor and trust as you might imagine."

After Dijksma introduced us to the general in Javanese, he nodded politely to each of us and then took a step towards Efendi. "*As-salamu alaykum wa rahmatu allahi wa barakatuh,*" he said in a soft voice.

"*As-salamu alaykum wa rahmatu allahi wa barakatuh,*" Efendi replied while placing his hand over his heart.

"What was all that about Mustafa?" I asked.

"A customary Islamic greeting," Efendi explained. "May the peace, mercy and the blessings of Allah be upon you."

When Agung clapped his hands, seven men magically emerged from the shadows carrying six chairs and a single table. The general motioned us to be seated as more servants carrying silver trays with plates of assorted fruits and pastries entered the hall. One man brought a silver pot with delicate glass cups wrapped in gold and silver ornamentations. After the servants placed the trays on the table and left, Agung lifted his sleeve to pour the coffee himself and as he poured, he resumed his conversation with Dijksma.

"Agung is honored," Dijksma said after the two men had exchanged many words, "to make your acquaintances. He has met

Turks before but has never met anyone from Ireland or Scotland or from the Caribbean and hopes to learn more about these lands. He has never met a woman from Europe, nor has he ever heard of a woman with ships and men-at-arms under her command. You in particular Elizabeth intrigue our good general."

"The general has never heard," I asked, "of the Muslim Pirate Queen of Tétouan, al-Sayyida-al-Hurra of Morocco? Her title, or so I've been told, means *the noble lady who is free and independent, the woman sovereign who bows to no superior authority* or something of the sort. I fear I know not her name but certainly he has heard the stories of this extraordinary woman? And let us not forget the fabled Amazon warriorsesses of old. Some say their kind can still be seen up in the mountains of Anatolia."

"*Touché, ma dame!*" Dijksma exclaimed with a wide grin then turned to the general to translate my words.

Agung smiled politely. "Her name my lady," Agung said in good Portuguese as he poured me more coffee, "was Lalla Aicha bint Ali ibn Rashid al-Alami, Hakimat Titwan."

Agung then stood and began pacing back and forth as if some weighty matter was troubling him. He spoke to Dijksma for some time in Javanese again and as he spoke, I could see the color draining from the Dutchman's face. When the general finished speaking, Dijksma took a moment to collect his thoughts.

"The gist of things is this," Dijksma explained solemnly in English. "The man who was killed at the tavern yesterday was one of Prince Ratu's cousins, his favorite cousin it would seem. The prince is overwhelmed with grief and will not see us. This is all a preposterous fiction. I suspect the boy barely knew his cousin. Earlier this morning, as we were being detained at the gatehouse, the minister of justice himself tried our men on charges of murder. After the minister heard the testimony of many witnesses from the tavern, he found our men guilty, except for your physician Stachel who he tried *in absentia*. The punishment is death. Our men will be taken to a place known as Execution Square this afternoon and publicly beheaded."

I looked at the general aghast and sprang from my chair to protest until Dijksma gently grabbed my arm. "The matter Elizabeth," Dijksma said delicately, "is closed. I've already beseeched Agung to intercede with Prince Ratu on our behalf, to ask his Highness for leniency. I've even offered gold in exchange for a royal pardon. Agung deeply appreciates our wish to help our men. I suspect he is even sympathetic. But there is nothing he can do."

"This is not justice!" I blurted out in anger. "There must be something we can do Ewoud to save our men!"

"No, Elizabeth, I'm sorry. Regrettably, there are palace intrigues at play here beyond our understanding. Agung is a friend to the Dutch. There are those amongst Prince Ratu's retinue however who would see we Dutch expelled from Java, indeed from all of Indonesia."

Sensing my ire, before walking off, the general nodded respectfully to me as if to offer an apology.

Word spread quickly throughout the city. Seven murderers - foreigners to boot - were to be put to death before day's end. Hundreds of curious spectators had already gathered at the place known as *Alun-alun Eksekusi*, Execution Square, when we arrived. I stood quietly in the midst of the crowd with my fellow officers and Dijksma at my side, soaked to the bone in rain.

Stripped of everything but their trousers, four of Atwood's crew, new lads, young, foolish boys who had no experience of the world outside of Ireland, and three of Dijksma's men, savored the last few moments of their lives in a strange land on their knees in filth and mud. A block of wood had been placed before each man. Behind them, dressed in purple tunics with white trousers and crimson sashes, with gold spikes atop their black turbans and odd shoes that curled at the toe, stood their executioners.

When shafts of golden light suddenly pierced the angry clouds and the rains briefly subsided, the boy prince, wearing robes of golden silk, golden sandals and a matching *tarboosh* with a single, gold feather pinned to the center, strolled into the square with a dozen of his viziers trailing behind him. Agung, now dressed in resplendent armor, walked with them. His polished breastplate of gold worn over a tunic of rich purple nearly blinded me in the sunlight. He wore golden greaves with golden boots and cradled in one arm he carried a magnificent golden helmet in the shape of an eagle's head.

The prince climbed onto a wooden dais underneath a green canopy with silver tassels along the fringes. He quietly took his seat on a highbacked throne of gold with red cushions, the only chair on the dais. As his entourage hurried to take their positions behind him, he stared blankly out at the crowd, showing no emotion one way or the other.

An absurd, childish rhyme suddenly took ahold of me, madly circling around and around in my brain. I couldn't shake the words off. *Tick-tock, tick-tock like Anne Boleyn I lay my head upon the chopping block; tick-tock, tick-tock I lay my head upon the chopping block; when the clock doth strike my head will fall and who will wed me then, who will bed me then; tick tock, tick-tock like Anne Boleyn I lay my head upon the chopping block...* I caught the giggles and had to pinch myself to regain my composure. MacGyver thought I was weeping and handed me his handkerchief.

When Agung moved to the edge of the dais and raised his hands, a great hush settled over the multitude. But for the pennants fluttering in the breeze, and the birds of prey circling overhead, squawking with anticipation, the world turned deathly silent.

With a simple command from Agung the executioners removed their turbans in unison and fastened them to their sashes. They drew their long, curved scimitars honed to a keen edge and forced our men to rest their necks against the blocks. When one of our lads, a fresh-faced boy with freckled cheeks struggled to break free two burly attendants dressed in black rushed forward, grabbed him by his arms and held him firmly in place.

When Agung turned to the prince, the boy turned to look over his right shoulder at a grey-bearded fellow standing behind him. I thought his highness would stand to address his people, serve up some nonsense about the evil barbarians who had defiled his kingdom or insulted Allah, but no. With a simple nod from the grey-bearded fellow the awful deed was done. The blows were swift and clean.

The crowd erupted into a wild frenzy. People roared and cheered and danced. They hurled ugly insults at our poor dead. But when his majesty stood, all fell silent again.

Without fanfare the executioners sheathed their soiled swords and followed the prince and his entourage out of the square. Once the prince was gone, the mob tossed the severed heads into wicker baskets and rushed down to the city gates and then to the river beyond. We followed them and watched as they gleefully mounted their trophies atop iron spikes planted along the riverbank.

"There was no justice done here today," MacGyver noted softly and made the sign of the cross.

Dijksma nodded. "We've paid a heavy price to keep ourselves in the prince's good graces. Leastwise our friends did not suffer much. I can assure you, there are far worse ways a man can meet his end in Banten."

Atwood looked at me with disdain - as if I was somehow to blame. "Small comfort Ewoud. A black day for us all. I for one am eager to leave this godforsaken land behind us."

Spirits plummeted throughout our tiny squadron as word of the executions spread. Our voyage had suffered a terrible blow. Men despaired and grumbled. Many longed to return home and said so openly. But under our commission with the Company, we were obliged to sail to the Spice Islands first and I still had my heart set on Macau.

As we sat around the table in my great cabin, MacGyver and Efendi both wavered. Henry and Kinkae, forever trying to please me, stood with me while Atwood, Maurice and Shaw were firmly opposed.

"That's it then," Atwood said as he helped himself to more wine. "The issue is settled. After we've concluded our matters with the Dutch, we sail for home."

"The issue is not settled Jacob," I said forcefully and stood to open a window. My cabin had turned hot and stuffy and I needed fresh air.

"Zeus' balls, Elizabeth!" Atwood exclaimed loudly. "We're split. Under the Ten Rules the vote must be unanimous."

"Why? Why must the vote be unanimous? I'm not putting the men or the ships in excessive danger. There is nothing extraordinary or particularly perilous about a trip to China. As my loyal officers, I expect you to support me."

Atwood vigorously shook his head. "We are not *your* officers."

I did not care for Atwood's callous tone, or for his insolence, not one bit. But I held my tongue. Though I considered myself to be Mary's heir apparent - she had shared as much with me in so many words - the others, to my great annoyance, often deferred to Atwood over me. I needed more time to win them over.

"Very well Jacob," I said. "You, Michael and Maurice can sail on to the Spice Islands with the Dutch whilst I sail to China with *Ghostrunner*. We can rendezvous here in Banten before setting out for the Netherlands."

Atwood drained his glass. "No," he said and sighed. "I see your mind cannot be turned. So be it. We keep the ships together. After the Spice Islands we sail for China."

"Excellent," I said joyfully and returned to my chair. "Shall we procure fresh victuals and prepare to sail?"

"Two days should be sufficient to do what must be done," Atwood replied.

"Friday then," I responded with a triumphant smile.

But we did not sail that Friday. An outbreak of the bloody flux kept us in port for another week. Little James fell ill with a high fever and could keep nothing down. Night and day I stayed by his side. I wanted to bleed him but Stachel convinced me otherwise. He had me administer cool compresses to the boy's skin and made James drink wine mixed with cinchona, a coarse, brown powder made from the bark of the fever tree found in the jungles of Venezuela. With God's good grace, James' fever broke a few days later. I fell to my knees and thanked Jesus. Even so, the mysterious malady claimed forty unfortunate souls in all, thinning our ranks alarmingly.

Chapter Ten

The master of my new world gingerly stepped down from his carriage. He removed his hat and closed his eyes just as I had done to savor the cool, mountain air brushing against his skin. I studied Salamanca as he ran his fingers through his long mane of silver hair, as he stretched his arms out taut above his head to relieve cramped muscles.

"Juan, I smell supper," he called out to Carlos while patting his belly and sniffing the air to sample the aromas drifting from a kitchen. "Will you join me?"

Carlos grinned. "With pleasure, sir, with pleasure."

"Good, good," Salamanca said, then turned to me and smiled. "I think we'll eat outside on the porch tonight, Juan. 'Tis such a pleasant evening. Filipe, take the Irishwoman to Catalina. Attend to our new blacks after that. Feed them, see to their clothing, assign them their living quarters and the rest. You know what to do."

Filipe nodded dutifully then led me inside the house and down a long, narrow hallway of plain white walls, devoid of any furniture or decorations, devoid of a woman's touch, and into a kitchen in the back of the house where a thin, stern looking woman, a Blackamoor with short, grey hair, stood next to a wooden cutting table slicing carrots. She took in my clothing, the rough attire of a rugged seaman, and frowned. She pointed her knife at me as she turned to Felipe.

"Who's this?" she asked indignantly.

"The master purchased her in Trinidad," Filipe replied as he pilfered a carrot slice. "She's Irish, Señora Catalina. She's a convict on the run."

The woman snickered. "So, the master has taken a fancy to gutter trash now?"

"I ask no questions Señora. I ask no questions. I was told to bring her to you. I did as I was told."

"What," the old woman asked me, "were you convicted of?"

"I wasn't convicted of anything," I replied in a respectful tone. "I was kidnapped by pirates who sold me to Señor Salamanca on a lie."

She took a menacing step towards me with the knife still in her hand and slapped me hard across the face with the other. "That's for lying to me," she said with a scowl.

I had to suppress the urge to strike her back, not an easy thing for me to do. I had to bite my tongue.

"Well, it matters not to me you know," she said, waving her knife in my face. "You look like a whore in those rags. I've dealt with all manner of scoundrels over the years. Oh yes, I've dealt with liars, thieves and rapists, with murderers and the lowest of the low. I've dealt with the meanest miscreants who slither across this earth. I've gelded more than one man too. Outside in the backyard there's a washtub and soap. Go clean yourself up. We don't allow pigs inside the Master's house. Filipe, burn her clothing. I'll find a dress for her to wear. Then we'll see what she can do. Or perhaps you Irish are better at working in the fields? That creamy white skin of yours will burn quick enough outside. It matters not to me you know. You'll pull your weight I promise. You'll tow the line or else. And if you break my rules, God have pity on you Irish for I will show you none..."

For the next few months, I worked inside la casa grande, the big house as it was called, cleaning, cooking and washing clothes alongside the other household slaves. I was the only white woman. The others, at least in the beginning, kept me at a goodly distance. I understood and took no offense. On occasion at harvest time Filipe would send me into the fields. I relished these brief moments outdoors, working underneath the shadow of breathtaking Pico. The snow crowned mountain reminded me of home, of Cruach Phádraig, the place where people say Saint Patrick fasted for forty days and forty nights if you believe the legends. Whenever my men and I returned from the Caribbean to Westport, I'd borrow a horse to escape to the mountain for a bit of solitude. I drew strength from those fond memories as I toiled in the fields.

And though I was careful to give Catalina no reason to be cross with me, she would, from time-to-time, without cause or warning, backhand me across the face or strike me with a rod or with whatever kitchen utensil was in reach just to remind me of who was in charge. Even so I was lucky. Salamanca had forbidden whipping me.

I also enjoyed some measure of privacy. Salamanca had given me a corner in the root cellar of the big house all to myself. I had my own bed with a canopy, a mosquito net and a nightstand and in the evenings after my chores were done, I spent my time reading books mostly, books I had secretly borrowed from Salamanca's modest library. On occasion Salamanca, a widower, would venture down into the cellar claiming he was looking for one thing or another but in truth he came to spend time with me. I have no doubt he would have made me his mistress but for the frailties of old age. Mercifully, he limited his familiarity with me to idle prattle, sharing a glass of wine or two and harmless flirting.

The days passed by slowly as I went about my monotonous, daily chores and though I was an obedient worker, I kept my mind busy. While I do not consider myself an extraordinary person, I do have two extraordinary gifts.

I discovered the first of these God-given gifts on the day-of-days, on the day I was transformed from a moth into a butterfly, on the day the child in me died and I was liberated and reborn a woman. When confronted with a dilemma, a problem or a puzzle, my mind begins churning out ideas, possible solutions to the problem, at a dizzying rate of speed. Some have remarked on this gift. They say I am quick, that I am clever and this is true. I am quick and quite clever. But I think the word clever is inadequate, too broad a term to describe this particular gift of mine. For many people are broadly clever. This gift is more refined, more limited in breadth. This gift makes me unusually adept at concocting schemes and plans.

This first gift of mine goes hand-in-hand with a second wonderful talent. Under times of tremendous stress, or even when danger is swirling all around me, my mind continues functioning with great clarity of thought, calmly, dispassionately and with little emotion to distract me. I remain composed at all times.

As I worked inside the big house or in the fields, I applied both of my gifts with vigor. I studied every aspect of Salamanca's hacienda while plotting my escape. I learned as much as I could about his routines and customs and of those of his lieutenants. I paid particular attention to the days when the supply wagons rolled in and to the times when Salamanca would send his wagons out to market, loaded down with the bounty of his land. I befriended several Blackamoors worthy of trust and learned as much as I could about the surrounding territory, about the roads and nearby villages. I even made a crude but useful map of the entire province of Veracruz.

Long days slipped by as I bided my time and schemed. And when an opportunity at last presented itself, I did not squander the moment. My plan was simple. My plans are always simple as I distrust complexity. Too many things can go awry with plans devised with too many moving parts.

I only needed to reach Havana or Santo Domingo where I knew people who could help me. The distance was not great. But first I needed to make my way to Veracruz to find a ship I could hide aboard, or pilfer a small boat for myself. Both options had risks of course. I could only conceal myself aboard a ship for so long dressed as a man before the crew discovered me and then, well... And even with a seaworthy boat, I could never hope to cross nearly one thousand miles of open water to Havana on my own. But if I sailed along the Yucatán coast, if I could reach the small Spanish village of Mérida, I knew I had a chance from there. From Mérida to the easternmost tip of the Yucatán Peninsula, a godforsaken wilderness known as Kan Kun, is only one hundred miles and the distance between Kan Kun to the windward shores of the Island of Cuba is even less. The problem was whether I could acquire fresh water and victuals along the way, particularly in or near Mérida.

Ashaki, a comely, young thing with large, intelligent eyes, flawless skin and a brilliant smile, handed me a leather knapsack and a purse as we conspired together down in the root cellar. We had taken an instant liking to each other. We had become fast friends.

"It's not much Mary," she said anxiously.

I peeked inside the purse, saw the fistful of coins and was deeply touched. I threw my arms around Ashaki's neck and hugged her.

"Where did you find these?" I asked.

"The master keeps spare coins in a tin box upstairs in the blue room for the evenings when his friends come over to play cards."

"You've taken an awful risk Ashaki."

"Nah Mary, the master won't miss these few pieces. Catalina keeps a jar of coins in the kitchen too for when she goes into the village, but that woman keeps a close count of every peso. Are you sure Mary? Are you sure you want to do this? I'm scared for you."

The day was wet and cold. Salamanca had left earlier for the city called México and had taken Carlos with him. Catalina had taken a wagon and a driver on one her rare trips into nearby Orizaba, for what reason I did not know or care, while Felipe was using his short-lived freedom to get himself inebriated on a cask of ale instead of going into Córdoba to deliver a cartload of coal as Catalina had instructed him to do. Filipe decided to send one of the hired hands, a freeborn mulatto, to make the delivery for him. From Córdoba, Veracruz was an easy walk away. The odds were fair. The timing was good. This was my chance and I'd never been shy about rolling the dice.

"I understand the risks Ashaki, but I'm sure," I said. "And all that I have told you about myself is true. God willing, I'll make it back to Ireland and if I do, I will return someday to secure your freedom."

I could see the tears welling up in Ashaki's eyes. She was frightened and in truth so was I. But Ashaki, though barely more than a child, was also very brave. She hugged me tightly as I kissed her cheeks. She took a deep breath and took my hand after I slung my knapsack over my shoulder. She led me up the stairs.

While Ashaki employed her charms to distract the driver, a

careless, slovenly man, I slipped into the back of the cart and hid myself with the coal underneath an old, filthy tarp. My thin dress and threadbare cloak offered little protection from the elements and an hour or so into the ride, soaked to the bone from rain, I couldn't stop my teeth from clattering. When we reached the outskirts of Córdoba in the late afternoon, I carefully slipped off the back of the cart with the driver none the wiser. I was only seventy miles from the sea, seventy miles from freedom and allowed myself a thin smile.

I did not tarry or rest in Córdoba. I started walking east in the fading light towards Veracruz. Ashaki had packed bread, fruit, a round of cheese and a skin of wine for me. I ate and drank as I walked. Staying off the road as best I could, which slowed my progress some, I walked well into the nights and rested only in the mornings, hidding in the brush. I reached the outskirts of Veracruz four days later with the rising sun, hungry and exhausted but excited too for I could taste the ocean.

I quickened my pace with renewed vigor. I walked down the city's narrow streets towards the waterfront, keeping to the shadows, and when I spied a carving knife imbedded in a block of wood outside a butcher's shop, I deftly pocketed the blade for myself.

With aching feet and a grumbling stomach, I needed a place to rest without being noticed. I found a sleepy, little tavern, an unclean place but with a good view of the water if one sat outside on the terrace. I asked for coffee, bread and jellied fruit from a hard-looking woman standing behind the bar, a strumpet in all likelihood, with unkept, grey hair and an all too friendly smile. She wore her dress overly tight to accentuate a generous bosom and had applied a white unguent to her face to hide the ravages of time. Her bosom and mask did little good. Her beauty and youth had deserted her long ago and I took pity on her, though I too must have made a pitiful sight in my mud-splattered shoes and cheap, soiled dress. When she smiled sweetly at me as if we were kindred spirits, I pressed an extra coin into her hand.

As the first patron of the day, I had my pick of tables and took a table outside. I sipped my coffee and ate my breakfast while leisurely watching the fishing trawlers and merchant ships sailing in and out of the harbor. I was in no hurry. Though my absence from Salamanca's hacienda would certainly have been noticed, no one could be certain of which road I had taken.

By midmorning a few frisky seamen with money to spend began dribbling into the tavern in twos and threes looking for food, drink and perhaps a little pleasure. I had pilfered a play entitled *The Taming of the Shrew* by the English poet Shakespeare from Salamanca's modest library and absently flipped through the pamphlet's pages pretending to read while I listened to the conversations around me. Men talked freely about their ships and cargos, about the ports they'd sail to next.

In the early afternoon I ate a bowl of hardy stew, a pickled cucumber and treated myself to a pint of ale. And then, having learned nothing of interest and feeling stiff and frustrated, I decided to take a stroll along the waterfront to look over the ships and boats while I still had the light.

I saw an army of seamen, laborers and dockmen loading and offloading cargo. I considered the freighters of all sorts sitting in the bustling harbor along with the fishing trawlers coasting back into port with their catches for the day. When I finally decided that hiding myself aboard a ship as a stowaway and relying upon the tender mercies of the crew was too risky, I focused my attention on the fishing boats moored against the piers. Any one of them would have served my purpose, but I saw very few boats left unattended and none that I could easily steal.

With lovely Venus rising over the water hand-in-hand with a sliver of moon, with daylight quickly fading, I could feel time slipping away from me and decided to return to the tavern for supper. I knew I had to make my move soon.

When I saw three soldiers walking my way as I headed back, I thought nothing of it. I kept my head down and briskly walked past them.

"Stop!" I heard a voice shout out behind me.

I pretended not to hear the man and kept walking.

"Stop woman or I swear I'll draw my pistol and shoot you where you stand."

I took a deep breath, spun around and offered the three men a pleasant smile.

"State your purpose here," demanded one of the soldiers with a corporal's insignia pinned to his collar.

"Supper," I replied, trying to conceal my accent.

"Supper, where?"

I pointed to the tavern to avoid speaking.

"Tell me your name!"

"Elizabeth."

"Elizabeth, eh? Elizabeth what?"

"Cortés."

"What is your village?"

"Córdoba."

"What's your purpose in Veracruz, Elizabeth Cortés?"

"I've come to purchase medicines for a sickly husband sir."

The corporal grinned as he turned to face his mates. "This is a happy day boys! She's the one. Seize the Irish bitch. We have a bounty to collect and Salamanca pays well I hear."

I slipped my fingers in-between the buttons of my dress and caressed the handle of the butcher's knife I had stolen. The curved blade was long and sharp. My training with Efendi had included knives. I was better skilled than most and confident I could dispatch all three men easily with rapid stabs to the heart and quick slashes to the liver and neck. Without hesitation, without compunction, I can kill. But I'm no murderer. I had no quarrel with these Spaniards. Neither was I under the protection of Queen Elizabeth as one of her privateers in England's war against Spain. I had heard about her death.

The horrible truth struck me hard. I had underestimated Salamanca and the Spanish. I had badly miscalculated. After a century of practice, the Spanish had mastered the art of hunting down runaway slaves. News of a runaway, no matter how lowly or useless the slave, triggered alarm bells throughout the land. Slave owners quickly marshaled their resources, put any differences aside, and banded together as one. Search parties scoured the territory relentlessly, efficiently night and day. Often the army joined in. Nothing was spared to catch a single, fugitive slave. An example had to be made to discourage all others. Stern measures were needed to preserve the good order of things.

I said nothing. I did not fight or run. I lowered my head in shame instead and quietly handed my knife to the corporal.

Chapter Eleven

After we buried our dead Atwood, in a most disagreeable manner, renewed his objections about China. He insisted upon another council of war to discuss the matter before we set off for the Moluccas, for the fabulously rich Spice Islands. I was most displeased.

"Circumstances have changed Elizabeth," Atwood said bluntly while absently adjusting his eyepatch, often a precursor to sharp words between us. "'Tis unwise to sail deeper into the unknown when we're shorthanded."

Sitting around the table in my great cabin, my officers quietly sipped their beer while watching Atwood and I spar. The ale was almost gone, the beer had turned bitter and I would have preferred wine but we had only a few bottles left. Large raindrops thumped against my cabin's windowpanes. Showers seemingly without end had been with us since our arrival to Banten.

"Shorthanded?" I asked with no kindness in my tone. I hadn't heard the word before.

"Aye, one of those new-fangled words," Atwood said. "We've lost many a good lad. Our ranks have been cut thin. I blame myself. Mary always believed in the curative powers of soap. We've been lax in scrubbing the ships and ourselves down clean."

I nervously drummed my fingers against the table. "True, the men we lost is most unfortunate. But we're hardly shorthanded."

"Should trouble find us Elizabeth, we'll miss the men we lost. We'll miss their courage and their swords. I very much doubt Mary would approve of a voyage to China considering our lean numbers. I doubt she'd sail to Macau without knowing more about what awaits us there."

"Mary's dead," I said more harshly than I meant to. Atwood's hostility, the sour beer and the incessant rains had made me irritable. I longed to feel the sun against my face again and was bored of being confined to the ship. Atwood looked away, hurt or annoyed I knew not.

"We should finish what we agreed to do for the VOC," he continued, "and then sail for home. There's growing discontent amongst the men. Morale is in the shitter."

"Perhaps aboard your ship, Jacob, not mine. After we take delivery of our cargo in the Spice Islands, you can return to Banten and enjoy the dismal weather if you like. Stay here, pout and be bored. I'm sailing on to China."

"Elizabeth, my brothers, please," Maurice interrupted in a conciliatory tone as he placed his hands palms-up on the table. Maurice had become the peacemaker amongst us.

"Other than causing discord," he continued, "this conversation is accomplishing little. We did agree to sail to China though Jacob is also right. 'Tis fair to say that circumstances have changed. I only know this: whatever we do, we must do as one. We must keep the ships together. Perhaps we should draw cards?"

I ignored Maurice's ridiculous proposal. I'd not leave something so important to me to chance. I stood to move to the door.

"Gentlemen, I have Ewoud standing by up on the quarterdeck. I've asked him to speak to us, to explain in greater detail what we should expect in the Moluccas. Perhaps he can tell us something about Macau as well."

The Dutchman hurried down the companionway to my cabin when I called his name. He squeezed in-between Shaw and Efendi and took the last empty seat at the table. I handed him a pewter tankard filled to the brim with the last of our ale.

"Ewoud, how many of your people will be sailing with us?" I asked.

"We lost forty-nine poor devils to whatever pestilence hit us," Dijksma said flatly. "Koopman and I are agreed. He shall keep ninety-three men with him in Java whilst I take the rest to the Moluccas, one hundred and fifty men in all."

I reached for a sea chart of the East Indies on my desk and unrolled the parchment across the table. "Which of these islands is our destination?"

Dijksma tapped his finger on an island named Ambon. "This one."

"Is this where," MacGyver asked, "Drake and his men landed in 1580 whilst circumnavigating the globe?"

"No, Michael. Sir Francis visited this small island to the north, Ternate. They say his ship *Golden Hind* was loaded down with so much Spanish treasure he had to decline the sultan's generous offer to provide him cloves."

"What's in Ambon?" Atwood asked.

"Too many Portuguese, Jacob. Then there are the Bantenese, the Chinese, the Japanese and the Ottomans living amongst the Ambonese - all of whom hate the Portuguese. With a well-protected, deep-water port, and only a day's sail from the Banda Islands where most of the spices grow, Ambon is an important island. We can purchase considerable quantities of cloves, nutmeg, mace and cubeba peppers in Ambon's spice markets."

"Why are the Portuguese hated so?" MacGyver asked.

"Not only are the Portuguese arrogant and greedy, their cruelty knows no bounds."

"After we take delivery of the spices," I asked, "what do you plan to do in Ambon?"

"We Dutch intend to displace the Portuguese throughout the Spice Islands. In time, we intend to run the Portuguese out of the whole of the East Indies and Asia. We start with Ambon."

"You're talking about war." Atwood said.

"War. Exciting, yes? Perhaps you haven't heard. The Company refers to these expeditions to the East as *oorlogsreizen*, as war trips. The Portuguese have been conquering bits and pieces of the East Indies for nearly a century now. They've stripped the Ottomans of their monopoly over the spice trade and have taken it for themselves. With the blessing of Sultan Saidi Berkat, the ruler of Ternate, the Ambonese have asked for Dutch assistance in ending Portugal's grip over their island. Saidi has even granted us a tract of land at Hitu Larna where he is allowing us to build a citadel. Not only does his excellency wish to see Portugal's trade monopoly broken, he also wants to curb the spread of Christianity. Saidi is tolerant of all religions within his kingdom but resents the heavy-handed, clumsy methods the Portuguese and Spanish monks have used to try and convert his people. Wealth, power, jealousy and religion are the seeds of conflict. War is coming to this part of the world with or without Dutch intervention."

"As I recall," I said, "you have brought a Calvinist minister with you."

Dijksma smiled. "True, true. But the good pastor is here to tend to his Dutch flock, not to convert the native peoples. We Dutch Protestants have no interest adopting the insufferable tactics of Rome to win over souls."

"The Portuguese," Shaw asked, "have no allies in the Spice Islands?"

"Oh, they do. The Portuguese are allied with Mole Majimu, the Sultan of Tidore, and maintain a strong presence there. Ternate and Tidore, with barely a mile of water between them, have been bitter rivals for years. Both Saidi and Mole have claimed the Spice Islands for themselves."

"My colleagues and I," I said as I went around the table refilling empty tankards, "are again discussing a visit to Macau before returning to Europe."

"Why?" Dijksma asked. "Why would you attempt such a risky voyage? The Portuguese own Macau."

"To purchase whatever strikes our fancy of course."

"But your ships will be loaded down with the Company's spices Elizabeth."

"We promised the Company three ships Ewoud and we have delivered three ships. The fourth ship is ours to use as we see fit."

"I fear the Company may not see things the same way Elizabeth.

This circuitous route home you are contemplating is asking for trouble."

"That is our concern."

"Very well. If you do decide to make this journey to Macau, I would not disclose your association with the Dutch to the Portuguese."

"No, of course not."

"Might I make a suggestion?"

"Please."

"I'm hardly disclosing any national secrets by stating the obvious. We Dutch intend to become the dominant power in the East Indies. Java, the Spice Islands, Malacca and Macau are all worthy prizes. I suggest you gather as much intelligence on the Portuguese in Macau as you can. Useful information about the strengths and weaknesses of the Portuguese there might offset any recriminations the Company may wish to bring against you upon your return to Amsterdam."

"Recriminations?" I asked indignantly. "Recriminations for what?"

"I did not intend to give offense Elizabeth. Perhaps my concerns are misplaced. I will say no more on the matter except to say that with regard to the terms and covenants of its contracts, beware, the Company is a stickler for compliance."

"We shall fulfill our end of the bargain Ewoud," I said firmly and stood to end the matter.

With our meeting adjourned, we spent the rest of the day procuring good water and fresh victuals. We did not need much as the next leg of our journey was not far. We weighed anchor the next morning in pouring rain, dropped our sails and set a course for the Moluccas. I brought the Chinaman Arslan with me.

We sailed east hugging the coast of Java, passed the Lesser Sunda Islands and when the island of Wetar appeared off of our starboard bow, we cut north straight across the Banda Sea for Ambon. Despite the relentless squalls and contrary winds following us from Banten, we reached our destination in only fifteen days and suffered no losses. Dijksma had us skirt around the north side of the island until we came to a modest inlet with dozens of outrigger canoes sitting in a line along the beach.

"Beyond those palm trees," Dijksma said casually while sipping coffee up on *Ghostrunner's* quarterdeck with Shaw, little James and me, "where you can see smoke rising from the cooking fires, is the small fishing village of Hitu."

Dijksma laid a friendly hand on James' shoulder. "As you can see Master James, Ambon is a mountainous island covered in lush forest. There's good water here and the soil is fertile. It is a pretty island don't you think?"

The boy nodded. "It is sir."

"And the sun is shining," I said happily.

"Yes, the monsoons tend to pummel the islands to the west and north before turning this way."

"Those mountains in the distance - volcanoes?" I asked.

"At one time, I believe so. There are live volcanoes on several of the islands in the East Indies. The volcanoes on Ambon are thought to be extinct, though I've heard there are a few hot springs sprinkled about the island. Something is simmering deep below the ground."

"The native peoples," Shaw asked, "are friendly or warlike?"

"Both. Ambon's natives are a dark-skinned people known as the Melanesians. The Melanesians inhabit many of the islands across the East Indies, though not as one tribe or nation. The Ambonese happen to be a peaceful folk. But Saidi has capable men in his army. He has brought in tough Moors from North Africa, seasoned Arab mercenaries from Persia and has battle-hardened Tanimbar warriors on retainer. Being a jealous man, the sultan keeps a tight reign over his realm."

"Tanimbar?" I asked, being unfamiliar with the word.

"Yes. I know not the lands they come from. They are wanderers. I've not seen them fight, but the Tanimbar are reputed to be utterly fearless in battle. Their bravery and unflinching loyalty are legendary throughout the islands."

"They're Indians, sir?" James asked.

Dijksma chuckled good naturedly. "In this part of the world my young friend Indians are from India. I believe we shall find the sultan's men waiting for us at Hitu. You may very well come face-to-face with a Tanimbar warrior, something few Europeans can say they've done."

"How," I asked, "did Saidi know to send men to this place to meet us here?"

"On our first day in Banten, Prince Ratu dispatched one of his ships to Ternate carrying one letter from the Company to the sultan and another from myself. I asked the sultan to send men to Ambon to help us fight the Portuguese and suggested we rendezvous at Hitu, away from the Portuguese fortifications in the port of Ambon. Saidi agreed. The Portuguese rarely venture far from the city and with the Almighty's blessing the Portuguese will not know we've landed men and arms on the island. Shall we?"

We took two longboats ashore. I decided to take Atwood, Efendi and Shaw with Dijksma and myself, along with forty well-armed men. I recalled Mary telling me stories about her first encounters with the gentle Taíno and later with the warlike Carib and the joy that filled her heart on both occasions. I felt the same elation when I spotted a platoon of twenty lean, Tanimbar warriors waiting for us on a crude jetty. Wearing nothing but grass skirts, elaborate necklaces and round headdresses garnished with feathers and bones, the Tanimbar came armed with spears and oval shields of bamboo. A monkey's skull, like some crown jewel, adorned the headdress of the lead man.

I was surprised when Dijksma spoke to the Tanimbar in Dutch. Dijksma and the man with the monkey's skull shook hands as friends do while exchanging pleasantries.

"This fine looking fellow," Dijksma said smiling and turned to me, "is Wibawa and the man at his side is Utari. We became well-acquainted with one another during my last visit to the East Indies."

"Wibawa is a chief?" I asked as I shook hands with the two men.

"No, no, Wibawa is the equivalent of a captain and Utari is his lieutenant."

"I see. The captain I pray understands my men and I are with the Company and pose no threat?"

Dijksma laughed. "They do indeed, and they are quite impressed by the four fine warships you've brought with you."

"Wonderful," I said and then turned to the captain. I spoke slowly to allow Dijksma to translate my words from English to Dutch.

"Wibawa, I am honored. I'm Elizabeth. This big fellow is Jacob Atwood from Scotland. The gentleman at his side is Mustafa Efendi from Istanbul and this young man standing next to me is Robert Shaw from Ireland."

Wibawa turned to Efendi and offered the same customary Islamic greeting I had heard Agung make. Efendi replied in kind with his hand over his heart and bowed.

After Wibawa and Dijksma finished exchanging more words in Dutch, Dijksma rested his hand on my shoulder. "Wibawa knows of Turkey as the Ottomans of course have been sailing to the Moluccas for centuries. I gave him a quick geography lesson on Scotland and Ireland and informed him that you are Spanish, but that you are not with the Spanish, that you are a friend."

"Excellent, ah, *uitstekend, dank u mijn vriend*," I said, practicing a little of my woefully inadequate Dutch. "With the introductions behind us, what happens now Ewoud?"

"Before we lose the light, we should bring my men and our supplies ashore. Wibawa will lead us into the village where we Dutch can make camp. You and your men are welcome to join us for supper. Wibawa has offered to host a fine feast in our honor."

Atwood, Efendi, Shaw and I agreed to keep twenty men with us and sent the rest back to the ships with the longboats to start ferrying the Dutchmen and their supplies ashore. After the first wave of Dijksma's men started landing on the beach, we followed Wibawa to the village.

Hitu is a small, unremarkable place of dirt footpaths and small huts made of bamboo with ornamental thatched roofs shaped like steeples. The villagers, though curious to see who had landed on their shores, kept their distance from us. I sensed no hostility in their words or deeds. Even so, I had primed and loaded my musket and my brace of pistols. Wibawa led us to a nearby field where the rest of his men, I saw about fifty warriors in all, were relaxing around their campfires. I was encouraged when I saw muskets and reflex bows stacked around the camp. The muskets were Turkish matchlock arquebuses, a heavy, outdated weapon and often unreliable but far better than any spear.

As Dijksma's men started trickling into the village, they promptly went about pitching tents next to the Tanimbar camp and gathering firewood and as they labored dozens of Ambonese women carried baskets of food and jugs of water over to a nearby clearing. Lithe, lean and pretty, the women were dressed in brightly colored robes with matching sandals and wore unusual hats resembling tall drums.

I sat between Dijksma and Wibawa as we feasted on roasted fish and boiled shellfish, on steamed beans and sago palms. A half-dozen Ambonese men started beating on drums they call *kendhangs* while others made their instruments - something called an *angklung* made from metal or bamboo tubes of different lengths strung across a wooden frame - sing by striking the tubes with wooden mallets. And while the men introduced us to their strange island music, the women entertained us with lively folk dances of a cheerful nature, a blend of Hindu, Buddhist and Islamic movements or so Dijksma claimed.

I had caught the envy in Wibawa's eyes back on the beach when he first saw our German snaphance muskets, a far better, lighter and deadlier weapon than the outdated arquebuses. "Ewoud," I said and handed my musket over to Wibawa, "please thank Wibawa for this grand celebration. One gift deserves another they say and I hope Wibawa will accept this musket as a token of my esteem for the Tanimbar and in honor of our new friendship."

Wibawa offered me a broad grin and nodded appreciatively after Dijksma translated my words. "Wibawa," Dijksma said, "is most pleased with this splendid gift. You are a shrewd ambassador, Elizabeth. The Company would approve."

"You have a strong force on Ambon now," I noted. "What is next part of your plan Ewoud?"

"Tomorrow, I'll accompany you into the port of Ambon. We should enter the harbor with one of the smaller ships and hide the other three so as not to attract attention."

"We go to Ambon to purchase spices?"

"Yes, and to do a bit of reconnaissance."

"Very well, my men and I will return to our ships tonight and we'll see you bright and early in the morning. Agreed?"

"Agreed."

At dawn the next day, with our four ships peacefully riding anchor in a tight circle, I stood next to Atwood at the bow of his ship watching eight Ambonese men wade into the surf to launch their outrigger canoe with a single passenger onboard. With water under her keel, the men hauled themselves into their boat, took up their oars and pulled as one while singing a lively ditty. They approached our ships with good speed.

I handed Dijksma a tin of fresh coffee as he stepped aboard *Homeward*. "I trust you are in fine spirits Ewoud on this lovely morning," I said cheerfully.

"I'm in splendid spirits indeed madam," Dijksma replied with a warm smile and nodded to Atwood. "Jacob, I never tire of setting out on a new adventure."

"Mornin' Ewoud," Atwood said as he reached over to pat the Dutchman's shoulder.

"Did you enjoy last night's banquet Jacob?" Dijksma asked.

"But for the lack of booze I did. The Ambonese are fine, hospitable folk."

Dijksma nodded in agreement. "Roughly half the people of the East Indies are Hindu and half are Muslim. The Hindus frown upon the consumption of alcohol and most of Islam of course forbids it. The Bantenese, being more worldly folk, don't strictly adhere to these rules. The Ambonese do. But for this flaw, they truly are a fine and hospitable people." Dijksma then paused to lift a waterskin strapped across his shoulder over his head and handed the skin to Atwood. "Have a taste of this my friend."

"Water?" Atwood asked.

"Ha! No, *zoopie*. Zoopie is Dutch for little drink."

Atwood took a swig and smacked his lips. "Ah, that's not bad, that's not bad at all," he said and handed the skin to me.

"Zoopie, or known as *anggur persaudaraan* by the islanders, meaning brotherly wine, is a favorite drink throughout the Moluccas though the sultan frowns upon it."

"What's it made from?" I asked out of politeness and handed the skin back to Atwood. I did not care for the taste.

"Zoopie is distilled from sweet palm sap mixed with crumbled husor root and then fermented inside bamboo stalks. Some prefer to drink zoopie slightly sweet. Some infuse the drink with herbs and roots such as ginseng. I like the sweet. Wibawa sent a small barrel of zoopie back with me as a parting gift."

Atwood took another sip and smiled. "I'll have this godsend brought aboard straight away."

"Do you," I asked Dijksma, eager to set out, "wish us to leave the other three ships here?"

"I suggest you bring them with us. There are two tiny islands off the western tip of Ambon just outside of Ambon Bay - if these islands have names I know them not - where your ships can safely anchor out of sight. Once we conclude our business in port, you can rejoin your squadron and then head south for the Bandas to take delivery of the spices.

"But how will you make your way back to Hitu and your camp?" I asked.

"How far must we sail Elizabeth to reach port?" Dijksma asked playfully.

"Thirty-five, forty miles give or take by my reckoning if the charts are accurate."

"The charts are most accurate. Dutch cartographers are renowned around the world for their exceptional skills at mapmaking. The winds are blowing-up from the southwest and are a bit tricky today. We'll need to do some tacking I think as we circle around the island. We have perhaps a nine-to-ten-hour journey ahead of us?"

"Aye," Atwood answered. "Sounds about right."

Dijksma grinned. "The distance between Hitu and the port city by land is only about five miles. I'll walk back."

After Atwood shouted the plan over to Maurice, MacGyver and Shaw, we set out at once sailing west in a line under a pale blue sky with Ambon only a few hundred yards off our port bow. When we reached the two small islands Dijksma had described in the late afternoon, we dropped anchor in-between them for the night and in the morning, with Atwood at the wheel, we took *Homeward* into Ambon's sleepy bay, leaving *Ghostrunner*, *Cerberus* and *Achilles* behind.

Dijksma and I stood with Atwood on the poop deck, taking in the chalk cliffs around the bay as we coasted along. The day was deliciously warm and bright. We sailed without any flags or pennants. We kept our gun ports closed. After traversing the bay, we entered a harbor crowded with many vessels, mostly canoes, boats and barges but we also floated past a good number of junks too flying flags with Chinese or Japanese markings and we spotted one handsome Portuguese merchantman of middling size anchored close to shore, armed with an impressive array of cannon.

"Ewoud, what the devil is that vessel sitting over there?" I asked and pointed to a massive outrigger canoe, by far the largest canoe of any kind I'd ever seen.

With a dragon's head in gilded gold fitted to her long, curved prow - like one of the Viking longships of old - and a matching serpent's tail rising over her stern, she made a fearsome sight. Though I thought her lateen-rigged main mast unremarkable, her single bank of one hundred oars made a good impression. Dozens of colorful pennants and long streamers fluttered in the breeze from her rigging and I counted six fat guns sitting on her deck.

"Ah, that magnificent beast is a *kora-kora*," Dijksma answered, "though I've never seen one that big or lavish before. She's quite impressive. I suspect the vessel belongs to the sultan. Perhaps she is Saidi's flagship. Kora-koras are used as warships and as freighters throughout the Moluccas. Plainly this vessel was built for war."

"Saidi is here in Ambon?" I asked, surprised.

"Most unlikely. My guess is one of his ministers is visiting the island regarding trade or taxes or perhaps the fellow is here on a diplomatic mission."

"A diplomatic mission?"

"The island belongs to the sultan. Under one treaty or another, the city belongs to the Portuguese and though the Portuguese control the spice trade, they pay taxes to the sultan for the privilege."

"The Melanesians are accomplished seafarers?"

"They are. They've been traveling between the islands long before we Europeans ever stepped foot in the Far East. The islands are a testament to their skill and courage at sea. I suspect a good number of the crew aboard that kora-kora though are Moors employed by the sultan. The Moors use condemned men at the oars. When she's on the move you'll hear the oar master bellow *mena muria, mena muria, mena muria* over and over again to the beat of a single drum. *Mena* means front and *muria* means back. Front, back, front, back, front, back and so forth. Those poor devils chained to their sweeps will row to the oar master's cadence until their hearts give out. Nasty business."

As we eased our way slowly through the maze of ships and smaller craft at anchor, I caught my first glimpse of the city. Ambon was not what I had expected. I had thought to see crude huts and dirt trails like Hitu but instead saw European style buildings, some as high as three stories, in ivory stucco with red tiled roofs standing along streets paved in stone. As a young girl I had traveled from Barcelona to Lisbon with my father before he took me across the Atlantic and to the New World. Ambon reminded me of Lisbon, only in miniature. Far less grand perhaps, but charming just the same. We drifted under the shadow of an impressive citadel named Forte de Nossa Senhora da Anunciada, the Fort of Our Lady of the Announced, or known as Kota Laha by the natives, with thick stone walls, large calibre harbor guns and watchtowers of heavy timber.

I turned to Dijksma as we dropped anchor and pointed to the fortress. "I think you might need more men."

"How the Spanish and their Portuguese lackeys love their fortifications," he said with a wry smile. "Stonewalls and heavy artillery will not stop a determined foe."

"You Dutch," Atwood quipped, "have swagger. I'll give you that."

"How many men-at-arms," I asked, "can the Portuguese muster in Ambon?"

"An excellent question my lady. Not enough, I think. The sultan keeps many spies in his service. The Portuguese are spread thin throughout the East Indies and though their commander, a man named Captain André Furtado de Mendonça, is no fool they say, it matters not. Caesar himself couldn't hold Ambon without more ships and men."

Atwood rolled his eyes. "A man I once knew, a fellow gifted in warfare, once told me there be a razor-thin line between bold talk followed by prudent action and imprudent talk followed by reckless action or something of the sort. I will confess though, the Dutch have won remarkable victories over the English, the French and the Spanish. You Dutch do know how to fight."

Dijksma nodded. "Anything can happen in war my friend. Though we are a tiny country, we are entering our golden age and we Dutch must press our advantage with full conviction whilst our good fortune lasts. Speaking of shifting fortunes, I smell rain in the air. Shall we go ashore and take a stroll through the city whilst we are still dry?"

"The Portuguese will trade with a Dutchman, Ewoud?" I asked.

"No," Dijksma replied grinning. "But they will do business with a Frenchman. Our ship is a French freighter from Boulogne. She is, say, the *Cherbourg*. Good name, yes? She's heavily-armed to be sure which will raise eyebrows, but such precautions are necessary to defend ourselves in these dangerous waters. I am a successful merchant from Dunkerque. My name is Henri Dupuis and I'm traveling with two of my favorite investors, the beautiful Lady Micaela de Romero from Barcelona and a one-eyed brigand from the hills of Ireland named Ryan Flynn."

"But I'm from Scotland," Atwood protested.

"I think you'll make a fine Irishman Jacob. Everyone knows the Irish have greater loyalties to Spain than to England."

Atwood, Dijksma and I took the ship's small skiff over to a modest shack standing at the end of a long pier extending well over the water with a sign with the words *Entrada Para Ambon - Capitão Do Port* painted in large, crude letters above the door. After we secured our skiff, we stepped inside the shack to declare ourselves to the harbormaster, a man of few words and unforgiving eyes. Dijksma handed the fellow an official looking document, a letter of introduction with the forged signature and counterfeit seal of Maximilien de Béthune, the Superintendent of Finance serving the French King, Henry IV. Satisfied with our credentials, the harbormaster happily let us pass once we paid him for the privilege of anchoring our ship in the harbor - along with a little something extra for himself.

While considerably smaller than Banten, Ambon had been thoughtfully laid out in orderly city blocks like Banten, though her streets were surprisingly clean and tidy and her architecture was more interesting. We walked past a variety of shops and pretty gardens and houses kept in good repair. We saw one large building called the Senate of the House and passed by two Christian churches, one a humble parish church named São Paulo and the other, a larger church run by the Jesuits, named Sant'Iago. When we reached a three-story brick building resembling a warehouse, Atwood and I followed Dijksma through a pair of large, blue doors with a sign overhead with the words *Bem-vindo à Casa da Índia* in gilded gold lettering carved across the wood.

"This is the king's brokerage house where all trade for mace and nutmeg is conducted," Dijksma explained as we paused in the middle of the ground floor to take in the crowd of men haggling with one another over stacks of crates, boxes and barrels. "The House of India is Portugal's equivalent to Spain's Casa de Contratación, the House of Trade, in the Americas."

"State your business," a squat, little fellow with receding hair and thin goatee commanded impatiently in Portuguese as he rose from behind one of several desks standing against the back wall. The man marched towards us with authority. He liked to dress well.

"I am Monsieur Henri Dupuis from Dunkerque," Dijksma replied. "And these are my associates in merchantry, Senhora Micaela de Romero from Barcelona and Ship's Master Ryan Flynn from Dublin. We've sailed from France for cloves, mace, nutmeg and pepper. I understand Ambon is the place to buy such things. And who do I have the pleasure of addressing sir?"

The squat, little man extended his hand. "I am Manuel de Pomte, the king's commissioner of this house. The man-o'-war anchored in the bay - yours I assume?"

"Quite so, but she's no warship," Dijksma answered as he shook hands with the Portuguese. "She's a freighter."

"She packs an unusual amount of heavy artillery for a freighter."

"We've not come to plunder your fine city. We're honest merchants come to trade. Our ship's guns bark only when pirates come sniffing around."

"You've travelled far."

"We have."

"From what city?"

"Cherbourg."

"And you say you're in Ambon to purchase spices?"

"We are."

"We shall see. For pepper you must sail to Banten. For the rest I assume we are speaking about acquiring cargo by the ton?"

"But of course."

"How many tons do you wish to purchase?"

"Two hundred, two hundred tons in all."

"Two hundred tons? It is not every day a trader strolls into the Casa da Índia proposing to make such a large transaction. How do you intend to pay?"

Dijksma removed a roll of banknotes from the inside pocket of his jacket. "What is the day's market price?" he asked.

The Portuguese motioned us to follow him over to his desk. He grabbed an abacus and after he finished manipulating the beads, he tilted the abacus to show Dijksma the result.

"You wish to rob me blind?" Dijksma howled indignantly. "Do you take me for some backwoods bumpkin? We are purchasing in bulk my good fellow and are entitled to a twenty percent deduction off the customary price at the very least."

Pomte shrugged his shoulders, reached for a cigar on his desk and used a candle to light it. He casually blew smoke rings up at the ceiling while casting an appreciative glance my way.

"I've quoted you a fair price Monsieur Dupuis. Take what has been graciously offered Frenchman or take your business elsewhere."

"Very well," Dijksma said with a heavy sigh. "We'll pay your scandalous prices but this matter is not over. No sir, it is not. The good Lady Micaela has friends at the royal Spanish Court. We shall petition King Phillip upon our return to Europe to redress this outrageous wrong."

"As you wish Henri. May I call you Henri? If you were paying in gold, I could perhaps propose a better price but you are offering banknotes."

Dijksma answered the commissioner by peeling off twenty notes and placing them on his desk.

Pomte quickly scooped the notes up, then glanced around the room. "Ah, Davitt, there you are. A moment if you please."

A peculiar looking fellow dressed in the plain, black frock of a monk hobbled towards us on a bad leg. The short, grey hairs on his head stood out like the bristles on a brush. The tips of his beard's thin, scraggly whiskers, he had no mustache, reached his belly.

"Gentlemen, my lady, this is Davitt ben Joseph. He is a Jew from Istanbul who once dabbled in banking whilst in the services of the renowned House of Mendès. He now represents the Sultan of Ternate, particularly in matters of trade. Davitt, allow me to introduce Henri Dupuis, Master Ryan Flynn and Lady Micaela de Romero to you. These good folks wish to purchase two hundred tons of assorted spices and have offered Mendès notes in payment. Can you validate the authenticity and value of these banknotes?"

Ben Joseph reached inside his frock to retrieve a pair of reading spectacles. He carefully balanced them on his nose and then proceeded to examine each note with care.

"The notes are genuine and are worth the stated amount," ben Joseph finally proclaimed while briskly pocketing four of the notes.

Pomte grabbed ben Joseph by the wrist. "Two notes Davitt, your master is entitled to ten percent."

"Twenty percent is the new rate, Pomte," ben Joseph said with a sneer and jerked his wrist away. "Your emissary in Ternate may protest the matter to the sultan directly if you like. I'll prepare a bill of lading at once. Gentlemen, my lady, please follow me."

We followed the former banker from Istanbul over to a desk standing against the back wall. We watched him draft a simple bill of lading for two hundred tons of spices. And after he dribbled melted wax from a purple candle onto the parchment, and impressed the royal seal of the Sultan of Ternate into the sticky goo, he handed the bill to Dijksma.

"You'll take this bill of lading, made payable to the bearer, to Banda Island," he explained, "where you will present this instrument to the harbormaster, a man named Kemal. He will oversee all the necessary arrangements."

"Excellent," Dijksma said. "Would that magnificent kora-kora in the bay be your vessel?"

"All such things belong to his Excellency Saidi Berkat and I am but his humble servant. I hear you have come to Ambon in a very handsome ship outfitted with batteries of heavy cannon. A most unusual vessel for merchants, yes?"

"I suppose that's true. A word to the wise Master ben Joseph, I wouldn't tarry long in Ambon. Find a reason to return to Ternate. Return to Ternate with haste."

"You suspect an ill wind blowing this way?"

"Across a troubled sea, yes."

"Blessings and peace be upon you *Dutchman*."

"*Shalom aleichem*, Master Davitt ben Joseph," Dijksma replied and bowed.

"I think," Atwood said after we left the brokerage house and started back towards the water just as it began to rain, "you paid too much to that Portuguese cur. Are the coffers of the United Provinces overflowing with so much gold you don't mind squandering some of it?"

"And we're short," I noted crossly. "We have yet to purchase cargo for the other ships."

Dijksma paused in the middle of the street. "With the sultan's blessing," he said with a broad smile, "Banda's harbormaster will secure eight hundred tons of spices for us under this bill of lading."

"Ah, I understand now," Atwood said. "With the help of the sultan's man, you've picked the commissioner's pocket."

"Yes, the four banknotes ben Joseph took for the sultan are authentic, the sixteen notes I left with Pomte are worthless paper, forgeries."

I placed a hand on Dijksma's arm. "Ewoud, we discussed this. We can fill three ships, not four. We're off to Macau after we've finished our business in Banda."

Dijksma shook his head and sighed. "I still advice against this course of action Elizabeth. As we discussed in Banten, you should return to Amsterdam with all four ships loaded down with Company cargo."

"I agreed to provide three ships."

"Yes, so you have said. May I make a suggestion?"

"Of course."

"Take delivery of all eight hundred tons of spices. Sell two hundred tons in Macau on behalf of the Company if you like and do what you will replacing the spices with your own cargo. Mind you, I do not and cannot approve of this action. The spices will fetch far higher prices in Europe than in China and I have no doubt the Company will hold you accountable for its lost profits. And be forewarned: two Dutch ships under the command of van Neck tested Macau's defenses not long ago in 1601. The Portuguese captured twenty of his men and executed all but three. If the Portuguese suspect you are affiliated with the Company, they'll hang you. Well, on that cheery thought, our journey together ends here. I extend my best wishes to you both."

I offered to shake Dijksma's hand but he leaned forward to kiss my cheek instead. "Until we meet again," he said.

"*Tot we elkaar weer ontmoeten*," I replied awkwardly as I felt myself blush. "I pray your mission in Ambon is successful."

"Good hunting, Ewoud," Atwood said as he shook hands with Dijksma. "Don't get yourself killed. I rather like you."

"Jacob, it has been a rare pleasure. My lady, I admit I was against allowing a woman on this voyage, especially one with authority. Over these past many months, you've won my admiration and my respect. I wish you and your men Godspeed. Before we go our separate ways, may I impose upon you for a small favor?"

"Certainly," I replied, basking in the afterglow of Dijksma's compliment. I found myself wanting the Dutchman. My blood was running hot. I imagined the two of us naked, grinding against each other. I imagined him ravishing me in bed. I felt no guilt. Dijksma was a smart, handsome and confident man. Any woman would welcome him into her bedchamber. Shaw was smitten with me, in love with me, or so he professed, and I was very fond of him. He was handsome, strong and kind and was hardly shy about pleasing me in the most intimate ways. But love? Love is neither here nor there. Love is a fleeting emotion like any other that comes and goes with time. I want what I like and take what I want when it suits me. I make no apologies for who I am.

"What would you have us do?" I asked.

"We have a wonderful opportunity to confuse the Portuguese and leave them uneasy."

"How so?" Atwood asked.

"After you return to your ship Jacob hoist the French flag with the three gold fleur-de-lis on a field of blue I left in your cabin up to the masthead on your way out of the harbor and run out your guns. Pour a broadside or two into the Portuguese freighter as a parting gift as you glide past her. With the fort so near, it is too risky to try and board her, to take her as a prize, so rip her guts open instead and let her sink."

I stared at Dijksma dumbfounded. "But -."

"But," Dijksma said, cutting me off. "I'm authorized to pay you a bonus of five thousand guilders under these circumstances. Let's have some fun shall we!"

"Gold or silver?" I asked.

"Ha! Why for you dear lady, nothing less than gold will do..."

Chapter Twelve

took in my grim surroundings in the root cellar as I stood with my back against a brick wall and my wrists chained to a rafter above my head. After Felipe had stripped me of my clothes, leaving me with only my undergarments, he removed my bed, my nightstand, anything I had called mine, and left me hanging in the cellar for several agonizing days.

I had caught the murderous look in his eyes when the soldiers from Veracruz had returned me to the hacienda locked inside an iron cage. Felipe had wanted to take me into the woods and kill me. After all I had escaped during his watch. But he had to content himself - for the prerogative of meting out any harsh punishment against a slave belongs solely to the master - with a few sharp cuffs across the face and a handful of hard punches to the gut. My left eye was swollen shut from one blow. He had cracked a rib with another. It hurt to breathe, sneeze and cough. I was chilled to the bone, hungry, alone and afraid - exactly the outcome Felipe had intended.

Ashaki had betrayed me. Not willingly and not that it mattered. Felipe had not been gentle with her during his interrogation. I could hear her whimpering from a room or a closet upstairs. Over the months Ashaki and I had been careless with our friendship. The time we spent together, the smiles, the laughter and the whispers, had not gone unnoticed. Catalina had eyes and ears everywhere. When my disappearance was first noticed Catalina went straight to Ashaki for answers and then she turned her over to Felipe.

I watched Salamanca gingerly make his way down the wooden staircase with Carlos and Felipe a step behind him. A chill ran down my spine when I saw the leather lash coiled around Carlos' shoulder.

"What in God's name was your plan once you reached the coast?" Salamanca asked gruffly as he stood before me with no mercy in his eyes. "Runaways go north or south or even west, not east. Perhaps you thought you could sell your cunt to some half-witted sailor in exchange for passage aboard his ship to one of the islands?"

I said nothing.

"Who helped you on the road to Veracruz?" he asked.

I said nothing.

Salamanca glared at me and clenched his jaw. "You have returned my many kindnesses with deceit. You have returned my respect with disrespect. The degree of your villainy astonishes me. The extent of your treachery repulses me."

I said nothing.

"I allowed you certain liberties not enjoyed by my blacks. Those liberties, my kindheartedness, poof, gone. It ends now. You've lost my respect. You've forfeited your good life here. You will sleep in the barracas with my blacks. If a man, any man, wishes to take you, he can have you with my blessing. If he wants to beat you, he can beat you with my blessing. You will toil in the fields until your hands bleed. You will work until your spine bends. That pretty, white skin of yours will turn to leather and crack. I'll make you a wrinkled, old hag. You'll suffer all manner of torments before I break your spirit. And when you die, I'll feed your carcass to my pigs. Thank your lucky stars I don't send you off to the mines."

I said nothing.

Salamanca retrieved a pocket knife from his trousers and started cutting away my undergarments. He paused when he saw the scar over my left breast, the scar of a coiled sea serpent poised to strike, the mark a monstrous pair of twins born of a she-wolf from hell had seared deep into my flesh with a red-hot branding iron many years ago. I had paid a terrible price for underestimating my enemy then. I'd pay dearly again for the same mistake with Salamanca.

"What's this?" Salamanca asked as he ran his fingers over the scar. "Who did this to you?"

Still, I said nothing.

"The brand of a pirate perhaps? Juan, Felipe, come see this. Does this mark mean anything to either of you?"

Salamanca's two bitches obediently came to heel to take a closer look but neither man had an answer.

"No matter," Salamanca remarked indifferently as he ripped off the last stitch of my clothing. While I stood before him naked, feeling nauseous and helpless, he looked me up and down as if he was inspecting a side of beef hanging from a hook. I could see the lust in his eyes. Only a pair of shriveled, old balls saved me. Then he spun me around to face the wall.

"I've met many beautiful women over the years," he said, leaning close to my ear. "But none to compare to you. Your youth perhaps is beginning to fade and yet you are still an exquisite beauty. 'Tis a shame to mare your flesh. I'm a merciful man. I'll not brand your cheek with the mark of a runaway. Juan, twenty lashes. Ten across her back and ten across this lovely rump. No need to be gentle. I wish to hear my lady scream."

While Carlos unraveled his whip Salamanca pulled a stool over, took a seat and poured himself a glass of wine. I grit my teeth and clenched my fists. I did my best not to cry out as Carlos laid into me with everything he had. But cry out I did. On the fourth or fifth blow I wept. A lash or two later I howled. I damn near fainted as Carlos whipped me harder and harder over and over again.

After Carlos finished his brutal work, he casually dipped his whip into a bucket of water to rinse away the blood, then quietly followed Salamanca up the staircase. Felipe remained behind. He unchained me, pulled me by my hair up the stairs, through the kitchen and outside into the backyard. He dragged me past slaves and hired hands who stopped whatever they were doing to gawk at my lacerated, naked body. Once we reached a shed used for curing tobacco Felipe pushed me inside. He tossed my torn undergarments in my face.

"Let's see how well you treacherous whores plot and scheme now," he said with a triumphant smile, then locked the door behind him.

I saw Ashaki sitting in a corner, naked, sobbing and holding herself by the knees while rocking herself back and forth. I crawled to her and took her hand.

"I'm terribly, terribly sorry," I said in a weak voice.

She stared at me in shock with a bruised and bloody face. After Felipe had finished beating and whipping her, he had sliced her left nostril open with a knife - the mark given to any slave who helps a runaway.

"I, I, I tried Mary, I tried to tell them nothing," she whispered and wrapped her arms around my neck.

"You did all you could," I replied and held her.

Ashaki and I spent our days in that filthy place with one privy bucket, two loaves of moldy, stale bread and a jug of unclean water to share. We sweat like race horses during the day. We froze at night and held each other close for warmth while we slept side-by-side in the dirt.

Then one morning we heard someone unlock the shed's door. We stared at that door filled with dread and braced ourselves for pain.

"Stand!" Catalina roared as she stepped inside.

Ashaki and I struggled to help each other up.

Catalina took a step closer. She slapped me hard across the face with one hand and backhanded Ashaki with the other.

"Irish bitch. Barraca Number Five is your new home. Ashaki, you've got the brains of a sow for helping this white gutter trash. Take her to her new lodgings and then clean yourself up. You stink. At the first cock of the crow in the morning return to the big house."

"You want me back at the big house?" Ashaki asked, confused.

Catalina removed a rolling pin hidden within the folds of her skirt and rested the pin against Ashaki's shoulder. "The master believes you are nothing but a stupid child with no good sense, therefore your punishment is light," she said coldly as she narrowed her eyes. "Myself believes otherwise. Had the master handed you over to me, I would have cut your fucking nose off instead of leaving you with that pretty, little scar. Then I would have sent you off to the mines to work alongside this one. You best believe I would have. Now ask me another question - I dare you."

I followed Ashaki quietly up a dirt trail leading away from the big house to the place where the slaves were billeted. Though I had walked past the barracas many times I had never actually stepped inside one. Salamanca had a dozen barracas on his land laid out in three neat rows, though he left one building unoccupied to quarter the Spanish soldiers who often stopped for a night or two while on patrol. The buildings were long, one-story structures with clay-tiled roofs and bare wood planking with adobe applied to gaps and seams. The windows, though unglazed, were fitted with snug shutters to keep out the wind and the rain. Each barraca had two brick chimneys, one at each end, a stone well for water and two privy shacks close by, one for the men and one for the women and children.

Ashaki's family lived in Barraca Number Five with eight other families. They all shared a single great room with no partitioning walls or privacy. The room was clean and tidy and I could smell the sweet fragrance of pitaya petals in the air. Two rows of rough-hewn timber pillars supporting the rafters for the roof ran down the center of the barraca. Each pillar had two oil lanterns. Bunkbeds stacked three high stood against the walls with hooks in-between the beds for hanging clothing and such. I saw an ample number of sturdy tables and chairs and five spinning wheels scattered about. I saw colorful rugs on the floor and two large, brick ovens for cooking and heat.

Ashaki's family was kind to me from the very start. Aminatu, Ashaki's mother, carefully cleaned and dressed my wounds with linen soaked in a honey paste mixed with crushed mustard seeds. She wrapped my ribs tight. She made a bed of fresh straw for me as all the bunkbeds had been taken and fixed-up a little space for me to call my own close to one of the ovens. After Ashaki's twin sister Lololi cleaned and properly stitched Ashaki's nose, she helped her mother serve us a wonderful vegetable soup with warm bread and cool, fresh milk.

As it happened to be Easter Sunday, a holy day of obligation for Catholics, Salamanca in his benevolence had given every soul under his dominion a half day's rest. Between the holiday and the cold rains, the barraca was crowded with men, women and children. The men kept their distance. The women eyed me suspiciously. The children mostly grinned and considered me with curiosity. I offered a weak smile or two in return to try and break the tension.

The next day Ashaki returned to the big house and a few days later, once I could walk, I was sent into the fields where Felipe was gleefully waiting with his brass-tipped cane resting across his shoulders. Carlos had whipped him a dozen times for his negligence in my escape. Felipe had a grudge to settle and wasted no time thinking of ways to kill me. He spoke openly about his options. Ashaki's father, a quiet, thickset man named Quaco, a man with powerful arms and legs, kept a watchful eye over me and but for Quaco, I'm certain someone would have found me lying in a ditch somewhere with my skull staved in.

I spent my days toiling in the fields from sunrise to sunset working side-by-side with the other slaves picking corn, chilis, avocados tomatoes, melons, jicama, amaranth, sweet potatoes and the leaves off the chaya herb. We filled bushels beyond count and then helped the men till the soil and planted. My hands blistered and my fingers cracked and bled. My back ached and sometimes my determination wavered but, despite Salamanca's promise, my spirit never broke.

Sitting in a chair outside the barraca, Aminatu greeted me one evening with a broad smile after I returned from a long day in the corn fields peeling husks and pulling weeds. The air was crisp and clean and free of insects. The sun was just beginning to dip below Pico's snow-covered crown as the Milky Way and all the stars in heaven revealed themselves across a twilight sky without blemish.

Aminatu was not only kind, she was also extraordinarily wise. And because she was both kind and wise, she had ascended to become the grand matriarch over all the families in all the barracas. The other blacks addressed Aminatu, out of respect and something akin to reverence, as Abuela, as Grandmother. Filipe and Catalina both avoided Grandmother. Even Salamanca showed her his deference.

"Come sit with me, Mary," Aminatu said as she drew on her long stem pipe. Tobacco, as far as I could discern, was Aminatu's only vice.

"Gladly, Grandmother," I replied as I plopped myself down on a stool next to her and prepared myself for the unexpected. Aminatu's ability to know what was in the hearts and minds of others was uncanny, often unsettling.

After she exhaled a ring of smoke, Aminatu set her pipe aside. She took my hands in hers and began rubbing a soothing salve into my wounds. When she finished, she patted me reassuringly on the knee while she tossed her head back to take in the night sky.

"Highborn kings and lowly slaves alike," she mused, "can all savor God's infinite glory on such a night. We can all revel in His boundless, perfect love, the love He has for each of us."

"If you say so, Grandmother."

"You have a restless soul, Mary. I see it."

"I'm mad."

"Mad? Mad at who? Salamanca?"

"No. I am mad at the world Grandmother, at the whole world."

"Imagine such a thing. Mad at the whole world, huh. Do you wish to know what I think?"

"Certainly."

"I think you are biding your time and plotting again."

"No, I've learned my lesson."

Aminatu reached behind her chair, grabbed a burlap sack and placed the sack in my lap. "I found this hidden underneath the floorboards near your bed. Recognize it?"

I looked down at the burlap sack, but said nothing. Ashaki and I over many days had stuffed warm clothing, ch'arki, dried fruits, vegetables, nuts and the like into that sack - enough supplies to last me for two weeks or more.

Aminatu chuckled. "You need not worry my dearheart. Your secret is safe with me. And I understand. Truly I do. You'll die in this wretched place if you linger here much longer. Some spirits cannot be caged or tamed. I've seen men, big, healthy men, men as strong as oxen, wither away and die in slavery. I fear you'll wither away and die here too. And Felipe's hatred for you has poisoned his soul. His mind is tormented by thoughts of killing you."

I looked down at my shoes, uncertain of what to say.

"Are the stories you've shared with Ashaki," Aminatu asked,

pausing to reach down and hand me a tin cup of *octli*, an ancient Aztec drink made from fermented agave, "about your past true?"

"As God is my witness, aye, what I've told Ashaki is all true."

Aminatu drew on her pipe again, exhaled slowly and nodded. "A mere woman, leading fighting men across the vast oceans in great ships - my, my, my... Imagine such a thing."

"Fantastical, I agree."

"I doubt you not. I was born in Africa a happy child. After men from a rival tribe sold me to the Portuguese, I was overcome with sorrow and spent my days wallowing in self-pity. I yearned to see my home and family again. Years slipped by before I was able to accept my fate as a slave. Now, old and grey, I am content with my life here. Though Ashaki and Lololi were born on this very land, this is not their home. Ashaki has beauty. She has a pure and fearless heart. But she lets dreams fill her silly head. Dreams can kill you here. Lololi is more like you. She's a thinker. She's practical in all things and keeps her feet rooted firmly to the ground."

"You have two very fine daughters to be proud of."

"I'm doubly blessed to be sure. To business then Mary?"

"Beg pardon?"

"Ashaki meant well when she helped you escape the first time," Aminatu continued. "But your plan was doomed from the start. You left too much to chance, you had no resources. I don't fault you. You were desperate. I'm sorry to say this, but this new plan of yours is as foolhardy as the first. You will fail. You'll be caught again and Salamanca will end your life this time. In exchange for a favor, I can improve your odds."

"Oh?"

"Do you know of the Cimarron peoples?"

I smiled broadly. "I know the Cimarron quite well. I have Cimarron amongst my crew. One Cimarron, his name is Maurice, is the master of his own ship. He is my brother as I am his sister."

Aminatu stared at me wide-eyed. "These Cimarron come from Veracruz?"

"No. From a village called Ronconcholan that once stood on the

Chepo River in Panama."

"Panama, you say? These Cimarron are former slaves?"

"Yes. A great man, a slave named Bayano led hundreds of rebellious slaves into Panama many years ago and built a nation."

"I know this name Bayano."

"Not long ago the Spanish destroyed Ronconcholan and slaughtered the Cimarron. I was able to rescue a few survivors and found homes for them in the islands."

"Ah, ha, we have Cimarron in México."

"They're highway bandits, yes?"

"Oh, no. They're far more than bandits. They're an army."

"Indeed? Why have the Spanish not hunted them down and crushed them?"

"Amongst the Cimarron is a great war chief, a sly fox and a skilled fighter with many fine soldiers. This man's name is Gaspar Yanga. The Spanish fear him and keep their distance."

"Interesting. And you are offering to help me, Grandmother?"

"I am."

"Why?"

"You've been a kind and loyal friend to Ashaki. You could have betrayed my daughter when Carlos whipped you. You chose not to."

"Even so, she was badly punished."

"Someday Felipe will be made to answer for his cruelty against his own people."

"And this favor you speak of?"

"I see you. You're a warrior, yes, but you have a good and noble heart."

"No, Grandmother. I can take a life without hesitation, without remorse or shame. At my core I'm a cold-blooded killer. My heart is vengeance; my sword is unforgiving."

"If pushed too hard Mary any of us can kill. In the end only one question matters: do I leave this world a better place than I found it?"

"Hmmm, something to ponder Grandmother. You believe this Yanga fellow might help return me to my people?"

"I do."

"And this favor you speak of, I suspect you want me to take Ashaki and Lololi with me?"

"Just so. What mother doesn't want to see her children free and happy, to see them make their own destiny? I trust you. I know you will do your utmost to protect my girls. This is why I help you now."

"When, how?"

"Patience child, patience. A week, a month, the turn of a season or two perhaps but soon."

I laid my hand on Aminatu's shoulder as we locked eyes. "I swear Grandmother, if I succeed in making the journey back to Ireland, I will return for you and for all who wish to leave this Godforsaken place."

"There you see, your first failure to escape was a blessing. God's plan."

"I know not of such things."

"You don't believe in God's plan?"

"I'm unsure. A priest once told me a story though when I was a young child of an English king who lived many hundreds of years ago. The priest's story has never left me. May I tell you?"

"Of course."

"This king, a devout man, prayed no less than three times a day. One day a powerful fleet of heathen Danes sailed up a river and threatened his kingdom. The king had to choose between paying the Danes in gold or war. The king chose war. The Danes were fearsome warriors, superior to the English in every way except one. The king had horse. He had fine, splendid cavalry. But to employ his horsemen he needed hard, dry ground. Despite the king's prayers for good weather a terrible storm swept over the land on the eve of battle, turning the fields to mud. The king couldn't understand why God had forsaken his people. But in the morning, as the clouds parted, the king looked down upon the river and saw hundreds of dead Danes floating on the water next to their shattered longships. His kingdom was saved, his people spared. We cannot know how God will answer our prayers."

Aminatu tilted back in her chair. "Imagine such a thing," she said and smiled.

Chapter Thirteen

Atwood and I stood next to each other in a soft, warm drizzle against the quarterdeck rail under skies of dappled blues and greys while we watched his crew scurrying about. We set out with only our jib, fore and main topgallants to catch a light wind. A tall Swede named Larsson, a good man at the helm, took the wheel and deftly steered us through the maze of ships and smaller craft anchored in Ambon's cluttered harbor. Once we cleared of the worst of it, Larsson spun the wheel around to point us towards the open sea while Atwood had the topmen raise the gaff and stay sails for a bit more speed. And when we came within one hundred yards or so of the Portuguese freighter, Atwood quietly gave the order to ready the guns for action.

His crew moved out smartly. Topmen scrambled up into the rigging and trimmed the sails as gunners hustled, priming and loading their great guns with solid shot. There was no need to mount the swivels. Atwood's lads moved about confidently and worked as one. I saw no lack of discipline aboard his ship.

Atwood himself hoisted the French ensign up the mizzen gaff and then had Larsson bring us up close to the carrack. And when the three golden lilies on a field of blue unraveled, I saw curious town folk rush to the water's edge to take a closer look. No doubt Dijksma was amongst them, relishing the moment.

With less than fifty yards of water between us, I could plainly see the faces of the Portuguese sailors casually going about their daily chores, oblivious to the approaching danger. The carrack's gunports remained closed. Her guns sat secured against the bulwarks with no gunners on deck to work them.

This was my first action at sea. I could feel the exhilaration rising in me, enveloping me, robbing me of any compassion for the men about to die. I found the expectation of battle as pleasurable as the anticipation I feel just before a bout of raucous debauchery, before rolling between the sheets with my lover.

"Port side gunners!" Atwood bellowed with a voice like rolling thunder. "Guns One and Two target her rudder, the rest of you aim for her waterline. Try not to kill anyone. Larsson, keep her straight and true. Gunners, ready, wait, *NOW*! Run out your guns and *FIRE*!"

Tongues of flame and puffs of smoke reached across the water for the carrack followed instantly by BOOM! BOOM! *BA-BA-BA-BOOM-BOOM-BOOM*! *Homeward* shuddered as her battery of eight nine-pounders - twelve hundred pounds of wood and metal each - barked and recoiled.

One broadside did the job. At such close range our solid shot blew gaping holes in the freighter's hull. I watched the sea pouring into her belly and was taken aback by how quickly she began listing to one side. Dozens of her crew rushed up on deck cursing and screaming and with no time to lower away the boats, men frantically jumped overboard to swim for shore.

As we left the doomed ship behind us, Atwood calmly gave the order to secure the guns and after his lads set the course and tops'ls, after they raised the flying jib, he joined me at the stern rail where we stood silently together sipping our morning brew while watching the carrack sink. But when she vanished in a whirlpool of bubbles, my exhilaration vanished too, leaving me feeling oddly sad and empty.

Once we cleared the bay, we swung around to the north to collect the rest of our tiny squadron. I returned to *Ghostrunner*, brought our ships about and led us south as one. When I stepped on deck the following day, just as the first rays of light began painting the horizon in brilliant yellows, blues and reds, I was overwhelmed by a mix of awe and terror when I saw an enormous plume of cinder and ash spewing into the heavens, dwarfing everything around us. Gunung Api, Mount Fire, was angry. Every man rushed up on deck to marvel at the spectacle, to gaze upon what looked like the end of the world.

We drove our ships towards the largest island, Banda Besar, where the *Myristica Fragrans* grow, the aromatic evergreens, the Nutmeg Trees, which bear the seeds that men will kill for and dropped anchor just off a village of simple grass huts called Lonthoir, directly across from Mount Fire. I led us ashore in the first of four longboats, one longboat from each ship, with eighty men in all. Ben Joseph had told us where to anchor and who to see. Atwood, MacGyver, Maurice, Efendi, Henry, Kinkae and Shaw all insisted upon coming with me.

The island's elders, the *orang kaya*, meaning rich men, had wandered down to the beach to greet us. The air smelled of nutmeg mixed with the pungent odor of rotten eggs, of sulfur, even though the volcano had quieted down. I presented our bill of lading to the three elders who in turn handed the document over to a tall, bearded fellow dressed in oriental apparel, in clothing befitting a nobleman.

"This man," Efendi whispered into my ear, "is an Ottoman. Judging by his attire and weapons he is a person of prestige and rank."

"He certainly looks like royalty to me, not a harbormaster," I whispered back.

The Ottoman wore a livery collar of heavy gold around his neck and a striking ruby on his left ear. His kaftan and elaborate, feathered turban, both scarlet, were richly embroidered in gold thread. On one hip he carried a *scimitar* with a jeweled hilt and on the other he carried a long, curved dagger, called a *jambiya*, with strange markings like runes etched along the blade. He wore black, baggy trousers and heavy, black boots, the kind favored by horsemen.

"I'm Ramazan Reis bin Mehmed," the Ottoman said in good Spanish after he had translated the bill of lading to the elders and bowed. "I recognize the signature of Davitt ben Joseph and the royal seal of the Sultan of Ternate. I've advised the elders to accept this bill and the orang kaya are pleased to welcome you to their island."

"We were instructed to seek out the harbormaster," I replied.

"Kemal is in route to Ambon. I speak for the elders in his stead.

You may wait for him to return if you like."

"No. How much time do the Banda people require to make delivery?"

"The Banda hold significant quantities of nutmeg and mace in nearby storehouses, but not the eight hundred tons the sultan has agreed to. They will need to harvest more to fulfill your requirements."

"How long will the harvesting take?" Atwood asked.

"Six to eight weeks."

"Six to eight weeks!" I exclaimed.

Mehmed caught the disappointment in my tone, he smiled politely as he rubbed his earlobe with the ruby. "Yes, I fear this is so. And yet you are most fortunate. The fruit is just reaching maturity and may now be picked. Some time perhaps can be saved if you are willing to allow your crew to assist the Banda in the harvest."

"We have urgent business in Macau," I said, unwilling to spend two months languishing in Banda. "We can return when the Banda are able to deliver all eight hundred tons."

Atwood grabbed me by the arm and pulled me aside. "Elizabeth, no," he said sternly in English.

"No what?"

"We must honor our agreement with the VOC."

"We shall, in six to eight weeks."

"A lot can happen in six to eight weeks."

"Such as?"

"Dijksma could lose his war in Ambon for one. Someone could land on this island after we set out for Macau and take the spices. We cannot risk losing our cargo. We dare not offend the Dutch. We are here and we should not leave this place until we have secured what the Dutch are paying us to acquire."

"Jacob is right," Efendi said gently.

MacGyver nodded in agreement while the others stood by and said nothing. I bit my lip to keep my composure, but inside I was seething.

"Fine, you boys can stay and burn on the beach for the next two months for all I care whilst I take *Ghostrunner* on to Macau."

"My dear lady," Mehmed interrupted in fair English, surprising us all, "though it is perhaps not my place to say, I shall say it anyway. Your friends have offered you wise counsel. The waters between here and Macau are infested with barbarous men. Macau itself is a very dangerous place unless you are Portuguese or Chinese or have strong alliances with one or the other. You have four fine vessels anchored off shore. They make a formidable force together. A single foreign ship sailing on her own in these waters is to invite a terrible end."

Once again, I was forced to backdown. I felt hurt, even betrayed, when not one of my brothers, not even Shaw, offered to stand with me. I nodded reluctantly to Mehmed, then stormed off in a huff towards the longboat to retrieve my backpack and gear.

We brought more men and supplies ashore. We pitched our tents close to the village. In the evening the elders held a banquet on the beach, a simple affair, in our honor. The Banda served us a kind of English posset, a blend of hot milk, sugar and spices, but without the ale and they make their brew with coconut milk as the island has no cows. The drink turned my stomach and once we toasted our new friends, I discretly poured the rest in the sand.

Atwood plopped himself down between Shaw, little James and me in front of our campfire and handed me a full flask of wine. "I'm sorry Elizabeth if you're cross with me," he said.

"I am disappointed, not cross," I replied and took a sip of his peace offering. Atwood's gift was thoughtful as we had finished off the last of our wine aboard *Ghostrunner*.

"The time will pass by quickly," Atwood promised. "You'll see. Our new Ottoman friend has offered to take us to the top of Mount Fire if such a venture is of interest you. The experience, he promises, is not one you'll forget."

I gazed over at the volcano across the water barely two thousand yards away. The mountain was only a dark silhouette against the fading light, and though the great cloud of smoke had dissipated, I could still see slender tendrils of steam and a thin, orange ribbon glowing around her crown. The idea of climbing to the top of the mountain very much appealed to me.

"Such a trip intrigues me," I said while watching Mehmed walking towards us carrying a basket of fish.

"I come bearing gifts," he said. "May I join you? I have baked marlin, swordfish, yellow fin tuna and wahoo, each prepared with a variety of wonderful spices."

"We'd be honored," I replied. "Sit next to me and my little man. The boy's name is James."

"Happily, dear lady."

"Are you the sultan's man or are you with the Dutch? I pray you're not with the Portuguese!"

Mehmed laughed. "I would never serve those Portuguese devils. I know very little about the Dutch and there are many sultans in these parts. I am my own man. If I have any master, as the land called Turkey is my home, he would be, if he still lives, the Sultan of the Ottoman Empire, his Excellency Mehmed III, Ottoman Caliph, Amir al-Mu'minin, Kayser-I Rûm and Custodian of the Two Holy Mosques, may Allah bless and grant him long life and wisdom."

"Would you care for some wine Ramazan?"

"Ah, happily. A thousand blessings my lady. It has been too long."

Atwood nodded his approval as I passed the flask over to Mehmed. "Our own Turk, Mustafa," Atwood said with a wide grin, "you met him earlier, often enjoys a round or two."

"The Muslims of the East Indies are Sunnis Muslims and fermented drink is forbidden to them," Mehmed explained and took a sip from the flask. "Mercifully, I am Alevi Muslim. Many Turks are Alevi Muslims and we Alevi are more tolerant about worldly matters, more liberal in our interpretation of the Quran."

Atwood laughed. "You'll get along just fine with the Dutch."

"No Christians in the Banda Islands?" I asked.

"I believe not. There are no Portuguese settlements or monasteries here. The Banda are fiercely independent and have many fine, skilled warriors, enough warriors to keep the Portuguese away for now. Besides, the Portuguese don't need to establish a settlement in these islands as long as they are able to control the spice markets from

Ambon."

My men had brought four young sheep ashore for slaughter earlier. We had a leg of lamb roasting on the spit next to a griddle of pancake fritters made from flour and lard. I sliced a strip of meat off the bone and offered the tender morsel to Mehmed.

"*Tesekkür ederim*," Mehmed said and eagerly bit into the roasted flesh.

"Those two words are about the only Turkish I know," I said. "You are most welcome. What can you tell us about the people who live on these islands?"

Mehmed washed his lamb down with a generous swig of wine before answering. "The Banda are a content and happy people. And why should this not be so? Truly I say unto you, we are sitting in paradise on this Earth. We are surrounded by great beauty and the Banda possess all the world's nutmeg and nutmeg is worth more than gold. The will of Allah. For centuries the Banda were able to keep the location of their nutmeg a secret. Then nearly eighty years ago Portuguese explorers came to the East Indies and did not rest until they found the Nutmeg Trees. To keep what they have without bloodshed, the Banda agreed to give the Portuguese a monopoly over the nutmeg trade. Now the Dutch are here. Like the desert sand shifting beneath one's feet, power across the world is shifting too."

"The Dutch and the Sultan of Ternate are allies we've heard," Atwood declared. "Which sultan rules the Banda people?"

"Ah my friend, now there is an excellent question. The Sultan of Ternate, who does indeed favor the Dutch, and the Sultan of Tidore, who is allied with the Portuguese, both claim these islands. The Banda don't recognize either man as their sovereign. I've heard the boy prince of Banten recently claimed the Spice Islands for himself. Kings come and go. The Banda have been here for centuries."

"We've already met Prince Ratu," I said sharply. "So, there will be war?"

"There is always war, my lady."

"True. I'm still unclear where your allegiances lie."

"Ha! When I know myself, I shall gladly tell you. I know you are allied with the Dutch."

"We sail," Shaw said as he reached into Mehmed's basket for a fish, "under contract for the Dutch, Ramazan. Nothing more."

"My mistake," Mehmed replied and bowed his head apologetically.

Shaw peeled the skin of his fish back and took a bite. "Mmm, delicious," he said and smacked his lips approvingly.

"Are there other ships in the Bandas?" Atwood asked.

"Oh yes many though you are the only Europeans. My own galley is anchored nearby. Banda offers more than nutmeg. Banda enjoys a significant entrepôt trade. Cloves from Ternate and Tidore, exotic bird-of-paradise feathers from the Aru Islands and massoi bark from Papua, which is used to make medicines and salves, all transit through Banda."

"The Banda," Atwood said as he helped himself to a fish, "are an enterprising people."

"They are," the Turk replied, nodding in agreement.

"How is the nutmeg prepared?" I asked.

"I thought you might ask this question," Mehmed said and reached into his kaftan. "I came prepared. This is the fruit of the Nutmeg Tree. As you can see, it is similar in shape and size to an apricot." Mehmed paused to pull his dagger from his belt and cracked the fruit open on a rock with the hilt. "When the fruit is fully matured it splits in two like so. This red part is mace. Peel the mace away and you have this shiny brown seed, the nutmeg. The mace is flattened on tables and allowed to dry for ten to twelve days. Mace is a delicate spice and can be used to enhance the flavors of many foods. Mace is also used as a preservative. The nutmegs are dried in the sun to shrink the shells. The women turn the shells over twice a day for six to eight weeks - until you can shake the shell and hear the nutmeg kernel rattling inside. Then they take wooden truncheons, break the shells open and extract the kernels. The kernels are later ground into a fine powder and packed into burlap sacks and crates for transport."

"How many Banda partake in the harvesting?" I asked.

"To fulfill your requirements, hundreds."

I reached into Mehmed's basket for a fish. "In the morning," I said, "we'll bring more men ashore to help with the harvest."

Mehmed smiled and took another sip of wine.

We spent six full weeks in the Bandas while the villagers gathered and prepared our nutmeg and mace. We spent the days resting, helping the Banda and working on the ships. We found an excellent stretch of sand in a quiet cove to finally grave their bottoms. The men beached the ships one at a time and toiled out in the open under a scorching sun in torrid heat scraping off barnacles and repairing the damage made by hungry seaworms. The work was tedious, dirty and hard.

With Mehmed as our guide, we also spent a few days cruising around the islands aboard his war galley to take in the stunning beauty all around us. The famous islands of spice sparkled before us like jewels on a sea of shimmering jade. The beauty of Rhun, Gunung Api, Neira, Banda Besar, Ai, Hatta, Syahrir, Karaka, Manukan, Nailaka and Batu Kapal will not soon fade from my memory.

We also accepted Mehmed's offer to climb Mount Fire. I found the experience sobering and thought of the Italian poet Dante Alighieri's description of hell in his famous *Divina Commedia* as I peered down into the volcano's crater, as I stared transfixed at the pools of bubbling lava.

Upon our return to Banda, Shaw and I disappeared into the woods from time-to-time to indulge our lusty cravings. We'd been celibate far too long. With uninhibited, wanton desire, Shaw rode me long and hard amongst the Nutmeg Trees like a wild stallion. He brought me to ecstasy each time, the kind of pleasure that leaves a woman quivering from head to toe and wanting more. But once our passions cooled, on each occasion, I struggled to find much to say and grew bored.

Chapter Fourteen

It is for our past transgressions I suppose that we are banished to this wretched prison of relentless loss, of pain and sorrow, to this world where everything - no matter its beauty or age - is dying or decaying. We all must make do as best we can until death comes to free us.

Such were my darker thoughts as ten brawny warriors, heavily armed with muskets, machetes, long daggers and swords, led Ashaki, Lololi and me up a steep trail into the hills in the dead of night during a driving downpour. Howling winds swirled all around us. Lightning above our heads split the sky open as thunder pounded the very ground we treaded upon.

"How much farther?" I asked the lead Cimarron. I had a pebble in my shoe and badly needed to stop.

Lololi, suffering from a nasty chest cold, had been coughing, wheezing and struggling to keep up. I worried she might catch the chills. And then there was Ashaki. She seemed remarkably indifferent to our hardships. She walked ahead of us with purpose, with boundless energy and oblivious to any danger. Every so often she'd spin around to offer me a reassuring smile. That one was like steel.

Many weeks had passed since Aminatu and I had sat outside underneath the stars together drinking octli. How she communicated with the Cimarron, I know not. Who planned our escape, or helped us by setting Salamanca's mill on fire during the dead of night, I cannot say. I only know that as flames devoured the mill and spread to several nearby shacks, Aminatu's husband Quaco awakened Ashaki, Lololi and me and led us to the far edge of an unplowed field during the hurly-burly where the Cimarron were waiting.

"Six, seven days if we keep moving," the lead man replied gruffly and handed me a skin of water. "We can stop and rest here. I left men behind to cover our tracks, to make certain we aren't followed. We'll be safe in this place for a bit."

We rested long enough to catch our breath. Then the Cimarron handed us fresh clothing. They made us strip and change, even our undergarments, giving no reason why. When we resumed our march again up into rugged country, I tried to engage our new friends in casual conversation but these men were not for talking.

We walked through the night, stopping only long enough here and there to rub sore feet and to relieve ourselves, and kept moving until we came upon an apple orchard in the morning where the Cimarron finally let us rest. The girls and I sat against an apple tree and gobbled down a meager breakfast of hard biscuits and dried fruit before the Cimarron had us up and walking again, always moving us uphill. The morning was overcast and pleasant but by noon the sun dispersed the clouds and caught us passing through open country with little shade. We trudged on in heat and humidity for hours. At least Lololi was on the mend.

Each day from dawn to dusk we walked and then some. The Cimarron treated us with respect but pushed us hard, constantly leading us up to higher and higher ground.

Sometime before midnight on the eighth day, we reached a Cimarron encampment, a war camp of many tents and huts laid out in a defensive ring with stacks of arms scattered about. And though I saw sentries with torches in hand patrolling the camp's perimeter, security seemed lax to me. I saw no walls or earthworks or barricades of any kind. The ground was flat, exposed and campfires were plentiful, fires that could be seen for miles around.

The lead man wished us well after he left us at one of the campfires near the center of the camp. Ashaki, Lololi and I wearily plopped ourselves down on the grass. The air smelled of smoky, green wood and roasted chicken and I heard someone playing a lute nearby. The musician had talent.

"Mary," a deep voice called out behind me.

I turned to find an older man with the most extraordinary eyes I'd ever seen hovering over me. He stared hard at me as if he was peering into my soul.

"I am Mary," I said as I struggled to my feet.

"And I am the one you seek," the man said while extending his hand to help me up. "I am Gaspar Yanga."

Like the soldiers we had traveled with, the infamous bandit, the man revered by slaves everywhere throughout New Spain, was a rough looking fellow with rippling, hard muscles. He was neither handsome nor homely and but for his eyes, eyes of haunting power, he appeared altogether unremarkable. Deep wrinkles cut across his brow. His cropped curly beard and short hair had long ago turned grey. He looked like a peasant farmer in his ragged, ill-fitting clothing. I guessed him to be about sixty years of age.

"I'm honored to meet you, sir," I said and took his hand.

"I'm pleased you made the journey to our camp without incident," Yanga said. "I sent good men to keep you safe."

"Thank you for helping us. Thank you for allowing my friends and me into your camp."

Yanga smiled politely as he considered me, as if appraising my qualities - good and bad. "Any day a man, woman or child can breathe the air in freedom is a good day," he said. "I don't believe I've ever helped a white woman before."

"A tale to tell your grandchildren someday perhaps."

"There is much I would know from you, Mary. Please, sit. Ah, this must be Ashaki. Your mother has told me of your great beauty. Quaco boasts about your fearlessness. Beauty and courage, fine, fine qualities. And lovely Lololi, I understand you are a thinker. I understand you are practical and clever. Your parents speak of you both with great pride."

Yanga leaned down and kissed the girls affectionately on the forehead as women brought us wooden bowls of hot food. "I've known your parents for many years. They are very dear to me and so you are very dear to me. Come ladies, eat. You must be famished and exhausted from the long journey."

We greedily stuffed ourselves on a fine stew of roasted chicken, black beans, corn and tomatoes. Yanga sat with us and passed a bottle of good Spanish wine around. He listened thoughtfully as we told our stories in turn. Being older and more worldly, I of course had the most to say.

"I know little of Ronconcholan," Yanga said after I finished my tale. "We've all heard the stories about the great rebel Bayano, the man who built a kingdom in Panama with thousands of Indians and escaped slaves. I do not know this Alonso, this Chidimma fellow you speak of but I've heard of the Aztec warrior who calls himself Zekowtah. You say some of the Cimarron who evaded the slaughter at Ronconcholan are now in Guadeloupe?"

"Aye. Over three hundred men, women and children. I was sailing with Sir Francis Drake in the winter of '95 when he invaded Panama. A good number of my men and I went ashore with the English army when they marched on Viejo looking for Spanish treasure. And whilst I marched with the English, I sent some of my boys on to Ronconcholan to look for Cimarron survivors."

"Imagine such a thing. I hear you have a clever mind. Are you an educated woman?"

"Not in the formal sense you mean. My education has been the trials and tribulations of day-to-day life and I began my schooling at a very young age."

Yanga nodded approvingly. "There is no better school in all the world."

"Can you tell us your story?" Lololi asked.

"Whatever you've heard about me my young Lololi is I'm certain much exaggerated," Yanga answered with an easy smile.

"They say you were born a prince, is this true?" she asked.

"This much is true. I was the son of Nyanga of the House of Gabon. My father was chief of the Yang-Bara people in a land the Portuguese now call Gabāo on the west coast of Africa. When my father died, I was, as the eldest son, to become chief. But I had a brother who was a jealous man. He wanted to be chief. My brother - to this day I cannot speak his name - approached the hated enemy of my people, the ruler of the Songhai Empire, Askia Daoud, and sought Daoud's help in furthering his depraved ambitions. In exchange for an alliance between the Yang-Bara and the wretched Songhai - surely an act of evil in the eyes of our Lord God - Daoud agreed to make my wicked brother chief. One day Daoud's men entered my village. They dragged me from my bed, beat me, broke my nose and fractured a bone in my wrist. They took me to the coast with my arms tied to a yoke across my shoulders and sold me to the Portuguese."

"Good God," I said. "Your own brother betrayed you?"

"As I have said."

"And the Portuguese brought you to Veracruz as a slave?"

"Yes. I worked in the fields on a hacienda not far from where we sit now called *La Tierra de las Cinco Holinas*, a place not unlike Salamanca's lands. One day I killed my master. The reasons no longer matter. I ran for my life of course. A dozen slaves fled with me. We took refuge in the wilderness, up here in the highlands. That was back in 1570 and we've been sparring with the Spanish ever since. As you can see, we've survived and prospered. Today we are thousands strong. We are a union of farmers, herdsmen and hunters, of blacksmiths, apothecaries, cooks, teachers, craftsmen, women, children and many fine soldiers."

"'Tis no small feat to keep a step or two ahead of the Spanish army for so many years," I said with sincere respect. "But I wouldn't want to defend this position."

Yanga chuckled. "Nor would I dear lady, nor would I. We'd be far away from here before any Spanish force approached. I have many spies and many scouts scattered across the land always on the lookout for trouble."

"Is it true," Lololi asked, "the Angolan Francisco de la Matosa and his men have joined you? Some say the Spanish fear this man more than any other."

"Do they now?" Yanga asked and laughed. "I'll introduce you to this Goliath when he returns. Francisco is leading a large raiding party up north and should be back in a day or two, God willing."

And then, with some trepidation, I asked the question dearest to my heart. "Can you, will you help me?"

Yanga looked at me perplexed. "Did not Aminatu say I would?"

"She did."

"God pity the fool who crosses that woman," Yanga said obliquely and looked away. "Sanchez, to me!"

A one-armed man, a light-skinned mulatto, hurried over to our campfire.

"You heard the Irishwoman tell her story?" Yanga asked.

"Oh yes. Yes, I did Gaspar."

"Do you recognize her?"

The man took a step closer to me. "No, Gaspar. I only saw the Irish woman from afar but this must be her. All she has said about the Cimarron in Panama is true. Every detail is correct. I knew Alonso. I knew Zekowtah. Her descriptions of both men are accurate. Zekowtah once lead a war party with a strong force of Irish and French sailors led by an Irish woman named Mary, a real beauty they say with long, raven hair, to search for lost treasure."

"This treasure you speak of," Yanga asked, "is the treasure the notorious Englishman Drake and his men robbed from the Silver Train in '73 but had to leave behind in Panama when the Spanish army began closing in on them?"

"The same Gaspar."

Yanga turned to me. "Sanchez survived the slaughter at Ronconcholan. He and a few others made their way here to join us. Your friendship with the Cimarron and the Carib was not unknown to me. I wished to hear your story for myself and Sanchez has now confirmed what I thought to be true. You are most welcome here Mary. Yes, I will help you."

I took a moment to compose myself, I brushed back a tear. "I will forever be in your debt," I said and reached over to squeeze Yanga's hand.

"You owe me nothing. I have my own debts to settle with Grandmother. I once knew a Bantu man. He gave his life for mine but before he died, he told me the name Yanga in Bantu means pride and because of this he expected great things of me. Amongst my people you will be known as Mary Yanga. You are now Cimarron and I expect great things of you."

"I'm deeply honored," I replied in all sincerity.

"Good. Ashaki, Lololi, you've risked everything to make the long and perilous journey to freedom and I welcome you with open arms. You too are now both Cimarron."

"My sister and I are grateful," Lololi said. "But we worry what will become of our mother and father? Salamanca will blame them for our escape. He'll whip them without mercy, or worse."

Yanga picked a stick up off the ground and started drawing trifling shapes in the dirt. "I don't think so."

"Why?"

"Because you did not escape."

Lololi shook her head. "Beg pardon?"

"Ladies, the story Salamanca will hear is this: the villainous Cimarrons who raided his lands and the lands of his neighbors came looking for livestock, gold, silver, strong spirits and women. Have you ever seen your mother cry?"

"Our mother does not cry," Ashaki said staunchly. "She's as hard as the hardest stone."

"How true. And yet your mother knows how to cry. She is a woman of many gifts. By now Aminatu has fallen to her knees in tears. She has wrapped her arms around Salamanca's legs and begged him to find you and Lololi. She has begged him to bring you home. By now the men Salamanca sent out to try and catch the raiders have returned to the hacienda with your old clothes, soiled, torn and splattered in blood - proof of evil doings. By now Salamanca has excused your mother and father from their labors for a day or two to let them grieve. If Salamanca whips anyone, it will be that dog Felipe for allowing the mill to burn, for allowing bandits to runoff with his slaves and livestock."

"Won't the Spanish army retaliate against your people?" I asked.

Yanga tossed his stick into the fire and smiled before he turned to me. "For over thirty years they've tried."

We spent the next few days resting and intermingling with Yanga's people until Matosa, or the Angolan as many liked to call him, strolled into camp with two dozen oxen pulling a dozen two-wheeled carts loaded down with burlap sacks bulging with smoked meats, corn, flour and tobacco and with casks of freshly brewed ale. I counted over fifty newly liberated men, women and children walking alongside the carts.

Being the only white woman in camp, Matosa hastened over to our campfire when he saw me, just as the girls and I were about to eat our morning meal. Matosa was no Goliath. He was a short, barrel-chested man, a younger fellow with a large head who liked cigars. I could smell the tobacco on him. He had the arms and legs of a wrestler and a tree trunk for a neck. He reminded me of a battering ram.

"I'm Francisco," he said and offered his hand.

"I'm honored," I replied and stood to shake hands. "I'm Mary."

Yanga quickly joined us. "Welcome back Francisco," he said and embraced the Angolan. "This is the woman Grandmother spoke of and these two fine ladies are Grandmother's daughters, Ashaki and Lololi. Come sit and share breakfast with us. You've returned with many splendid gifts I see."

"Compliments of our generous Spanish hosts up north," Matosa replied with a wide grin.

"Why do they call you the Angolan?" I asked as I moved around the campfire to pour everyone more coffee while Ashaki followed behind me with a hot skillet of cornbread cakes.

"Because I come from a land in Africa the Portuguese call Angola."

"Where is this Angola?" I asked. "I've not heard of it."

"Angola is on the west coast of Africa."

"Near Gabāo?"

"Yes, a little farther south. Before the Portuguese came to Africa, those lands were a province of the Kingdom of Kongo."

"Were you a prince like Gaspar?" Lololi asked.

Matosa and Yanga exchanged knowing glances before they roared with laughter. "Gaspar enjoys telling anyone who will listen to his babbling nonsense that he was born a prince! Pure drivel. Look at the man. He's ugly. He's a lowly peasant like the rest of us. Why anyone would even boast about such a dishonorable thing baffles me. I myself was born a thief, a most excellent thief who takes great pride in his work. A good thief is worth a hundred princes in this world."

"Not such a good thief," Yanga said in-between his fits of laughter. "The Portuguese caught Francisco lying in a ditch outside his town in a drunken stupor with a bag of stolen goods, with trinkets of little value! For this horrible offense the magistrate sentenced him to a lifetime of slavery."

"Lies, all lies," Matosa said and spit into the fire. "I cannot be caught! No, no. I stole a Portuguese galleon for myself and I sailed her to the New World seeking high adventure and plunder."

"Without a crew," Yanga proclaimed and slapped his knee. "Francisco boasts he sailed this galleon all by himself, that he survived terrible storms with waves as big as mountains and fought off great sea monsters trying to eat him, slaying them all with his bare hands as the sea had taken his sword and musket."

"I'm surrounded by mice," Matosa scoffed, "with no understanding of the world of a giant."

"Your Christian name Francisco and your surname de la Matosa," I asked smiling, "are Portuguese, yes?"

"Ah, this is true my lady. In 1575 or thereabouts the explorer Paulo Dias de Novais landed in Angola with four hundred soldiers and one hundred Portuguese families to settle and tame the land, land that had already been tamed and settled by the native peoples there centuries before. The Portuguese built a port on the coast with a fine harbor and named the place São Paulo da Assumpção de Loanda. My father was Portuguese, one of Novais' lieutenants. My mother was African. She gave me my father's name hoping I suppose that this might somehow protect me from evil. I was born in Loanda."

"When Mary," Ashaki interjected, "tried to escape earlier from Señor Salamanca, her plan was to find a boat in Veracruz, one large enough to reach Cuba. Mary has friends in Cuba, friends who can help her return to Ireland, an island across the ocean near a great kingdom called England. Gasper says you have a boat. Can your boat cross the ocean to Ireland?"

Matosa shook his head. "To Ireland, no girl. To Cuba, yes. I've traveled to Cuba and back again to Veracruz many times."

"You must be a most excellent sailor," Ashaki said.

"I have some skills. I've been lucky too. If the gossip I've heard around camp is true, Mary is herself an able mariner. She understands the challenges and the dangers."

"Do you," I asked, "keep to the coast?"

"Yes. The land between Veracruz and the small village of Mérida on the Yucatán Peninsula is mostly wildness with abundant sources of sweet water and food. From Mérida to the tip of Yucatán is about one hundred miles and from this point to Cuba is a meager ninety miles or so. No need to sail far out to sea."

"From Kan Kun," I said softly to myself, pleased for having devised a good and proper plan when I had first tried to escape.

"Excellent, Mary. Yes. You've studied your maps and given this matter some thought I see. From Kan Kun to the western shores of Cuba is a two-day journey over open water. This is how we reach Havana if we wish to keep the odds of surviving in our favor."

"What type of boat is she?" I asked.

"She's no galleon. She's a two-masted lugger, about thirty feet in length from stem to stern. The old girl is slow and clumsy but she gets the job done. Because she's a squat, ugly thing, I named her *Gasper Yanga*! Ha, ha! If she's not to your liking we can sneak into Veracruz and pilfer another."

"A lugger you say. How is she rigged?"

Matosa beamed. "Ah, the lady wishes to test me. Most wise, most wise. Her lugsail is rigged forward with vangs and a bonnet to give her a bit more speed. She's fitted with a stubby bowsprit but has a generous spritsail and handles well in rough water. Her lateen mizzen is sheeted to an outrigger for good balance."

"You know your boats, sir. I apologize for questioning you."

"No need. I respect you for it."

"So, you will take me to Havana?"

"I will, I will indeed with room to spare for these two lovely companions of yours. Be good to leave the dust of this land behind and taste salt air again."

"No, no, just me."

The twins simultaneously whipped their heads around and glared at me with dismay. "What do you mean Mary?" Ashaki demanded. "We are traveling with you."

"Ashaki is right," Lololi said. "We are all agreed."

The sisters surprised me. I had expected them to remain behind with the Cimarron.

"Girls, we are not agreed. This journey to Cuba will be long, difficult and dangerous. You are too young. I'll wager neither of you has ever stepped foot inside a boat before, let alone sailed across the ocean. Besides, a poor white woman traveling with two young Blackamoors would attract unwanted attention. Your place is here. Stay and savor your newfound freedom."

"We'll find you some pretty clothes," Lololi said, ignoring me. "We'll make you a lady. We'll travel with you as your slaves, obedient in all things."

"No!" I said aghast. "You mustn't say such things! I pray you live long and happy lives as free women here in New Spain."

Ashaki defiantly placed her hands on her hips. "Lololi and I are of like mind. We sail for Cuba with you."

"What would your mother say?" I asked. "She'd cringe at this proposal I'm quite certain and admonish you both. Do not be so careless with your new lives."

Ashaki shook her head. "You're mistaken about our mother, Mary."

Lololi jumped to her feet to stand next to her sister. "We are decided."

Yanga raised his hands, calling for silence. "Ladies, please. Ashaki, Lololi, Mary is older and far more worldly than either of you. It is good and proper you respect her wise counsel. This is the order of things. And yet - Mary - what is freedom if one cannot choose his or her own destiny?"

"But," I protested, "what will these two do in Havana?"

When Yanga shrugged his shoulders and said nothing, I turned to the girls. "Well?" I asked.

"We'll prove our worth to you," Lololi said. "By God we will, you'll see. And one day we'll be at your side when you return to Veracruz with your great ships and brave soldiers to free our people."

"This," Ashaki added, "was your solemn promise to Aminatu."

"Such passion and determination in ones so young!" Yanga exclaimed with father-like pride and clapped his hands. "You are our future and give me hope. Bravo ladies, bravo!"

"I have," I said in mock anger, narrowing my eyes as I spoke, "dealt with twins before and matters did not end well for them..."

The girls knew they had won the day and needed to say no more though Ashaki, to add insult to injury, stuck her tongue out at me before turning and walking away. I couldn't help myself and smiled.

Another week slipped by before all was ready. With chests full of fashionable women's clothing, with a fortune in gold doubloons for food, lodging, bribes and passages for one lady and her two maids-in-waiting to cross the Atlantic to Europe - the Cimarron had plenty of Spanish treasure to share - Ashaki, Lololi and I said our farewells to Yanga and his people. As Yanga could spare no horses, we headed for the coast on foot with Matosa, his crew of five and three pack mules. Twenty well-armed men marched with us to see us safely to the coast. For the first time since I found myself floating on the ocean in the dark, clinging to a splintered ship's rail, I felt confident about my chances.

Chapter Fifteen

hina. The thought of reaching Macau filled me with shifting spells of joy and dread. I know not why. With our four ships loaded down with exotic spices, with a fortune in nutmeg, mace and cloves - eight hundred tons in all - we left the Spice Islands behind us, skirted around the leeward side of Seram and headed due north into the China Sea with a friendly wind at our backs and fair skies overhead. We made good time, reaching the coast of China after only twenty-one days of easy sailing.

I gave the order to furl sail near a cluster of small islands several miles off the mainland. I had Henry raise the checkered yellow and green pennant up the main mast, the signal for the others to join me in my great cabin. Atwood, MacGyver and Maurice rowed over to *Ghostrunner* in one longboat and as they stepped aboard, I greeted each of my brothers with an engaging smile and a warm embrace.

"Let us review the plan once more," I said as all my officers, along with one Chinaman, took their seats around the table. "But before we do, the ships are sound, the men are well?"

"I lost two men overboard during the night," MacGyver reported. "I know not how."

"Foul play?" Efendi asked. "We encountered no storms. We sailed through no rough seas."

"Quite possibly," MacGyver answered. "Perhaps a quarrel of some sort. Perhaps someone was careless. The mishap could have been nothing more than an unfortunate accident with no one to blame. I found no evidence of evil doings. Both lads were new men. I doubt we'll ever learn the truth of it. You know how it goes Mustafa."

"Most unfortunate," I said. "Jacob, Maurice, all is well aboard your ships?"

"All is well Elizabeth," Maurice answered, followed by a dour nod from Atwood.

"Good. Mustafa, Kinkae, Henry, Rob, anything to report?"

The four men quietly shook their heads.

"Good, good. I've asked Arslan to join us as he has a part to play in the coming days."

"You still propose," Atwood asked, "to sail into Macau with all four ships? Such a sight is bound to raise an eyebrow or two, stir up gossip."

"Yes, Arslan and I think it best," I replied.

Atwood turned to face Arslan with an unfriendly smile. "What the Chinaman's thoughts are on this or that or on any matter is of no interest to me. We don't know this man. We don't know his intentions. He shouldn't be sitting at this table."

"Well Jacob, if we wish to sell our cargo, we need to sail into port with all of our ships and I believe Arslan can be of great service to us."

"*Our* cargo?" Atwood asked indignantly. "I'll wager the Dutch will have something to say about that inasmuch as they purchased every sack, crate, box and barrel of spices we carry."

"As you know full well Jacob," I answered defiantly, "the Dutch paid the Sultan of Ternate off and stole the spices from the Portuguese."

"The spoils of war, a bit of trickery between rivals, call it whatever you will but not theft. That's how the Dutch will see things."

"We must," Efendi insisted, "honor our contract with the Company Elizabeth or risk incurring the wrath of the Company, perhaps even invite the displeasure of the Dutch government."

I placed my hands on the table, interlocked my fingers and chose my next words with care. "Gentlemen, I do understand your point. I understand your point quite well. I'm not suggesting we make an enemy of the Dutch. We can sell our cargo in Macau and turn the profits for six hundred tons over to the Company upon our return to Amsterdam. By doing this, we can load our ships down with Chinese goods for ourselves."

"Beg pardon?" Atwood asked wide-eyed. "You propose we sell the Company's cargo to the Chinese and use the proceeds from that sale - money that unquestionably belongs to the Dutch - to finance the purchase of our own cargo? Utter foolishness, pure chicanery. You can't be serious."

"Two hundred tons of spices is ours to sell as we see fit and proper and as long as we pay the Dutch back the profits on the rest, who's to care?" I asked rhetorically in a testy tone, then took a moment to translate the exchange of words between Atwood and myself into Portuguese for Arslan as he struggled with English.

Atwood vigorously shook his head. "Elizabeth, I'm sorry. I do not wish to be contentious, but no. The spices will fetch far greater profits for the Company in Europe than in Macau. And let's not forget our English friend Martin's hand in all of this. We not only risk offending the Dutch government, we could incur the wrath of the English Crown as well. Who can say what politics or schemes are at play between the two nations? Both countries despise the Spanish. Neither King James nor Maurice of Nassau can be too keen about leisurely sitting back whilst Catholic Spain and Portugal carve up the world between them."

I stared hard at Atwood as he glared back at me. The cabin turned uncomfortably quiet. Mary never would have tolerated such insubordination. But I did not have her power - not yet. Again, I took a moment to translate the words between Atwood and me to Arslan as well as to cool my own ardor.

"Gentlemen," Arslan offered cautiously, "I assure you such trans, act, transactions are not uncommon in this part of the wor, world. Do you Christians not sometimes rob Peter to pay Paul? I can help you sell your spices. I can help you purchase excep, exceptional goods at very de, de-sir-able prices."

Atwood placed his hands on the table with a menacing glint in his eye and leaned forward. "Shut your hole Chinaman," he commanded, then turned to me. "Elizabeth, you're ambitious and headstrong. I understand. You're young. But this notion of yours to sell every pound of cargo we have is folly and I'll not agree to it. We have all agreed, with no enthusiasm in our hearts mind you, to sail to Macau. We have all agreed to sell one shipload of spices, though I fear our Dutch partners will disapprove of our actions as Ewoud warned. I'm prepared to do this much and no more. I'll not take my ship into Macau. This is my final word on the matter."

"I'm sorry Elizabeth," MacGyver interjected. "I must agree with Jacob."

When Maurice aligned himself with Atwood and MacGyver - all three captains - I once again found myself alone. We were on the brink of achieving great riches. But for me, but for my audacity, we'd be sailing aimlessly around in circles in the Caribbean and growing poorer by the day. I had the urge to say as much but once again I decided to bite my tongue.

"So be it," I said, annoyed. "We'll enter Macau with one ship. We're leaving money on the table, a substantial amount of wealth. Kinkae, you and your Blackamoors must stay out-of-sight for it is unclear how the Portuguese would look upon free Africans serving aboard a European vessel. Henry, it is best you and your Carib do the same. I'll go ashore with Michael and take Arslan with me. Arslan will be your navigator Michael and I shall play the part of ship's purser. I'll use the alias Ortiz and Michael you can be, say, Flannigan. Do you have any objections to this plan, Jacob?"

Atwood rolled a chart across the table. "I've said all I need to say. Maurice, Rob and I will anchor the ships at this island sitting off our starboard bow called Dawanshan Dao. We'll wait for you there. According to the notations in the margins here, the island is home to simple fishermen and their families. If trouble finds us there, we'll move the ships south to this island named Shangchuan, an island the Portuguese once used as a base until they abandoned the place some years ago for Macau. Either island should have a suitable roadstead."

I nodded. "This is all fine and well. We should be in Macau for no more than a few days, a week at most. If we encounter complications, I'll hire a boat to send word out to you."

MacGyver eased *Achilles* into a harbor swarming with vessels, a harbor far more congested than Banten and Ambon combined with ships of every sort and kind. Amongst them we saw three Portuguese warships, one light frigate and two modest caravels, all with their guns run out and double the watch standing guard. Plainly the Portuguese had heard about the loss of one of their ships in Ambon.

MacGyver, Arslan and I took the skiff ashore without a crew. We tied our little boat off against a newly built wharf and asked a passing dockman, a Spaniard, where we could find the harbormaster. The man pointed to a modest, wooden shack not far off with a wood shield nailed over the door. With its five azure escutcheons charged with as many plates in saltire - representing the five holy wounds of Christ and forming a cross in the center of a rounded shield with a red bordure containing seven golden castles with triple towers - I instantly recognized the royal coat-of-arms of Portugal.

We found the harbormaster, a stout fellow with a ruddy complexion and several days of grey stubble on his chin, sitting behind a barrel chewing on the end of an unlit cigar while playing a game of chess against himself. He casually waved us inside.

"*Um bom dia para você senhor, eu sou a Senhora Elizabeth Ortiz,*" I said to the man and then translated my words to MacGyver as he spoke very little Portuguese. "A good day to you sir, I am Lady Elizabeth Ortiz. *Nosso navio é o Aquiles e você vai encontrar os papéis dela em ordem, se você se importa de olhar. Eu sou o armador do navio, ah, tesoureiro. Este senhor à minha esquerda é o mestre do Aquiles, Michael Flannigan, e o chinês é Arslan, a quem contratamos como navegador.* Michael, I told the harbormaster our vessel is the *Achilles* and that he will find her papers in order if he cares to look. I introduced myself as the ship's purser and introduced you as Michael Flannigan, the ship's master. I told him we've hired Arlsan as a navigator."

"*Um bom dia para você, senhora,*" the harbormaster replied. "*Bem-vindo à Cidade do Nome de Deus de Macau. Indique seu negócio.*"

"The man wishes us a good day Michael and welcomes us to the City of the Name of God of Macau. He wants to know our business."

I dropped my knapsack on the floor and took a step closer to the harbormaster. "*Somos comerciantes que vêm ao comércio. Poderíamos falar em espanhol para que meus companheiros possam nos entender melhor?* We are merchants come to trade I told him Michael and I've asked him if we can speak in Spanish."

"Yes, happily," the harbormaster replied. "You bring a lot of firepower into port for merchants. That ship of yours looks more like a ship-of-war than a freighter."

"A dangerous ship for dangerous waters, sir."

"How true, madam, how true. Fair enough. What is your country?"

"We're Irish. We come from Ireland."

"Oh? You speak Portuguese with a Spanish accent my lady."

"Yes, I was born in Spain, though I lived in the West Indies during my youth and now call Ireland home. You may inspect our ship if you have a mind to, you'll find an Irish crew on board."

The harbormaster scratched at the whiskers on his chin. "Can't say we've ever had any Irish drop anchor in our fine harbor before today."

I smiled sweetly at the man. "Then today is a happy day as we've made a bit of history together."

"How does a woman become a ship's purser?"

"She's born of noble blood and her family has important friends at the Spanish Court."

"Ah, Ortiz is the name of a noble Spanish family?"

I placed my hands on my hips. A touch of Spanish arrogance, not too much, was needed to put the Portuguese in his place.

"Do you question my integrity sir? You think me some peasant or a waterfront harlot? I am the cousin of Íñigo López de Mendoza y Mendoza, the Fourth Conde de Tendilla. Before his death, Mendoza was one of King Phillip's favorites. The Conde and his wife, the Marquesa María de Mendoza y Aragón, have three daughters: Ana, Isabel and Mencía. Sadly, Isabel died whilst in childbirth. I know this because Ana and I were once good friends and we enjoyed exchanging letters. Mendoza and my father were partners in a joint venture or two in the West Indies and profited nicely together."

Everything I told the harbormaster about Mendoza was true, though I was no relation to the man and had never met or exchanged any letters with any of his daughters. I knew these things about Mendoza and his family because my father had indeed done business with the man some years ago.

The harbormaster nodded approvingly. "I am vaguely familiar with the House of Mendoza. What you say about the Conde and his family I believe is correct. And you Master Flannigan, what lands are you from?"

"I come from a small fishing village north of Dublin called Rush. That makes me Irish."

"I see. Who rules Ireland these days Master Flannigan?"

"A Stuart, King James of Scotland. When Queen Elizabeth died childless, he inherited both the English and Irish crowns through his great-grandmother, Margaret Tudor, the elder sister of King Henry VIII."

"Very good. As it happens, I was a junior officer aboard the galleon *São Marcos* when she sailed with the Great and Fortunate Fleet in '88. I've been to Ireland."

"You're lucky to have survived the experience," MacGyver said cautiously. "*São Marcos* foundered off County Clare in the great Atlantic storm of that year as I recall."

"She did indeed. The Irish, under strict orders from the English, slaughtered many of her crew, leastwise those who survived the rocks and made it to shore."

MacGyver nodded. "The evils of war I'm afraid. I had no part in that."

"You need not be concerned Irish. I hold no grudge. It was an Irish family with loyalties to Spain who helped me and a few of my lads escape back to Portugal. I was a young and foolish buck back then. Dreams of glory filled my head. Had Admiral Medina Sidonia won the day and taken London, many Protestants would have been burned at the stake. The Spanish are no better. The evils of war indeed."

"Happily, I'm a simple sailor, not a soldier."

The harbormaster then turned to me. "Lady Elizabeth, do you have a letter of introduction you wish to present?"

"No," I replied. "We are beholden to no man or country. We sail for ourselves. May we pay the required tax and go about our business my good sir? I think we are keeping you from your game."

"Patience, my lady, patience. I must inspect your knapsacks first."

"Certainly, we carry just clothes, soaps, unguents, powders and such."

"What will I find in the cargo holds of your ship?" the harbormaster asked while casually looking through our bags.

"Spices."

"From the Moluccas?"

"Yes."

"Perchance did you put in at Ambon?"

"Why no. We sailed here from Banten. We purchased our spices in Banten. Why do you ask?"

The harbormaster shrugged his shoulders. "There was some mischief in Ambon recently. The French, more likely the Dutch, may be stirring up trouble."

"Oh my. This is distressing news."

"I will," he warned, "inspect your ship and cargo on the morrow. If you've not been forthright with me, I shall impound your vessel, seize your cargo and arrest your crew in the name of the King of Spain. Then I'll toss you and your friends into prison."

"As I have said, you will be most welcomed aboard our vessel."

Once the harbormaster finished inspecting our bags, he started scribbling our names across the bottoms of three official looking documents, one document for each of us. "These," he said, "are your passeports."

"Passeports?" I asked, unfamiliar with the term.

"Yes, your letters of entry. You have ten days to conduct your business in Macau. Keep these letters on your person at all times. If you fail to have your passeports with you, or if you fail to return to me within ten days you, my lady, will be arrested for sedition and most likely hanged as you are a subject of the Spanish Crown. Your two companions will be charged with subversion as co-conspirators and hanged alongside you. All is clear? Questions?"

I stared at the man dumbfounded. "Certainly, you jest sir? What if our letters, our passeports, are lost or stolen? Such an offense hardly warrants execution."

"Don't lose your passeports. Don't allow anyone to steal them. We have a new commander in Macau, Captain-Major João Caiado de Gamboa. The good captain has a reputation for strict obedience to the rule of law. I would not test Gamboa if I were you."

The harbormaster then paused and turned to Arslan. "You look familiar Chinaman. Yes, I'm quite certain I've seen you before. You're acquainted with Macau and our ways, yes?"

Arslan bowed his head respectfully. "Yes."

"You understand then that what I've said is true. If you have any interest in the well-being of your companions, as well as your own neck, you'll ensure no laws are broken. You understand, yes?"

"I understand."

The harbormaster craned his head around to look at me again. "As a purser, you understand the value of things, yes?"

"I do."

"Excellent. For me to issue these papers, I require two hundred gold ducats, or I'll accept fifty taels of silver, the equivalent of about four pounds of silver in the current markets."

I turned to Arslan for guidance. The amount the harbormaster was demanding seemed an outrageous sum to me.

Arslan pulled me aside and leaned close to my ear. "This man is the nephew of one of the senators in Macau's Loyal Senate," he whispered. "Offer him fifty gold ducats. He will refuse fifty but he'll settle for one hundred. Still a shameful amount I know."

"This far exceeds any proper tax for anchorage," I whispered back. "He's demanding a bribe, an exorbitant bribe at that. What if I report this man's dishonesty to the captain-major instead?"

"No, no. No good will come from that my lady. The harbormaster is collecting this amount on behalf of his uncle the senator who is a powerful man. No doubt a portion of this sum, let us call it a gratuity, will find its way to Gamboa."

"All foreigners entering the city must pay such a price?"

"No. Because of the grandeur of your ship sitting in the harbor, this man now picks your pocket. Welcome to Macau my lady."

After returning from *Achilles* with a box of one hundred gold ducats - an absurd amount - the harbormaster, smiling triumphantly, handed us our passeports and our knapsacks and then waved us into the city. Moments later I made my first purchase when I spotted a Chinese merchant pulling a two-wheeled cart up and down the streets selling parasols. I had seen many women in Amsterdam with parasols, parasols imported from China, to protect themselves from the sun, a new fashion on the Continent. With my parasol in hand, I had chosen a white parasol with dainty pink and blue flowers painted around the fringes, Arslan took us on a leisurely tour of the island.

The streets of Macau were teeming with throngs of people. We passed Portuguese and Chinese men and women of course, along with a sea of Tanka boat people, but we also saw Japanese, East Indonesians, Indians from India, Turks, Arabs and a surprising number of black slaves the Portuguese had brought across the ocean with them.

I was astonished by the many European style stone, stucco and brick buildings with red tiled roofs we saw. One house with three majestic stone turrets, the home of a rich Portuguese merchant I assumed, resembled a small palace. We walked by the Church of St. Dominic built by the Dominicans in the Baroque style in the '70s, but with Chinese teak doors and a Chinese roof, and passed by the foundation of a new cathedral being built by the Jesuits to be named São Paulo. We saw Chinese homes and shops of course but they seemed oddly out-of-place. The Chinese prefer timber over stone and use glazed tiles made from yellow potter's earth to make their roofs, curved upwards along the eaves and at the corners to shed the rain. One Chinese building, a handsome structure, reminded me of a piazza. Three levels of shops enclosed a spacious courtyard garden bursting with colorful flowers and sculptured bushes. A thin wooden wall surrounded the city though I saw no fortifications or watchtowers or cannon, information that I knew would interest Dijksma.

Like Ambon, only grander, Macau was very much a European city. It was as if God had scooped-up a Portuguese seaport with his hands - homes, shops, churches, cobblestone streets, parks and docks - and placed it all in China.

We stopped at a Chinese tavern for our afternoon meal where I had my first taste of Chinese ale and sampled Japanese rice and plum wines. The proprietor served us roasted duck with steamed dumplings and gave us thin sticks sanded down smooth called *kuàiz* in place of spoons, forks or knives.

"Arslan, who is the governor of Macau?" I asked as I clumsily tried lifting a dumpling with my sticks.

"Zhu Yijun, the Wanli Emperor of the Great Ming Dynasty rules all the provinces," he replied.

"No governors?"

"Macau falls within the Province of Guangdong but no, this emperor has chosen to rule all of China directly, without the assistance of governors, of men who often will undermine their master for their own self-interests. Under a trade agreement known officially as the Acordo Luso-Chinês de 1554, negotiated by **Leonel de Sousa of Portugal and by Admiral** Haitao Wang Bo on behalf of Wanli's father, Emperor Lóngqìng, China agreed to lease Macau to the Portuguese in exchange for five hundred taels of silver each year. China has also granted the Portuguese exclusive rights to several important trade routes. The most prized route is **Macau-Malacca-Goa-Lisbon** but the **Portuguese also have the rights to Guangzhou-Macau-Nagasaki and Macau-Manila-Acapulco.** For these lucrative monopolies the Portuguese pay the emperor an additional customs tax of twenty percent on all goods flowing in or out of the city. Think of Macau as an immense trading house for the world."

"Macau is under Chinese or Portuguese law?" MacGyver asked.

"Though the Chinese remain subject to Chinese law, Captain-Major Gamboa and the Loyal Senate are the law here."

"How many Portuguese live in Macau?"

"At least one thousand men and women with as many slaves to

serve them, perhaps more."

"And the Chinese population?"

"From the last census, twenty-five thousand or so I believe."

"We saw no fortifications, I thought that odd."

"Under the trade agreement, the Portuguese are forbidden to fortify the island. The Portuguese are merely tenants of Macau, nothing more."

"What," I asked, "are the most valuable goods imported and exported through Macau?"

"Ah, the Chinese export great quantities of silk of course, along with the finest teas, porcelains, furniture, teak and sandalwoods. The Chinese import raw cotton from Egypt, finished textiles from Spain, Portugal and France, crystal and marble from Italy, spices from the East Indies of course, beautifully crafted silverwork, swords, lacquerware and fans from Japan and hardwoods, minerals and all manner of foodstuffs from the Americas."

After I pushed my plate away, I poured the last of the plum wine into Arslan's glass. "Under our own accord between you and me Arslan, I was to give you free passage to Macau in exchange for your help obtaining the best prices for our spices and in negotiating the best prices on the goods we wish to purchase and you agreed to help us avoid any import and export fees and taxes. You showed skill with the harbormaster. Now the real work begins. I've honored my part of the bargain, are you prepared to honor yours?"

"You will not be disappointed. There are many trading houses in Macau. We can visit as many houses as you like but, you shall see, we only need concern ourselves with one, one very old and noble house - a house of trade which enjoys the emperor's favor."

"Please, lead the way."

After Michael and I paid for rooms at an inn above a tavern in the center of the city and left our baggage behind, we rejoined Arslan outside and took to the streets again. A huge eight-wheeled wagon, a mammoth beast the likes of which I'd never seen, being pulled by a team of ten enormous draft horses lumbered past us towards the docks with a heavy load of twelve giant barrels, each larger than man. We saw many oxen, horses, donkeys and even a camel - my first - pulling wagons and carts of every description across the city. We even saw a palanquin or two ferrying the rich about.

A great multitude of people, who all seemed to be in a hurry, cluttered Macau's streets. We walked past scores of shops and dozens of trading houses but Arslan ignored them all and led us straight to a deceivingly modest warehouse close to the waterfront on the east end of the city with a wooden black eagle, with outstretched wings and talons as if descending upon its prey, angrily hovering above a pair of tall red doors.

We came face-to-face with an army of Chinamen sitting behind many rows of tables working abacuses and recording numbers into black, leather-bound ledgers when we stepped inside. I took a moment to observe a young woman sitting on a stool off in one corner playing a *pipa*, the Chinese version of a lute, while she sang to the men at the tables. Her voice must be how angels sound I thought. And though I did not understand her words the melody, at once both beautiful and hauntingly sad, stirred my soul.

"Ahhhhhhhhhhh..." a much deeper, cruder voice thundered from behind a curtain in the back of the warehouse. A great mountain of quivering flesh, the fattest, tallest man I had ever seen, pulled the curtains back and stepped out of a small office.

"*Ā'ěr sī lán, nǐ zhè biàn chī tūjiù, huānyíng huílái!*" the man bellowed. Dressed in a plain beige tunic, brown baggy trousers and cheap sandals, the mountain began moving towards us with slow, ponderous steps like a man riddled with gout.

"What did this man say?" I asked Arslan.

"I said," the Chinese giant replied in good Portuguese as he clasped Arslan by the shoulders, "Arslan, you shit eating vulture, welcome back!"

"Elizabeth, this is Féng Wú," Arslan said. "Nothing, no beast of burden, no person or thing, moves through Macau without the knowledge and approval of this monstrosity."

Wú cocked his huge, bald head back and roared with ripples of laughter, forcing the folds of fat overlapping his massive belly to wiggle and shake. "Nothing," he said as he looked me up and down with curiosity, "moves through Asia without my knowledge. I see all. I hear all. You are Elizabeth Ortiz from Spain and you are Michael Flannigan from Ireland. You have crossed the wide and perilous oceans in great floating castles and of all the warehouses in Macau, you have chosen to visit mine. You honor me. Ha! Ha! Ha! And you Arslan, you half-breed ass-licker, I hear you're now a navigator! By the gods, I thought you dead!"

"And yet," Arslan replied, "I stand before you with a beating heart and have brought with me the prospect of good fortune for your consideration."

"Hmmm, did anyone survive the shipwreck?" Wú asked as he released his grip on Arslan.

"None."

"Good, good," Wú said pensively, nodding with satisfaction as he caressed the tips of an exceedingly long mustache resting against his chest. "I'm most pleased."

"What is good about men dying at sea?" I asked.

"Depends upon the man," Wú replied casually while licking his lips. "Someone stole something from me. They thought they could steal from me and find sanctuary under a young prince's roof. Fools. I'm told you've been to Banten and to Ambon my lady, though under the name Cortés. I hear you sail with four ships, four impressive warships. I hear you have Dutch friends."

"You seem well-informed," I said and took a step backwards with alarm - yes - but the Chinaman also reeked of bad odors. "Arslan?"

"I've told Féng Wú nothing about you Elizabeth," Arslan replied. "As he has said, he has eyes and ears in every port."

"Do not concern yourself dear woman," Wú whispered. "Your true identity and your friendship with the Dutch will be our secret."

"Your discretion is most appreciated."

"Over many centuries we Chinese have perfected the art of discretion. I understand you brought only one ship into our fine harbor. A ship heavy in the water with spices."

"We have one shipload of spices to sell, two hundred tons in all."

"Only one? Pity."

"We have commitments to sell the rest to others. Think of any transaction between us as a sampling."

"A sampling?"

"A small taste."

"Huh. What cargo do you wish to buy?"

"What do you have of quality to sell?"

Wú beamed with delight. "Everything the other trading houses can offer I can offer and more and I will give you better terms, terms no one in Macau can match."

"Féng Wú," Arslan interjected, "does not exaggerate. But he will not be offended if you put his boast to the test. Prudence requires we visit other emporiums. We have time."

"I will not be offended in the least," Wú readily agreed and looked away. "I expect no less from savvy merchants from Europe. Ling! Come stand by me my lovely, golden dove!"

The young woman with the angelic voice, dressed in a simple but flattering white gown, called a *changpao* I later learned, with a splash of purple flowers embroidered down one side, sat her pipa against the wall and hurried over to Wú's side. Barely more than a girl, she was as delicate and as enchanting as her music. If there was any blemish in her great beauty it was her eyes, eyes cast in sorrow not unlike Maurice's.

Wú cupped the young woman's chin firmly in his hand. "This delicious creature is Ling. Is she not heavenly? And yet she's the unfortunate offspring of a poor pig farmer and his ugly sow. This rarest of jewels, this enchanting beauty with the exquisite voice was born and raised in pig shit. Imagine such a thing if you can. The gods are not without humor!"

Ling stared blankly past Wú and said nothing.

"Arslan," Wú continued as he released his fat fingers from Ling's chin. "You know how I abhor crowded places and trite levity. You will entertain our guests in my stead. Take them away from this abortion we call Macau. Let them sample a small taste of true, mother China."

Wú paused to reach into his tunic and removed a purse. "Take this Arslan. Ling my treasure, three is an awkward number. You shall accompany Arslan and our two guests. This charming woman is Lady Elizabeth Ortiz from Spain and this fine-looking fellow is Master Michael Flannigan from a place called Ireland, a faraway island on the other side of the world. Introduce our new friends to our incomparable Chinese hospitality. My lady, Master Flannigan, this night is yours to enjoy. The *House of a Thousand Pleasures* awaits you. Tomorrow you will return here and then we shall speak of trade."

As Wú sluggishly ambled back to his office, after I translated the gist of what Wú had said to MacGyver, Arslan led MacGyver, Ling and me to a maze of piers with interconnecting footbridges not far from Wú's warehouse - to a floating village on the water - where I saw more Tanka boats than I could count. The industrious Tanka use their boats as homes and to fish and as shops to buy, sell and fix things. We walked up and down the piers until Arslan found a flat-bottom river barge to his liking. He hired the vessel from a grey-bearded Tanka man and we set out at once with the fellow's six strapping sons. As the father worked the tiller his sons quietly pulled as one at their oars.

Ling and I sat underneath a sheer canopy at the bow on a hard bench across from Arslan and MacGyver as the barge glided across an estuary of smooth, black water. Once we circled around Macau, we turned north into a narrow river flanked by dark woods and with very little traffic. An uneasiness settled over me when I began wondering if I had trusted Arslan too much. MacGyver and I were isolated and alone and had Arslan, in league with the Tanka men, wanted to kidnap us for ransom, or worse, there wasn't much we could have done. When I asked Arslan how much farther, he simply smiled, closed his eyes and napped.

When the sun dipped below the treetops the six brothers set their oars aside to light the lanterns and after the boys hooked their lighted lanterns to iron staffs and mounted the staffs to the rails, they took up their oars again and began humming a lively tune as they rowed in perfect harmony. And as we continued our lazy journey upriver under a clear and moonless sky, as I listened to the boys crooning, to the splashing of the oars and to the crickets and frogs singing along the riverbank, I passed the time reminiscing.

Another hour passed before we reached an immense four-story building of white clapboard, awash in the light of a thousand candles, torches and lanterns, standing on a small island in the middle of the river. I counted twenty dormer-windows along the roof. I saw scores of people laughing, drinking and dancing to strange music along an outside balcony, a balcony that stretched around the entire length of the second floor. Our Tanka crew turned their barge towards the island and we floated by dozens of ferryboats and their slumbering boatmen. Other boats sat beached along the right riverbank near a footbridge linking the island to the shore. We pulled up next to a narrow wharf where two men dressed all in black, black trousers, tunics, boots and head-gear, stood waiting. I took note of the double-edged swords hanging on their hips and the crossbows and quivers packed with deadly armor-piercing bolts strapped against their backs. One man grabbed the stempost at the bow and held the barge in place as the other offered his hand to help Ling and I step off.

Arslan and the two men exchanged a few brief words and after Arlsan mentioned Wú's name and pressed a gold coin into the palm of one man, the men bowed and escorted us up a gravel path lit by many candles in glass bowls to a broad, brick staircase leading up to the front portico of the great house. Two enormous monkeys of grey stone, staring down and laughing ominously on all who walked by, stood guard on each side of the staircase. I wondered what the pair knew that we did not.

We climbed the stairs, passed through a pair of massive double doors decorated with carvings of dragons and other exotic beasts and stepped into a spacious, well-lit foyer where a line of male and female servants dressed in simple white robes of linen greeted us with polite smiles and bowed. The men had obviously been chosen for their fine looks and muscular physiques, the women for their beauty and trim figures.

"Welcome to the *House of a Thousand Pleasures*," Arslan said with a broad smile. "It is very rare to see foreigners at this establishment. Wú does you great honor. Here we may relax and enjoy ourselves with the best food, the best wines and with wonderful entertainment. You may even sample a taste of paradise if you are game, or not. All are free to choose. First, as is our custom, we bathe. The ladies will take the hallway to the left, the gentlemen to the right."

I followed Ling into an anti-chamber of red walls with an oval pool of white marble in the center of the room where female attendants stood waiting for us holding pitchers, towels, bars of soap and trays of perfumes, face paints, colored pastes for the lips and blushes for the cheeks. Ling unabashedly stripped off her clothing in front of me and waded into the pool. Her breasts were full and perfectly round, her waist and hips were small, not the best hips for childbearing I think, but shapely just the same and pleasing to the eye. Her skin was without flaw. She smiled alluringly at me and waved for me to follow.

When I hesitated, two attendants giggled and hurried to my side. They gently began undressing me and though I did not resist, I covered myself with my hands for modesty's sake before stepping into the pool. The water was warm and soothing. Petals of fragrant rose, jasmine and lily surrounded me. A third attendant removed her robe and stepped into the water with soap and a handcloth and began washing Ling. Another did the same for me. Then two more women holding straight razors joined us. They carefully scraped the hair off our arms, legs and thighs. After Ling and I had been thoroughly scrubbed clean and rendered smooth, other attendants dried us, set our hair and applied color to our faces. They wrapped us in robes of golden silk and placed golden slippers on our feet. Even with slaves to attend me as a child in my father's house, I had never been so pampered.

With our transformations complete, a young girl led us by the hands down a narrow hallway to a small dining room, to a private room with dark paneled walls, where we found Arslan and MacGyver lounging on silk cushions around a low table. The men were preened and perfumed and dressed in glittering silver robes and slippers. I'd never seen MacGyver without his beard. I'd never seen him wear his hair swept back over his forehead. He was surprisingly handsome.

"You are refreshed from your bath?" Arslan asked and handed me a cup.

"I am."

"Drink?"

"What is it?"

"Black tea."

I took a sip and winced. "Good God, this tea is bitter!"

"This is a very special blend. Please, enjoy."

MacGyver smiled. "Good, yes?"

"I think I'd prefer wine," I said as I set the cup aside.

"Wait a bit," MacGyver suggested with a wry smile. "There, do you feel it?"

After a few moments I felt a pleasant warmth spreading across my chest, across my arms and legs. A sudden sense of bliss embraced me.

"We call it *nga-pin,* the tears of the poppy," Arslan said.

"You mean opium?" I asked, alarmed.

"Yes, I've added just a drop or two to your tea."

"When Stachel set my arm last year," MacGyver said, "and gave me the opiate Paracelsus' Laudanum, I felt this same lightness of thought and peace. Well I recall this small taste of ecstasy."

Mary had warned me about the evils of opium. She had told me how the drug can rob one of their wits and self-control. And yet, I suddenly felt the ache in the small of my back, a consequence of sitting too long on a hard bench, melting away. I felt wonderfully mellow and content. I found the sensations intoxicating and pleasing.

"I'm famished," I said and took another sip of tea despite myself.

We ate a delicious meal of roasted pig ribs, steamed shrimp, noodles, eggs fried on a griddle, raw oysters and boiled cabbage served with a sweet, red sauce. We drank good wine and ate fresh, black bread with butter and jellied fruit. And while we feasted, Arslan amused us with his wild tales of his many adventures. He had traveled throughout the East Indies. He had been to Japan, India, Egypt, Jerusalem, Turkey and to a port called Acapulco on the Pacific coast of New Spain, places

I longed to see. I thought him amiable, witty and an excellent host. I found his rugged good looks appealing. As Ling knew no English and Portuguese was difficult for her, she said very little throughout our meal - though a woman with her stunning beauty hardly needed to say much. In her own quiet away, she too was charming.

After supper we followed Arslan up a wide, circular staircase to the second floor. The main room was very large and crowded with couples sitting around small tables talking, drinking and laughing. The air was thick with smoke. Everyone seemed to be enjoying themselves. And though all the *House's* guests were dressed in robes of silk, only we wore silver and gold.

Everywhere I turned I saw couples passing long stem pipes back and forth. Against a far wall I saw a troupe of actors on a stage performing a comedy of some sort judging by the chuckles around the room while musicians hidden behind a curtain played music. Against the other walls I saw gaming tables for those who liked to gamble and out on the balcony I spied a man and woman passionately kissing and groping one another, oblivious to the world around them. No one seemed to notice or care.

"Does this floor interest you Elizabeth, or would you like to ascend to the next level?"

"I thought," I asked, "or so I've heard, the emperor has forbidden tobacco?"

"He has indeed. But the emperor is in Beijing and Beijing is very far away. The tears of the poppy are more potent when mixed with tobacco and inhaled."

"Ah, I see."

MacGyver grabbed me by the arm. "A drop of opium in tea is one thing Elizabeth. This is something else. We should not tarry here. I don't like it."

Sensing MacGyver's reluctance, Ling slipped an arm around his waist and pulled him closer. "There much jo, joy here," she said in her broken Portuguese, struggling with the words. "Many pleasures to share."

"I don't fault you for being wary, Michael," I said. "But I wish to try a pipe, just once. Where's the harm in a bit of fun?"

When Arslan snapped his fingers, a servant rushed to his side carrying a pipe on a silver platter. Arslan drew on the pipe first and then handed the pipe over to Ling. After she inhaled, she handed the pipe to me and I did the same. MacGyver declined when I offered the pipe to him.

"What, what is on, on, the other floors?" I asked Arslan, choking on the tobacco fumes as I spoke.

"The fourth floor is forbidden to us," he replied with a mischievous grin, then waved for us to follow him. "But on the next level - well come and see."

We were met by soft, rhythmic music with a sensuous beat on the third floor. We walked down narrow passageways and past poorly lit rooms with no doors and I was horrified by what I saw at first but my horror soon gave way to arousal. I could feel my inhibitions melting away with each breath. In one room after another we saw men and women in various stages of undress, shamelessly absorbed in different acts of debauchery. We passed one room with four women reclining on large cushions while sharing a pipe. Three women, already naked, were undressing the fourth. In another room I stopped to watch two men pleasing a woman lying on one couch while on an opposite couch I saw two women chained at the ankles together pleasing each other.

Ling then led MacGyver by the hand down a long, dark hallway and after they disappeared Arslan leaned over and began nibbling on my neck, slowly moving his way up to my lips. I welcomed his kiss with my own and when he slipped his hand inside my robe and down between my thighs, I closed my eyes and moaned as I my body rose up to meet his.

I don't remember much after that. In the morning I awoke back at the inn in Macau in my bed alone with a terrible pounding in my head. Someone had dressed me in a dainty, silk nightshirt and had left my clothes, washed, dried and neatly folded, on a table near the bed. A note from Arslan, informing me that MacGyver and I could find him outside the tavern whenever we were ready, had been left on top of my clothes.

Chapter Sixteen

ur march to the sea took us eleven days by foot through dusty, rugged country. Ashaki and Lololi endured the fatiguing pace, the heat, the dust and all of our hardships without complaint and I was proud of them. Once we reached the coast we turned south and treaded carefully across wild, uninhabited lands for another two days until we reached a quiet spot of water, a secluded lagoon surrounded by pretty coconut and royal palms where Matosa gave the order to unpack and make camp.

It did not take Matosa long to find the lugger where he had left her, buried nearby underneath a pile of sand covered over in fronds, branches and debris. After he scooped away handfuls of sand and brushed away the rest, he turned to me with an unlit cigar in his mouth and a mischievous grin.

"Eh? I did warn you Mary," he said and slapped the boat's side. "She's an ugly, old seabird. She's been beaten down by the elements and time and could use some sprucing up but she's sound. What say you, Mary?"

"Hmmm. How far are we from Veracruz, Francisco?"

"Ah, about thirty miles. Why? You do not like my boat? You wish to find another?"

"Without any masts, I think we have a very long row ahead of us," I replied warily. I could see a good bit of her hull poking through the branches, but saw no masts or spars or canvas. At one time, long ago, she had been white but now she was the color of dirty snow with more bare wood than paint.

Matosa pointed to a sand dune about fifty yards away. "Buried over there, we'll find the rest of her."

After a day of digging and putting ship parts together, we had ourselves a sturdy lugger with masts, spars, rope, tackle, blocks and sail. With the help of Yanga's twenty men, serious, burly lads, we carried Matosa's boat out into the lagoon the next morning and then loaded her down with barrels of fresh water and victuals, as much we could carry, saving room for my trunk packed with plain dresses for the girls and lady's refined clothing for myself along with a tidy sum in gold. After Yanga's men set the mules free, bid us a safe journey and started back to the Cimarron war camp, I turned to face the girls.

"Ladies, it's not too late to change your minds," I said, pointing to the lugger. "That boat will be home for the next two or three weeks, perhaps longer. Chances are good we'll sail through storms. I've been in seas with waves taller than her masts. I've seen the bravest man quake with fear during the worst of it. There's no oven to warm our food or to make hot coffee. There's no cabin. You'll find no privacy aboard that boat. You'll piss and shit in a bucket in front of these men and sleep alongside them in damp clothing on a hard deck as they snore the night away, as they belch and break wind."

I saw the gleam in Ashaki's eyes as she looked past me and considered the lugger and the ocean beyond. My words had no effect on her, none at all. That one was itching for adventure. But I caught Lololi craning her head around to catch one last glimpse of Yanga's men as they marched off.

When she looked at me apprehensively, I slipped my arm around her shoulder. "Lololi, there's no shame in remaining here in New Spain. Kiss your sister farewell and go now. I know Gaspar will take very good care of you."

She turned to face her sister, looked back at me again and then glanced over at the lugger. "I'll prove me worth, I swear it," she proclaimed boldly and before I could say another word, she slung her knapsack over her shoulder, bit her lip and headed towards the boat.

Between the two sisters I wondered, who was the braver?

Matosa started laughing and grabbed my knapsack off the sand, he followed Lololi then turned to me and winked before stepping into the water. Would you like to take her out?" he asked.

"I believe as master of this fine vessel the honor belongs to you Francisco," I replied. "I obey your commands."

Matosa shrugged his shoulders indifferently and waved us all into the boat. With everyone onboard, he took the tiller firmly in his hands and confidently eased us out into the lagoon while his crew went about raising the lugsail, the spritsail and lastly set the mizzen sail. We entered the untroubled, sparkling green waters of the Golfo Mexicano with a stiff breeze at our backs and a flock of grey, puffy clouds overhead giving chase.

Matosa had not lied, his lugger was no galleon. With nine souls on board, together with our provisions, we lived and slept shoulder-to-shoulder and hip-to-hip across a narrow, thirty-foot deck. She was a clumsy craft and the outrigger slowed us down, but she was robust enough and sailed true. Across the Caribbean smugglers favor luggers for their stability, for their ease of handling and shallow drafts. Smugglers can beach their boats with ease or sail them up shallow estuaries - far from any prying eyes or nosey tax collectors. Matosa's crew worked the lugger with skill and mercifully were respectful to the girls, even kind. I had no need to consider the knife I had tucked inside my boot, a quality knife I had quietly pilfered from Yanga's camp.

On the first day out, we traveled as far as Veracruz while we had the light. We saw the sails of many a ship along the way but none took an interest in our poor vessel. With the help of a radiant full moon, we continued sailing south for several hours in the dark and then, sometime past midnight, Matosa turned us into shore and drove the lugger up onto a narrow, deserted stretch of beach.

"What is this place?" I asked Matosa as he jumped off the boat just as I stepped up on the bulwark to do the same.

Matosa offered a hand to help me down. "A patch of sand south of Veracruz with no name where we can safely stretch our legs and rest. No one lives in these parts."

"Do you carry a watch, Francisco?"

"I do," Matosa replied and pulled a small watch with a cracked crystal from his vest pocket. "'Tis nearly two hours past twelve of the clock."

"Any idea how far we've traveled?"

"We've been on the water for a little over sixteen hours. I'd say we've put about fifty miles behind us, give or take."

"That would mean we're making roughly three knots each hour."

"She's no racehorse."

"You've landed here before?"

"Yes, there is a lake with good water close by. Banana and papaya trees are plentiful here. My men and I once found a large sea turtle sitting atop her eggs near this very spot. By God, we ate well that night!"

"How long do you intend to stay?"

"Say, until sunrise? Just long enough to refresh ourselves."

"Good, we shouldn't linger here," I said and turned to the twins. "Girls, do not wander far off."

"Snakes," Matosa said, "are not uncommon in these parts ladies. I'll light you a torch. If you wish to go to the lake or pick fruit, take one of my lads with you."

With just the hint of a breeze rolling across a quiet sea in the morning, we all pitched in to push our lugger out into the surf. Matosa gave me the tiller and I kept us close to shore as we continued on our southerly course. And when we reached a small, insignificant village named Villa del Espíritu Santo, our course veered easterly as I kept us parallel to the natural curvature of the Yucatán.

With no other sails in sight, I called the twins to me as they finished sharing a bowl of cold, black beans for their noonday meal. "Ashaki, Lololi, 'tis time. If you wish to live in my world, you must learn about the sea. You must acquire some basic skills. Come stand by my side and I shall teach you about sailing, at least a little. Lololi, you first. This is the tiller. The tiller is attached to the rudder and the rudder is what turns the boat to port or starboard, to the left or to the right. There now, take the tiller."

Lololi stared at me wide-eyed and froze. "No, Mary, I might tip us over. Ashaki and me can't swim."

Matosa and his men howled with laughter. "When we make land

again," Matosa said after he caught his breath, "I'll teach you girls how to swim. I've never lost a man to the sea because he couldn't tread water. Now Lololi, Mary is in command of this vessel at present and you are obliged to obey her. This is the first rule of the sea. José, Miguel, the sun turns hot. Whilst the girls are at play, let's raise the canopy before we all fry."

Lololi tentatively took the tiller from me. Soon she was steering us across the easy swells and smiling and I took pleasure in watching her overcome her fears. An hour later Ashaki took the tiller without hesitation and with little instruction from me. She was born to sail.

As the girls took turns steering, I sat down against the bulwark under the shade of the canopy. I unrolled Matosa's chart across my knees, made some crude calculations in my head and then waved Matosa over to me.

"Francisco, I would put us about here."

Matosa handed a coiled line to one of his men and plopped down next to me. "Yes. I think that's about right."

"You've taken a pencil and drawn a square around this place called Ciudad del Carmen. Will we bring the lugger ashore there?"

"No, no! We must avoid Carmen. Indeed, before sunset we'll turn north and head out to sea. We must keep well clear of Carmen and the men who frequent those waters."

"Why? What's in Carmen?"

"The waters around Carmen are infested with devilish marauders. From Carmen the pirate clans are well positioned to intercept and plunder ships sailing in or out of Veracruz or Campeche or both."

"Ah, I see. I do not know these waters well and was unaware. God help us if brigands catch us out here. We cannot run. We cannot fight."

"No, but we Cimarron have done some business with many of these men over the years. They like our Spanish gold. And we share a common enemy, the Spanish, which makes us natural allies. Even so, I wouldn't want to risk mingling with any of these men with you and the twins onboard. These men are - unpredictable."

"Thank you."

"For what?"

"For your wisdom. Had I succeeded in stealing a boat from Veracruz during my first attempt to escape from Salamanca, I don't believe I would have survived this voyage on my own."

Matosa reached over and squeezed my hand. "I wouldn't bet against you."

"As we'll be far from land, do we have any instruments onboard to help us navigate, a compass perhaps or an astrolabe?"

Matosa smiled and removed a compass from a wooden box sitting next the tiller. "We have this magnetic compass and my watch. We have sea charts and we have the sun and the stars. If we lose the sun or the stars, we'll sail by dead reckoning."

"Dead reckoning? I do not know these words."

"I heard a Dutch sailor use the phrase not long ago. The words mean we'll navigate by calculating time and speed and trust to luck."

"Ah dead reckoning, I see," I said and committed the newfangled term to memory. "You've circled Campeche. I've never been there, but I've heard Campeche is an important seaport for the Spanish. We should avoid Campeche?"

"When Francisco Hernández de Córdoba landed at Ah-Kim-Pech many years ago, the name means abundant ticks and snakes in Mayan, Córdoba saw value of rebuilding the sleepy village into a Spanish port and the name Ah-Kim-Pech became Campeche. Campeche rivals Havana, Veracruz and Cartagena in importance. From Campeche the Spanish export gold, silver, farm goods and hardwoods to Spain. We can safely take on food and water there if we are discrete."

"And I see you've drawn a square around this other Spanish settlement, Mérida. We must avoid this port?"

"Yes, we must stay clear of Mérida, or Ichkanzihóo, meaning the City of Five Hills because of the five pyramids the Mayans built there many lifetimes ago. Nothing good waits for us in Mérida."

Matosa then relieved Ashaki at the tiller. He turned us north, taking us out into deep water, and we sailed for many hours far from any land before he turned us east again. We sailed through the night and when the sun peeked over the horizon in the morning, we were within sight of land again and well past Campeche. Though we had lost a full day sailing out to sea and back again, the Angolan had shown skill and good judgement and I would have gladly welcomed him into my clan. I was even more certain than before that I never would have survived the journey on my own. God's plan or just good fortune, I do not know.

Around midday, Matosa guided our boat into a small inlet where we saw many canoes resting in a line against the shore with dozens of mudbrick huts built in squares just beyond the beach in plain view. The land was flat and covered in palm, scrub pine and red cedar trees.

"Mayans," Matosa said simply as he beached our boat within shouting distance of the village.

The Mayans, humble fishermen, farmers and friends of the Cimarron, hurried down to the shore to welcome us. We ate and rested with the Mayans for two days. They are a gentle folk, more like the peaceful Taíno of the Caribbean I thought than like their neighbors, the warlike Aztec to the north. At daybreak on the third day, after Matosa, good to his word, had finished teaching the girls how swim, we replenished our stores of food and water, said our farewells to our friendly hosts and once again launched our lugger out into the water.

We sailed past Mérida and landed at Kan Kun next. Kan Kun, meaning a den of snakes in the Mayan tongue, is a desolate, unpleasant land of swamps, mosquitos, mangroves and dense jungle. We tarried there only long enough to take on more supplies and once we stowed away our bananas, coconuts, papayas and fresh water, we set out on our journey again.

Cruising under a blazing sun reigning over a cloudless sky, I relished watching the land behind us slipping away over our stern. And when New Spain finally vanished over the horizon, my nightmare vanished too.

It begins harmlessly at first with a stray raindrop or two on the nose, a sudden chill against the cheek. The day turns bleak. The clouds thicken and start swirling around and around as blustery winds, often from the east, increase in ferocity. Waves turn into angry whitecaps. Swells rise and fall with mounting fury. Halfway between Kan Kun and Cuba our luck ran out.

Our lugger pitched ominously to and fro with heavy rains pelting us hard. When water began spilling over the rails, the girls and I grabbed the bailing buckets while Matosa and his men stowed away the canopy and double-lashed our provisions down.

I used my hands to ask Matosa if we should take in canvas. He shook his head no and shouted back over the howling winds that the lugger did not handle well in rough seas without sail.

Though we were past the season of the huracán, the storm overtaking us was no less frightening. Roaring winds and heaving seas savaged our tiny boat. Blinding rains and something I'd never seen before in the Caribbean - chunks of hail - hit us hard. We were taking on water at an alarming pace. And when a gust of wind suddenly ripped away our spritsail, the lugger whipped around and lost her balance, spilling most of our precious provisions over the side. At the worst of it giant waves - the very kind I had warned Lololi about - threatened to topple us. We nearly capsized twice.

Ashaki and Lololi clung to me for comfort as we rode up and down the daunting rollers, as the lugger creaked and groaned in agony. We held each other tight. We did not sleep. We did not eat. We said our prayers and bailed.

Chapter Seventeen

opened my door ever so slightly with my pistol in hand when I heard a light rapping. I found MacGyver standing in the hallway casually leaning against the far wall, taking a bite out of a glossy, green apple.

"Michael, good morning. What is the time?"

"And a good morning to you, Liz," MacGyver replied while he chewed. "'Tis nearly noon. I must say, you look no worse for wear. I trust you're well-rested and in good spirits."

"I slept well enough, thank you."

"I'll not soon forget last night," he said with a devilish grin and winked at me, something I'd never seen MacGyver do before.

I suddenly felt a sinking feeling in my gut as I stared hard into his eyes. "I don't recall much of last evening. I don't even remember returning to the hostel. Did we, did you and I, um?"

"Did we what? Oh, that. No, no, Ling led me to a private room to introduce me to a few of her friends whilst you remained behind with Arslan. You were out cold when we returned to the barge. Over the years I've heard some mighty fanciful tales about China and Chinese women, sailors' tavern gibberish or so I imagined. Sweet Jesus, there's nothing bashful about these Chinese is there?"

"No, I think not."

"How's your head Liz?"

"It hurts something wicked."

"Mine too. If you're hungry there's a platter of fruit and a basket of fresh biscuits downstairs in the tavern. I also saw a bulbous pot of Turkish coffee hanging over the fire near the bar when I was in there earlier. Strong coffee will help. Arslan waits for us outside."

"I should have heeded your good advice, Michael. I should have been more temperate in my indulgences. Too much wine and perhaps a little too much opium has undone me this day."

MacGyver chuckled. "*In nomine patris et filii et spiritus sancti, amen,*" he said as he made the sign of the cross. "A Hail Mary or two Elizabeth and all our sins will be forgiven."

"You might," I said, rolling my eyes, "need an ordained priest to help with that act of contrition and those Hail Marys of yours."

"I'd rather rake out a shitter on a hot summer day than see a priest to confess my sins. I feel no shame about what I've done."

"Nor do I, Michael. Even so, I think it best if we keep last night's indiscretions to ourselves. What say you my good captain?"

"Most wise Elizabeth. I doubt anyone would believe us anyway. No, I'll not soon forget last night. Ahhh, my beautiful, sweet Ling, exquisite in every way and the fabulous *House of a Thousand Pleasures*, mmm... I can't help but wonder, was it all just a dream?"

"'Twas no dream. Fair warning Michael, I'm quite certain Ling belongs to another. If you wish to keep your head, you'll steer well clear of those hazards. Now we have work to do and as for last night it never happened and we should speak of it no more - to anyone."

"Agreed my lady."

When we returned to the warehouse, Ling was back on her stool plucking away at the strings of her pipa and singing to the men hunched over their tables, men diligently working their calculations and tallying up the master's money. I thought her music magical and I committed the melody to memory. Ling was as lovely and as elegant and as fresh as the day before and I found myself intrigued by the young beauty and wanting to know more about her. It was easy to see why MacGyver had fallen under her spell.

Wú greeted us with open arms and a broad grin. I found the man repulsive but forced my best, engaging smile.

"I trust you both enjoyed our Chinese hospitality last night?" he asked.

"Most certainly," I answered. "Master Flannigan and I enjoyed ourselves immensely and we thank you for your generosity. The *House* is beyond imagining. The place must be experienced to be believed."

"How true, how very true."

"We have nothing in Europe to compare to the *House*, none leastwise that I know of."

"No? How sad. Perhaps you and I should combine our resources and build one together, as joint proprietors."

"In Europe?"

"Certainly, why not? Cultures may differ around the world but people are more or less the same. We all enjoy good food, good drink and stimulating entertainment. And I've never known a man or woman, not even a Shaolin, who didn't crave the forbidden pleasures of the flesh."

"A tantalizing proposition."

"To ignore opportunity is to insult the gods. To the business at hand then? This morning I went down to the harbor to see your ship. Length multiplied by beam multiplied again by depth and then divided by one hundred equals tonnage capacity. She can carry between two hundred fifty to two hundred seventy-five tons of cargo?"

"An excellent estimate," MacGyver answered in Spanish after I finished translating Wú's words for him. "That is indeed the calculation we mariners trust. My compliments. *Achilles* though is not your common freighter. She's armed with heavy cannon and carries ample stores of iron shot and gunpowder. I also have an exceedingly large crew. A larger crew requires additional provisions, especially as our journey is long. All this additional weight reduces our cargo capacity considerably. I wouldn't care to take on much more than one hundred seventy-five tons or so, two hundred tons at most."

Wú seemed to understand MacGyver's words, at least the numbers, and nodded. When Wú bellowed out something in Chinese, a short, baldheaded man with a bent back, dressed in the same garb as all the others at the tables, black baggy trousers, plain black tunic and cheap wooden sandals, rose from his desk and scurried over to Wú's side carrying a scroll in his hands. He bowed his head reverently as he offered the parchment up to Wú.

"This," Wú said, turning to me, "is a list of luxury goods that will fetch the best profits. The document is written in Chinese as I seem to have misplaced my translator. Arslan can translate the document into Portuguese for you later. I will give you a price, a very good price considering you will pay no export taxes, on two hundred tons of cargo. If you like what I am offering I will happily accept your banknotes as payment. I am also prepared to purchase your spices. No other trading house in Macau, not Chinese or Portuguese, will match my offer. Be forewarned: selling your spices in Macau will yield less profits than what you would reap in Amsterdam. Now I must speak with Arslan privately on another matter of some urgency. Ling shall accompany you and Master Flannagan to a teahouse nearby. Arslan will join you there shortly after I've concluded my business with him. I promise not to detain your navigator long."

The teahouse was not far. Ling, MacGyver and I took seats around a small table in the midst of a modest dining-room of paneled walls, roughhewn timbers and a floor of polished stone. Chinamen, grey-beards, playing cards or *wei ch'i*, a game of strategy where men move white and black pebbles across a paper board, surrounded us. Though cramped, I found the teahouse clean and comforting.

As we waited for Arslan, I quietly enjoyed a cup of plain, green tea. The pounding in my head was beginning to subside, as was my guilt. The wickedness of the night before now seemed like a distant memory. Then again, I felt my passions stir and my pulse quicken whenever I glanced over at Ling, as I imagined myself returning to the *House* arm-in-arm with the bewitching beauty.

"Ah, Arslan, there you are," I said as the fine-looking nomad, the traveler between worlds, stepped into the dining-room.

Before acknowledging me, Arslan leaned close to Ling's ear and whispered something to her in Chinese. She nodded politely to Arslan, smiled sweetly at MacGyver and me and then abruptly left the teahouse.

"All is well?" I asked.

"Yes, yes," Arslan replied curtly as he plopped down in Ling's seat.

"Can you tell us what is on this paper Féng Wú gave us?"

M. McMillin

"Wú is offering you," Arslan replied as he handed me another sheet of pale-yellow paper with several columns of numbers written in Arabic numerals, "the finest Chinese porcelains and silks, magnificent Chinese folding screens of exceptional quality together with other unique and beautiful furniture made by Chinese artisans highly prized throughout the land for their skills. He is offering you the best in Japanese silverwork, swords, art and jewelry. He is presenting all these things to you at excellent prices. The amount Wú is willing to pay for your spices is regrettably disappointing, but such is the market. When considered as a whole, this opportunity is better than satisfactory. It is indeed very, very good. You'll prosper handsomely if you choose to accept Wú's terms."

I passed the paper over to MacGyver. I had just enough in banknotes to cover most of what we needed if Wú didn't discount the face value of the notes too steeply.

"Michael and I still wish to visit the other major trading houses," I said.

"Of course, Elizabeth. This is prudent. It will be my pleasure to escort you both to as many houses as you wish. You shall see. None can match Wú's offer in quantity, quality or price."

"And why," MacGyver asked after I finished translating Arslan's words, "does Wú favor us with this bounty? We are strangers, foreigners to him."

"Strangers, foreigners or not, Wú is a shrewd, practical man. He hopes to lure you back to Macau someday with all four of your impressive ships. Should you return to China, you would become his most revered customer."

When MacGyver nodded his satisfaction with Arslan's answer, Arslan turned to me. "Elizabeth," he said with a flirtatious smile. "There is one more thing Féng Wú requires from you."

"If he thinks I'll take him into my bed," I scoffed, "he's badly mistaken."

"By the gods, no!" Arslan replied and laughed. "You need not worry there. Wú is immune from the charms of your sex. To say it delicately, his appetites lie elsewhere."

"Oh my. Such relationships are not *jìnjì*?"

"Ha! Very good Elizabeth. You remember the word jìnjì from last night. Your pronunciation is excellent! No, such relationships are not forbidden or thought to be unclean. The Chinese are far more tolerant than you Europeans about such matters. Indeed, men for example are permitted to marry other men in the Province of Fujian."

"Surely you jest!" MacGyver exclaimed with a pained expression.

"I do not Master Flannigan."

I shook my head. "Astonishing. I would say the laws of Fujian are indeed most tolerant. In our world, the Holy Roman Catholic Church burns sodomites at the stake. Wú perhaps should refrain from traveling too far west. But tell me now, what is this thing Wú requires of me?"

"Wú is in need of transportation to Banten."

"We can accommodate him gladly," I said.

"Not for himself. He must transport men to Banten. I can improve the price of the arrangement between you both if you will agree to ferry these men. Java is on your way. You would not be inconvenienced."

"These men are merchants or sailors?"

"No."

"Artisans, craftsmen?"

"Nooo! A ton of cow shit has more value to Wú than these men. These unfortunates bound for Banten are poor farmers and simple laborers. They're desperate men, men who need to feed their families. Drought and beetles have devasted this year's harvest. There is great suffering amongst the people of Guangdong. Starvation ravages the province and work is scarce. Banten however is a rich city with an ambitious prince with ambitious plans. Ratu intends to build new roads and new cities across all of Java but he needs an army of workers to help him."

"Why not hire Javanese?"

"Chinamen are far more plentiful - and cheap. Ratu can employ ten Chinaman for the cost of one Java man. And if a Javanese is killed whilst working, Ratu must pay his widow a stipendiary for one year under the laws of Banten or, if he is only injured, Ratu must pay the man's wages until he recovers. If a Chinaman is killed, maimed or injured, Ratu pays nothing."

"You will accompany these men to Banten?"

"Regrettably, I cannot. I must remain in China."

"How many men?"

"Seventy-five men for Prince Ratu. And, as you lost a good number of men in Banten, I have taken the liberty of assembling twenty-five seamen for your inspection. These men are veteran mariners of good character. They are obedient and hardworking. They'll sail to Europe with you without complaint."

I turned to MacGyver. "Jacob will not like taking on Chinese sailors."

MacGyver shook his head. "No, I'm quite certain he will not approve Elizabeth."

Arslan helped himself to my tea. "Take these men. Pay them whatever you like. If you are not pleased, leave them behind in Banten with the rest and pay them nothing. I have no doubt Prince Ratu will make good use of them and **Wú's moneymen will be counting more gold for the twenty-five** additional laborers."

"That seems fair," I said.

"Good. Then it is settled. There is one more matter. When the harbormaster asked if we had been in Ambon, you said no. There is talk in Macau of a European warship sinking a Portuguese freighter in the harbor at Ambon. They say this warship sank the freighter without cause or provocation. This is the "mischief" the harbormaster first spoke of."

"Oh?" I said with mock surprise. "How odd."

Arslan smiled. "You left me aboard *Ghostrunner* when you slipped into Ambon's harbor with *Homeward Bound*. Robert and I were eating breakfast when we heard the boom of cannon. At first, we thought we heard thunder and then we wondered if the Portuguese at the fort were practicing their gunnery skills."

"Yes, I heard the sounds too. Pirates perhaps?"

"Perhaps. Some say this incident is proof that war is here."

"More likely the sailors aboard the merchantman were careless with the ship's stores of gunpowder. Such mishaps are not uncommon. Stowing powder away properly can be a tricky business."

Arslan grinned, stood and extended his hand to help me to my feet. "As you say, my lady! Still, you did put a good number of Dutchmen ashore in Ambon and they are a meddlesome, troublesome people."

"Why do you dislike the Dutch?"

"They wish to upset the order of things. Change is always dangerous."

"Oh? I've found the Dutch to be reasonable, good folk."

"I fear I may have taken a wrong fork in the road with you. My apologies. Let us call upon a few of the Portuguese trading houses, see if we can strike a better bargain."

Over the next few days, we introduced ourselves to the larger Portuguese emporiums in Macau. Wú though had not exaggerated the quality of his offer. The Portuguese saw us as competitors. They were arrogant and abrupt in their negotiations and insulted us with their paltry proposals. They seemed happy to see us leave empty-handed - believing no doubt that once we found no better options, we'd be forced to return to them on bended knee to accept whatever meager scraps they tossed our way. And while Arslan and I visited trading houses, MacGyver often disappeared mysteriously and would be gone for many hours. I did not ask.

After Wú and I came to terms, we moved *Achilles* over to a wharf across from Wú's warehouse where he had men already standing next to a long line of assorted wagons and carts parked along the waterfront. His men helped our men offload our spices and then they began the tedious task of carefully loading one hundred eighty tons of luxury goods onboard. I had to settle for less than two hundred tons as despite the money Wú was paying me, I didn't have enough banknotes to purchase the rest. As men labored, MacGyver quietly slipped ashore for his own reasons while Arslan and I sat together up on the quarterdeck, flirting with each other and sharing a pot of delicious black tea - a few cups of the *House's* special blend.

Chapter Eighteen

n the morning of the third day, as shafts of golden light pierced the angry clouds and the wild winds subsided, we found ourselves surrounded by empty water with no idea of where we were. And though the sea had made peace with the world, the storm had blown us far off course. The logical thing to do would have been to continue sailing due east but Matosa and I - on nothing more than a sailor's whim - both agreed to head south-by-southeast.

Another day past and then two. Matosa and I began to fret. We had lost most of our food, had only a half barrel of fresh water and after the good thumping we had taken, we had ourselves a leaky boat without a spritsail for balance. We were hungry, exhausted and utterly miserable. The twins did not complain, not once, and again they made me proud. More hard days slipped by as Matosa coaxed as much speed out of our crippled boat as he dared.

Lololi was the first to see it. She jumped to her feet excitedly and twirled around in a circle while wildly waving her arms in the air as if she had gone mad. Once she composed herself, she pointed to a dark smear on the water off in the distance, to a smudge of land off our starboard bow. We all cheered, hugged each other and thanked our lucky stars. Vague shapes took form as we approached the coast and soon the shapes turned into rounded mountains the Spanish call mogates. Before long we could see fat cattle grazing on tall grass in the green pastures nestled in-between the mountains.

I could hardly believe my eyes and smiled for I knew the place. This was the very spot where Drake had landed in '95 to provide his men with fresh beef before sailing on to Panama with his powerful invasion force. We had reached the northwestern shores of Cuba and

Havana wasn't far off.

Matosa guided our battered lugger into a stream a few miles west of the city. After he beached the boat on a sandbar upstream, the twins and I grabbed our packages wrapped in oiled parchment and walked a little ways until we found a secluded grove of tall cedars where we stripped off our filthy clothing and washed ourselves in the stream as best we could as we had lost our soap. We rinsed the sea out of our hair and the stink off our skin and slipped into our stylish dresses after we had dried ourselves off. We laced up our polished boots and donned our fancy hats.

Matosa crossed himself and howled with laughter when Ashaki, Lololi and I returned to the boat wearing our finest. "Are you divine goddesses come to visit Earth, or are you mortals simply blessed with great beauty? I do not recognize you. Pray tell me, what have you done with my sisters?"

I curtsied. "Francisco, you've risked everything to bring us here. My debt to you and your men is huge."

"We have matters to settle in Havana. This voyage was long overdue. You and the twins have been no trouble, no trouble at all."

"Even so, I hope to repay your kindness someday," I said, then paused to kiss Matosa and each of his men on the cheek. "Should the Fates allow it, I'll return to New Spain someday and when I do I pray we meet again. When do you intend to return to Veracruz?"

"In a week or two I should think once our business is concluded," Matosa replied and then reached over to embrace Ashaki and Lololi in turn. "Girls, remember who you are. You are the children of the Anlo-Ewe tribe. Your ancestors were fierce, proud warriors. But you are not free, not yet. You have no papers. Never let your guard down. You must play your parts convincingly. You must give no offense, give no cause for suspicion. The Spanish are well-practiced at spotting runaways. Understood? Good. And what part will you play Mary?"

"If asked, I am the Lady Mary of Edenborough, Scotland, a minor noblewoman come to the Caribbean to settle the estate of my beloved, deceased husband with his Spanish merchantry partners. I know many entrepreneurs in the Caribbean and if tested I am intimately familiar with how trade works throughout the islands. As for my two ladies, I purchased them years ago at the auction blocks in Trinidad when they were very young."

"Good, very good. We'll patch the lugger up and hide her away over by that boulder. Should anything go awry, you take her if you have the need. My lads and I can always procure another."

"Thank you, Francisco. Fare thee well my friend."

"May God ease your burdens some and protect you."

Having said our farewells, the girls and I slung our knapsacks over our shoulders, heavy with clothes and gold, and took deep breaths before we set out for Havana on foot. I've been to the *Pearl of the Caribbean* on many occasions and each time I've found the port larger, busier and more important than before. Over twenty thousand souls inhabit the city, or so I've heard, and as we strolled down the city's broad, cobblestone streets, we saw new construction at every turn. All around us we passed the trappings of wealth, prosperity and power. We witnessed the magic of commerce at work.

Having never seen a city before, the sisters walked alongside me in awe. With her three great fortresses, Castillo de los Tres Reyes Magos del Morro, Castillo de la Real Fuerza and San Salvador de la Punta, with the ocean-class galleons bristling with heavy guns sitting in her harbor flying the Cruz de Borgoña, the ensign of the dreaded Spanish navy, there was no mistaking Havana's preeminence in the New World.

We found a suitable hostel, treated ourselves to proper baths and a fine supper and then I sent a letter - the Spanish run an excellent post service throughout the Caribbean - to my business partner Cortés at his hacienda some twenty miles outside of the city. I addressed the letter in care of his trusted steward, a man named Jesús, in the event Cortés was away traveling. I had men and women of different races and from different nations - my eyes and ears - scattered across the New World secretly in my employ. Jesús had been one of mine for years.

Several days later an older man with a familiar face, a man as black as night with pure white hair and matching eyebrows, stepped into the tavern where Ashaki, Lololi and I were sitting at a table leisurely drinking our morning coffee. He moved gingerly with the help of a walking stick, something I'd never seen him use before, and acknowledged me with the faintest hint of a friendly smile.

"Lady Mary, I received your letter," Jesús said in English as he knew my awful skills with Spanish. "*Querido Dios misericordioso, oh, lo siento*, eh sorry, I heard you were dead!"

I stood to embrace the old man. "It is so very good to see you Jesús!" I replied in Spanish. "My Spanish has much improved over the years. I understand your words. Please sit, rest yourself. This young lady is Ashaki and this is her sister, Lololi. They are my, ahem, companions."

"Indeed," Jesús said and raised an eyebrow as he took a seat.

"How did you learn of my death?" I asked and braced myself for the worst.

"Señorita Elizabeth came to Havana to see her father, to tell him that you had perished at sea somewhere off Florida in a terrible storm."

"So, Elizabeth is alive! Praise God! The others? My ships?"

"Misfortune only took you."

"Ohhh, my prayers have been answered thank God!" I exclaimed relieved and wept. "Lucky for me we were close to shore. Your master must have been pleased by the news of my demise."

"On the contrary Mary, Señor Cortés always admired you and, in his way, thought of you with affection. The news of your death distressed him greatly."

When the tavern's proprieter stopped by our table, I dried my tears and smiled sweetly at the man. But when he wiped his hands on his apron and placed them on his hips, I knew something was amiss.

"Señora, forgive me," he said nervously, "I know you are an outlander from Scotland and perhaps not accustomed to our ways. Out of courtesy, I've ignored your two young blacks. But I cannot have three blacks sitting at your table. This simply will not do. You'll agitate my other patrons."

"Oh, I am humbly sorry," I replied with feigned politeness. "You are right of course. Please, forgive me. I keep my girls close as I have a weak heart which renders me prone to fainting spells. This gentleman is the property of Señor Rodriguez Miguel de Cortés y Ovando, the same Cortés who owns the large hacienda west of the city. As you can plainly see from his fine apparel this man is no field hand. He is Señor Cortés' loyal steward and I have important matters of business with Cortés."

"All the same, please Señora, this is most unseemly."

"I understand," I said as I reached into the pocket of my dress to retrieve a coin. "Might we," I asked as I pressed a large silver piece into the proprietor's hand, "have another cup for Señor Jesús? When we have finished our coffee - I promise we shall not tarry long - I'll send this man on his way."

"Of course, of course," the proprietor replied gleefully as he scrambled off with his newfound wealth.

Jesús laid his stick on the floor and leaned close to my ear. "Lady Mary, Señor Cortés passed away a day after Señorita Elizabeth's arrival."

I felt myself stiffen. Cortés had been a good and faithful partner in merchantry with me for many years. And even though he had betrayed me once he had, at the cost of his little finger, redeemed himself. I had always been rather fond of the Spaniard. His passing brought me sorrow.

"I am sad to hear of it. How did he die?"

"Peacefully, in his sleep. He had been ailing for some time."

"Do you know the whereabouts of Elizabeth or my men?"

"No Lady Mary."

"Esmeralda is aware of Cortés' death?"

Esmeralda was Cortés' Jesús in Santo Domingo and oversaw his estate there.

"Yes."

"Who owns the hacienda now?"

"After her father died, Señorita Elizabeth sold all of his properties and possessions in Cuba. A gentleman named Jerónimo de Landa purchased the hacienda lock, stock and barrel, including the slaves."

"And Cortés' properties in Hispaniola?"

"I do not know."

"Does this Landa fellow," I whispered, "treat you well?"

"He does. He is a moral man."

"I have gold. If you wish your freedom, I will see it done."

Jesús took my hand. "No, Lady Mary. My days at *La Serenidad*, this is what Landa calls his property, are easy and comfortable. I was born there. I will die and be buried there. It is my home."

I turned to the twins. "Ladies, I've already checked the departure times for the packet ships sailing between Havana and Santo Domingo. One vessel leaves Havana later this afternoon. Let's collect our things with haste. Jesús, I have a story to tell as you might imagine but the girls and I are on the run, possibly in danger. We cannot linger here. I'm truly sorry. Until we meet again my friend."

Jesús kissed my hand and smiled. "Mary, I've never known you not to be in danger or not to be in a hurry. Ashaki and Lololi have no papers?"

"No."

"How did you get past the harbormaster?"

"We entered the city on foot from the west. No one challenged us."

"Ah, good, good. If we had more time, I know a man, a talented fellow, who could forge the necessary papers for you. I'm certain Esmeralda will know such a man too. I'll pray for your safe journey."

"And you Jesús, my friend, I pray you live out the rest of your days happy and content."

Chapter Nineteen

ith our precious cargo stowed away and our decks awash in eighty Chinamen, with another twenty Chinamen sitting in the longboat we had in tow, MacGyver gingerly eased *Achilles* out into the China Sea under half sail with a flotilla of Tanka children in small canoes accompanying us for a mile or two. We headed due south for the island of Dawanshan Dao, an easy sail away, and found our friends exactly where we had left them a week before.

"God's wounds, Elizabeth!" Atwood shouted as he leapt up onto *Homeward's* main mast shrouds. "What are all those Chinamen doing aboard *Achilles*?"

"'Tis good to see you too Jacob," I shouted back cheerfully. "Grab Maurice and let's assemble aboard *Ghostrunner*. All is well."

Returning back to my own ship was like returning home, returning to a snug place of comfort, safety and peace. And I was delighted to see my brothers again. I missed and loved them all. We sat around the table in my great cabin sipping fresh, Chinese ale, ale Atwood had purchased from local Dawanshan fishermen only days before.

"Our business in Macau was wonderfully successful," I began to say before Atwood cut me off.

"Buying Chinamen?" he asked sarcastically.

"No. I'll come to that matter in a moment Jacob. We sold our spices for a fair price and purchased one hundred and eighty tons of finished goods of exceptional quality. I expect we'll make a tidy profit back in Europe. I trust your days on the island were leisurely and uneventful?"

"Leisurely and uneventful, aye," Atwood replied flatly. "Some might say dull and tiresome. We've had eyes on us the whole time. So, tell us Elizabeth, who are those Chinese you brought with you?"

"Part of the bargain Michael and I struck with a man named **Féng Wú, he is the proprieter** of one of Macau's great trading houses, was to deliver seventy-five Chinese workers to Banten."

"I think," Efendi interrupted, "you brought more than seventy-five Chinamen back with you."

"Yes, Mustafa. We've also hired twenty-five Chinese seamen to augment our crews for the long journey home."

"Zeus' balls, Elizabeth!" Atwood grumbled while vehemently shaking his head. "You can't be serious! What in God's name possessed you to agree to such a thing?"

"We can use the additional muscle."

"We can make do without these strange folk roaming freely about the ships. You don't know these men. You know not their skills or loyalties. I can believe a Chinaman or two might be willing to sail around the world with us, but twenty-five souls? No. We should put them ashore on Dawanshan and depart these waters at once."

"Famine is ravaging the lands to the north and west of Macau, Jacob. Work is scarce. Men are desperate to feed their families."

"Sorry to hear it, Elizabeth. Bad luck for them. But we're not a charity for downtrodden souls."

"Please Jacob, let's not bicker. The deed is done."

"The deed can be undone. Is Arslan with them?"

"No."

"Good. That one's a slimy toad and I trust him not."

"Jacob, we have Cimarron, Blackamoors and Carib sprinkled amongst our crews. We have men from Ireland, Scotland, France, Sweden, England, Germany, Turkey, Italy, Holland and Spain. We have Christians, Muslims and Jews and God knows what else sailing with us. Why not a few Chinamen?"

"This is true, Jacob," Kinkae offered softly. More and more Kinkae had assumed the role of peacemaker between Atwood and myself when Maurice became less inclined to do so.

Atwood nodded. "Aye Kinkae, over the years we've eased a few outlanders into our ranks here and there and we've prospered for it. This matter with the Chinese is different to my way of thinking. Do any of them speak English, Elizabeth?"

"A handful," I replied, "speak Portuguese."

"Wonderful."

"They'll learn."

"What say you, Mustafa?" Atwood asked. "You're the law over all the men."

Efendi shrugged his shoulders. "Elizabeth hired them."

"Jesus Christ!" Atwood scoffed and rolled his eyes. "That's no answer! At times I think I'm sailing with a bunch of feeble, old men and one silly girl. Fine, fine. But at the first sign of trouble - if just one Chinaman looks at me cross-eyed - I swear by Christ I'll leave every fucking one of the little, lizard-eyed shits stranded on the nearest strip of land and I'll give no thought or care as to whether they live or die."

"*Ghostrunner*," I said, "has the most space. I'll take the Chinamen and their gear aboard with me. If the sailors fail to measure up, we can leave them in Banten with the others."

"I'll see it done," MacGyver offered quickly, eager to cut the tension in the air.

The sun was bright and pleasantly warm as our squadron plowed across the ocean's rolling swells towards Banten. I stood next to the rail on the quarterdeck with not a care in the world sipping my strong, black tea, sweetened a little with the gift Arslan had thoughtfully left behind with me. I relished the comforting warmth spreading across my body and the joyfulness filling my soul. I lost myself in happy thoughts.

"You seem to be in a cheerful mood," Shaw said as he moved to my side.

"I am," I agreed. "Life is good. Lovely day don't you think Rob? Oh, look, a pair of young dolphins at play! A good omen."

"Life is good Liz and it is indeed a beautiful day. I've missed you."

I tossed my head back and laughed.

"What amuses you?" he asked.

I took Shaw's arm in mine. "The world amuses me, Rob. Come,

let us go below and fuck. I long to feel your stiff cock throbbing inside me."

Shaw looked at me aghast and pulled away. "What the devil has gotten into you Liz? I've never heard you speak so crudely."

"I want you. What's wrong with that? Don't you want me? Don't you want to take me below and ravish me?"

"'Tis only midday! For discretion's sake we must wait until nightfall before playing nug-a-nug."

"Discretion's sake?" I asked and scoffed. "Discretion holds no sway over me," I said and blew my lover a naughty kiss. "I'm hot for you now. I yearn to feel your naked flesh pressed against mine, to feel my legs wrapped around your waist. Let the entire crew hear our wild passion."

When Shaw, disarmed and too stunned to speak did nothing, I took his hand in mine and dragged him down the companionway to my cabin. He did not resist.

Seized with animal lust, afire with unrepentant desire, we furiously traded kisses as we stripped away each other's clothing. I pushed Shaw on my bunk and straddled him. I started riding him with vigor, savoring the intoxicating pleasures washing over me. I couldn't help myself and thought of the *House of a Thousand Pleasures*. My arousal heightened and I rode him harder, as I thought of Arslan and Ling. I rolled underneath him, held my lover's hips tightly against my own and crassly begged him to fuck me deeper and harder. I had to bite my lip to stiffle my moaning as he eagerly did my bidding.

"*Sails ho!*" we heard a voice cry out followed by the clanging of the ship's bell.

Shaw inexplicably rolled off me without a word and quickly slipped into his trousers.

"What's wrong with you?" I asked, put-off by the interruption.

"You heard the lookout, Liz. We must hurry up on deck."

"These waters are teeming with ships, Rob. 'Tis nothing. Come, don't go soft on me now. Not now! Let us finish what we started."

Shaw ignored my pleas and finished dressing. "Something has spooked the lookout enough to sound the warning bell - we must go

Elizabeth."

"What is it, Mustafa?" I asked crossly after Shaw and I stepped onto the quarterdeck together.

When Efendi answered me with disapproval in his eyes, I immediately understood. Our disheveled appearance, our flushed cheeks and beads of sweat had betrayed Shaw and me. I didn't care. I put my hand to my mouth when I caught the giggles.

"Look Elizabeth!" Shaw said excitedly and pointed. "A large fleet, ten, seventeen, twenty-three, twenty-seven, thirty - I count thirty ships in all hastening this way!"

"Elizabeth, where's your Spanish glass?" Efendi demanded.

"I'll go fetch it," Shaw volunteered when I failed to answer and raced down the companionway to my cabin.

Efendi narrowed his eyes and took my hand. "Have you," he asked sternly, "been hitting the bottle Elizabeth?"

"No!" I replied indignantly and yanked my hand away. "Why do you ask such an impertinent question?"

"You seem indifferent or out-of-sorts. Perhaps disoriented?"

"I'm none of those things. I'm tired. I did not sleep well in Macau. Otherwise, I'm fine, couldn't be better, and you need not concern yourself."

When Shaw returned a few moments later with my glass, we each took turns looking through the small end of the tube and saw, in close detail, Chinese junks and luggers with six impressive Portuguese carracks mixed in coming down from Shangchuan. The vessels appeared well-armed, were under full sail and moving fast straight for us. Companies of armed men stood shoulder-to-shoulder up in the rigging of each ship - always an ominous sign. But I saw nothing amongst the pack to rival our battlecruisers.

I had my men hoist our battle flag up the main mast - Mary's ensign of yellow-gold with a coiled, red sea serpent emblazoned in the center, at one time the war banner of the monstrous Twins, of the wicked *Síol Faolcháin* - and then went below to make myself another cup of strong, black tea with a drop or two of Arslan's gift to calm an odd anxiety spreading across my chest and arms. I returned to the quarterdeck just as Atwood was bringing his ship up alongside *Ghostrunner.*

"Elizabeth," the one-eyed Scot called out from his ship's poop deck. "Watcha thinkin'? Why raise the battle flag? If we continue sailing south, we can outrun whatever trouble is sailing this way."

"We can just as easily sink those ships if they wish to test us," I replied in a cocky tone and took a sip of tea.

"Why? There's nothin' to be gained by getting into a brawl with these rascals."

"I'm no coward."

"No, of course not. You're a brave and skillful fighter. You have the respect of all the lads. Now let's lose these rabid dogs before we push our luck too far."

But my mind was firm. I'd not slink away again as I had off Madagascar and forfeit an opportunity to prove myself, to win the admiration of my brothers.

"We go straight at them Jacob!" I said defiantly. "A man who runs from a fight is no man at all and deserves no respect. This is doubly true for any woman who would lead them. You can follow me - or not."

Atwood rubbed the bridge of his nose and sighed. "Mustafa, for the love of God talk some sense into her. I'm at my wit's end."

Efendi gently laid a hand upon my shoulder. "Elizabeth, what you propose is most unwise. Why do this? Did something happen in Macau? Was some insult given? Did you suffer some offense?"

"No."

"What have I taught you over the years, eh? Unless you are certain you can win a fight, or you are cornered and you have no choice, run. There is no dishonor in choosing to live to confront your enemy another day when the odds are in your favor. I beg you to reconsider."

"Relax and have a cup of tea Mustafa," I said. "All shall be well, I promise. Rob, let's bring our warhorse about. We'll charge straight at these heathen devils. We'll scatter them like chaff in the wind. They'll shriek in terror and run by God or they can all share a watery grave!"

Shaw stared at me with a hurt expression but did as he was told.

Atwood said no more as Efendi coldly turned his back on me, rudely ignoring my offer of tea.

I had been with Mary in a few skirmishes before, all minor tussles, never in any meaningful action. But I had heard the stories of her near legendary prowess in battle. Shift right, shift left. Take in the wind, consider the currents. Bide your time, seize the weather gauge when you can. Maneuver and fire, maneuver and fire. Use your wits against your opponent as much as your brawn. Deception is your friend. Hesitation is your enemy. Simple plans are nearly always best Mary liked to say. And then luck, the Devil's own court jester, has a part to play in any tragedy too. Luck can favor a champion in the morning and desert him in the afternoon. Trust not in luck.

Oh yes, I had heard it all before. But I had no patience for such things, not when we were facing mere Pygmies sailing flimsy bundles of sticks armed with measly smallbore cannon, three-pounders at best I figured. In Ambon after all we had sent a carrack to the bottom with just one broadside. I led our four sturdy battlecruisers, double-planked with the hardest woods and bristling with heavy cannon, manned by crusty veterans of cruel, unforgiving war, straight into the jaws of the beast bearing down on us. And as we raced headlong towards righteous, glorious war, the peaceful joy I had savored earlier now blossomed into sublime exhilaration.

Sailing in a cluster like a cloud of angry bees the pirates - and that is what they proved themselves to be, godless, wicked, filthy, villainous, godless pirates, a wretched scourge upon the earth - fired first with their bow chasers. Puffs of smoke and tongues of flame reached out across the water for us while all around the sea erupted with tall geysers of white water.

After I gave the order to turn to starboard, the crews readied their ships for action. We'd form a wall and bring all of our guns to bear against the swarm of ships charging at us, a favorite tactic of Mary's.

While Kinkae and his men brought up shot and powder and cleared the decks, while Henry and his men worked the rigging and trimmed the sails, Efendi's gunners primed and loaded their great guns then ran the barrels out over the side. But they did not fire, not yet. We needed the enemy to close the distance with us. At a thousand yards Mary had taught me our men would start hitting things. Shooting at anything farther out was a waste of precious ball and powder she had said. At five hundred yards our guns could cause real damage and at two hundred yards we would mount the swivels to the rails and load them with grape or chain shot to inflict some truly horrific damage against sail, flesh and wood.

We were about ten miles off Shangchuan when Efendi, leaning over the rail near the main mast, checked the range with his gunner's quadrant one last time. When he glanced up at me on the quarterdeck and nodded, I nodded back, giving him my blessing.

"Gun captains!" Efendi roared. "Pick your targets. Mind the swell. Remember your training. Steady, wait for it, wait for it..."

I watched our gunners, four men to a gun, standing at the ready. I watched the gun captains leaning over their gunner's sights with their slow-burning linstocks in hand, coolly waiting for the command from Efendi.

Not me. The honor was mine and I took it.

"*FIRE!*" I screamed.

BOOM! the first gun thundered followed by a bolt of excruciating pain shooting through my head - I had neglected to stuff my ears with strips of cotton and paid the price for my stupidity. I placed my hands over my ears before the next gun bellowed.

BOOM! BA-BA-BOOM! BA-BA-BA-BA-BOOM! BOOM! BOOM! BOOM!

The ship shuddered. Clouds of choking smoke rolled across the decks while gunners sprang into action to recover the guns on the recoil.

"Stop your vents!" Efendi shouted. "Swab your barrels down! Jump to it! Prime and load, prime and load. Faster, faster I say if you want to live through the day!"

Cerberus fired her guns next followed by *Homeward* and then *Achilles*. Our ships hurtled dozens of six, nine, and twelve-pound shot across the water. I watched in awe as we unleashed hell. I found the violence intoxicating.

We poured broadside after broadside into the ships charging at us. We hammered the lead ships hard. One ship lost her fore mast and clumsily turned away with her shattered mast dragging in the water behind her. When a large lugger of one sort or another burst into flames like a tinderbox two ships close by, trying to avoid the conflagration, collided. Both ships sheared-off the bowsprit of the other. In the twinkling of an eye, we had put four enemy ships out of action. What a wonderous mess I'd made of things I thought to myself and caught the giggles.

Our pugnacious foe did not lack courage though. With twenty-six ships still in the fight, our enemy ignored the hail of deadly iron raining down on them. The pirates continued closing the distance with us and shot at us with their bow chasers, though none of their gunners showed any great skill at gunnery. They fired haphazardly with haste. Their marksmanship was poor. None of our ships suffered any real damage.

Then... a disquieting melody with an evil cadence from the depths of hell came floating across the water. With war drums beating *doom-doom-da-da-doom*, *doom-doom-da-da-doom*, *doom-doom-da-da-doom* and longhorns blaring *ooo-whooooo*, *ooo-whooooo*, *ooo-whooooo* over and over again, more than one man lost his nerve. I saw one of the newer lads lean over the rail and heave. Another boy, not much older than James, crouched low behind a barrel and wept.

And then I heard Efendi give the order to mount the swivels to the rails. He sent musketeers up into the rigging. But before I could find out why, I heard the sickening crack of wood behind me followed by a dreadful scream. Debris flew past my face as I spun around just as our helmsman toppled over. An iron ball had split the poor fellow in two. Worse, after passing through him, the ball had shattered our wheel.

"Liz, Liz!" Shaw shouted frantically as he shook me by my shoulders.

Covered in the helmsman's blood and entrails, Shaw thought I had been wounded. "I, I'm fine Rob," I said, "but the ship's wheel..."

"Aye, I see the broken pieces," he said while bending down to wrap his neckerchief around my leg. "You're bleeding."

"What?" I asked surprised. I felt no pain - but I could feel the ship losing speed and straying off course. Without her rudder *Ghostrunner* began wobbling to and fro, staggering between the swells like a drunken sailor stumbling down a crooked alley.

And then I heard Kinkae's strong voice. "Ready yourselves for close combat!" he shouted. "Prepare to be boarded!"

I hurried over to the ship's rail to have a look around and was shocked to find a carrack from out of nowhere pulling up alongside us. Her men were already tossing out grappling hooks and snagged our ship on our starboard side. Portuguese sailors by the score began climbing over the rails as musketeers up in the carrack's rigging peppered our decks with bullets.

And then I heard a great commotion at the bow. Dozens of Wú's Chinamen, armed with spiked maces, clubs and axes, started rushing up onto the forward deck to join us. Brave lads all I thought at first. But in utter disbelief I watched as the two-faced fiends began attacking my crew! From stem-to-stern *Ghostrunner* turned into a killing arena. Men fought hand-to-hand like gladiators in a vicious struggle to the death.

"Rob, quick, the wheel!" I shouted. We needed our rudder, we needed speed to break free from the carrack and had precious little time.

Next Henry bolted up the quarterdeck ladder with three of his Carib warriors behind him. "Mustafa sent us!" he blurted out excitedly and had his men form a protective semicircle around Shaw and me as we dropped to our knees to fix our broken wheel.

A musket ball whizzed past my ear. Another passed through my vest and struck a plank near my knee. Shaw and I both ignored the danger. We used rope and straps of leather to tie broken pieces together. We worked feverishly amidst the chaos. Once we did what we could do patching broken fragments together, we lifted the wheel up onto its pedestal and slipped the hub through the spindle.

Then one of Henry's warriors stumbled on top of me when a musket ball slammed into his shoulder. After I helped the man to his feet, I stepped over to the forward quarterdeck rail to get a better look at things. The forward and main decks were awash in a sea of desperate, angry men splattered in grime, blood and gore. Men were shooting, stabbing, gouging, biting, bludgeoning and hacking away at one another with ungodly zeal. The Chinese were fighting Kinkae and his men around the bow. The Portuguese were pressing Efendi and his gunners back across the main deck. The desperate tug of war for *Ghostrunner* hung in the balance as men surged forward and then fell back again. The cries of dying men filled my ears. Smoke stung my eyes. I wondered if any of us would survive.

I frantically looked for hope across the water. I scanned the sea in every direction and to my astonishment, not far off, I found what I was looking for. Atwood, Maurice and MacGyver, realizing that something was terribly wrong aboard *Ghostrunner*, were driving their ships hard to reach us. Their gunners had started lobbing bow shots at the carrack tied alongside us - but the Portuguese build some of the finest warships in the world and the carrack shook each blow off. Portuguese gunners returned fire, concentrating their efforts on *Cerberus*, the largest of the three ships closing on them. They launched three broadsides at Maurice's ship in quick succession.

But then, as Atwood, Maurice and MacGyver drew closer, the carrack's captain lost his nerve. He gave the order to cut the ropes securing his ship to ours. He gave the order to drop sail. I could hear the panic rising in his voice as he screamed at his men aboard *Ghostrunner* to fall back to the carrack. Sailors tripped over themselves trying to reach their ship. The captain didn't wait for stragglers though and left dozens of his men behind.

Next my brothers swung their ships around to bring all their guns to bear against the fleeing Portuguese. One broadside from each ship at close range did the job. Great chunks of wood and metal went soaring through the air. The carrack began sinking by the bow and vanished moments later.

Like a wild beast cornered on all sides, the stranded Chinese and Portuguese ferociously lashed out in desperation. To my astonishment six Portuguese sailors managed to claw their way up to the quarterdeck as Shaw and I worked the wheel. Henry and two of his men, one Carib lay dead, bared their fangs, ripped off their shirts - exposing tattoos of weapons, fearsome animals and heroic deeds in battle - and rushed headlong into the Portuguese as they shouted a ferocious war cry while wielding their battleaxes above their heads. Short in stature and slight in build - yes - but exceptionally skilled at killing, Henry and his warriors brutally cut all six sailors down with ease.

With the quarterdeck secure, I left Shaw at the wheel and returned to the forward quarterdeck rail again. I saw Kinkae with a swivel cradled in his arms advancing with his Blackamoors on a good number of Chinese trapped against the bow. A Chinaman or two dropped their weapons. The rest seemed determined to fight on. Kinkae leveled his swivel and fired, leaving none alive. And in the center, I saw Efendi, splattered in blood and gore from head to toe, jump atop a barrel holding a severed head in one hand and his sword in the other. When he pointed the sharp steel at the nearest Chinaman, the man dropped to his knees and tossed his axe aside. Another did the same followed by another and another until every Chinaman had surrendered. The Portuguese wisely did the same.

"Merciful God," I cried out to Shaw. "We've taken the ship back."

"Maybe so Mary," Shaw replied. "But look around us."

Everywhere I turned I saw ships firing at each other at close range. Though our enemy's plan to take *Ghostrunner* by treachery had failed, though they were outgunned and outmatched and had lost many ships and men, the pirates had more to show us. Their tenacity, their fury and thirst for blood perplexed me.

"Henry," I called out. "Go below and find the carpenter. He must fashion us a new wheel. Then see to our wounded. Quickly now!"

"I will Elizabeth, but first," he said as he stood over a bloodied Portuguese crawling across the deck on his belly. Henry flipped the sailor on his back, plunged his knife into the man's bowels and twisted.

While Kinkae and his men bound our prisoners and took them below, Efendi's gunners returned to their stations and soon had

Ghostrunner's gun batteries belching smoke and fire again. We were back in the fight and our frightful power gave me hope the worst was over.

But no. When I heard Shaw call out my name I spun around and watched him spinning the ship's wheel around and around in his hands with no effect.

"The shot that broke our wheel must have shattered the rudder stock too," he declared. "The helm no longer answers. We best shorten sail Elizabeth."

I stepped over mangled bodies and puddles of blood to make my way down to the main deck to reach Efendi. "Mustafa, we've lost our steerage," I said flatly without emotion.

The Turk used his shirt sleeve to wipe the soot and sweat from his eyes. He stared contemptuously at me, but said nothing.

"I know what you're thinking," I said. "Say it, you're right - I've made a royal mess of things."

"What's done is done," Efendi replied wearily without any malice in his tone. "There's more killing yet to do. Over there, look. Jacob, Maurice and Michael are forming a circle around us. Let these bastards come and beat their heads against a wall of iron if they dare. By all that is holy, we must hold this patch of water until our good carpenter finishes his work. Then, when night comes, we can quietly slip away."

"Yes," I said awkwardly and lowered my head to avoid his harsh gaze.

Efendi saw the scarf tried around my leg, the trickle of blood running down my ankle. "You best have Stachel take a look at that wound."

"I will," I replied absently and turned to walk away. But I didn't go below to see our surgeon. After I gave the order to shorten sail, I returned to the poop deck to stand with Shaw.

When the carpenter joined us with two other men, I helped Shaw lower the three men over the side in a boatswain's chair. We handed them their tools, wood planking and a bucket of bolts and screws. We watched them fashion a makeshift rudder while the battle raged on all around us. With our prisoners secured below, Kinkae and his

Blackamoors returned to the main deck and began tossing dead pirates over the side while Henry and his lads brought up more shot and powder. And once those tasks were done, both divisions went around the ship splicing snapped lines, patching torn sails and mending any damaged wood of importance.

And then a strange lull then settled over the action. The pirates pulled back - not to retreat as I first imagined - but to regroup and when they were ready, they sailed out in a single line of battle and began circling around our ships. I counted twenty-two enemy ships still in the fight. Our foe launched one broadside after another at us with frightening ferocity, desperately trying to find some weakness to exploit. They circled around us three times, keeping up a steady rate of fire. We took some hits. A few men fell. And yet for all their shots and bluster our foe gained no real advantage. Our guns had longer range, punched harder and we disabled two more vessels.

Down to twenty ships, the pirates once again withdrew. Still, they did not retire. This time they pulled their ships into a tight cluster and started clumsily floating towards us under half sail. This new tactic baffled me at first.

At about a thousand yards the pirate ships picked-up good speed once their crews raised every stitch of canvas. With the big, powerful war carracks out in front the snug formation came at us like a battering ram tipped in bronze. I thought the plan sheer madness at first. And then I understood. Our enemy wasn't coming for *us*, they were coming for *Achilles*.

Without our rudder there was little my men or I could do. We couldn't sail towards *Achilles* or turn to give Efendi's gunners targets. *Ghostrunner* was adrift and barely in the fight.

Atwood and Maurice moved their ships in closer to protect *Achilles*, the prize the pirates seemed to desire most. *Homeward's* guns made short work of one flimsy Chinese junk and sent her to the bottom and after *Cerberus'* gunners raked the deck of another ship with brutal grapeshot, her crew turned their ship around and fled.

The pirate commander coldly disregarded his losses. He ignored *Homeward* and *Cerberus* and brazenly continued driving his fleet straight at *Achilles.*

Efendi, Kinkae and Henry joined Shaw and me at the aft rail to watch the action. We stood side-by-side as cannons boomed and muskets crackled, as clouds of smoke wafted across the water.

Achilles fired a full broadside into a galleass of sixty oars closing in on her, splitting the galleass in half. Her bow drifted one way and her stern another and when both halves disappeared with all her crew, my men raised a thunderous victory cheer. Two lesser ships quit the battle. Another vessel burst into flames. I took pleasure in watching her men burn as they frantically tried to save themselves. Atwood, Maurice and MacGyver were inflicting horrendous carnage.

But then our enemy found cause to gloat. A lucky shot struck *Achilles'* main mast at the base. The great stick wobbled for a bit, groaned and toppled over, taking rigging, canvas and sailors with it. *Achilles* lost her speed and the pirates, down to fourteen ships, pounced on MacGyver's crippled battlecruiser like a pack of ravenous wolves. In matter of seconds, in no time at all, the tide of battle had turned against us and all seemed lost again.

But Atwood, that magnificent Scot I grudgingly admit knew no fear, madly charged straight at the heart of the pirate formation in a desperate, selfless, glorious attempt to drive our foe away from *Achilles.* Maurice followed close behind. But neither man had the wind and their ships struggled making headway.

The pirates ignored the sluggish counterattack of my brothers. With unbelievable recklessness two galleys with blunt bows like barges - one with fifty oars and the other with twice that many - rammed into *Achilles* with great violence. I felt my heart skip a beat when *Achilles* rolled over on her side. I grabbed the rail to steady myself when my knees buckled. I swallowed the bile rising in my throat. And though *Achilles* was able to right herself in my gut I knew, I knew the double blows had killed her.

We all watched helplessly as wave after wave of ruthless barbarians wielding all manner of weapons crossed over a wide plank from the first ship and boarded *Achilles* at the bow. The pirates fanned out across the forward deck like locust, murdering every defender in their path. They seized *Achilles* from her bow to her fore mast and then pushed the rest of MacGyver's men back. Then men from the second ship stormed aboard *Achilles* at the stern. They quickly took the quarterdeck and then the poop deck, forcing the survivors below. With a sword in each hand, we watched MacGyver rally the tattered remnants of his crew around the stump of the main mast to make a final stand.

Then Atwood and Maurice arrived. They brought their ships up behind the pirate pack. Their guns shredded sail and blew gaping holes in wood. Two more junks peeled-off and quit the battle. A column of black smoke, like fumes belching from a chimney, began billowing from the deck gratings of a third ship. Her crew lowered away the boats and bolted. Even with all their courage and bravado though neither Atwood or Maurice could reach *Achilles*.

Despite my sex I've never been one to weep. I wept now. I couldn't staunch the flow of tears as I watched the pirates cut MacGyver and all his men down. No quarter was asked and none was given.

Shaw pressed my head against his chest and let me sob when the last man fell. Then some fool decided to torch *Achilles* before returning to his ship - or perhaps one of MacGyver's men heroically set the blaze before he died. The fire spread rapidly. Flames raced up *Achilles'* rigging, crawled across her yardarms and leapt over to the other two ships entangled with her. Scores of men jumped over the side as the wild conflagration engulfed all three ships. A handful of men, theirs or ours I could not tell, managed to slip away in a single longboat.

And then... A burst of brilliant light blinded me followed instantly by a horrific boom. A wall of searing heat knocked me off me feet. When Shaw and Efendi helped me stand, I saw only a smoldering skeleton of ribs floating on the water where *Achilles* should have been. No living thing could have survived that blast. Efendi, Shaw and I watched in silence as *Achilles* slipped beneath the waves, dragging the two other ships down with her. I searched the heavens and prayed in earnest for a stray bullet or piece of flying debris to kill me. My prayers went unanswered.

Finally, having paid a terrible price for *Achilles*, our mysterious adversary turned his ships around and slithered off to the north. Atwood and Maurice did not give chase.

It was late afternoon. The winds had subsided and the day had turned uncomfortably hot. An unbearable weariness gripped me. I blamed the heat. I wanted to return to my bunk and rest. I badly needed my tea, but dared not leave the deck. An hour slipped by before *Homeward* and *Cerberus* pulled up alongside us. An eternity passed before Atwood and Maurice stepped aboard *Ghostrunner* and slowly made their way up to the quarterdeck where Efendi, Shaw and I stood waiting. I braced myself for the worst.

I expected the big Scot to charge me with some crime, or perhaps dispense with charging me with anything at all and simply execute me on the spot. I imagined him drawing his sword and screaming ugly words in my face before plunging his blade into my belly. I had exhausted every tear. I felt numb. I had nothing left to say or give, not even to save myself. I was ready. But when Atwood stepped in front of me, staring down at me with his one good eye, he simply bit his lip and nodded.

Efendi handed both men a tin of *uisge beatha*, or what some men are calling whiskey. "Did anyone survive?" he asked solemnly.

"We fished one of ours out of the sea, a boy named Heath," Atwood replied wearily and sighed. "We searched the water for some time. Except for the boy, *Achilles* went down with all hands after her powder magazine blew. We gave the scum who slipped away in the longboat a taste of grapeshot."

Overwhelmed by a toxic mix of grief, guilt, relief and exhaustion, the world around me started spinning. My legs gave way again and I started falling until Maurice caught me.

"Rob, when can you have *Ghostrunner* under sail?" Atwood asked evenly, ignoring me.

"Another hour or two," Shaw answered.

Atwood clenched his jaw as he surveyed the damages to *Ghostrunner*. "Very well. As soon as *Ghostrunner* can get under way, we sail for Java. We'll refit and reprovision in Banten before setting out for home. The Chinamen, Arslan's men, they turned on you?"

"Yes," Efendi replied.

"All of them?"

"Yes."

"Sons of whores," Atwood said under his breath and spit. "Where did they get their weapons?"

"They had them hidden inside their knapsacks, knapsacks we thought carried clothing, tools and such," Efendi answered. "They brought their weapons aboard in pieces and assembled them when the pirate ships appeared. This attack was clever and well thought out. How many lads did you both lose?"

"I have nine dead and seventeen wounded," Atwood answered.

Maurice knocked his whisky back. "Six souls lost and twice as many wounded. Two at least will need Stachel's particular skills with his saws and blades - assuming our good surgeon still lives. You, Mustafa?"

"Twenty-seven dead, about as many wounded by my last count. Stachel is below with his medical instruments and medicines. By all means take the good doctor with you when you're ready."

"A hard day to get clear of," Atwood offered wistfully to no one in particular. "Thank God we kept the Chinese confined to one ship. Had we sprinkled them amongst all four ships, well, who knows. We have no time to dawdle. Not much daylight left. We can bury our dead on the move. Elizabeth?"

I swallowed hard and braced myself for death again. I was certain my moment of reckoning had come. I fixed my gaze on my shoes.

"What say you?" he demanded, peering down at me.

I said nothing.

"Elizabeth?" he asked again, pressing me hard for an answer.

"After what I've done," I mumbled, "I have no right to say much of anything."

"After what you've done?" Atwood asked. "What did you do? Did you violate one of our revered Ten Rules?"

Atwood's question surprised me. I had to think for a moment. "No, I don't think so."

"You don't think so? But your heart is heavy with guilt?"

"Yes."

"Well, you best purge this guilt of yours. You best purge it quickly too. The journey ahead will be long and hard. Guilt is a heavy burden that will only fester and gnaw at you if you let it."

I looked up at Atwood confused. "What?"

"I'll not mince words with you Elizabeth. I think you've been extraordinarily rash on this most unfortunate of days. I think you've shown poor judgement. Perhaps I am mistaken. Had we done what I wanted to do and run, those brazen rascals might have picked us off one-by-one during the night. Or perhaps they would have raced ahead of us and ambushed us in Banten. Who can know for certain? You've not dishonored the Ten Rules and you are our sister. Some years ago, I learned a hard lesson. Judging others is like stumbling down a narrow, crooked mountain path in the dark, covered in ice with sheer cliffs on either side of you. I'll not judge you. If Mary were with us now, I think she would approve of all I have said, the bitter and the sweet."

Atwood leaned down to kiss me on the check. "Then again, I could be wrong. At midnight, when we're under sail, we'll offer a toast and our prayers to our brother Michael and the others. Brave lads all worthy of our praise."

We had left Ireland with four ships and four hundred souls. Disease and war had claimed nearly half our numbers. MacGyver was dead. *Achilles* was lost. Our precious cargo of exotic luxury goods sat on the bottom of the China Sea. In the blink of an eye, in no time at all, our world had changed forever. To add insult to injury, when I went below, I found the beautiful hand mirror Dijksma had given me had fallen off a cupboard. I saw pieces of mirror scattered across the floor.

During the voyage to Banten, I languished alone in my great cabin. I even shut Shaw out. One matter alone consumed me. As Mary once had the Twins and the *Síol Faolcháin* to contend with - a feud to the death she had always said - I now had unfinished, violent business of my own to settle with one grotesquely fat Chinaman and his loathsome, half-breed dog. The two men never strayed far from my thoughts. Day after day I fell in and out of black and blacker moods. At the darkest hour, when my sorrow cut me to the bone and apprehension filled my soul to bursting, I turned to my soothing, black tea, the *House's* special blend, for comfort.

Chapter Twenty

The voyage from Havana to Santo Domingo, to the *Gateway to the Caribbean* as the port is often called, was pleasant and uneventful. Our Spanish caravel was a good ship with a competent master and we made excellent time. After only eight days at sea the master expertly guided us into the Ozama River, past the impressive harbor guns at Fortaleza Ozama and docked his ship not far from the city's main gates.

Though I had been prepared to bribe the harbormaster to let us pass, the man showed no interest in the twins or me and waved us through. After we collected our baggage and our knapsacks, I led the girls straight to Cortés' house on the outskirts of the city. We strolled down the Calle de Las Damas, walked past the Basilica Santa Maria la Menor where they say the great Christopher Columbus is entombed and skirted around the Alcázar de Colón, the New World's first palace.

Cortés' house was spacious, well-built and stood apart from the others. The exterior walls were brick the color of sand. The roof was finished in alternating red, brown and orange tiles. The windows were fitted with expensive lattice glass and fancy wood shutters.

A plump, handsome woman with intelligent, kind eyes, with smooth skin and fine, grey hair pulled back into a bun greeted us at the door when I knocked. A Castilian Negro Ladino, Esmeralda was as refined and as cultured as any European noblewoman and like Jesús, she was one of mine. She had been one of the very first to join my ring of spies in the New World.

Once she overcame her initial shock, Esmeralda welcomed me with open arms and tears. "¡*Capitána Maria, Dios es bueno!* You live!"

I held her tightly as we embraced. "Yes," I said and kissed her on both cheeks. "'Tis a great joy to see you again my lovely Esmeralda."

"But how? Señorita Elizabeth and Jacob told me you perished in a storm!"

"Aye. But as you can see..."

Esmeralda pushed me away, looked me up and down and shook her head with disapproval. "Tsk, tsk, tsk, you are so thin Mary!" she exclaimed, then turned her attention to the girls. "And these two pretty, little things, your ladies-in-waiting?"

"Ha!" I replied with a wink. "I'm hardly royalty. For now, they are my slaves. In truth they are my friends. This is Ashaki and this is Lololi. Though they do not look alike, they are twins from a town in México not far from Veracruz. Ladies, this is Esmeralda, the woman I told you about. She is most dear to me. Esmeralda, we can share our stories with you later if you have the time and patience. We met Jesús in Havana. I am aware Rodriguez is dead."

"Yes, Señor Cortés has passed. Elizabeth had him buried in a cemetery nearby if you wish to visit his grave and pay your respects."

"I'm not much for looking in on rotting corpses. May we visit with you awhile, either here if we can talk or someplace in the city?"

"Come, come in ladies. I must feed you first and then I'll listen to everything you have to say."

The girls and I followed Esmeralda inside and down a hallway to the back of the house. The interior walls were finished in marmorino, a popular Venetian plaster amongst the rich. The floors were expensive, polished slate with marble tile accents. Cortés' home had luxuries like bronze door handles, a water closet imported from Córdoba and several elegant chandeliers of fine, Italian crystal. Esmeralda took us into a backyard planted thick with shade trees and over to a redbrick building, the kitchen, with double stone chimneys. Beyond the kitchen stood small shacks for curing meats and tobacco along with a half dozen barracas for housing slaves.

Esmeralda had the cook prepare one of my favorite dishes. We ate at a rough-hewn wooden table on simple wooden stools in the kitchen's modest dining room. We feasted on smoked pork, fried plantains, Spanish rice and boniatos and for dessert Esmeralda treated us to sweet chocolate, or *chocolātl* in the Aztec tongue, served warm over delicate crêpes stuffed with slices of banana, prickly pears and chunks of pineapple. I smiled when I caught the sparkle in the eyes of Ashaki and Lololi. My reaction to my first taste of chocolate had been much the same. Esmeralda excused the cook and the two women helping him once we finished our dessert. She poured after dinner cordials for each of us and then coffee. Ashaki told her story first followed by Lololi and then I told mine.

"Such is my sad tale," I said when I had finished.

Esmeralda, a devoutly religious woman, crossed herself. "Merciful God, Mary. You, a slave, working in the fields and living in a barraca?"

"Aye."

Esmeralda turned to the sisters. "I would like your mother Aminatu ladies," she said. "You have traveled far and have endured great hardships. Take heart, God must have a plan for you. These two are strong like you Mary. I see it in their eyes."

I nodded. "From an early age they've suffered humiliations and indignities untold. They've suffered the master's lash. And as you know full well my dearest Esmeralda, adversity makes one either weak or strong and these two are very strong indeed. They've become as precious to me as any kin. Who owns this place now?"

"A wealthy, wine merchant from Italy bought the property."

"Ah, that is why the wine is so delicious. Where is this wine merchant of yours presently?"

"He should be returning from the Port of Spain any day now."

"When did you last see Elizabeth?"

"Oh my, it has been some time ago. Nearly two years."

"That long?"

"Yes. After Señor Cortés died, his business interests died with him and with you gone, well, Elizabeth and your men struggled."

"Have you received any letters from Elizabeth? Could my ships still be somewhere in the Caribbean?"

"In the Spring of last year, I received letters from Elizabeth to pass along to the families of your men in Guadaloupe to let them know she intended to sail to the East Indies and would be gone for a very long time."

"Good God, the East Indies?"

"Yes."

"Have you heard any news about my son James?"

"When I last saw Elizabeth, she told me your son was a healthy, happy boy. This is all I know. I'm sorry."

"Your new master, how does he treat you?"

"Signore Savona, silly man, prefers being addressed as signore over señor and is the only Italian I've ever known. The Italians are a crude, boorish peoples if the rest are like him. He enjoys boasting about the great triumphs of his ancestors and takes pleasure in reminding us daily that the Romans conquered and enslaved half the civilized world. He is an irksome, difficult man."

I shook my head. "The man sounds like a pompous fool. Gloating over the past glories of an empire that turned to dust and ash many centuries ago is feeble-minded. The modern Italian kingdoms are divided and weak. The man does have excellent taste in wine though."

"How may I be of service to you and these two lovely young women? You must get back to Ireland, yes?"

"Yes. We had no trouble sailing from Havana to Santo Domingo. No one asked me for papers for Ashaki or Lololi to prove, forgive me ladies, ownership. Securing passage to Ireland or to some other kingdom in Europe for them might prove more difficult. I simply don't know what is required. I'm not accustomed to sailing as a passenger or traveling with slaves."

"You might need a bill of sale to cross the Atlantic. You might not. No matter. I can make you the proper documents. I still have Cortés' seal."

"Wonderful, but this simply will not do."

Esmeralda looked at me confused. "Beg pardon Mary?"

"As Savona is not here, I cannot legally buy your freedom. Make me three bills of sale and come with us."

"No, no, Mary. Too many people know me in Santo Domingo. Such a thing would be too risky."

"Please Esmeralda."

"I will not. You know I am right."

Yes, I knew Esmeralda was right as I slowly turned the matter over in my muddled head. I had lost my tolerance for strong drink.

"Very well then. I'll leave a letter for Savona and offer to buy you from him."

"And tell him what? No one has any desire to purchase an old crone like me. Such an offer might provoke suspicion. He may ask troublesome questions."

"I'll tell him the truth. I will tell him that Cortés and I were friends and partners in trade and that over the years I've grown fond of you and wish to make you comfortable in your old age."

"I am grateful Mary. At my age I should be a bargain. But I'm certain Savona will see an opportunity to fleece you if he understands my importance to you."

"He'll accept my offer - I promise."

Not many ships sail between Santo Domingo and Ireland but luck was with us. The *Dublin Merchant*, a large English freighter out of Liverpool was in port and accepting passengers. Her master intended to leave by weeks' end for Dublin before sailing on to England.

The girls and I took rooms at a pleasant hostel. We whittled away the days exploring the city and playing cards. One evening I took them to a tavern known for its gambling tables where I tripled our gold and then some playing French Ruff, a game of cards I had mastered years ago.

Once Savona returned to the city, I purchased Esmeralda from him at a fair price and then I set her free. I placed a small deposit on a modest but comfortable house within the city walls for her and bankrolled a small, new trading company with interests in imports and exports with the two of us as equal partners. She fought me at first but my mind was firm. I was merely repaying a debt for her years of dangerous and faithful service and told her so.

With my bills of sale for the twins in hand, imprinted with

Cortés' seal, and our passages paid for in advance, we boarded *Dublin Merchant* without difficulty. I used our days at sea to teach the girls English and how to read and write. And then - at their request - I added navigation and mathematics to their studies. The sea had seduced Ashaki. Learning navigation was her idea. As for mathematics, Lololi possessed an inexplicable natural talent, a God given gift for numbers. Both girls were hungry to learn and often kept at their studies well into the night. Where Ashaki was bold, carefree and wild like me, Lololi was more circumspect and excelled at shrewdness. I cherished them both like daughters.

Chapter Twenty-One

twood took Maurice and me ashore along with twenty men to find Koopman after we reached Banten. The season of the monsoon still cursed the land. God seemed determined to drown that part of the world. We trudged through ankle-deep mud in heavy rains as we made our way along the outer east wall of the city. We followed the river to the Dutch trading post, which was little more than a cluster of modest log cabins surrounded by a simple palisade, where we were surprised to find Dijksma waiting for us there instead of Koopman.

The handsome, personable Dutchman greeted us with open arms and a friendly smile. He invited us inside the main cabin and served us cinnamon tea with freshly baked biscuits as we took seats around a bench table. He was eager to hear our tale. Atwood and Maurice did most of the talking. They recounted our battle with the pirates in great detail. They spoke of Chinese betrayal and Wú. I told Dijksma all that I had seen and heard in Macau. Well, I found no need to mention Ling or the *House of a Thousand Pleasures*.

"A tragic story," Dijksma said sorrowfully after I had finished. "I am grieved to hear about the loss of your men and *Achilles*. I'll need to send the Company a full report concerning these most unfortunate matters. As luck would have it there's a Dutch merchantman sitting in the harbor and she's ready to depart for Amsterdam on the morrow."

"And what precisely will you put in this report of yours?" Atwood asked.

"What you have each told me certainly, along with my own observations. As for Macau, we have our spies in the city of course.

Even so, the information you've provided Elizabeth may have value. I cannot say how my masters in Amsterdam will receive this news of lost cargo. I did warn you about the risks in sailing to Macau whilst under contract with the Company. Rest assured, I hold each of you in high esteem and that too will be in my report."

"Outlaws ambushed us!" I blurted out angrily and pounded my fists on the table.

"True, true, but the question will be why Elizabeth? Why did you sail to Macau without approval and why did these villainous scoundrels attack you? How is this Féng Wú fellow or Arslan involved in all this intrigue? Or perhaps the Portuguese were the architects of this treachery?"

"Wicked does as wicked will," I said indifferently and shrugged my shoulders. "Who can know the why of it? We may never learn the truth. We've disclosed everything we know to you and besides, since when do we hold one man accountable for the evil deeds of another in which he played no part?"

Dijksma shook his head. "The men I answer to do not accept failure well. Make no mistake Elizabeth, the Company will conduct a formal inquiry into this matter. The Company will demand answers. At the very least the Company will demand indemnity."

"Indemnity? Ha! What about our losses, who will indemnify us? If the Company wishes satisfaction it should run down the brigands who attacked us!"

"I admire your passion Elizabeth but I don't think you quite understand the seriousness, um, well, never mind. I do understand your position. Did you capture any prisoners?"

"We did," Atwood replied. "We took nearly forty Chinese and Portuguese prisoners in all. You can have them. We interrogated them of course but they seem to know very little. Thank God we weren't fighting professionals. The Chinese are farmers and tradesmen, not soldiers. The Portuguese are merchant sailors, not navy men. These scoundrels appear to be nothing more than someone else's lackeys. No one knows who bought their services or for what purpose. They were promised plunder and were willing to kill for it."

Dijksma nodded. "I shall happily relieve you of these vermin. I have a man, a rather odd fellow who has, shall we say, a peculiar gift for extracting the truth. How long do you intend to stay in Banten, Jacob?"

"Just long enough to overhaul our ships and take on fresh provisions. We repaired what we could at sea. But with the long voyage ahead, we'll need our ships in prime condition."

"Prudent as always. Well, I know a tolerable tavern nearby where we can wash away the grime and numb our sorrows. I can write my report later. Shall we? I'm buying."

In the morning I watched the Dutch freighter carrying Dijksma's report slowly negotiate her way through the maze of ships anchored in Banten's bay with an uneasy feeling in the pit of my stomach. As my special tea from Arslan was nearly gone, I quietly went ashore in the skiff to purchase more for the long voyage ahead.

We spent the next few days working on the ships. The men, longing to return to their families, were of good cheer despite our losses and the incessant rains. They plunged into their work with purpose. And then one morning Dijksma rowed out to *Ghostrunner* to see me. I gladly welcomed him aboard.

"This is a pleasant surprise Ewoud," I said as I offered my hand to help him up the rope ladder dangling over the side.

After he stepped on deck, he tenderly kissed my hand with obvious affection. "Elizabeth, 'tis always a joy to see you."

"The sentiment is mutual."

"I fear I've not come to exchange pleasantries today."

"Oh? That sounds ominous. Will you join me for breakfast? You can tell me what is on your mind as we eat."

"Happily, yes. You may wish to have Jacob and Maurice join us."

"You seem determined to spoil my good mood."

"I bear news all three of you must hear."

"Very well, I'll see it done."

Dijksma bowed. "Thank you," he said as he tenderly kissed my hand a second time.

After Atwood and Maurice stepped into my great cabin, I moved around the table to pour each man a tin of coffee. "Ewoud has weighty matters to discuss with us," I said cheerfully, though I found the suspense excruciating.

"You, I'll wager," Atwood said, "need us to take you back to Ambon."

"No, I'm afraid that is not why I'm here. We questioned your prisoners. We didn't learn much more than you did but it would seem one of these villains is the nephew of Prince Ratu. We returned the man to the palace yesterday as a courtesy."

"What is this to us?" I asked. "The prince should be pleased we spared his nephew's life."

"Prince Ratu is indeed pleased Elizabeth, though the man did lose a foot to an axe during the mêlée with your men. Ratu's nephew, his name is Mohamed Ishmael Ratu, swore before Allah on his hands and knees that your ships attacked his ships. He claims most fervently that you are bandits roaming the seas in search of slaves and plunder."

"That's utterly absurd," Atwood growled.

"Drivel to be sure. But look at this through Ratu's eyes, or rather through the eyes of his uncle the regent, Mandalika. You are foreigners who have come to the East Indies with four powerful ships, ships better suited for warfare and marauding than hauling freight. In his mind, your men have shown themselves to be unruly and have committed murder once already in his kingdom. He has no reason to trust you over Mohamed Ratu, a Muslim, a Javanese subject and a person of royal blood ‑ or leastwise it serves Mandalika's political purposes for others to believe these things to be so for now."

"Fuck the prince and his nephew," Atwood blurted out harshly. "Our lads, whatever they may have done that night at the tavern Ewoud paid dearly with their lives as did yours. Elizabeth, we should weigh anchor and leave this odious place. This port has an unpleasant odor about it that no longer agrees with me."

Dijksma shook his head. "Jacob, I strongly advise against such action. Mandalika has already sent gunboats out into the bay to prevent you from sailing off."

"We'll blow them all to hell!" I said testily.

"Yes, even with one less ship you have the power. And yet these gunboats - their crews are securing them together with heavy iron chains as we speak to form a barrier - could damage your ships, could cost you lives. There is risk. And even if you succeed in bludgeoning your way out of the bay, you'll never be able to trade in the East Indies again. Mandalika, though an unsavory fellow and a schemer, is also a practical man. I've taken the liberty of brokering a peaceful resolution to this crisis on your behalf - should you wish to take it."

"Oh?" I asked.

"Mandalika has promised to investigate this matter more thoroughly. He is suspicious of his great-nephew's story and well he should be for this is a man not known for his scruples. Mohamed Ratu involves himself in a variety of illicit enterprises. I'm confident, nay I can promise you, Mandalika will discover the truth in the end if he hasn't already. Mohamed Ratu will be disgraced, most likely severely punished, and you will all be absolved of any wrongdoing."

"How can you be so certain?" I asked.

"Because, when all is said and done, Mandalika must bend to Dutch will. He fears the Portuguese and he likes the generous tribute we Dutch pay him. He is also keenly aware that we could seize the young prince's throne by force at any time if we wished to."

"An investigation," Maurice observed, "could take weeks or longer."

"True. But we must take the long view my friend. You may remain in Banten until Mandalika completes his investigation - or - he will allow you to sail whenever you like provided you leave ten men behind to guarantee your return. One of your men must be an officer."

Atwood grunted. "Hostages? No."

"Think of them as guests of his majesty. I assure you, no harm will misbefall any man. Mandalika has already agreed you may leave your men in my care and custody and I give you my word they will be well-treated and returned to you unharmed."

"Ah, you want us to leave men behind," Atwood said. "Because you need us to sail immediately."

"Yes. The clock is ticking. Each day you delay your voyage to

Amsterdam costs the Company money. Forgive me for saying the obvious. Weeks have been squandered already because of your - I say it bluntly - ill-advised excursion to Macau. You must not delay your departure further. Truly, I have only your best interests at heart."

After Dijksma rowed back to shore, after a long and heated debate amongst my officers, we decided to accept Mandalika's offer. Atwood, Maurice and Shaw voted no. Efendi, Kinkae and Henry voted with me and in this instance, a majority vote was all I needed under our Ten Rules. Efendi upset us all however when he stubbornly insisted that he be one of the ten. We each took turns trying to dissuade him, but Efendi would not bend.

With our ships in good repair and fully reprovisioned, we said our farewells to Efendi and the nine volunteers as they piled into a Dutch boat with Dijksma at the tiller. We trusted Dijksma to keep his word and keep them safe. And after the Bantenese withdrew their blocking boats, after we raised our anchors and dropped our sails, with heavy hearts we pointed our ships towards Amsterdam.

Chapter Twenty-Two

Seven weeks after departing Santo Domingo, we landed in Dublin along the River Liffey in a cold, fine drizzle without any mishaps. Despite the dreary weather, I was overcome with joy as we stepped on Irish soil. Though I thought of the Caribbean as home, my Irish roots run deep.

Not far off was my stepfather's butcher's shop, the place where I was born. But painful memories prevented me from ever stopping by to see the old place again and so we hired the first coach and driver we could find to take us on to Westport. After a tedious trip of seven days, resting at small, unpleasant coach inns along the way, at guesthouses that were little more than hovels, I led the girls straight to *Banshee's Lament*, to Shaw's splendid tavern.

We entered the tavern hungry, filthy and chilled to the bone from the cold, relentless rains that had followed us from Dublin. We longed to enjoy a wholesome, hot meal next to a good fire and a hot bath. Tom Flynn, a bald, thin fellow with an easy smile and a neatly trimmed beard, the *Banshee's* barkeep and a loyal friend, dropped a clay pitcher of ale when he saw me walk through the tavern's double doors.

"Hello Tom," I said with a playful smile.

"Mary, but..."

"I know, I know."

"The saints preserve us," he said wide-eyed as he made the sign of the cross. "'Tis a miracle!"

"No miracle Tom. Just good luck. I'm hardly on good terms with the Almighty, leastwise not good enough to be the beneficiary of one of His miracles."

"Come my lady, we still keep the backroom closed to the public. I'll bring you a warm blanket and a hot supper and we can speak freely, away from prying eyes and ears. Ahem, what should I do with your two companions?"

Though my adopted brother Robert Shaw owned the tavern the backroom, a windowless private room with a long dining table, a stash of gold hidden inside a wall that not even my men or Elizabeth knew about and a secret unground passageway to the harbor, was reserved for me and for me alone.

"Tom," I said as I removed my gloves to brush the rain off my cloak, "this young lady is Ashaki and this is her sister Lololi. They are my friends and will join us. I expect you to treat them with courtesy and respect."

Flynn nodded uneasily as he grabbed a lantern and led us to the backroom. He removed a large, silver key from his vest pocket to unlock the room's heavy oak door, a door impenetrable to musket balls and resistant to fire, and waved us inside.

"I'll fetch some hot stew and warm bread to chase away the chill," he said. "Ale, beer or wine? Or something with a bit more kick?"

"I'll have whiskey Tom, thank you. The girls will have wine mixed with an equal measure of water. But first, where are my ships? We walked by the harbor and I did not see them."

"At sea."

"And my son James?"

"He's with Elizabeth."

"She took James with her?"

"Aye."

"They set off for the East Indies?"

"Aye. Your men sailed to Amsterdam first and from there they sailed to the Orient for the Dutch East India Company. Leastwise that was the plan as best I know."

"The Dutch East India Company? What is this?"

"I don't rightly know. A trading house of some sort, I think. 'Tis new."

"When did they depart?"

"I remember the day well. They left Westport the day after *Lá Bealtaine* in May of last year."

"Jacob is in command?"

"No, Elizabeth."

"Elizabeth?"

"Aye."

"Jacob and the others agreed to this?"

"I suppose so."

I loved Elizabeth. She was plucky, headstrong, full of Spanish fire and raw ambition but she was also very, very young.

"Did the Englishman Martin meet with Elizabeth or the others?"

"Aye, he was here briefly."

John Martin. Though Martin liked to pass himself off as a gentleman adventurer, he was in truth a provocateur and a spy. He had been one of Queen Elizabeth's most trusted captains and had been my ardent champion at Court. I knew he had close ties with the Dutch and reasoned that he must have been the one to introduce my men to this new trading company. I needed to find Martin, or travel to Amsterdam and introduce myself to the Dutch.

I left the twins in Westport in Flynn's good care before departing for London to look for my friend Martin. But before setting out, I introduced Ashaki to the master of a fishing trawler, a good man and a fine seaman named O'Neill who had sailed with me to the New World back in his youth before he chose to settle down. He agreed to take Ashaki on as his apprentice, to hone her skills at sea. Westport's little fishing trawlers never ventured out too far. As for Lololi, I handed her all my books and records. Flynn did a splendid job of running Shaw's tavern but was a terrible accountant. I charged Lololi with the task of finding whatever monies I might still have and learning the intricacies of the business as best she could. I put her talent for numbers to the test. The girls accepted their new assignments with cheerful hearts and vigor.

When I could not find Martin in London, I immediately caught a ferryboat to Amsterdam where six burly, Dutch soldiers surrounded me the moment I stepped off the boat and grabbed me roughly by the arms. They ignored my protests. They pulled me down the streets past scores of gawking men, women and children and took me to an abandoned building nearby, at one time used as a warehouse I think, where they dragged me up three levels of stairs and pushed me into a dark, cold room.

Two stout fellows bound my hands and then my legs to together. They tied me to an uncomfortable chair in the center of the room. As I took in my grim surroundings, I did my best to look unperturbed and unafraid.

Vagrants or perhaps ruffians working the alleys at night appeared to use the room for shelter. Off in one corner stood pieces of an armoire next to the charred remains of a small campfire. A shattered mirror hung lopsided against one wall. Trash and shards of glass from broken windows littered the floor. Directly above my head, through a gaping hole in the ceiling, I could see blue sky.

The Dutch left me tied to the chair within reach of a privy bucket, a loaf of bread and a jug of water. My predicament appeared bleak. But I did not panic. I would not give my captors the satisfaction. I whittled away the hours deep in thought, plotting my escape.

Chapter Twenty-Three

he return voyage to Europe was long and hard. Beset by one punishing gale after another, coming at us from all directions, the ships suffered tremendous wear and tear - ah, a clever new phrase I had overheard the sailors use - and we lost another dozen men. Some died from the sweating sickness after we landed at the Cape of Good Hope to replenish our provisions. Six men perished on the sands of West Africa when swarms of angry natives ambushed us while we looked for fresh water. Another two men disappeared one night off the small Dutch island of Gorée while we were refitting our battered ships. We lost two days lingering on the island in sweltering heat fruitlessly trying to find them.

During the last leg of our voyage our luck changed for the better. We enjoyed fair weather and calm seas. We suffered no meaningful mishaps. Eighteen months almost to the day after embarking upon our journey to the East, we slipped back into Amsterdam's crowded harbor flying the Company's bold colors. And though we had returned to Europe and were nearly home, no one was in a mood to celebrate after having lost so many friends and having left our fortunes on the bottom of the China Sea.

I savored the day as my men pulled on the oars. The sky was clear and bright. The air smelled of autumn. I needed to make arrangements with the Company to deliver our cargo and to be paid, money I'd need to fund a new expedition to the East Indies. I saw no need to bring Atwood or the others ashore with me.

For the first time in a long while I felt happy. But when I stepped off the longboat and up onto the pier, a squad of Dutch soldiers, a rabble of undisciplined ruffians, immediately grabbed me. They slipped a hood over my head, tied my hands behind my back and dragged me off. My men were powerless to stop them.

The soldiers pushed and prodded me down streets and alleys. They dragged me into a building, forced me up three levels of stairs and strapped me to a chair inside a drafty, cold room. I could hear water dripping down from a hole in the ceiling above my head. I heard the soldiers leave and lock the door behind them.

I did not know where I was or what to think. I had no plan. I was alone and afraid and without my tea, the *House's* special blend, demons - wrathful, vile creatures as black as night - are free to roam about in my dreams as I slumber.

Chapter Twenty-Four

After a long and uncomfortable night tied to a rickety, old chair, a stocky little fellow with a red goatee stepped out of the shadows holding a pewter candlestick holder in one hand and a thick wad of papers in the other. The man came dressed in a fashionable slashed doublet in blue satin, in red silk stockings and breeches the color of cream. He wore various gaudery accoutrements to show-off his wealth. He had fastened his cloak with a long-stemmed, gold tulip. He wore fancy gold cuff boutons in the French style on his sleeves. A gold pocket watch on a long chain of gold dangled from his belt. The man reeked of money and self-importance.

He set his candle on the floor, removed his black copotain hat trimmed with a long, black feather and nodded. "I am delighted to meet you at last Mary," the man said in good English. "My name is Houtman, Jan de Houtman."

Certain there had been some misunderstanding, I smiled sweetly at the Dutchman.

"You are Lady Mary of Westport, also known as Captain Mary or Captain Bloody Mary?"

"You have me at a disadvantage, sir. You know my name and title, but I know you not."

"Patience. All shall be made clear. Now again I ask: are you Captain Mary of Westport?"

"Some call me Captain Mary or Lady Mary, aye."

"Very fine, very fine. We begin with honesty."

"I have no reason to lie. And you are?"

"I am Houtman as I have said."

"Why have you kidnapped me Meester Houtman?"

"Kidnapped? No, no, not kidnapped. You're being detained for questioning and I am your inquisitor."

"Questioning?"

Houtman tucked his hat underneath his arm and started flipping through the wad of papers in his hand. "You own four ships, yes? Let me see. Ah, here we are: *Ghostrunner*, *Cerberus*, *Achilles* and *Homeward Bound*. You employ or are otherwise associated with one Spanish woman named Elizabeth Cortés, a Scot named Jacob Atwood, an Irish fellow named Michael MacGyver and one Frenchman, a Blackamoor, probably from the Americas originally who calls himself Maurice. Correct?"

The Dutchman knew the names of my officers holding captaincies but, except for *Cerberus*, not the names of my ships. I did not recognize the other three. Then again, Flynn had told me that Elizabeth had purchased three new ships to replace *Phantom* and *Diablo*.

"You appear to know a little something about me. Yes, I know these men. I know the young woman too. What of it?"

"Ohhh, I know more than a little about you madam. The papers I hold contain quite a few particulars on you. We Dutch are meticulous about gathering information on people of interest, people who might someday be useful to us - or become our enemies. Information bestows power after all."

"I pray you tell me sir, who do you represent?"

"'Tis no secret. I represent the Company, the *Vereenigde Oostindische Compagnie*, the United East India Company, as I suspect you already know."

"I know very little about this enterprise and I know nothing about you. Why would I? As I have said, we've never met."

"Come, come dear lady. I'm not one for playing games of cat-and-mouse. You know me because you sent your factors to Amsterdam in the spring of last year to broker a deal with the Company on your behalf. I facilitated the transaction myself directly with your officers."

"Facilitated?"

"Ah, one of those new modern words. I helped consummate the

contract between us."

"I know nothing about any contract. I've committed no crimes against the United Provinces or against this Dutch company of yours. I'm no enemy of the Dutch. If anything, I am an ally. Truly, I don't understand why you've brought me to this wretched place."

"We shall see. Why now have you chosen to visit our fine city?"

"My sole purpose in Amsterdam is to find my ships and men. I was told an Englishman named Captain John Martin, a mutual acquaintance between us I am guessing, may have introduced my companions to you and the Company. I understand they sailed to the East Indies. I'm merely here to find my friends."

"I'm acquainted with Martin and it was Martin who did indeed arrange the introductions. According to my sources, including the very Martin you speak of, you perished at sea off the coast of Florida some two and a half years ago."

"Plainly your sources are mistaken."

"So it would seem. Imagine our astonishment when you magically appeared in Westport several weeks ago alive and well."

"Ah, you have eyes and ears in Ireland. I'm not surprised, but I've made no secret of my return."

"The Company has resources everywhere. Did you contrive your own death in furtherance of this illicit scheme?"

"Mr. Houtman, this interrogation becomes tedious. What illicit scheme are you referring to?"

"A scheme to deceive the Company of course."

"For what purpose?"

"To cheat the Company out of monies owed."

"How ridiculous. Who has filled your head with such nonsense?"

"Then tell me."

"Tell you what?"

"Tell me about Florida."

I gladly recounted my tale to Houtman, beginning with the Tequesta fishermen who saved me. I told him about Schmidt and the auction blocks in Trinidad, about my time in Veracruz and my escape to Havana in a small lugger with the help of Yanga's men, though I saw no reason to mention the twins or my promise to Aminatu.

"A fascinating if preposterous tale Mary," Houtman declared after I had finished. "You, a white woman, sold off as a slave with blacks? Ha! You have a lively imagination. Well, no matter. To the business at hand. All this time I thought I was dealing with Elizabeth Cortés but now I understand the truth. In reality I've been dealing with you and you, my dear lady, owe the Company substantial sums of money."

"My story is true and I owe the Company nothing."

The Dutchman leaned down and came nose-to-nose with me, close enough for me to smell the licorice on his breath. "I beg to differ," he said with a twisted, arrogant smile. "As you say, this sordid matter between us is becoming tedious. You are keeping me from a hot breakfast and my warm, cozy bed. My mood turns foul. If you fail to make good on your obligations to the Company, you'll suffer terribly for it. Ohhh, indeed you will. That much I can promise you. The men I've brought with me are not known for their tenderness."

I narrowed my eyes and clenched my teeth. I stared long and hard at the Dutchman without blinking. My menacing demeanor had the desired effect. I decided to strike when Houtman hesitated, when he returned my gaze with uncertainty.

"You wish to threaten me? You think you know who I am because of a few notes scribbled across some scraps of paper? You think you hold the upper hand because you have me bound to a chair in this fucking shithole?"

"I am the interrogator and I shall ask the questions, not you," Houtman interrupted with a forced smile.

"Shut your hole and listen," I commanded. "Ask Martin who I am. Ask him about the Twins and the *Síol Faolcháin*. I am the slayer of monsters and the destroyer of clans. I am the bitch men dread. I was a friend to a queen until her death. I sailed with Drake in '88 against the Spanish Armada. Drake sent my little squadron north to Dunkerque to support Nassau's thirty flyboats during the battle. The following year I -."

"If you had sailed with Admiral van Nassau," Houtman

interrupted, "I'd certainly know it."

"It appears your records are incomplete Houtman, which has led you to an incorrect portrait of me. Nassau stole two prizes from me, the galleons *San Mateo* and the *San Felipe*. Ask him. He'll disagree about the theft but he'll remember me. Now as I was saying, I sailed with Drake again in '89 when the English Counter-Armada invaded Spain and I sailed with Drake again in '95 when he invaded the West Indies. Martin was there, he'll verify the truth of what I say. I've ended the life of many a man. More men than I can count. No, you don't know who I am for if you did, you'd shit your breeches and run. Harm me and my wrath, even from the grave, will be swift and sure. My brothers will not rest until they find you, as far as into your warm, cozy bed if needs be. That much I can promise you."

Houtman turned pale. He took a step backwards and stood motionless for a moment to collect his thoughts before scampering off. He did not go far for I could hear him questioning another in a room close by.

Chapter Twenty-Five

When someone behind me removed my hood the next morning, I found Houtman standing in front of me holding a candle in one hand and a wad of papers in the other. "Welcome back to Amsterdam, Elizabeth," he said with a grim smile.

"How dare you!" I shouted angrily, still half asleep.

"How dare I? No, how dare you! You've plotted against the Company woman. You've betrayed the United Provinces. Did you truly imagine you could swindle the VOC?"

"That's a lie," I said as I thoughtlessly lunged at the Dutchman. A pair of strong arms behind me pushed me back into the chair.

"A lie?"

"Yes. We've returned to Amsterdam in good faith with six hundred tons of spices."

"True, but you lost *Achilles* and her cargo. I've read Ewoud Dijksma's report. You sailed to Macau without authority and sold two hundred tons of the Company's spices to finance your own illicit, private deal with the Chinese. Your astonishing stupidity and greed have caused the Company significant losses. We demand you compensate us at the current market price for the spices you sold. In addition, you'll cover our lost profits on eight hundred tons caused by your tardy return and you'll pay the Company a substantial fine as punishment for your disobedience and dishonesty. You'll make the Company whole and then some."

"What lost profits? The Company hoodwinked the Portuguese and stole those spices!"

"How we acquired the spices is irrelevant."

"I pledged three ships. I've returned with three ships. I've honored the contract between us."

"I beg to differ. You embarked upon this enterprise with four ships. The contract between us was exclusive. You knew this. You cannot sail for yourselves whilst employed by the Company."

"I disagree."

"Do you now? Well, disagree all you like. Disagree to your heart's content as the English poet Shakespeare might say. Your refusal to accept responsibility for your folly only makes this sordid business between us worse."

Houtman was being difficult. I fidgeted in my chair. I had no cards to play, no leverage. I longed to sit back on a comfortable couch and relax with a cup of my strong, black tea.

"I will," I finally offered meekly after a long pause, "make good on all your losses. But first you must let me go."

"How will you pay? You're ruined. As we speak, the Company is confiscating your ships and incarcerating your men until we decide what to do with you."

"No, no, no! Stop! Please, please stop! I can make things right. I can, I can. I swear it."

"I trusted you, Elizabeth. I vouched for you. I walked out on a limb for you with my superiors - with men who were against hiring a woman, a Spaniard at that, and who distrust the Irish. You Spanish, always such a troublesome, villainous people and the bumkin Irish, well..."

I couldn't stop myself from shaking. I couldn't help myself and started crying, something Mary never would have done in my predicament. I felt ashamed at my own weakness.

"Please have pity," I pleaded.

"You'll receive no pity from me. Now I wish to know what role Mary played in all of this?"

"Mary? Mary's dead."

"Tell me about Mary. Tell me how she died."

"What? Why? We lost Mary in a storm in the Americas long before you and I met. What does it matter now?"

"Humor me."

"Very well," I said and answered Houtman's questions.

The Dutchman seemed satisfied with my answers and then began pacing around the room for a time as if he was working a problem. "Did Ewoud not warn you against sailing to Macau?"

"Yes, yes, it's, it's true," I mumbled in-between my fits and tears. "Ewoud was against our sailing to Macau. In hindsight I admit the voyage to China now looks like a mistake. But we were betrayed and but for that betrayal the Company would be whole and I'd have a fortune in luxury goods. Ewoud promised he would include all the good work we have done in his report."

"Ewoud is a fair and decent man. He kept his word to you. This is why you are still breathing. For the life of me I don't know what to do with you."

"I beg you, be merciful."

"We Dutch are an exceptional breed of people. Though we are a small nation, we've beaten all the great kingdoms on land and at sea. Around the globe, Dutch supremacy and Dutch prestige are on the rise. We are entering our very own golden age. The Company however is still young and fragile. To increase our own power and prestige, we must rely on outsiders, on mercenaries like yourself. We cannot afford to appear weak or indecisive. If we are to succeed, we must build and nurture a strong reputation, a reputation to inspire respect and loyalty from those who would serve us and strike fear into the hearts and minds of any who would oppose us."

I stared blankly at Houtman, he sounded like a military man on campaign. "What are you talking about?" I asked in barely a whisper. My throat was parched. My lips were cracked. I badly needed to piss. "The Company is a trading enterprise, not an army. We've lost a bit of cargo to pirates which I've promised to make good on. I don't understand the rest."

"Nonsense. You understand full well. Dijksma is a part of the Company is he not?"

"Yes."

"He arranged for the purchase of the spices?"

"Yes."

"So, the Company does engage in trade. But did you not also help Dijksma with his invasion plans for Ambon?"

"Well, yes. I suppose."

"At his behest did you not sink a Portuguese freighter in Ambon's harbor?"

"Ye, yes."

"Well, there you have it then, war. Is it not fair to say then that Dijksma is more than just a merchant? That he is a soldier too?"

"I, I suppose so."

"You seem to think the breach of a merchantry contract between you and the Company is a piddling matter. I assure you it is not. The Company is more, far more, than a simple trading enterprise. The Company is building its own navy. The Company is recruiting men for its own army. The Company is appointing its own administrators to oversee conquered territories. We do all of this with the blessings of our Stadholder, Maurice of Nassau. You are one of the Company's soldiers and you have disobeyed your orders."

"Orders?"

"Yes, orders. I must leave you now. I'll return in a day or two. You should use this time wisely to reflect on your grievous transgressions, of which there are many."

"What will become of me?"

"Ah that is the question of the moment, a question yet searching for an answer."

"What do you intend to do with my men?"

"I must confess, I do not yet know. We must make an example of you certainly for all those who would follow after you and sail for the VOC. Something more than a light touch is needed here. A strong statement, one without equivocation is required."

I pulled against the ropes, a silly thing to do. I lowered my head in shame and soiled myself. Houtman smirked and then abruptly left, leaving me to wallow in my melancholy, leaving me to suffer my heart-wrenching despair alone and in the dark. He did not go far for I could hear him questioning another in a room nearby. I supposed he had Atwood or Maurice tied to a chair like me.

Twenty-Six

An hour passed before Houtman returned to ask me curious questions about Elizabeth. I freely answered his questions. He had his men to untie me. He had them bring me a cot, a pillow and a blanket before he turned on his heels and left. He did not go far for I could hear him again questioning another in a room close by.

When he returned a few days later his demeanor seemed far less hostile - and he brought me gifts, a peace offering. He handed me a covered pot of hot vegetable soup, a loaf of freshly baked bread wrapped in a warm cloth and a bottle of cold beer. I quickly devoured it all.

"The dispute between us," he began with forced resolve, "is a civil matter concerning a breach of contract, not a criminal one. My words the other day perhaps came off a bit too harshly. I was threatening legal recourse, not bodily harm. We are the Company after all, not murderous villains. We do not kill for money."

"I'm glad to hear it," I said indifferently but in truth I was relieved. "So many these days seem less squeamish about killing, especially for wealth. You'd be wise to let me go."

"All in good time. But first, I have in my hand a report from my man in Java delivered to me just a few weeks ago. Your arrival in Amsterdam at this moment in time is most fortuitous. Let me tell you a story, a sad story of incompetence and betrayal. Let me tell you what your men did to incur the Company's wrath."

I listened carefully as Houtman read a report to me from someone named Ewoud Dijksma. The document was a dozen pages long and rich in detail. Elizabeth had led my ships and men from

Amsterdam to Africa, to Java, to the Spice Islands and then all the way to China. Her audacity impressed me. But when Houtman explained the reasons for the Company's displeasure, I understood full well. When he informed me of the loss of *Achilles*, when he told me that MacGyver and all his crew had perished in a battle at sea with brigands, it was if someone had ripped my heart out of my chest. I lost all focus and wept.

Houtman handed me his handkerchief and waited patiently for me to regain my composure. Once I dried my tears and caught my breath, his men escorted me to a modest hostel a few blocks away. They walked me up four levels of stairs to an apartment with several agreeable rooms. I had an ample fireplace, chairs, a comfortable bed and a water closet. I even had a large washtub to bathe in. A basket of fruit, cheeses and fresh biscuits sat on a dining table along with wine and beer in corked, long-necked bottles, a new type of bottle I'd never seen before. Houtman's men locked the door behind them after they left me alone in the dark to wallow in my grief.

A day went by, then two and then another and though my rooms were clean and comfortable I was nevertheless a prisoner. Other than a Geneva Bible printed in Dutch, I had no books to read. I had no visitors to talk to, not even Houtman. Each day two guards with ne'er a word to say between them brought me food, more wine, beer, clean spring water and fresh clothing. They kept my door locked and stood vigil quietly outside in the hallway. Another three days went by with always the same routine and I began wondering if the Dutch were trying to kill me with boredom. I considered breaking a window and escaping but my room sat four stories above the street.

And then on the morning of the seventh day I heard a soft rapping at my door. I was surprised to find the door unlocked. I was even more surprised by my visitor.

"My God, John Martin!" I blurted out when I saw the Englishman standing before me, smiling. I threw my arms around Martin's neck. I kissed him wildly on his cheeks and forehead.

"Mary, Mary, Mary," he said and held me. "What a story I hear you have to tell."

"Houtman? Houtman must have sought you out."

"He did. You put the fear of God into that poor fellow let me tell you. May I come in?"

"Of course, by all means, please."

After Martin removed his distinctive broadbrimmed hat trimmed with an exceedingly long ostrich feather, the only fashionable thing about him, and stepped into my room, I stuck my head into the hallway to take a quick peek around. I saw no guards.

"The Dutch have left," Martin said and helped himself to an apple. "You are no longer being detained. You are free to leave whenever you please. You are now a guest, not a prisoner of the VOC."

"Thank you."

"You can thank yourself. Houtman needed no persuasion from me to set you free. After speaking to me and conferring with Admiral van Nassau, who serves Breda as governor now, together with a few others, he knows your story to be true. So, I hear the sea took you, found you altogether disagreeable and spat you back out!"

I smiled. "An amusing way to describe my close brush with death."

"Though Houtman told me what you told him about the storm, Florida Indians, Trinidad, your time in Veracruz as a slave - dear God - and your remarkable escape in a small lugger to Havana, I'd like to hear your story firsthand, from start to finish. We have plenty of time. No need to spare any details. I want to hear it all. And then we must talk about your future."

I obliged Martin gladly. I handed him a bottle of beer, a tasty beverage brewed in Leuven, as we took our seats at the table. He produced a flask of good whiskey instead and filled two glasses. I began my tale with the night I was swept overboard off the coast of Florida and ended my tale with Amsterdam. I hid nothing from Martin. There was no need. I trusted him with my life. I even told him about the twins and my promise to Aminatu.

Martin sighed after I had finished and refilled our glasses with the last of the whiskey. "Remarkable, Mary. I was deeply saddened when I heard of your end. The death of our good Queen Bess last year was an equally heavy blow. I do not know this Salamanca fellow. I've never heard of Francisco Matosa, but I do know something of Gaspar Yanga. He enjoys quite a reputation. By God, he has caused the Spanish a pain or two over the years and the Spanish have honored him by placing an impressive bounty on his head. How he has survived this long I do not know."

"Yanga has lived in the wildlands of New Spain, or what he and his people prefer calling México, for thirty years and has thousands of loyal followers. He's a clever, resourceful fellow and was very good to me."

"Now there's a man I'd like to meet. And you intend to return to the province of Veracruz to help Yanga and his runaways out of New Spain, out of México?"

"No, Yanga has no desire to leave México whilst there are slaves to free. I must return for Aminatu and her people."

"I see. Well, had anyone else told me this fantastical tale of yours Mary, I would have beaten them with a hickory switch for their deviousness and sent them on their way. I've never known anyone with better luck than you."

"I'm blessed to be sure."

"Yes. I was sorry to hear about MacGyver and his crew. Michael was a good man."

"Aye, Michael was a good man. He was one of the first to affix his star to mine. I shall miss him dearly. Are you in the service of King James now?"

"I do indeed serve his majesty."

"Still up to your old tricks then?"

"I do enjoy my work."

"You've never been one for small talk John. You now know my story and I know better than to ask you about your own adventures. You've always been, and I suspect shall always be, a man of many secrets. As I have said, I looked for you in London before setting out for Amsterdam. I hope I've not inconvenienced you much."

"Not in the least. I happened to be in Zeeland as a guest of the

Dutch navy."

"How interesting. Tell me though, why have you come to Amsterdam?"

"To repay a debt to an old friend."

"Hmmm. I'm sorry to have involved you in this untidy business."

"My work here is a far easier task than the day you stormed Belém Tower."

"Lisbon was a long time ago."

"Seems like yesterday."

"You mentioned my future. There is more to this visit than a simple reunion of good friends, yes?"

"You still possess that wonderfully astute mind. Yes, we have weighty matters to discuss. But first, I have a gift for you."

"Oh?"

"By remarkable happenstance your ships sailed into port hours after your own arrival. Jacob and Maurice are waiting in a building nearby. Shall I go and fetch them?"

Jacob, Maurice and I stood in a circle locked arm-in-arm. We kissed and wept and held each other for a very long time. I suddenly felt lightheaded and needed to sit. Drinking whiskey on an empty stomach with Martin hadn't helped, neither did my fading youth and diminishing stamina.

"As John led us here," Atwood said while pouring me a glass of spring water, "he told us the short version of your story. Incredible, truly incredible. We searched for you for days after you fell overboard. And now here we are, nearly three years later, reunited in Amsterdam of all places."

I took a long sip of water before speaking. "And I know something of your story too Jacob. A man named Houtman read a report to me from some fellow named Dijksma. Do you know this Dijksma?"

"Aye, we do."

I nodded. "But there's more to tell, I think. We have much to discuss. What of my son James, is he well?"

Maurice took my hand and smiled. "He is Mary. James has blossomed into a tall, strong lad and is every inch a mariner. You'll be very proud."

"No doubt, no doubt I will be. And Elizabeth, where is she?"

Martin cleared his throat. "Houtman still has Elizabeth in custody," he answered. "Which brings us to next steps."

"Next steps?" I asked, confused.

"Yes. The offer is simple really. Unlike their French neighbors, the Dutch relish simplicity. The Company has decided to entrust a man named Matelieff with a powerful fleet. I met the admiral the other day. He strikes me as a capable commander. He is also one of the prestigious Gentlemen Seventeen, a member of the Company's Board of Directors. He intends to sail from Holland to the Indonesian Archipelago in the spring. His mission is one of trade, or so the Dutch claim. It's all nonsense of course."

"Nonsense?"

"I'm not privy to Matelieff's specific mission, but it's easy to imagine his true objective is the Portuguese stronghold at Malacca. Why else would he set off with ten war galleons, a new heavy frigate that is very fast I hear and six companies of professional soldiers - fourteen hundred men in all? Certainly not for trade."

"Ten galleons?"

"Yes, an impressive array of naval power by any measure."

"And what is this to me?"

"Well, the Dutch -."

"John," I interrupted. "Before you say more, I have no interest in sailing with the Dutch to fight some war for them half a world away."

"Mary," Atwood interjected and took my hand. "Before John explains the Dutch offer, there is something you must know which may hold sway over the decision you must make. We had to leave Mustafa and nine of our lads behind in Java. The Crown Prince of Banten, a boy named Ratu, is holding them."

"What? Mustafa and the others are prisoners?"

"No, more like hostages to guarantee our return."

"Why? Why does this boy prince want you to return to Java? Houtman made no mention of this to me."

"That's because Houtman doesn't know. Dijksma had already sent his report back to Amsterdam with a Dutch merchantman before we learned of a certain, ahem, situation."

"What situation?"

"When we reached Banten, we turned our prisoners over to Dijksma. One of those men happens to be the prince's nephew, a fellow named Mohamed Ishmael Ratu. During questioning Mohamed Ratu swore to the prince that we are the pirates and attacked his ships. It would seem the prince, or rather his uncle, a fellow named Mandalika and the kingdom's regent, was suspicious of Mohamed Ratu's story and ordered the minister of justice to fully investigate the matter. Mandalika forbid us from leaving Banten before the minister completed his investigation - unless we agreed to leave ten men behind to guarantee our return."

"Since when have we ever agreed to leave men behind?" I asked crossly, too crossly, and looked away. Efendi would trade his life for mine and I could do no less for him.

"They're all in Dijksma's care Mary and Dijksma is a good an honorable man. He's a man we can trust."

Martin, not one to show emotion, affectionately caressed my cheek with the back of his hand. "Mary, I owe you my life. I am and shall always be your humble servant and your very dear friend. But you, we, must one way or another make amends with the Dutch."

"Aye. What, what pray tell is this Dutch offer?"

"Your men and ships, Elizabeth too, will be returned to you and all your debts and any grievances against you will be forgiven, a full pardon if you will, provided you agree to sail with Matelieff in the spring."

"I knew it. Houtman intends to use us as an auxiliary squadron to support this Dutch campaign."

"That's the gest of things, yes."

"And if I refuse?"

"The Dutch will not keep your men, but they will keep your ships."

"Fuck..." I whispered under my breath, the only word that came to mind. After my last voyage with Drake in late '95, after settling my feud with the *Síol Faolcháin* shortly thereafter, I thought I had made peace with the world. I thought I was done with war. I thought I had retaken control of my own destiny. I shook my head in disgust at the reality.

BOOK II

Mary & Fùchóu
(复仇)

Chapter Twenty-Seven

Late Winter, 1605

With the rising sun comes the slaughter. Filth defiles hallowed ground. Blood corrupts good water. Tongues of flame reach out to scorch the very heavens. Surely God must weep at the barbarity of man. The dead - indifferent - move on, leaving the wreckage behind for the living.

New beginnings. Elizabeth.

As if holding court, I sat on a chair on top of a box my brothers had placed in the middle of the room earlier. The woman I had adopted as my sister after fleeing from her father stared at me in wide-eyed disbelief. Elizabeth dropped to her knees before me. She wept and groveled at my feet.

My heart broke when I realized how gaunt and frail she was. Her beautiful dark eyes had lost their luster. Her luxurious black hair was now a tangled mess with flecks of straw and bits of dirt. She looked like a street urchin in her soiled, ill-fitting clothing.

I had a sudden urge to lift her up, to hold her in my arms and wipe away her tears, to tell her that all would be forgiven, that all would be well again. But the terrible urge to strike her down was just as great. I remained coldly seated on my makeshift throne with Atwood standing rigidly on my right and Maurice on my left.

"Rise," I said sternly.

Elizabeth struggled to her feet. She searched my face with the saddest eyes I'd ever seen and stretched her arms out taut, reaching for me, begging me to embrace her. But I made no gesture of friendship or welcome. I offered no pity. I resisted all temptation to show her the least bit of kindness.

Her lips quivered as she stood before me. Her shoulders shook. After she used her shirtsleeve to wipe the tears and snot from her face, she let her arms dangle awkwardly by her side.

"Ha, ha, how, how," she asked, choking back her tears, "how did you survive Mary?"

I met her woeful deportment with a scowl. "I shall ask the questions Elizabeth and you shall do the answering. Jacob, would you see to Elizabeth's comfort and bring her a chair. Maurice, would you be so good as to fetch my lady a glass of wine mixed with an equal measure of water."

Elizabeth took her seat across from me. She took a sip of wine and glanced down at the floor to avoid my gaze.

"Elizabeth, look at me!" I commanded. "Not long ago a man named Houtman read a report to me from a man named Dijksma. Houtman graciously provided a copy of this report to me yesterday, leastwise those portions that pertain to us. I've heard from Jacob and Maurice already. I've spoken with Rob, Henry and Kinkae too. Now I would hear from you."

"I, I, I don't understand," she replied nervously while scratching at her arms. "What can I possibly say that you haven't heard already? I'm so very, very tired Mary. I wish to close my eyes and rest."

"Tired? You've been languishing inside a Dutch jail for nearly two weeks. How can you be tired? We leave for Ireland in the morning. You'll have plenty of time to rest and reflect during the voyage home."

"The Dutch are releasing us?"

"Yes. Why are you scratching at yourself? Do you have a rash, some infection? Should I call for Stachel?"

Elizabeth cocked her head to one side as if embarrassed. She slipped her hands underneath her thighs.

"Elizabeth, answer me."

"I, I'm fine," she said, forcing a faint, pathetic smile. She looked at me briefly before turning her head away to face the wall.

"Good, so speak. I know about your father's death and I am sorry for it. I know you and your brothers struggled in the Caribbean after he passed. I know you had hard choices to make. You may begin your story in Westport when you first decided to sail to Amsterdam to meet with the Company."

Elizabeth took another sip of wine before speaking. She took a deep breath. I noted her peculiar scratching, her trembling hands and occasional slurred speech. I saw the listlessness in her eyes and her lack of vigor as she recounted her tale. She talked at some length, rambling almost incoherently at times, telling me nothing I didn't already know.

Shaw and Kinkae had told me about Elizabeth's persistent anxiousness, of her odd behavior during their voyage back to Amsterdam. They had told me about her fleeting moments of joy followed by sudden, inexplicable spells of severe depression. She had shut herself away in her cabin they said and reluctantly informed me that she had forsaken her responsibilities of command. Henry had declined to raise a contrary word against Elizabeth when I had asked him for his account. I could not fault his loyalty and did not press him. Atwood and Maurice, who had seen very little of Elizabeth during the long voyage home, were unaware of her troubling behavior.

I had seen such symptoms before. Opium was nearly always the culprit.

"I think I have," I said, "a better understanding of matters now. I understand the reasons why you thought it best to sail to the East Indies. I might have done the same. Had you sailed back to Europe after taking delivery of the spices in Banda, you would have had a prosperous, good run. You would have returned with all four ships and most of your men. This voyage to Macau perplexes me though. Your decision to stand and fight thirty ships puzzles me."

"Well, I -."

I put my finger to my lips. "Hush… I'm in no mood to hear more about Macau, Chinamen, or pirates, leastwise not yet. But tell me Elizabeth. Have you perchance tasted the tears of the poppy during your time in the East?"

"You mean opium?"

"Aye, I mean opium."

"No."

"Nooo?"

"No. Well, I, ahem, well perhaps a little Mary. I find a wee bit of opium helps me sleep."

"No matter. There is a room, a comfortable room, next to mine prepared for you. You'll find a hot bath scented with fennel and bay waiting for you You'll find fresh clothing. Maurice, would you see Elizabeth safely to her chambers."

"Certainly," Maurice replied.

"Go and rest now Elizabeth," I said. "Maurice, once Elizabeth is settled, please secure the door to her room and then gather the others for me."

Elizabeth turned to look at me before following Maurice out the door. "Mary, I'm terribly, terribly sorry about Michael and all the others. Men betrayed us. I'm not to blame! Do not think poorly of me, I beg you."

"You are very young and inexperienced Elizabeth. Perhaps I am to blame, not you. Perhaps I expected too much. But do not suppose I am satisfied with all your answers. You and I still have much to discuss."

Atwood laid a hand on my shoulder after Maurice led Elizabeth away. "What do you intend to do Mary?"

"What do *we* intend to do Jacob. She is after all one of us. We do not abandon our own."

"Opium, eh? I did not see that."

After climbing aboard *Ghostrunner*, I hurried over to James when I saw him and wrapped him in my arms. Maurice had described him fairly. He had grown tall and lean and was blossoming into a fine, fine man. I made the rounds with all the men, shaking hands, exchanging hugs and tears and kisses and then I went below and found Elizabeth's stash of opium hidden away in dozens of little bottles. I pitched all of it out the stern windows. And when she stepped aboard, I searched her too and found two more bottles sewn inside her coat and tossed those over the side as well.

"You've let yourself become a slave to this poison Elizabeth. I found the other bottles. I shall free you from this evil my love - even if it kills one of us."

"Where's Jacob and Maurice?" she asked indifferently. "I do not see their ships."

"I've sent them south to Boulogne."

"For what purpose?"

"Kinkae," I called out, ignoring her, "please show Elizabeth to her new quarters."

I restricted Elizabeth to a tiny cabin, a space little more than a broom closet, next to my great cabin as we started our easy passage back to Westport. She endured great pain during the twelve-day voyage. I rarely left her side. She suffered from the sweats, from cold spells, tremors, hallucinations, vomiting and often felt severe aches in her muscles, joints and bones. At times she lost control of both her bladder and her bowels. During the worst of it, Stachel persuaded me to administer small amounts of laudanum to ease her discomfort a little.

After we reached Westport, I gave the men two months' liberty, give or take, and put *Ghostrunner* into drydock to be overhauled and reconfigured. I wanted to increase her speed in preparation for the long voyage ahead. Between the gold Yanga had given me, the gold I had hidden away at the tavern in Westport and monies the Dutch had paid me - oh yes, they paid me the commission due on six hundred tons of spices and paid me for the destruction of one Portuguese carrack - I had enough to send the men on their way with a little something in their pockets. I still needed money for the ships and I'd need more money later to provision them.

Though I lamented her lack of speed, *Ghostrunner* was an exceptionally fine warship by any measure and *Cerberus* was a match and then some for most vessels. But *Homeward Bound* was too small for war and this is why I had sent Atwood off to Boulogne with a skeleton crew before he returned home to Scotland.

Prior to departing the Netherlands, I had summoned Messrs. Ink and Blot, the Dutch and French marine architects renowned for their bold ideas in shipbuilding, the same two men who had once transformed *Phantom* into a marvel and had built *Ghostrunner* for Elizabeth, to Amsterdam. Unbeknownst to Elizabeth, or my brothers, some years back I had purchased a modest shipyard in Boulogne and had made the two architects my junior partners. When we met in Amsterdam, the two men eagerly agreed to sell *Homeward Bound* and give me another, something more to my liking, and agreed to refit *Cerberus* while Maurice and his crew spent their days of leisure in France - all at no cost to me as recompense for having foolishly accepted commissions from Elizabeth, money they had no right to take even though they imagined me dead. My partners were lucky I didn't take a pound of flesh as well.

While my men travelled home to friends and family, with my ships laid-up in drydock, I did not sit idly by in Westport. I had my Blackamoors and my Carib with me. I had Ashaki and Lololi. And I had a map.

Lololi shook her head as she sat next to me on a stool at the bar, as one of Flynn's barmaids brought us each a bowl of hot porridge, flavored with a dusting of cinnamon and sugar. "Mary, you're nearly broke. I found only one account with four hundred, twenty-one pounds sterling and eight shillings."

"And eight shillings you say?" I asked, amused.

"Yes, Mary, only eight."

"Well, 'tis not the best news but thank you Lololi," I said while pouring her a cup of tea, an expensive luxury few Irish have tasted, tea Elizabeth had brought back from China. "This," I continued as I flipped through ledger pages, "is wonderful work Lololi. From this day forward, I am entrusting you with all my books and records - that is if you want the job."

Lololi had organized, corrected errors and had made sense out of a dizzying array of crude, nearly illegible notations scribbled across the margins of each page. Her eye for detail, her accuracy and thoroughness impressed me.

"Yes Mary, thank you!" Lololi exclaimed with a gleam in her eye.

Then Ashaki, wearing a black skull cap pulled down over her ears and dressed in seaman's rugged clothing, with a dagger tucked inside her belt and a gold ring pinned to one ear, strolled into the tavern with long, confident strides. She made a formidable sight.

"Old Tom Flynn tells me Ashaki," I said while pouring her a cup of tea as she plopped down on a stool next to me, "that Master O'Neill told him that you gave a splendid account of yourself at sea."

"Master O'Neill is a wonderful tutor Mary," Ashaki replied. "His men treated me with patience and kindness."

"No doubt they did. No one in Westport will trouble you girls as you are under my care and protection. Even so, the Irish have never tolerated foreigners well so do not stray too far. I do have men quietly keeping an eye out for you."

And then Kinkae strolled into the tavern. "I've found a suitable yacht for hire Mary, a forty-foot sloop," he said as he walked over to us and helped himself to my tea.

The girls looked Kinkae up and down with curiosity.

"Ladies go and pack your knapsacks with warm clothing along with your foul-weather gear. We're going on a little adventure."

"We sail for México?" Ashaki asked.

"No, my dearest," I answered and chuckled. "Not in a forty-foot sloop. We sail for the *Na Sailtí*, the Saltee Islands, two small, islands just off Kilmore Quay between Waterford and Wexford on the other side of Ireland. I realize these names and places mean nothing to you now, but I expect intelligent girls with ambition to find themselves a good map and learn these things for themselves. Ladies this is Kinkae, he is one of mine. Kinkae, meet Ashaki and Lololi."

Kinkae offered the girls a wide grin. "New grist for the mill, eh Mary?"

"Quite so."

Lololi looked at me aghast. "This man's black," she whispered into my ear.

"Is he now?" I whispered back. "I hadn't noticed."

"You keep slaves aboard your ships?"

"God forbid no. I employ men. I employ men of skill and talent and young ladies too it would seem."

"He's a free man?"

"We need not whisper," I said out loud and laughed. "Aye, Kinkae is a free man. He is my friend and my brother and he is one of my officers. Kinkae and his men were once slaves. On this little trip of ours, you'll meet a man named Henry too, a Carib Indian."

"You have blacks and Indians in your crew?" Ashaki asked nonplussed.

"I do indeed. They've sailed with me for years. I even have Cimarron and a few Spaniards sailing with me, including a woman named Elizabeth, whom you'll meet soon enough. But Ashaki, Lololi, I do have sad news I am compelled to share with you now. I'll keep my promise. I will return to México for your mother and father and for all those under Salamanca's cruel dominion who wish their freedom. But I have urgent matters to deal with in the East Indies first before I can return to the West Indies. Truly I am sorry my loves."

"I'll be sailing with you Mary," Ashaki said, pausing to brush a tear from her cheek.

"And me," Lololi added.

"Girls, the journey I must make is much longer, much harder and more dangerous than any voyage to the Americas. You'll be safer and far more comfortable here in Westport. But let us put this matter aside for now. I need time to weigh matters. Go now and fetch your things."

I stopped along the narrow footpath for a moment to catch my breath after a long and arduous climb. I looked down the side of the cliff to catch a glimpse of the yacht Kinkae had hired peacefully riding anchor in the cove below. Once we reached the summit the land flattened out and I could see the Irish Sea for miles in all directions. Visibility was excellent and I saw no ships nearby to give me any worry. My Blackamoors and Carib, armed with shovels and pickaxes, followed me in a single file while the twins and young James walked alongside me.

The Great Saltee is little more than a desolate pile of rock covered over in sand, in wild grass and patches of scrub brush. Small lizards scurrying about and seabirds, thousands of squawking birds of different kinds and colors probing the ground for food, inhabit the island. No people live there and few every visit.

We marched towards the southern tip of the island at a leisurely pace until we came upon a cluster of boulders surrounded by a thicket of scraggly thorn bushes. This is the place where I had recovered the treasure of a pig named Dowlin many years ago. A few years back, on nothing more than a whim, I had buried some of my own wealth in almost the same spot. I had all but forgotten to mention this modest hoard of gold, silver and precious baubles in my last will and testament.

After returning to Westport with our loot, I summoned Elizabeth to the *Banshee*, to my private room. I waved her over to a chair across from me at the table. I poured her a glass of good Spanish wine neat, without water, and handed her a plate with assorted cheeses and a loaf of freshly, baked bread.

"Your health seems to have improved," I said. "Your color is back. You are looking fit."

"Yes."

"Is that all you have to say?"

"I, I know not what else to say Mary."

"Before my mishap off Florida, you and I could talk for hours. Have a sip of wine. That's better. You seem nervous. Relax, put your mind at ease."

"What are your plans?"

"Once our lads return, we sail for the East Indies. We must free Mustafa and the others marooned in Java. This much is certain. I'm less certain of what to do with you."

"You are sailing for the Dutch?"

"To secure the release of our ships and men, including you, this is the deal I had to strike with the Company."

"I see."

"Do you have any monies left from your father's estate?"

"No, Mary. I spent everything I had to fund our last voyage."

"You're penniless?"

"*Sí*. Why? Do you intend to send me away, banish me? I have nothing."

"After the terrible tragedy in the China Sea, what did you think might happen?"

"I, I do not know."

"Surely you must have thought Jacob at the very least would be angry?"

"I suppose."

"You suppose? Hmm. When he boarded *Ghostrunner* following the battle was he angry?"

"No."

"He proposed to make haste for Banten once the carpenter had repaired *Ghostrunner*'s rudder did he not?"

"*Sí*, yes."

"He asked you if you agreed?"

"Yes."

"And how did you respond?"

"I, I, I said nothing."

"No, that is not quite true. I understand you replied that after what you had done you had no right to say anything. Then Jacob asked you what it was you thought you had done. Is this not so?"

"Yes, yes. I remember now. That is true."

"He asked you if you had violated any of the Ten Rules?"

"Yes."

"You said no and he agreed?"

"Yes."

"But you felt guilty?"

"Yes."

"And then Jacob told you what?"

"He told me not to feel guilty."

"And?"

"And?"

"And..."

"And, well, um, Jacob said he thought I had been rash, that I had shown poor judgement by confronting the pirates. He had wanted to run. But he also said he could have been wrong. I remember he said it is best to not judge. He thought you would agree."

"Agree to what?"

"That I should not be judged I suppose."

"Ah. And do you agree?"

Elizabeth began fidgeting in her chair and took another sip of wine before answering. "I'll accept whatever punishment you deem fit and proper without complaint."

"For all Jacob's strength and his tough hide, for all his bluster, he has a kind heart and he was being magnanimous to you on that ugly day. I'm not certain I would have been as charitable had I been in his boots. The Ten Rules are a bit fuzzy - fuzzy, a new word I picked-up here in Westport recently - on the subject. Every one of your brothers supported you then and they support you now. As there was no judgement, there can be no punishment."

"Thank you, Mary."

"Ohhh, don't thank me yet. This doesn't mean actions don't have consequences. If you wish to return to my good graces, you have much to prove. Well, in Amsterdam you asked me how I survived and I shall tell you. I floated on a piece of *Phantom's* railing for days after I was swept overboard. Fishermen of the Tequesta found me. I lived in Florida with the Indians for many months. They treated me well enough and eventually agreed to help me reach San Augustín, the only Spanish settlement on the Floridian coast I know of. With the help of the Tequesta, I reached San Augustín and from there I caught a freighter bound for Havana to find your father. Bad luck for me, the freighter's master, a German fellow, betrayed me for the gold doubloons I carried. He sold me off in the slave markets in Trinidad. A wealthy Spaniard named Salamanca purchased me and took me to his hacienda outside of Veracruz. I bided my time as I labored and eventually escaped to Havana with two sisters, Ashaki and Lololi, whom you'll meet soon. When I learned of your father's death from Jesús, we sailed on to Santo Domingo to find Esmeralda and from there she helped us make our way back to Westport. From beginning to end my odyssey was long and difficult with many challenges."

"You, a slave to a wealthy Spaniard?" Elizabeth asked incredulously.

When I saw the doubt in her eyes I stood, undid the buttons to my shirt, lifted my shirt over my head and turned to show her the scars across my back made by the cruel edges of a whip. "A gift from my master when my first attempt to escape failed. My rump bares the same marks."

Elizabeth put a hand to her mouth and gasped. "Mary, Mary, we, we searched for you for days trying to find you."

"You and your brothers did all you could," I said as I rebuttoned my shirt.

"How did you know to look for us in Amsterdam?"

"Esmeralda told me of your intentions to sail to the East Indies and Flynn told me about the Company. I figured you had reached out to Martin and that Martin had in turn introduced you to the VOC. I was looking for Martin in Amsterdam when the Dutch arrested me. Whilst Houtman was questioning you in one room in that dreadful building, he was questioning me in another room nearby."

"Oh."

"Well, from the moment I fell overboard until now, you will recount your story in full - every detail - in writing and I shall do the same and when our brothers are satisfied with both our accounts, our statements will be entered into the ship's master journal. Understood?"

"Why?"

"I know not why," I answered honestly and shrugged my shoulders. "For nothing more than posterity perhaps. Just do as I say."

"As you wish Mary."

"Are the charges against you true or not Mr. Benge?" I demanded, straight to the point. I had found Barnaby Benge hiding in Dublin. The plump, balding Englishman with rosy cheeks had been both a brewer and a victualler in Plymouth for the Stuart navy until he fled to Ireland one day after the king's men charged him with theft, specifically for using inferior malt and hops to make his beer and then filling the new beer into old casks. I had paid for his carriage from Dublin to Westport and invited him to supper in my private room at Shaw's tavern. I asked Atwood, who had coasted into Westport the day before with his new ship, to join us.

"As for using old casks, aye my lady, the charge be true. But the charge of using unfit ingredients to make my beer is a gross, detestable lie."

"Such an odious act of making inferior beer," Atwood mused, "would be more of a sin than a crime I'd say."

"That be true Master Atwood. 'Twould be an unpardonable, unspeakable sin to be sure."

"You cheated the Stuart navy then?" I asked.

"Not quite. A captain of the king's navy, 'tis best I not reveal his name, forced me to buy the casks along with the malt and hops from a purveyor who happens to be his brother. The casks were not new. I cannot deny that. Though the malt and hops I was obliged to use were of lesser quality, they were not unfit."

"If you are innocent, why flee?" I asked.

"Ha! And accuse a captain of the royal navy of helping his brother cheat the king? No thank you. Even if folks believed me, some nameless, faceless person would put my name on some secret list as a troublemaker. I'd be banished - or worse. Certainly, I'd never see another contract from the navy."

"You are a victualler too I'm told?"

"I am."

"What," Atwood asked, "are English sailors eating aboard their ship these days?"

"Common in a sailor's daily fare is one pound of sea biscuits and eight pints of beer. Each week every man is supposed to also receive four pounds of beef, two pounds of salted pork, three-eighths of a twenty-four-inch cod, two pints of dried peas, six ounces of butter and eight to twelve ounces of cheese. Salted fish, oatmeal and rice are permitted substitutes if other staples cannot be got."

"Well, I'm not the Stuart navy," I said. "I insist my men eat well. I insist they have belly-timber that is wholesome and pleasing to the tongue. I do not skimp on victuals."

"My compliments, madam. A well-fed crew is a happy crew."

"Tell me, how do you salt and pickle your meat?"

"Ah, 'tis best you dry-rub the pork, beef or fish with white salt first. Then you soak the meat for five days in brine to absorb the blood. Once the blood is completely removed, you can pack the meat into barrels - liberally sprinkling bay salt in-between each layer. The last step is to add fresh brine, brine strong enough to float an egg, and then you must seal the barrel tight."

"How do you make your brine?"

"For proper brine you mix three and half pounds of white salt to each gallon of good, clean water, no more, no less."

I turned to look at Atwood. "Jacob?"

"I'd say Mr. Benge knows his trade. I trust the man who vouched for him and this is why I suggested you meet him."

"What do you know of me, Mr. Binge?" I asked.

"Only quiet whispers spoken in the shadows, spoken in the dark corners of discrete backrooms and alleys."

"Huh. Very well. Welcome aboard Mr. Binge. You are our new victualler and chief cook. You do right by me and I'll do right by you. You'll see your rightful share of gold after we finish our voyage. You cheat me, you do injury to my lads to fatten your own purse and, well, I'll leave the unpleasant consequences of such folly to your imagination."

The Englishman smiled broadly as he extended his hand. "Please my lady, folks call me BB."

"BB it is," I said as we shook hands. "We sail in two weeks' time. You know our destination. You may begin acquiring sufficient provisions for all three ships. Let me know what you need in monies."

"Straight away my lady. Thankee kindly."

"Jacob, after we finish supper, I would see this new ship of yours. Have you chosen a name for her or is she the new *Homeward Bound?*"

Atwood beamed. "Ink and Blot have outdone themselves once again. Five hundred tons, frigate-rigged, twenty-six great guns, a mix of long barrel six and nine-pounders, sharp prow to slice the waves, upper deck and bulwarks reinforced with quebracho wood - she's a marvel to behold. In honor of Michael and his love of Greek mythology, I thought the name *Nemesis* after the Greek goddess of vengeance would do nicely but, instead, she's the good ship *Copulation.*"

"You're joking!"

"I am not. 'Tis the name my brave lads chose."

"Good God sir, you have a brazenly, bawdy crew."

Atwood roared with laughter. "Ah Mary, I got you there!"

I rolled my eyes in reply. Atwood had always enjoyed a bit of fun at my expense.

After Atwood wiped away a tear and collected himself, he drained his tankard of ale. "Whew, *Copulation* was indeed the name my crew suggested. But I told them I doubted you would approve. I asked them to pick another. *Shitfire* was their second choice."

"*Shitfire?*"

"Aye, from the Spanish word *cacafuego*, fire-shitter."

"And what is the significance of this name?"

"Bless me if I know. To a Spaniard fire-shitter means braggart. Some say the name was intended for Drake. Martha didn't much care for it. No, not at all. My good wife suggested I use the more polite word folks are using in its place these days, spitfire. My lads embraced the name at once and so she is now the good ship *Spitfire*. Good, strong name, eh? Far better than *Ghostrunner!*"

"I like this new name *Spitfire*, Jacob. I pray she is a good ship for us. I see you grinning Mr. BB. What is your opinion?"

"Strong name," the jolly Englishman with rosy cheeks agreed. "*Shitstorm* might have been my choice."

"You'll fit in well with my lads," Atwood said and chuckled.

"BB off you go," I said. "You have things to do and I need to speak with Jacob in private."

"In all these years Jacob," I said after our new victualler left, as I reached across the table for Atwood's hand. "You've never asked me for anything. While Maurice has *Cerberus* and Elizabeth did have *Ghostrunner* - I was generous with her, too generous it would seem - I thoughtlessly neglected you. *Spitfire* is my gift to you Jacob for all your years of fidelity and friendship. A belated Happy Christmas to you."

"Mary, you gave Elizabeth and me equal shares in *Phantom*, this gift is not necess -"

"It is done Jacob," I said, cutting my most loyal of lieutenants off. "And I rather like your idea of the name *Nemesis* in honor of Michael. As of today, *Ghostrunner* shall be *Nemesis*."

With our men trickling back into Westport, and our ships in fighting trim, with our new victualler doing a splendid job of requisitioning first quality provisions across Ireland for good prices - the man did indeed seem to know his business - I gathered all my officers for supper at *Banshee's Lament* as was my way before setting out on any new adventure. I had promised the Dutch I would be back in

Holland and ready to sail no later than the end of April and I was determined to keep my word. I invited Ashaki, Lololi and James to join us. When we had our fill of good food and strong spirits, when the mood in the room turned light, I stood and raised my hands for quiet. I took a moment to consider each face around the table.

"Well now, how odd life is. I did not know if I'd ever see any of you thugs again. Each of you is more beautiful to me than any sunrise, more striking than any sunset. Kinkae, Henry, I regret there is no time for us to return to the Caribbean for you and your lads to see your families. The ladies and I will write letters on behalf of any man who wishes to send word back to their loved ones before we sail. Have any of your lads decided to leave us, to catch a ship for home?"

Both men shook their heads.

"Very well. Once we've honored our obligations to the Dutch in the East Indies, we shall return to the West Indies."

"Cutting across the Pacific?" Atwood asked.

"Certainly, why not? I hear the Chinese and Japanese make the journey in their modest junks."

"At last, we circumnavigate the globe," Atwood offered facetiously and raised his glass of whiskey.

"A daunting task lies ahead of us to be sure Jacob. I wish it were not so. And then again, there are opportunities for us to the east. We make the best of things. We have three mighty battlecruisers, three companies of skilled fighters and we'll be fully provisioned by week's end."

"You've assembled a formidable force Mary," Maurice said affably. "Do you know what the Dutch expect of us?"

"I do not."

"Let us hope this Matelieff fellow is a better soldier than Drake."

"Aye, Maurice let us hope."

"What do we know of the man?" Atwood asked. "Did Martin give you any insight?"

"None. But rest assured gentlemen, ladies, we shall always look out for ourselves. Anything else Jacob? No? Maurice? Kinkae? Robert? Henry? No? Very well. **Elizabeth, Ashaki, Lololi, you've each expressed** your desire to sail with us. I've done my best to dissuade you. Young James has been no less ruthless pestering me with his daily pleas. I'm betwixt aye and nay." I paused to raise my hand when Elizabeth tried to speak. "After conferring with our brothers, I've decided to allow all four of you to sail with us. James you are of age now and I have no right to keep you from the world. Elizabeth, I'll not deny you the chance to redeem yourself. And as for you Ashaki and Lololi, we have unfinished business in México do we not? The lads are making a cabin for you three ladies to share. I'm told this cubbyhole will accommodate three hammocks if they are stacked one above the other. Snug, eh? Better than trying to sleep standing upright I suppose."

"What," Elizabeth asked gingerly, "is my command to be?"

"Command? Command is a privilege not a right. You forfeited that privilege in Macau."

"I am an officer! Under the Ten Rules, you have no authority to strip me of my rank."

"True, how true. And yet it is done. Kinkae will assign you, James and the twins your duties before we sail. In addition to whatever work Kinkae gives you, you'll also be responsible for teaching James and the twins the classic disciplines, the *trivium*, grammar, logic and rhetoric, and the *quadrivium*, arithmetic, geometry, astronomy and music. I've purchased the necessary books you'll need."

"But Mary," young James protested. "Liz and Rob have taught me everything I need to know. My schooling is complete."

"What James says is true, Mary," Elizabeth interjected in support. "There is nothing more I can teach the lad."

I ignored James and Elizabeth and turned to Atwood. "Captain Atwood, who is this loud-mouthed, adolescent boy who disrespects me now?"

"I know him not Mary," Atwood answered as he absently toyed with his eyepatch. "I thought the boy was with you. If not, then he must be a filthy stowaway and I'll see him put ashore this very night on the nearest deserted island."

I turned to James. "My God sir, who are you? Are you a stowaway or my obedient son?"

"I'm your obedient son," James answered sheepishly.

"What's that you say? I cannot hear you."

"*I Am Your Obedient Son.*"

"Much better. As for you Elizabeth, do not question me again my love. You shall bend to my will or I shall break you..."

Chapter Twenty-Eight

A representative from the Company met me at the waterfront as I stepped off the longboat. He welcomed me to Amsterdam with a posy full of red tulips and a friendly smile. The Company insisted I accept its hospitality as an honored guest he said and then he escorted me to an attractive hostel overlooking Dam Square. The spacious, comfortable lodgings took me by surprise. I was even more surprised by my visitors the next day.

"Why Captain John Martin, Meester Houtman," I said cautiously and waved both men inside. "Please, do come in."

When Martin leaned over and kissed my hand, Houtman followed his lead and did the same. "Mary, how wonderful to see you again, especially under more favorable circumstances," Martin said with a droll smile.

"Quite so, John. I'm so very happy to see you too. And Meester Houtman, I trust all is well with you?"

"I am enjoying good health and am in excellent spirits thank you for inquiring," Houtman replied. "Life is good. Please, put your mind at ease. This is a cordial visit."

"Good, I'm glad. John, are you coming or going?"

"Alas, I am leaving Amsterdam this very day. I took a quick peek at your well-armed ships in the harbor earlier this morning. Very fine, very fine. I'm certain they'll do you good service in the coming months ahead."

"Please gentlemen, sit. The tea will be cold by now. 'Tis a bit early, but perhaps a glass of wine? The hostel's proprietor has pampered me with an assortment of delicious wines including a good sherry, far tastier than the shipboard swill we mariners are accustomed to."

"Sherry would be splendid," Martin said. "Jan?"

"Yes, of course. I trust all is well with you Mary?"

"Better than when last we met," I said with a nervous chuckle, I know not why. "I have fine rooms and excellent wine. I'm surrounded by an array of lovely flowers and boxes of delicious, sugary treats, all compliments of the Company. I feel like pampered royalty."

"I pray there are no hard feelings between us."

"None at all. I understand the Company's earlier displeasure full well. I told you I'd make amends. I'm here to support the Company as promised with sturdy ships built for rugged war and fighting men of quality."

"Indeed, with three superb ships John tells me. I hope to introduce you to Admiral Matelieff de Jonge in a day or two. I think you'll be impressed by the man."

After I poured each of us a glass of sherry, I stepped over to the room's front windows to watch a mist rolling across the great city from the harbor. The lamplighters were already out, rushing about to finish their work before the last bit of daylight faded.

"What is that excavation across the way?" I asked.

Houtman joined me at the window. "Ah, men are beginning work on what will become the Bourse d'Amsterdam, Amsterdam's first true stock exchange," Houtman replied with a hint of pride. "Hendrick de Keyser, a renaissance man, the same fellow who designed the lovely Zuiderkerk church under construction over in Nieuwmarkt, is the principal architect. When finished the trading houses within the Bourse d'Amsterdam will face a colonnaded courtyard of forty-six columns, tall, majestic columns in the Greek style. The exchange will accommodate as many as five thousand people at a time. We expect every kind of product from all over the world, except for wheat of course, will be bought and sold there including the Company's own securities."

"An impressive undertaking Meester Houtman."

"Please call me Jan. We got off on the wrong foot Mary during our first encounter. I very much regret that but we are now fast friends. Yes, Amsterdam is being transformed. She'll be a magnificent city someday, perhaps even the crown jewel of Europe."

"Though yesterday was rather blustery, I took a leisurely stroll through your fine city Jan. A wonderful excitement fills the air. I found new construction at practically every corner. I saw an army of laborers at work. You Dutch are certainly an industrious people. John, tell me if you can, what brings you to Amsterdam?"

"We English and the Dutch are natural allies and friendly rivals," Martin replied vaguely as he ambled over to the window with his sherry to join Houtman and me.

"Friendly rivals John, how so?" I asked. "Your respective masters are plotting how best to carve-up the world between them?"

"Oh, that sounds rather diabolical when you put it that way Mary. I'd say England and the United Provinces share mutual interests. Ending Portugal's monopoly over the spice trade for one and reaching trade agreements between the EIC and the VOC in the East Indies for another - once the Portuguese have been evicted of course - benefit both our nations."

"The EIC?"

"Ah, the English East India Company, chartered by our good Queen Bess back in late 1600 before her death."

"Oh. I know little about this English company. The EIC as you call it is a private enterprise I believe?"

"It is. Wealthy English merchants who like to refer to themselves as Adventurers formed the company. Adventurers, a quaint description, yes?"

"So, these men crave adventure over profit?" I asked glibly.

"Not quite. The EIC has sent two expeditions to Indonesia. Sir James Lancaster led the first expedition in 1601. He sailed with the nine-hundred-ton war galleon *Red Dragon*, armed with two demi-cannons, sixteen culverins, twelve demi-culverines and eight sakers, a floating fortress of marvelous proportions to behold, accompanied by the three-hundred-ton *Hector*, the two hundred-sixty-ton *Ascension*, the two-hundred-forty-ton *Susan* and a small victualler, the *Guest*. The venture proved extraordinarily profitable. We English now have trading factories, or *entrepôts* as the French like to call them, in Banten and in the Moluccas. In the spring of last year Captain Henry Middleton departed Gravesend for Indonesia on behalf of the EIC with the very same ships. He should have reached the Far East by now and is probably stirring up some mischief. That one's a back-alley brawler."

"Are you John," I asked smiling, "trying to impress me or Jan?"

"Ha!" Martin exclaimed good-naturedly as he wrapped an arm around my shoulder in a protective, familial way for Houtman's benefit. "These Dutch do not impress easily Mary let me tell you! Well, the hour grows late and I must be off. May God watch over you Mary as you embark upon this new venture. Be a good lass and keep both feet planted firmly on deck whilst at sea this time. Jan, until we meet again *vaarwel* my friend."

"Happy travels my good Captain," Houtman replied.

"Godspeed John Martin," I said and kissed the Englishman on the cheek. "I know better than to ask you where you've been or where you're off to. Wherever the road takes you, I pray you return to England with success and in good health."

After he drained the last of his sherry, Martin embraced me and as he held me, he discreetly slipped a note into my hand before nodding goodbye to Houtman.

"You have a most persuasive advocate in John Martin, Mary," Houtman observed after Martin left the room and closed the door behind him.

"We have a long and colorful history together."

"I'm so very pleased you and your men have returned. I must confess I won a modest wager with my colleagues when your ships glided into our fine harbor. You do have a reputation for honoring your word and I find myself the richer for it."

"A reputation earned over the years at some cost in blood I fear."

After we exchanged a few brief pleasantries, Houtman excused himself while I poured myself another glass of sherry and took a seat by the fire to read Martin's note. "I very much like and admire the Dutch," Martin wrote. "Today we are fast friends and fair allies but I expect the Company's Gentlemen Seventeen will be ruthless in pursuing their ambitions in the Far East. Expanding trade is but one ambition. Building an empire is another. There will be war. Do keep your wits about you. Trust no one except Ewoud Dijksma. Make no mistake, Dijksma is a loyal patriot to his country but he is also one of those rare gems who happens along from time-to-time. He is to his core an honorable and courageous man."

I met Admiral Cornelis Matelieff de Jonge for the first time with Houtman in the drab, cramped offices of the VOC within an unimpressive warehouse in disrepair known as the Bushuis Armory facing the Kloveniersburgwal Canal. There was little to distinguish the commander from his sailors, two of whom stood guard outside the door of the room where Matelieff was waiting. A commoner and a man of simple tastes who had married well had come dressed in plain seaman's clothing. He wore no fancy accoutrements or jewelry of any kind. A long, sharp nose and a reddish-brown goatee with flecks of grey helped give an otherwise unremarkable face a bit of character. By the end of our meeting the admiral impressed me as alert, astute and serious. He used his words sparingly, his thoughts seemed focused and well-organized.

"Lady Mary, I am delighted to meet you at last," Matelieff said in broken Spanish as he stood to offer his hand.

"I'm honored Admiral," I replied as we shook hands.

"Forgive our offices. They're temporary. It was convenient to meet you here. The Company's new headquarters, the grand redbrick building under construction next to this building, is well underway. The Company will name the new building the *Oost-Indisch Huis* when completed. Not a very imaginative name perhaps, but practical and to the point."

I glanced around the small room and took in the three worn chairs, a badly chipped desk and the brooms and buckets stacked against walls covered in peeling paint and splotches of mold. "*Oost-Indisch Huis*, the East India House?"

"Yes, my lady."

"The Company's new accommodations I have no doubt," I said as Matelieff, Houtman and I took our seats around the room's rickety, old desk, a desk better suited for firewood than business, "will be a marvelous improvement when completed."

"Admiral, Mary," Houtman interjected, "I shall let you two become better acquainted and take my leave, but before I do I wish to be abundantly clear. Admiral, I've provided you with our files on Mary which will give you some appreciation of her quality. Mary, Captain Martin has given his blessing to your participation in this expedition, which is to say that King James has no objections. Our agreement is simple. Your three ships will sail to the East Indies with Admiral Matelieff's fleet and whilst in service to the Admiral, you will be subject to his command as if you were one of his own officers. Should the Dutch fleet encounter hostile action with the Portuguese or the Spanish or with any enemy whilst at sea, you shall support the Admiral in whatever manner he deems prudent. Once Admiral Matelieff releases you, you will seek out either Gerrit Koopman or Ewoud Dijksma. They'll make all the necessary arrangements to procure as much spices as your ships can transport whereafter you shall promptly return to Amsterdam - no deviations this time. The Company has agreed to pay you a commission of ten percent on the market value of the cargo you return with. This percentage is a substantially greater sum than our customary arrangements with our agents but reflects the additional risks you have agreed to accept. Is there anything I need to clarify? Are we in perfect agreement?"

I nodded. "All is clear Jan and we are in agreement, perfect agreement."

"Excellent. One last matter before I go. The English, ah how they love to play their silly games, insist there be no record of your participation in this particular voyage Mary. I know not why. No matter. Admiral, no reference to Mary or her ships or men is to be made in your ship's *leeskarte*, or in any of your official reports to the Company. Well then, I'll leave you both to it."

On the 12th day of May in the year of our Lord 1605, Matelieff departed Zeeland in fine weather with seven powerful warships and my three battlecruisers trailing behind them. A half dozen Dutch flyboats took the lead to see us safely out to sea. We glided unceremoniously past the harbor buoys in no particular order but after we slipped into the English Channel, after our escort fired off a single salvo in salute and then headed back to port, we formed a single line of battle and though our destination was a secret, no one could have mistaken our purpose. The Dutch had assembled a powerful squadron at great cost - over two million guilders I later learned - for war, not trade. Spanish spies in Amsterdam would most assuredly send word of our expedition back to Madrid by way of the swiftest horsemen.

We plowed through rolling waves in close formation under dove grey skies while hugging the English coast and when we reached Lizard Point, we made a hard left turn to the south. Matelieff's flagship, the seven hundred-ton *Oranje* with a man named Captain Dirk Mol in command, then assumed the lead. The three-hundred-ton *Nassau* under the command of Captain Wouter Jacobz, fell in behind the *Oranje* followed in turn by the six-hundred-ton *Middelburg* under Captain Simon Lambers, the five-hundred-forty-ton *Witte Leeuw* under Captain Claas Jansz, the six-hundred-ton *Zwarte Leeuw* under Captain Abraham Mathijsz, the seven-hundred-ton *Mauritius* under Captain Gerrit Klaasz and lastly the five-hundred-forty-ton frigate *Grote Zon* under Captain Gerard Hendriksz.

My three ships - the seven-hundred-ton brute *Nemesis*, rearmed with thirty-four guns, Maurice's swift and agile five-hundred-ton *Cerberus*, now mounting twenty-two guns, and Atwood's splendid new five-hundred-ton *Spitfire*, bristling with twenty-six guns - sailed abreast in a line close behind *Grote Zon*. My ships had been built for rugged war and speed and most of my men, nearly four hundred strong, were tough, seasoned veterans of cruel, hard war. Most had sailed with me before and quite a few had sailed with me for years. Men who had declined to sail with Elizabeth had eagerly volunteered to sail with me. I knew the mettle of my men.

Another squadron of four warships under the command of Vice-Admiral Olivier de Vivere was to sail from Texel a few weeks after us and rendezvous in Indonesia with us later. De Vivere would depart Holland with the seven-hundred-ton *Amsterdam* under the command of Captain Reynier Lamberts, the two-hundred-twenty-ton *Kleine Zon* under Captain Cornelis Jorisz, the five-hundred-ton *Erasmu* under Captain Osier Cornelisz and the four-hundred-ton *Geunieerde Provincien* under Captain Antoine Antoniscz.

We made slow but steady progress cruising due south along the coasts of France, Spain, Portugal and western Africa. The Dutch ships were large, well-built and weatherly but, except for *Grote Zon*, speedy they were not. To occupy my time, apart from the daily burdens of command, I spent my days reading and keeping a watchful eye over Elizabeth, the twins and James. Elizabeth kept her distance from me but seemed to have accepted her new role. Once she and the others had completed their daily chores for Kinkae, I often helped her school Ashaki, Lololi and James in the classic disciplines. Except on Sundays, they studied for four hours each afternoon and in the evenings, after supper, I handed the twins and James over to Shaw to train them in the martial arts as Efendi had trained us.

As for reading, I had found Elizabeth's copy of Jan Huygen van Linschoten's *Travel Accounts of Portuguese Navigation in the Orient* in my great cabin and spent many a day and night studying every page of Linchoten's work with meticulous care. I committed as much of the material to memory as my abilities would allow. I also had brought copies of several plays by William Shakespeare with me, including his newest work *The Tragedy of Hamlet, the Prince of Denmark* as I enjoyed the master poet's gift for storytelling. I also had a copy of Edmund Spenser's *The Faerie Queene* and followed his six knights with keen interest in their quest for holiness, temperance, chastity, friendship, justice and courtesy.

After forty days at sea, and with three thousand miles behind us, we dropped anchor off the Dutch-held island of Gorée across from the city of Ndakaaru. Gorée was where I first learned of Matelieff's orders while eating supper one evening aboard *Oranje* with the Matelieff and his senior officers. The sheer breadth and boldness of Dutch designs in the Far East astonished me. The Company intended to oust the Portuguese from all of Indonesia and then Asia. The admiral's instructions were to seize Malacca first and then Macau and then he was to grab all the pepper, nutmeg, mace and clove ports in-between. We spent three days anchored off Gorée making repairs and reprovisioning our stores of food and water before setting out again.

From Gorée to the Cape of Good Hope, where we put in at Table Bay to again reprovision, was another forty-five hundred miles of sailing. From the Cape of Good Hope to Madagascar - we were too powerful a squadron to worry about the many pirate tribes who infest those waters - and across the Indian Ocean, stopping only briefly to replenish our stores of food and water at the Dutch trading factory in Machilipatnam on the east coast of India, and then sailing around the northern tip of Sumatra and down into the Strait of Malacca, was another sixty-nine hundred miles.

The disappointing speed of the Dutch galleons, together with the constant gales, repairs at sea and passing through the Doldrums twice, once while sailing south on the way to the Cape of Good Hope and then again as we sailed north across the Indian Ocean, cost us a goodly amount time. After nearly eleven tedious months at sea, we finally sighted the fabulous center of trade for Asian goods, the prize the Dutch longed to have most, Malacca. The journey had been excruciatingly long and I swore to myself that if we ever made it back to Ireland, I'd never make such a voyage again.

We sailed a bit beyond Malacca to a large island at the tip of the Malay peninsula across from the Johor River called Pulau Ujong, meaning island at the end, where Matelieff found a secluded cove to his liking. With his squadron safely tucked away inside safe waters, Matelieff gave the order to make camp along the shore. But before he could move against the Portuguese at Malacca, Matelieff needed Vice-Admiral Vivere's four ships to join him and he needed a treaty of alliance between the Company and the Sultan of Johor, the ruler of the Malay people, Alauddin Riayat Shah III.

As I had no desire to sit on a beach for monotonous weeks fighting off insects, disease and boredom in the tropical heat, I had a longboat lowered away and went ashore to see the admiral before sending my own men in. As I stepped foot in Indonesia for the first time, I considered the palm trees, the beach, the flies, mosquitoes and humidity and found the land not much different from the Caribbean.

Matelieff, in fine spirits, happily called me inside his command tent when he heard me ask the two sentries standing guard outside for permission to enter. I was thrilled when the admiral readily agreed to let me to sail on to Banten with all my ships to recover my men being held by Prince Ratu. He handed me sealed dispatches to deliver to either Koopman or Dijksma and made me promise to return to his squadron no later than mid-June.

As the longboat crew pulled on their oars to return us to *Nemesis*, I craned my head around for one last look at the shore and caught a glimpse of Matelieff setting out on foot leading a company of soldiers for Batu Sawar, the capital city of Johor, to seek an audience with the sultan. I watched the admiral and his men disappear into the jungle and wondered if I'd ever see any of them again.

Chapter Twenty-Nine

I love all my brothers dearly. I'd kill or die for any of them. But for reasons beyond my understanding, Efendi and I had always shared, from the very beginning, a particularly special, inexplicable bond.

When we reached Banten I brought Atwood, Maurice and Shaw ashore with me and stepped onto the beach with mounting apprehension. But as we approached the Dutch trading post just beyond the city, my fear gave way to joy when I spotted Efendi sitting underneath a shade tree casually whittling away on a piece of wood. When Efendi's eyes met mine, we both shed tears.

"Mustafa, Mustafa, Mustafa!" I cried out as I rushed towards him, as I dropped to my knees next to him. I wrapped my arms around his neck and kissed his hands, his brow and his eyes.

"In my heart," he said and held me tight, "I knew this day would come."

"Thank God, we found you Mustafa."

Efendi clasped me by the shoulders and smiled as he helped me to my feet. "You and I are hunters always Mary, never the prey."

Atwood embraced Efendi next, followed by Maurice and Shaw. Four grown men, made hard from years at sea and gruesome war, stood in a circle holding each other and wept.

"Elizabeth is with you?" Efendi asked.

"She is," Atwood replied.

Efendi nodded. "She is very young."

"Mary has her answering to Kinkae for now."

"Come," I said, "we can tell each other our stories later. Gather the others and let's go see this child prince who rules this land to secure your releases, unless the fool wishes to test me."

"No need Mary," Efendi said. "Prince Ratu, under pressure from the Dutch tried his nephew, the man who had falsely accused us of piracy, six weeks ago. The court found his nephew guilty of treason. To the jeers and boos of a huge crowd the man was beheaded in the city square. We are free. We've been waiting for a Dutch ship to return us to the Netherlands. There are but six of us now. Two men succumbed to one illness or another. The other two simply walked off."

"Pity that, but you're alive."

"Allah is merciful. You've hardly aged a day, Mary. You come from fine, sturdy stock I think."

"Ha! My joints would beg to differ Mustafa and I've had to behead a few grey hairs. I must see a fellow named Gerrit Koopman or Ewoud Dijksma. Do you know where I might find one or the other?"

"Koopman is south of here building a Dutch settlement he has renamed Batavia but known as Jayakarta by the Javanese, meaning victorious city. Prince Wijayakrama, a vassal of Banten, rules the region. Koopman believes he can turn the place into a significant port for the Dutch with Wijayakrama's blessing as he doesn't fully trust Prince Ratu. Dijksma left for Ambon a week ago. If you have business with one of these men, between the two, I'd look for Dijksma."

"That is what we'll do then."

"But finding Dijksma in Ambon," Atwood interrupted, "may not be easy as Ambon is under Portuguese rule."

"No longer," Efendi replied, grinning. "The Dutch seized Ambon for themselves last year."

There was no reason to linger in Banten other than to celebrate our reunion. I sent BB ashore to purchase fresh fruits and vegetables to chase away any scurvy and plenty of new ale to ease any pain. I had Atwood, Maurice and Shaw bring most of the men ashore. We built bond fires against the sea, away from the city walls, and slaughtered chickens, pigs and sheep. And after we offered up our prayers, after we toasted our friends whose bones lay buried in the sand or at the bottom of the sea, we took our places around the campfires to eat and drink and sing while we told our stories in turn. My officers, the twins and young James too, sat in a circle with me as we celebrated. And when we had our fill of food and drink, when we had nothing more to say and the fires had burned to embers, Efendi stood and gave Elizabeth a reassuring embrace, an embrace of forgiveness for all to see before we returned to our ships in our longboats.

In the morning I called my officers to me. No one around the great cabin's table had much in the way of clear thought. I served strong coffee and tea, fresh, warm biscuits and passed around a bowl of powdered cinchona for any aching heads.

"Gentlemen, Elizabeth, good morning," I said as I tried to stiffle a yawn.

"We're off to Ambon to find Dijksma I take it?" Atwood asked.

"Aye, Jacob. I'm keenly aware we need to overhaul the ships and, as you know, I promised Matelieff we'd rejoin his squadron by mid-June. Can we refit our ships in Ambon?"

Atwood added a heaping spoonful of cinchona to his coffee before answering. "Aye. Ambon is not far and the harbor there has repair facilities that can accommodate ocean-class vessels. Earlier this morning the master of a Dutch merchantman rowed over to my ship to introduce himself. Jansen is his name. He's a likeable fellow. His ship brought provisions, foodstuffs, powder, ammunition and the like from Rotterdam. He sails for Holland in a few days and offered to take any mail our men might wish to send back home with him."

"Wonderful," I said. "I'll send Ashaki, Lololi and young James around the ships with ink, pen and paper to help any man who needs help writing letters. I suppose I should send a report back to Houtman too though there isn't much to say. Mustafa, I assume you're willing to resume your duties as both Captain of the Guns and Master Chief over all the men? Good, good. Elizabeth, I spoke to Jacob and Maurice last evening and we are agreed. As Maurice lost his first officer to an infection of the blood from a seemingly minor cut a few weeks back, the position is yours if you wish to have it."

Elizabeth instantly perked up. "Yes," she said in barely a whisper.

"I dare say I expected a bit more enthusiasm from you than a meekly proffered yes, but no matter. Rob, I also wish to see what you can do. You shall assume the captainship of *Nemesis*, which I suppose makes me an admiral now."

"And here I thought," Atwood quipped, "only kings and queens have the power to bestow titles upon themselves."

I chuckled good-naturedly but as I did, I caught the dark scowl passing across Elizabeth's face for promoting Shaw into her former position.

With favorable winds behind us, we set out for Ambon in the morning under full sail - we even ran out the studding sails, a rare treat - and flew cross the thirteen hundred miles between Banten and Ambon in remarkable time. I took Atwood, Efendi and Elizabeth ashore with me and we had no difficulty finding Dijksma. He had taken up offices inside the walls of Fort Victory, formally known as Forte de Nossa Senhora da Anunciada under the Portuguese.

Standing behind an elegant writing table in the new Baroque style, a table that had only recently belonged to the Portuguese commandant of the fort, or so I supposed, a handsome, cleanshaven fellow dressed in the unadorned black trousers and black coat favored by the Dutch Protestants welcomed us into his office with open arms and an engaging smile. His expression brightened even more when he saw Elizabeth.

"Elizabeth!" he exclaimed as he stepped over to her, grasped her by the forearms and affectionately kissed her on both cheeks. "I'm overjoyed to see you again. You must have come to some understanding with the Company?"

"I, ah, yes, ah, yes we did."

"Excellent. And Jacob you old goat, how very good to see you! You are looking fit my giant friend. The adventure's life agrees with you!"

Atwood beamed as he shook hands with the Dutchman. "Ewoud,

'tis good to see you haven't gotten yourself cleaved in two by a Moorish scimitar or pierced through the gut with a Portuguese blade! I trust you've got something stashed away to wash away the brine and dust?"

"Ha! I do, I do," he replied and looked over at the junior officer who had escorted us into the fort. "Hans, be a good fellow, find a few bottles and something tasty for our weary travelers to munch on. And bring more chairs. Mustafa my friend, I'm glad your people have finally come to liberate you. I'll miss your sage advice and good company. And you my dear lady, who might you be?"

"I am Mary."

"Mary?"

"This is our Mary back from the dead," Atwood explained. "Ewoud, meet Captain Mary, the grand matriarch of our little clan."

"Nooo... Incredible! By some unworldly intervention you survived Florida!"

"I have a story to tell," I said as I held the Dutchman's gaze. Dijksma had an easy way about him. He had pulled his long, blonde hair back in a tail. A strong, square jaw with several days of stubble gave him a playful, roguish look. I found his dignified bearing, his good looks and rugged physique appealing.

"And I would hear your story. I've been told a few fantastical things about you Mary. I'm honored to make your acquintance. Do you and your men sail for the Company?"

"We do."

"How many ships?"

"Three."

"Maurice and Rob have returned with you? They are well I pray?"

"Both men enjoy good health and aye, they are with us."

"Maurice and Rob are wonderful fellows. They are men of high quality."

"Each in his own way is a match for any man."

"Ha, not at cards!" Dijksma exclaimed and laughed. Those two scoundrels both owe me money. 'Tis the only reason I ask about them! Did you sail on your own or with Company ships?"

"We sailed from Amsterdam with Admiral Matelieff," I replied and handed the Dutchman the leather pouches Matelieff had entrusted to me. "He asked me to deliver these dispatches to you immediately. As you can see, the seals remain unbroken."

"Ah, *heel goed, dank u.* Where is the good admiral?"

"We left the Dutch squadron anchored off the southernmost tip of the Malay Peninsula."

"How many ships has he?"

"Seven warships, with four more on the way."

"The journey from Europe is quite arduous, yes?"

"Indeed. I'm told by a certain Englishman that you are a man who can be trusted. What say you to that sir?"

Dijksma took a seat behind his writing table, rested his elbows on the tabletop and interlocked his fingers. He considered me carefully before answering.

"My goodness dear lady, you are direct and waste no time."

"I am. I've never found much value in idle prattle."

"You must know John Martin."

"I do."

"Now there's a man worthy of trust."

"Nothing, no spice, silver or gold or jewel is more valuable than trust."

"The same can be said about a man's reputation."

"Or a woman's."

"True, or a woman's. How do you know Martin?"

"We sailed together with Drake."

"Remarkable. I hope you'll share your story. Well, 'tis no small feat for a person to be given a second chance by the Gentlemen Seventeen. I had my doubts whether the Company would ever employ your men and ships again. You must have extraordinary powers of persuasion."

"You'll find in me an exceptionally good friend whose loyalties do not shift with the wind or change with the tide or, should you prefer, you'll find me a very resourceful and dangerous opponent on land or at sea. I believe these qualities are what persuaded the Company."

"I doubt you not my lady. Ah, here comes Hans now with our refreshments and chairs. We have Portuguese and Spanish reds of course and some very delicious white wine from one of the German states. The wine is sweet but I'm rather fond of the clean, refreshing taste."

"What happened to the Portuguese?" Elizabeth asked.

"You missed all the excitement in February of last year my dear when Admiral Steven van der Hagen sailed into Ambon's harbor. The Portuguese soiled their trousers and evacuated the island with barely a shot fired."

"Are you Ewoud," I asked, "the captain-general of this island?"

Dijksma laughed good-naturedly. "God forbid, no. Think of me as a Dutch Martin, a far more affable and talented rendering I dare say!"

"How do you know Martin?"

"He did not tell you?"

"No, he was short on time and Jan Houtman was with us when we met in Amsterdam."

"Ah, well, I found myself in a difficult predicament awhile back, well before the Company was conceived. I was betrayed, falsely accused of being a double agent working for the Spanish. I was imprisoned at Rasphuis whilst awaiting my appointment with the headsman when Martin intervened and saved my life at a time when he could have profited from my death. He produced unequivocal evidence of my innocence and the identity of the true culprit who tried to do me in. When I asked Martin why he had interceded on my behalf, he simply referred to his actions as a "professional courtesy." The Stadtholder himself later handed me the honor of ending the true traitor's life. So, to betray your trust would be akin to betraying Martin, something I could never do."

"I understand you treated my men well during their time in Banten. You have my gratitude."

"'Twas my pleasure. Mustafa made quite an impression on young Prince Ratu, or should I say on his uncle, the regent. Mustafa was a most persuasive advocate at the trial of Mohamed Ishmael Ratu. His eloquence served him well and his Islamic faith certainly did not hurt our cause."

Dijksma paused to open the correspondence from Amsterdam. "Well, this is fascinating," he said after quickly browsing through several pages.

"The dispatches are not in code?" I asked surprised.

"Most of it is yes and I will decipher those portions later but there is a short section here pertaining to you and your men that someone neglected to encode. I am to sail with you to Macau at once."

"Macau? What the devil for?"

"I will happily tell you if I can once I decipher the rest."

"But I gave the admiral my word. I promised Matelieff that I'd rejoin his squadron no later than mid-June."

"I shall send the admiral your regrets. I'm quite certain he'll understand. The Company's wishes after all exceed his own orders to you."

I had mixed feelings about sailing to Macau. I wanted to avenge MacGyver and the others certainly, but I also feared becoming entangled in things I did not understand with people I did not know in an unfamiliar, foreign land. I still had time to think things through. Dijksma after all was only traveling to Macau to survey Portuguese strengths and weaknesses for Matelieff. His orders were to tread lightly and I saw no harm in doing the same.

After taking seven days in Ambon to refit our ships and rest, we raised our anchors, set our sails and headed north for Macau. Dijksma brought five men with him, men fluent in Spanish and Portuguese and one in Chinese, brave lads all who would be hanged as spies if caught. I took the Dutch aboard *Nemesis* with me as I wanted to get a better measure of Dijksma. My brothers had all agreed I would like the Dutchman.

"More coffee Ewoud?" I asked as we stood together on the quarterdeck, taking in a spectacular sunrise while relishing a brisk, playful breeze. We were cruising along the windward side of the islands of the Philippines, named by the Spanish explorer Ruy López de Villalobos in honor of King Philip II of Spain, and making good time.

"Please," Dijksma replied and raised his tin cup. "Did you know the Philippines are not governed locally by a captain-general as you might suppose but rather are governed by the Viceroy of New Spain from faraway Ciudad de México? Last I heard, Don Juan de Mendoza y Luna, the third Marquess of Montesclaros, holds the position."

"You are well-informed."

"To be uninformed is dangerous."

"Aye. A pickle I now find myself in."

"How so?"

"Elizabeth, Jacob and the others long to punish those who betrayed us. Elizabeth especially is obsessed with thoughts of revenge. But revenge against whom?"

"I did not know whether I'd ever see Elizabeth or any of your men again after they sailed for Amsterdam. For my own edification however, I discreetly asked questions about this mysterious man named Arslan and about the Chinaman Féng Wú. Sadly, I learned very little."

"This Arslan fellow knows Elizabeth and all my officers. I cannot risk sending any of them into Macau. My Spanish has much improved over the years though I speak the language with an Irish accent and my Portuguese is poor. I fear if I go into Macau on my own to discretly look around I may raise suspicions."

Dijksma smiled as he leaned over to kiss my hand. "This is what I do madam. Yes, if I can gather information on your behalf without jeopardizing my own mission I shall gladly do so."

"Wonderful. But I don't expect you to do it all. You and your lads intend to go ashore as Spanish merchants on your way to Japan?"

"Yes, that's the subterfuge we intend to use."

"And as our faceless enemy has seen both *Cerberus* and *Nemesis*, you'll want to take our new ship *Spitfire* into port?"

"Yes. I think we should remove most of her guns first and replace her crew with some of Maurice's Cimarron, men with light skin who speak excellent Spanish. A small crew sailing a modestly-armed Spanish merchantman shouldn't raise any eyebrows. We can rename your ship *La Dama de Madrid*, or some other suitable name if you prefer. I have the necessary paper to forge a proper Spanish commission."

"And as for you, hasn't this Arslan fellow seen your face?"

"He saw me from afar and then only briefly. I had a thick beard and short hair back then - and I was rather pale."

"Well, this plan of yours is a good disguise. I would like to join you."

"Oh? Did you not just say - rather astutely too I thought - that you would raise suspicions if you went ashore?"

"Not if I accompany you as your wife."

"Ha, ha! How quickly my fortunes have improved! Very well, you shall be the enchanting, beauteous wife of the esteemed Charles Serrano from the town of Burgos in Castile."

"Why Burgos?"

"Blonde men and women with fair complexions are not uncommon in northern Spain and I know the town well."

We pulled into a quiet inlet on the exquisite island of Mina de Oro to offload *Spitfire's* heavy artillery and to swap-out crews. Mina de Oro, meaning gold mine in Spanish, is a mountainous, lush island of great beauty, one of many islands in the Philippine Archipelago and I would have relished lingering there for a day or two had we not been in a hurry. I sent Kinkae ashore with forty men to cut down trees along a deserted stretch of beach and build us rafts. Once Kinkae's work was finished, Atwood's men used rope, block and tackle to ferry eighteen of *Spitfire's* guns over to the island on the rafts, a slow and laborious task. After Kinkae's men buried the guns in sand and hid the rafts behind the trees, we resumed our journey north.

"Again, Elizabeth," I commanded impatiently. I had brought Elizabeth over from *Cerberus* to *Nemesis* before departing Mina de Oro to allow Dijksma and I the opportunity to question her in my great cabin. "Let's review everything you saw and heard. Let's consider everyone you met during your days in Macau. Spare us no details, no matter how small or insignificant they may seem."

But Elizabeth claimed that there was not much to tell as she had seen very little. I found this odd inasmuch as she and MacGyver had spent a good number of days in port.

"So, after passing through the harbormaster's station," I asked, "you secured lodgings for Michael and yourself and then you visited Wú's warehouse and a few Portuguese trading factories with Arslan?"

"Yes."

"And you spent time taking in the city and visited different taverns and teahouses?"

"Yes. Michael and I also attended Sunday Mass at the Church of St. Dominic."

"And your only intercourse was with Wú, Arslan and a few Portuguese merchants?"

"Yes."

"What about the girl?"

"Girl? What girl Mary?"

I set my jaw and stared hard into Elizabeth's eyes. She began fidgeting in her chair as she knew I had caught her in a lie.

"In passing a few months back I overheard you mention a Chinese girl to one of the twins - a young woman of exquiste beauty with a bedazzlingly voice you said."

"Oh, well, yes, that's true. There was a girl at one of the taverns where Michael and I took our supper who sang for the patrons. I, I do not know her name."

"No?"

"No."

"Did you," Dijksma asked, "see Arslan with anyone other than Wú?"

"No."

"Did the man obtain a room for himself at the inn you and Michael stayed at?"

"No. I don't know what arrangements Arslan made for lodgings. Perhaps he had family in Macau."

"He told you he had family in Macau?"

"No."

"So why do you suppose he did?"

"I, um, I... I am only trying to be helpful Ewoud. I've told you everything I know."

I frowned and arched eyebrow as I knew Elizabeth had more to say. "This conversation has been most unsatisfactory," I said flatly and excused her.

I've never much cared for towns, cities or ports. The streets are always unclean as are the buildings and most of the people. Macau was no exception. For the life of me, I didn't understand Elizabeth's fascination with the place.

Walking arm-in-arm as loving husband and wife, Dijksma and I visited a number of trading houses both large and small. And while we stopped at various establishments owned by Portuguese, Chinese, Spanish and Japanese merchants, pretending to be interested in purchasing exotic wares for buyers back in Europe, Dijksma's men quietly went about the city gathering information on Portuguese strengths and weaknesses for Matelieff.

And then Dijksma and I stumbled upon a warehouse close to the waterfront on the east end of town where we saw a fearsome wooden eagle - a black eagle with outstretched wings and talons as if descending upon its prey - mounted above a pair of double red doors. The warehouse fit Elizabeth's description of Wú's factory perfectly.

We were met by an army of Chinamen sitting behind rows of tables working abacuses and recording numbers into leather-bound ledgers when we stepped inside. A young woman of exceptional beauty sitting on a stool off in a corner, preparing to play something that looked like a lute, immediately caught my eye and when she began singing with a voice from beyond this world - with a voice of majestic beauty that touched my soul - I knew at once this was the Chinese woman Elizabeth had spoken of.

A short Chinaman with stubby, bowed legs and an exceedingly long mustache immediately hurried towards us. He greeted us with a crooked smile, a perpetual, nauseating smile, and introduced himself in Portuguese as Lu-Li. When Dijksma asked the man for the proprieter, the Chinaman informed us that Master Wú was away on business on the mainland and would not return for several weeks. Dijksma asked Lu-Li for the next man in charge, thinking the Chinaman might offer up Arslan's name, but the little fellow with the endless smile replied that he was the man in charge. We dared not press our luck too far and ask for Arslan by name so we pretended to be interested in purchasing this and that for a time and then politely excused ourselves to meet an acquintance for a round or two of spirits, or so we said.

Dijksma poured more wine as we ate our supper at a nearby inn. "The fare is to your liking Mary?"

"Aye. I like this mix of Portuguese and Chinese food. Have you noticed the poorly dressed man standing against the wall in the far corner, the thin fellow wearing a bamboo hat?"

Dijksma smiled approvingly. "I have Mary. I was curious to know if you had. He followed us here from Wú's establishment."

"Aye. Should we be concerned?"

Dijksma laughed. "Not in the least. You've got your pistols and knives tucked away. I feel quite safe."

"And what if I don't know how to use my weapons? Or perhaps I'm a coward? Won't you be the sorry Dutchman then."

"According to the Company you can be, as you first told me yourself, a very dangerous opponent on land or at sea. Oh yes, within those dispatches you handed me in Ambon the Company included a brief, personal account on you. But in all candor, you need not worry because we are under the protection of Diogo de Vasconcelos de Meneses, the present Portuguese Governor of Macau. No Chinese will touch us. I handed the harbormaster a letter of introduction addressed to the good governor when we obtained our passeports. Which reminds me, I should stop by the governor's house to give Diogo my warm regards and thank him for his hospitality."

"You know this man?"

"I do. Some years ago, we served together aboard a Spanish treasure ship as junior officers. We became fast friends. I was Charles Serrano back then as I am now."

"You tease me sir with the prospect of a good story but if you are anything like our good friend Martin, you'll not tell me more."

Dijksma smiled. "Well, the hour is late. Should we return to the hostel?"

"Aye, I'm looking forward to my bed."

"Perhaps we should take a bottle or two of wine with us?"

"That sounds like trouble brewing. One could construe your intentions as an attempt at seduction." Dijksma couldn't help himself and started grinning like some bashful schoolboy, reminding me of another, reminding me of my first love.

"Well, if you were to invite me into your bed Mary, we could at long last consummate our blissful marriage."

"Ha! A favor for a favor?"

I could see the disappointment in Dijksma's eyes when he thought I would sell myself to him. I quickly disabused him of his error.

"Ewoud, I'm no harlot. You are a very fine-looking man and despite your heavy clothing, I can see you are fit and muscled. You'd be a prize for any woman and it has been too long since I've felt a man's touch. Aye, I'll invite you into my bed because I'm in a lusty mood - with or without the favor."

Dijksma's body was strong and taut. He had endurance. He was a tender, considerate lover. Though he lacked the playful imagination of an Englishman, or the fiery, reckless passion of a Frenchman, I thought him teachable.

"You are satisfied Mary?" Dijksma asked playfully as he rolled off me.

"Whew, I should say so," I replied a bit untruthfully so as not to offend. "You are a patient, thoughtful lover."

"As are you, Mary. This brand of the serpent over your left breast, this is the mark of the Irish beast?"

"Aye. I'm sorry if the scar repulses you."

Dijksma leaned over and kissed the old wound. "Not in the least. I know something of the story."

"And this round scar on your side Ewoud, a bullet wound?"

Dijksma smiled. "Yes, not a wound won in battle I regret to say but a lover's gift. I think she was aiming for my heart, or perhaps lower. And these stripes across your back and bottom? There was no mention of these wounds in the Company's file."

"No, there wouldn't be. These wounds are more recent. Ashaki bears the same scars across her back."

"When you are ready, I'd like to hear the story."

"Why have you not married Ewoud?"

"What woman would have me considering my work and the long months, sometimes spilling into years, I must be away from home?"

"A fair point."

"I could ask the same question of you Mary. You are a beautiful, clever woman. You have wealth and property. You could marry well if you wished."

"I'm too much of a free spirit to settle down. Tell me, from what little I've seen thus far you appear to be a very capable fellow. Why not strike out on your own? With a good ship under your feet and a loyal crew to command you'd do well for yourself I think."

Dijksma kissed me tenderly on the forehead. "I find my work most fulfilling. But I'll keep your suggestion in mind. Now that we have consummated our marriage, and I find myself the happiest of husbands, I am curious to know about this favor?"

"I would have words with the young woman we saw at Wú's trading house. I want to speak to her in private."

"Oh? You mean you wish to interrogate her."

"Aye."

"Why?"

"Honestly, I'm not entirely sure. A woman's intuition perhaps? I'm certain this is the girl Elizabeth spoke of. I'll need your help questioning her as I speak no Chinese and my Portuguese is woefully inadequate. If she knows nothing, no harm done. I'll send her on her way with a bit of silver for her troubles."

With the help of one of Dijksma's men, a fellow named Egbert who spoke tolerable Chinese, we snatched the beautiful, young China woman with the magical voice the following night as she left Wú's warehouse for home. We blindfolded her, hustled her into a cart and whisked her away to an abandoned Tanka boat moored against a quiet wharf nearby. We tied her to a chair inside the boat's small house cabin and left her blindfold on. To my surprise she did not beg or cry out.

"What is your name?" Dijksma asked in Portuguese. "Do not lie to me for I shall know it."

"Pardon? I talk small Portuguese."

Egbert repeated Dijksma's words in Chinese.

"Is the master testing me?" she asked nervously. "I am loyal. I have been obedient in all things. I swear. Please release me. I've done no wrong!"

"Your name."

"Ling, my name is Ling."

"Good. Wú is your master?"

"Yes."

"Good. Relax. Breathe. The truth will see you safely home this night. Do you understand Ling?"

"Yes."

"Excellent," Dijksma said and turned to me. "Madam?"

"Do you know," I asked in Spanish and waited for Egbert to translate my words, "a Spanish woman named Elizabeth?"

"Yes."

"And do you know an Irishman named Michael MacGyver?"

"No. I do not know this man."

"No?"

"No. Elizabeth was accompanied by a European man named Michael Flannigan. Perhaps this is the man you are asking about?"

"Yes, Flannigan."

"I know Michael a little."

"And who is Arslan?"

"You, my lady, speak with the same accent as Michael. You are Irish?"

"You have a good ear Ling. Ah, but of course you do. You're a musician."

"You are a friend of Michael? Michael was very kind to me."

"'Tis best for both of us if you let me ask the questions. Now, who is Arslan?"

"Please, please dear lady. If Master Wú learns I've talked with you he will kill me. He will kill my family. I am nothing but a lowly peasant girl. I know nothing. I am nobody. I sing for the men who count the master's money. Such is my sad lot in this sad life."

"Who is Arslan?"

"Please, I beg you have pity…"

"Who is Arslan? I ask again: who … is … Arslan?"

"He, he and Master Wú have business together. This is no secret. Arslan is a merchant. He once served the emperor, or so I've heard men say. Arslan travels between Banten, Malacca and Kyushu for Master Wú. This is all I know."

"Kyushu?"

"Japan."

"Where is your master?"

"He is traveling north. I know not why."

"Where's Arslan?"

"I do not know. I never know where Master Wú sends Arslan or for what purpose. I play the pipa. I am a singer of songs, poems and ballads, nothing more."

I removed Ling's blindfold to see her eyes. "Elizabeth and Michael agreed to transport Chinamen to Banten."

The young Chinese woman stared at me confused and fell silent. "Well?"

"You are the woman who walked into the master's warehouse yesterday."

"I would have my question answered."

"Yes, yes. And they sold spices to Master Wú and bought goods from him to take back to Europe."

"See, you do know some things about certain matters. How do you know this?"

"Michael, Michael told me."

"When?"

"As men moved cargo on his ship, he came to see me. He told me these things."

"Why would he leave his ship to see you?"

"We, eh, we, we loved each other," she said hesitantly and looked away. "He promised to come back for me one day. He will tell you."

Her answer caught me off guard, I took a moment to suppress my emotions, to retain my poise. "The Chinamen Elizabeth and Michael brought aboard their ship turned on them. Why?"

"I, I, I know nothing of these things," Ling replied with rising anxiety in her voice. "Is Michael, is, is he well?"

"After leaving Macau, pirates attacked Elizabeth and Michael. The Chinamen they were transporting joined the pirates. What do you know of this treachery?"

Ling lost her composure. She began fidgeting in her chair and I could see the terror spreading across her eyes.

"Well? Speak damn you!"

"I, I, I do not know. Please, please good lady, where is Michael?"

"Michael's dead."

The young beauty let out a loud sigh and looked away again. She started panting, gulped down air and wept as her body trembled.

I felt pity for her and yet I needed answers. I cupped her jaw firmly in my hand, forcing her to look at me.

"I believe the men who killed Michael may have been working for Wú. If not Wú, I want to know who gave the order and I want to know why."

After a long pause Ling collected herself and answered me in a woeful, defeated tone. "I, I know nothing of these things, madam. I swear. Kill me if it pleases you. I am ready. Michael was very kind to me. He won my heart. He gave me hope."

I continued pressing Ling for answers, gaining nothing, and then Dijksma tried. He gently asked Ling to recount everything she had seen and heard about Michael and Elizabeth and we learned about the *House of a Thousand Pleasures* for the first time, but little else.

Dijksma and I both agreed Ling had been honest with us. She was too young, too unworldly to spin a good lie. She asked me if Elizabeth had survived and seemed genuinely relieved when I said yes. Then I handed her a purse of silver and sent her on her way.

For the next few days Dijksma and I spent time enjoying ourselves while his men finished their work. We took long strolls around the city and sampled different foods at various taverns. On Market Day we stopped at one shop after another. I saw a mix of cheap babbles and common wares alongside things of exquisite beauty made by master craftsman. We spent one pleasant afternoon with the Portuguese governor at his home. In the evenings Dijksma and I played cards and drank and entertained one another in my bed. We very much enjoyed each other's company. But I had seen enough of China. I was ready to discard my dress, rejoin my men and put to sea again. I was disappointed that I had accomplished little more in Macau other than to satisfy my desires of the flesh.

And then, on the last evening of our stay in Macau, there was a light rapping at my door. Dijksma quickly slipped his trousers on, donned his tunic and warily opened the door holding a dagger behind his back.

"We have a guest Mary," he said casually in Portuguese and waved our visitor inside. "In fact, we have two guests. Well, step inside Ling and state your business. Who's the boy?"

Ling and a small, sinewy boy dressed in shabby clothing, a child of about eight or nine years I guessed, stepped into my room carrying burlap sacks over their shoulders. Ling searched my face apprehensively.

Dijksma closed the door and set the lock. "Ling?"

"Good sir, kind madam, this me sister, no, no, me brother, me brother Jian," she said slowly in her tortured Portuguese.

I quickly threw on my dress and hid my pistols underneath the sheets. I moved around the room to light more candles while Dijksma pulled two chairs over and motioned Ling and the boy to sit.

"You've taken a great risk coming here," Dijksma said. "Why?"

"I answer your questions truthfully," Ling replied nervously. "I know little. Me brother knows more."

"Oh?" I asked suspiciously, certain Ling and her brother had come only for more silver. "How would your brother know anything?"

"He clean, he sweep floors at warehouse for Master Wú. He run errands for Master Wú. He carry messages for Master Wú. Jian hear, see many things."

"How much?"

"How much?"

"Yes, how much? You come for more silver, yes?"

"No, madam. No silver. Take Jian. See him safe. Please. Jian have good information. You like."

"I trust," Dijksma interrupted, "you were not followed?"

"Ah? What?"

"Shhh..." I commanded as I put my finger to my lips and then sent Dijksma off to fetch Egbert. Once the two men returned, we resumed our conversation in Chinese.

"We," Ling answered after Egbert translated Dijksma's question, "were most careful and were not followed."

"I thought," I asked, "you told me the other evening that if you ever crossed Wú, he would kill you and your family?"

"After I told my mother and father about you, they begged me to find you and bring my brother to you. I gave them the silver you gave me. They left with a caravan traveling west. I pray to great, wise Buddha to keep them safe. Jian can help you find answers to your questions in exchange for safe passage."

"Safe passage? Safe passage to where?"

"Anywhere far from China."

"Our ship is not a pleasure yacht."

"I come in good faith. If you say no, if you turn Jian away, he will die."

"And what about you?"

"I am dead already. You take Jian. The man you met at the warehouse, Lu-Li, asked me questions after you left as if I was somehow to blame for your presence here. He knows I spent time with Michael and Elizabeth. I only did what Master Wú commanded me to do. Europeans rarely come to Master Wú's warehouse. You caused a stir. Lu-Li is suspicious and none, not the guilty or the innocent survive the suspicions of Lu-Li for long. I have friends amongst the Tanaka. Perhaps they can help me escape Macau."

Though furious with myself, I couldn't say no to Ling. I should have avoided Macau. There was no one in the port I could trust. The languages and customs were strange to me. I thought the Portuguese overbearing and arrogant and found the Chinese to be two-faced and untrustworthy. The Chinese, as Dijksma had forewarned me, like to speak in riddles. They often say one thing but mean another. I suppose this is true of all peoples but the Chinese seemed to excel at duplicity. Macau reminded me of Trinidad on the opposite side of the world - an island of lechery, treachery and villainy, a filthy abomination thriving on greed - and I was wary of becoming entangled with the East as Elizabeth had mistakenly done.

Dijksma returned to his room to grab a blanket and pillows. Ling slept with me in the bed while he slept on the floor with Jian and Egbert. At first light in the morning, Dijksma sent Egbert out to gather the rest of his men. He approved of taking Ling and Jian with us and when Egbert returned with the others, we cautiously made our way back to *Spitfire*, keeping to the shadows and back alleys.

Once safely back aboard our ship, we quickly left Macau behind and found our little squadron where we had left it. I waved to Atwood and Maurice to follow me and we made haste for Mina de Oro to retrieve *Spitfire's* guns. After four days of easy sailing, I went ashore with the first wave of men to make camp and then summoned my officers to me.

When Ling stepped off one of the longboats hand-in-hand with her brother, I watched Elizabeth race wildly across the beach towards her with open arms. A happy moment but, unhappily, I knew I would need to deal with Elizabeth and her deceit later.

"God's wounds," Atwood roared affably and laughed as he considered Ling and Jian while stepping off his own longboat. "Truly we now have ourselves a universal crew."

Atwood's good humor perplexed me. "I thought you disliked the Chinese, Jacob?" I called out to him from my tent.

"Only them who would do us harm Mary, only them who would do us harm. These two don't appear dangerous to me. The boy and the girl - brother and sister?"

"Aye. They may be useful."

Atwood took a few steps closer to Dijksma. "Did you and your boys take Macau, Ewoud?" he asked as he patted the Dutchman on the shoulder.

Dijksma tossed his head back and laughed. "No, Jacob, I thought I'd give you the honor of sacking the city and planting the Company's flag atop the governor's house."

"I'd rather sail to the top of the world, or do you Dutch have plans to add the Arctic to your empire?"

"No, no. We're not a covetous people. You are welcome to the Artic and any ice you find there."

I waved the two men over. "Ewoud, please come join my officers and me. I don't have any chairs, but we've laid blankets out across the sand - and we have wine."

"I'm delighted to be back with all of you," I said once everyone was seated. "Ewoud and his men accomplished what they set out to do whist I accomplished very little. Neither Wú nor Arslan were in Macau."

I paused to face Elizabeth. "We have," I continued, "two new passengers as some of you know. The boy may have information which might help us better understand the treachery that killed Michael and our lads. I've not spoken with the boy yet. His name is Jian. His sister's name is Ling. They left Macau with us seeking sanctuary from Wú.

Ewoud, what is the next part of the Dutch plan as pertains to my men and me?"

"We should sail to Banda Besar to make arrangements for the spices you will be hauling back to Amsterdam and then we must rendezvous with Matelieff. What happens after that is not for me to say."

"Very well Ewoud. Jacob, I'll give you your ship back. She's as good a vessel as when you first let me borrow her. Maurice, Rob, when can you both sail?"

"Let the lads have a few days of rest on shore?" Maurice asked. "The ships are in fine condition, but the men are weary."

"I agree," Shaw added. "Do the lads some good to be off the ships for a bit and this is a pretty spot."

"Good. Mustafa let's start rotating the men ashore. We can recover *Spitfire's* guns in the morning. Ewoud, say three days?"

Dijksma nodded. "Three days of rest it is Mary."

"What," Atwood asked, "can you tell us of your orders Ewoud?"

"Not much as I wasn't given much. I'll know more after I consult with the admiral and I'll be happy to share what I can with you when he does. Certainly, procuring the spices for your voyage back to Amsterdam is a priority."

"The sooner the better," Atwood said. "We have men who've been away from home for a very long time."

"I believe I overheard someone say you intend to sail to the Caribbean once you've fulfilled your obligations to the Company?"

"Aye," I answered. "We have business in New Spain."

"You will sail west across the Indian Ocean and retrace your steps back to Europe or do you intend to venture east across the Pacific?"

"We have yet to discuss that choice. What do you know about the Pacific?"

"Not much. The Portuguese have been hauling cargo across the Pacific between Macau and Acapulco for years. Spain has been doing the same from Manila to various ports in the Americas. But where the Portuguese and Spanish are sailing due east to the western coast of the New World, you'd be sailing south-by-southeast and then you'd need to circle around the whole of the South Americas."

"A longer journey to be sure," I said.

"Much riskier too I think."

"Why?"

"In 1553, in October of that year I believe, Francisco de Ulloa sailed from the city of Valdivia in the territory known as Chili with the first expedition to enter the Strait of Magellan from the west so it can be done. Just before I sailed from Banten in June for Ambon, Captain Willem Janszoon returned from Papua New Guinea with the barque *Duyfken* after discovering a new land to the south during his voyage. He named the new territory Kaap Keerweer, Cape Turnback. Who knows what other islands or continents lay beyond to the east or south? From Malacca to Papua New Guinea is at least thirty-five hundred miles. Then you'd need to cross a wide stretch of the Pacific to reach Chili, perhaps as much as nine thousand miles of open water with possibly no land in-between. From the Strait of Magellan, up the coast of Argentina and to Veracruz is another eleven thousand miles, though you'd be sailing close to shore with plenty of opportunities to make landfall. That's roughly twenty-two thousand miles of water and then you'd still need to return to Amsterdam with your cargo for the Company - another sixty-three hundred miles. Thirty thousand miles of sailing in all by my reckoning, give or take."

I nodded as I refilled Dijksma's pewter flagon with wine. "An arduous journey to be sure. By comparison, a voyage from Malacca to Cape Town is close to six thousand miles. Then sailing north along the west coast of Africa to Amsterdam is another seventy-four hundred miles and, as you say, a voyage between Amsterdam to Veracruz is roughly sixty-three hundred miles, though we could stop in Ireland first to rest and refit our ships."

"Yes Mary, twenty thousand miles give or take and then a voyage back to Ireland. You might encounter more favorable trade winds sailing east across the Pacific, but the currents will generally be against you. The choice to me seems clear. Take the traditional route west back to Europe."

"Most impressive," I said. "You've studied your maps."

"There's little revelry out here in the wild," Dijksma replied as he tipped his flagon towards me. "I read books to fill the emptiness of my days."

"You read books on navigation for amusement!" Atwood quipped. "I think you've been living out in these untamed lands too long lad. Perhaps you should find yourself a good woman who can better fill your days."

The Dutchman sighed. "Find a good woman you say? Here, deep in the untamed lands of Asia? Most unlikely Jacob..."

Chapter Thirty

ollowing three days of rest on the idyllic island of Mina de Oro, we broke camp, returned to our ships and headed west for the island of Banda Besar next to make arrangements for the Company's cargo. We spent only a day on the island before sailing north, passing by one volcano spewing a thin column of smoke and ash into the heavens, something I'd never witnessed before.

We enjoyed fair weather throughout our voyage towards Malaysia and encountered no mishaps. We made good time. But when we reached Pulau Ujong at the tip of the Malaysian peninsula, the place where we had left Matelieff and his squadron, his ships were nowhere in sight and the Dutch camp was gone. After circling around the island and finding no sign of Matelieff, we sailed on to Malacca and there we spotted the Dutch squadron, now reinforced by Vice-Admiral de Vivere's four warships, riding anchor a mile or two offshore. With the help of my Spanish glass, I could see Dutch solders outside the city's walls. Matelieff had landed his army and had Malacca surrounded.

"Ewoud, how good to see you again," the admiral said and stood to shake hands with Dijksma and me as we stepped into his great cabin. "It has been too long my friend. Mary, welcome back. I pray you found your men?"

"I did, thank you Admiral. And I see you've found the rest of your fleet. I see you've sent the army ashore."

"Quite so. We've been blessed with good fortune thus far. Mary, you've already met Captain Dirk Mol. Dirk, meet Ewoud Dijksma, one of the Company's rising stars. The gentleman looking over the charts on my desk is one of our junior officers, Lieutenant Christopher Perry. Please, sit and enjoy a glass of sherry with us. Did you reach Macau, Ewoud?"

"With Mary's help, I did sir. The Portuguese have built no fortifications or stonewalls. They have no redoubts. We saw no artillery. The treaty between the Portuguese and the Ming emperor which forbids the Portuguese from fortifying the city appears intact. We saw many insignificant galliots, galleys, caravels, pinnaces and junks. But we also saw two respectable war-carracks and one very large galleon sitting in the harbor, though we heard the galleon was preparing to sail for Japan. The Portuguese have perhaps as many as six hundred men-at-arms to defend the city. Defenses appear light. It is unclear what the Chinese would do if we attacked Macau. Whilst the Portuguese and the Chinese are hardly allies, their mutual trading interests are strong. I have a more detailed written report I'll leave with you Admiral."

"Excellent, Ewoud. On my part, I've secured the treaty we needed with the Sultan of Johor. His highness has readily agreed to support us. The Malay have no love for the Portuguese let me tell you. And as you can see, we have the city under siege. Nothing is getting in or out."

"If I may ask sir, what are the essential terms of this treaty between the Company and the Malay?"

"You are right to inquire Ewoud. Once we take Malacca, Aluaddin has agreed to lease the city back to us for nominal annual sum whilst all adjacent lands outside Malacca will be returned to the sultan. We've also agreed to respect each other's religions. The Malay will be permitted to rebuild their mosques within Malacca and worship freely according to the precepts of the Quran."

"Congratulations, Admiral," Dijksma said with a nod. "Victory is close at hand then?"

"We shall see. André Furtado de Mendonca, the Captain-General of India, commands Malacca's defenses and is a capable fellow they say. Furtado has placed a battery of heavy guns on the high ground overlooking the harbor, preventing our ships from entering. The city's defenses are formidable. The army has made several attempts to breach the city's walls without success. We have no siege engines and Furtado's men have been tenacious fighters. Furtado also has a small squadron of Japanese Red Seal ships supporting him. The samurai have their magnificent swords and are armed with Spanish long muskets too with a new trick borrowed from the Chinese - they've affixed long daggers to the barrels enabling the samurai to fight as musketeers or pikemen. Furtado also has large numbers of slaves at his disposal. The blacks may have little training but any man holding a weapon in his hands can kill."

"How many men defend the city?" Dijksma asked.

"Perhaps as many as three thousand men in all though I suspect no more than three hundred or thereabouts are professional Portuguese soldiers."

"And the Dutch army is eight hundred strong?" I asked.

"Well, it is the Company's army but yes Lady Mary, I have eight companies of seasoned professionals at my disposal."

"Has the sultan committed any men, Admiral?" Dijksma asked.

"Our new ally has only provided a token force thus far to support our noble endeavor. One can hardly blame his majesty. The sultan is being cautious until we Dutch prove ourselves. On the bright side the sultan's spies within the city have reported our siege is producing the desired results. The city's twelve thousand citizens are starving. Many are urging Furtado to surrender. Such is our present military situation."

"Malacca's collapse is imminent then Admiral?" I asked, a bit surprised as I had never heard the admiral string so many words together at one time.

"As you know Mary, nothing is imminent or certain in war. Perchance do your ships carry any provisions you can share? We are low on foodstuffs. Our army is especially in a desperate way."

"Aye, of course, sir. Tell me where you wish us to make the transfer and when and I shall see it done."

"I'm most grateful, thank you. I'll instruct Captain Cornelisz of the *Erasmu* to arrange matters. If you find yourself running low on supplies, you'll kindly let me know and I'll cut your ships loose to forage for more, yes?"

"Aye."

"Good. Alas Ewoud I've received catastrophic news which could have serious implications for your mission. I assume you've heard?"

"You are referring to the loss of the Moluccas?"

"Yes."

"I am aware."

I looked at Dijksma first and then at Matelieff. "May I ask what happened in the Moluccas?"

"A powerful Spanish armada from the Philippines," Dijksma explained, "of thirty-six ships with an army of two thousand men led by Pedro de Acuñah seized Tidore and Ternate last April. The Spanish have arrested Saidi and his royal family and have imprisoned them in Manila, though it would seem the sultan's son, Mudafar Syah, a mere boy, avoided capture. Spain now possesses Ternate, Tidore, Moti, Makian and Bacan and consequently controls the world's entire clove market."

"What will you do Admiral?" I asked.

"What can I do? My objective is Malacca. Once we take Malacca, I can redirect my attention to the Moluccas. The Company is sending more ships and men into Indonesia. The additional muscle should tip the scales of power in our favor. Then perhaps we can place the boy Mudafar on his father's throne as our ally."

Mol stood to refill my glass. "So, we wait for the city to fall. Christopher, I dare say you're going to ruin your eyes studying those charts in this light. Leave the charts. Be a good fellow and see to it that Cornelisz receives the admiral's instructions concerning the supplies Lady Mary has graciously offered."

I shared one quarter of what we had with the Dutch and prayed I would not live to regret my generosity. Matelieff had been respectful and courteous towards me since leaving Amsterdam, far more so than Drake had ever been, and I felt obliged to show him my gratitude in return. I wanted to keep the Company's goodwill for as long as I could.

We sat anchored off Malacca for long weeks, well out of the range of the city's large harbor guns, as the siege dragged on and on. And then one afternoon in mid-August a goodly number of ships appeared on the horizon to the north and suddenly the scales of power tipped -

but not in Matelieff's favor.

Some commanders might have panicked; some might have withdrawn. Not Matelieff. He promptly summoned his officers to *Oranje*, including Dijksma and me. Sitting behind his desk, the admiral waved Dijksma and me into his cramped great cabin where all his senior officers, including Vice-Admiral de Vivere, whom I'd not yet met, stood gathered.

"Ewoud, Mary," Matelieff said, "thank you for joining us. Our new, uninvited guests, the twenty Portuguese warships off Cape Rachado to the north, are most certainly the ships of the Viceroy of Goa, Dom Martim Afonso de Castro. Christopher, you may now read the particulars of what we know about Castro's fleet."

Perry, a bland, young fellow with a nervous demeanor grabbed a sheet of paper off the admiral's desk and cleared his throat. "Ahem, gentlemen, my lady, Castro we believe has the following principal great ships at his disposal: the forty-four gun, one-thousand-ton galleon *Nossa Senhora da Conceição*, captained by Manuel de Mascarenhas, the forty gun, nine-hundred-ton galleon *São Simeão*, captained by D. Francisco de Sotomayor, the forty gun, nine-hundred-ton galleon *São Salvador*, captained by Álvaro de Carvalho, the thirty-eight gun galleon *Nossa Senhora das Mercês*, also weighing nine-hundred-tons, captained by Dom Henrique de Noronha, the thirty-six gun, eight-hundred-ton galleon *Todos os Santos*, captained by D. Francisco de Noronha, the forty-gun, eight-hundred-ton galleon *São Nicolau*, captained by D. Fernando de Mascarenhas, the thirty-two gun, six-hundred-ton galleon *Santa Cruz*, captained by Sebastião Soares, the thirty-four gun, six-hundred-ton galleon, *de Guerra*, captained by Dom Duarte de Guerra, and lastly the eighteen gun, two-hundred-forty-ton frigate *Sancto António* under the command of Master António Sousa Falcão. The remaining eleven ships consist of modestly armed fustas, galleys and caravels for which we have little information but are most likely serving as troop transports and victuallers."

"Thank you, Christopher," Matelieff said. "Some of you have urged me to retrieve our army and fall back to Banten and wait for Castro to return to Goa, which he must eventually do. Once Castro is gone, we'd be free to resume our assault on Malacca without interference. I must admit this is sensible advice. Ewoud, you know something of my colleagues on the Company's board of directors. What do you suppose those fine gentlemen would urge me to do if they were with us now?"

"Speak your mind man," the admiral commanded when Dijksma hesitated.

"Admiral, I wouldn't presume to know your thoughts on the matter, or those of any board member but, as you have pressed me for my opinion as to what the other sixteen members might urge you to do, I doubt any of those fine gentlemen would look favorably upon any retreat or delay. They would, I believe, insist you keep on the offensive, that you do your utmost to run Castro out of Indonesia."

The admiral nodded approvingly. "Always the diplomat Ewoud and uncommonly shrewd too. Gentlemen, tomorrow we shall sail north and engage the enemy. Full attack. Christopher shall hand you your written orders as you take your leave. God be with you. God bless our just cause. That is all."

Mercifully, my orders were to keep Malacca blockaded and provide the army with artillery support if needed, tasks I welcomed. When the Dutch fleet weighed anchor and sailed north, I took *Nemesis* and followed the Dutch at a respectful distance to observe the action, leaving Atwood and Maurice behind to carry out Matelieff's instructions.

The first day of the battle was bright and clear, though the winds had turned blustery and unpredictable. The two fleets sat anchored across from one another off Cape Rachardo and contented themselves with lobbing shots at each other from afar. The second day was more or less the same with neither side gaining any real advantage. But on the third day, just as the first shafts of golden sunlight burst across the jungles of Malaysia to usher in a new day, the Portuguese raised their anchors, set their sails and attacked. With their bigger ships and larger crews, with favorable winds behind them, the Portuguese charged straight into the Dutch. Ships on both sides broke formation and engaged one another at close range. The struggle between the two titans quickly disintegrated into a disorganized, bloody brawl.

I've always preferred fire and maneuver, finesse, over brute strength. I watched aghast as galleons - slow, clumsy beasts - crudely rammed each other. My crew and I saw flames engulf one ship and then another, though we couldn't tell whose ships were burning. In the late afternoon we witnessed a horrific explosion obliterate one galleon. Dijksma, having decided to sail aboard *Oranje* with Matelieff, perhaps would have a good story to tell when he returned, if he returned. I found myself consumed with worry over his well-being and that annoyed me.

With the day's savagery drawing to a close, I had Shaw bring *Nemesis* about and we hurried back to Malacca to rejoin our own ships. If the Portuguese had won the day, I had a ready plan. I'd sail to Banda Besar in haste to collect our spices and then sail on to Amsterdam with as much speed as we could muster. I wouldn't linger in Malacca's waters and risk my ships to capture. The Dutch would need to fend for themselves.

As we approached the Portuguese stronghold, we saw six Red Seal ships in the distance flying the black and yellow crest of the Oda Clan attempting to run our thin blockade. *Cerberus* fired off a broadside followed by *Spitfire*. I had Shaw steer *Nemesis* close to shore to bring us up behind the Japanese and had Efendi fire our bow chasers to let the Japanese know we were coming. The reach of our long guns made a good impression. The Japanese commander promptly swung his ships around for the safety of the harbor when he saw our ship approaching and I for one was glad. I had no desire to watch good men drown, men with whom we had no quarrel.

But then the Japanese commander had a sudden change of heart.

He turned his ships north towards *Nemesis* and kept his squadron close to shore, thinking I suppose that he could slip past a single ship sailing his way.

I took the wheel from the helmsman, then looked for Shaw and found him standing next to Efendi on the main deck. "Rob," I called out. "I'll have the checkered yellow and green pennant raised up the main mast if you please." This was the signal for all my officers to join me in my great cabin for a council of war.

"Ah, that will bring Jacob and Maurice racing this way, up behind the Japanese - as you do what exactly Mary?" Shaw asked, clearly amused.

I couldn't help myself and answered Shaw with nothing more than a mischievous grin. How I love the game of battle.

Next, I spotted Kinkae standing at the fore mast and called out to him. "Kinkae, have your lads ready the ship for a hard turn to starboard!" I bellowed. "Once we complete the turn, furl all sail but the topgallants. Mustafa, clear the decks for action. See to your port side batteries."

When I gave the order to make our turn, we cut across the six Japanese vessels just as *Spitfire* and *Cerberus* started coming up behind them at a brisk pace from the south. The Japanese could go no farther north without running straight into *Nemesis'* great guns. They could not come about and go south without passing *Spitfire* and *Cerberus* and exchanging multiple broadsides. Nor could they sail west and out to sea for we had the Japanese pinned against the coast with a lively westerly wind to keep them there.

The Japanese commander understood his predicament. He had his ships form a defensive circle and made no effort to ask for terms. Japanese samurai I later learned do not surrender. Though we could have stood back and obliterated his ships with ease with our bigger guns, I signaled Atwood and Maurice to secure their batteries and fall in behind *Nemesis*. I had Shaw raise a white flag. The Japanese commander understood the gesture. He gave the order for his own men to secure their guns and allowed us to escort his ships back into the harbor. And as we parted ways in the fading light, I saw the

Japanese commander - I imagined him a proud and valiant man - climb up on the quarterdeck rail and nod his appreciation followed by a respectful bow. I donned my hat and curtsied back.

Once we cleared Malacca's waters, I gave the order to furl sail with our ships pointing south. We did not drop our anchors for I wanted us to be ready to flee in a hurry if it was the Portuguese, and not the Dutch, who came our way during the night.

But in the early morning it was the Dutch who appeared. *Oranje* limped past us with a diagonal red stripe on field of yellow flying off her royal main, the signal for us to follow, with eight battered warships trailing in a single line behind her. Her sails were in tatters, much of her rigging had been shot away and her hull was badly pitted. The other galleons looked no better. After my ships fell in behind the Dutch, Matelieff stopped to retrieve his army and then we returned to the Johor River where we formed a defensive line and dropped anchor.

A longboat from one of the Dutch ships soon rowed over to my ship with a dozen wounded. I felt my heart flutter when I saw Dijksma alive, sitting amongst them with his arm wrapped in a bloodstained sling. I sent James below to warn Stachel that he had work to do. After Efendi and I helped Dijksma and the others aboard, I sent Ashaki over to *Spitfire* and *Cerberus* in the Dutch longboat to bring Atwood, Maurice and Elizabeth back to my great cabin.

"I saw the gates of hell open before my eyes," Dijksma said soberly as I cleaned a nasty gash across his upper arm with beer. "I've been in battle before but never have I beheld such gruesome carnage."

"After he has tended to those with more serious injuries Stachel will need to do some stitching later," I said as I wrapped a length of clean linen around Dijksma's arm and tied the ends in a tight knot. "Fighting at sea is an ugly business. How were you wounded?"

"A piece of flying glass bumped into me."

"Hmmm. I'm bringing the others over. Are you able to tell us what happened off Cape Rachardo?"

"A dram of whiskey first might help revive me," Dijksma replied with a thin smile.

"Scoundrel, always poaching off me."

"Perhaps the feel of your fingers caressing my inner thigh might stimulate the blood and restore me to better health more speedily?"

"Christ, you're impertinent!" I said and giggled.

"What's so amusing?" Atwood asked as he ducked his head below my cabin's door frame with the others following behind him.

"The Dutch are amusing," I said. "They lose battles and laugh."

After my officers took their seats, I passed a bottle of good Scottish whiskey around. "Tell us Ewoud," I asked, "what happened?"

After Dijksma knocked his whiskey back, Atwood poured him another. "The battle was a bewildering affair," he began. "I suppose the Portuguese will claim a glorious victory inasmuch as they sank *Nassau* and *Middleburg* and have driven us from Malacca. But the Portuguese have paid a terrible price. From the causality reports prepared for the admiral, I understand we have over one hundred dead, twice as many wounded and a great number of men are missing. Even so, the Portuguese suffered heavier losses from what I could see and we sank *São Salvador* and *de Guerra*."

"Sounds like a draw," Shaw commented.

"Alas, no Rob. Tactically you are correct perhaps but we've been forced to abandon our siege. We've exhausted most of our ammunition, supplies are dwindling and our army is close to ruin. Castro has won this day."

"What is the Dutch plan now?" I asked.

"Matelieff is a lion. He'll repair his ships, acquire more ammunition and, if he still has the sultan's support, he'll attack."

"Can you describe the battle for us?" I asked.

"With no pleasure. The first two days we fought from a distance whilst at anchor, exchanging hundreds of rounds of shot. Barrels overheated and cracked. On barrel melted before my eyes. We lost a few men but no ships were seriously damaged. On the third day the Portuguese charged straight at us. Ships collided. Men fought hand-to-hand, clawing at each other like animals. Rivulets of blood flowed down the scuppers. *Santa Cruz* caught *Nassau* at anchor. *Oranje* maneuvered over to *Nassau* to give aid but a sudden shift in the winds drove *Oranje* into *Middelburg*. *São Salvador*, *Nossa Senhora da Conceição* and *de Guerra* all rushed into the fray to support *Santa Cruz*. *São Salvador* rammed into *Middleburg*. *Nossa Senhora das Mercês* rammed into *Oranje*. *Nassau* and *Middleburg* both caught fire and then - a great tragedy - *Nassau* exploded, killing Captain Jacobz and most of his crew. Like some crazed bull, Captain Klaasz then drove *Mauritius* straight into *de Guerra* and pushed her into the burning *Middleburg*. When Matelieff realized *Middleburg* was doomed, he gave the order to withdraw. As *Middleburg* sank, she dragged *São Salvador* and *de Guerra* down with her. I saw no lack of valor on either side."

"What a fucking muddle," Atwood said with a pained expression and shook his head in disgust.

"Matelieff and Castro," I offered coldly, "have set naval warfare back a thousand years. These are the tactics of the ancient world. Ships smashing into one another like battering rams, crude and unimaginative tactics. Fighting men deserve better."

Dijksma sighed. "The unpredictable winds Mary, raucous, mischievous winds, toyed with us for three days. Maneuvering was extraordinarily difficult."

"Good time to withdraw then, make repairs, replenish your stores and wait for more favorable conditions," I said testily with a clenched jaw. A waste of lives by callous commanders had always upset me.

"Yes, you make a profound observation my lady, but then again, you have the luxury. You don't have the Company to please..."

Chapter Thirty-One

Iexpected Matelieff to release my ships while his fleet licked its wounds, but no. Rather than showing his displeasure with his new Dutch allies for failing to take Malacca, Alauddin, the Sultan of Johor, impressed by Dutch tenacity and resilience during the battle off Cape Rachado, pledged to provide more men, more supplies and to replenish Dutch stores of gunpowder if Matelieff agreed to resume his siege of Malacca. Matelieff accepted.

I asked Matelieff for permission to sail to Banda to collect our spices but he said no. I asked Matelieff for permission to scour the coast to look for provisions but he said no. He needed every ship and every man for the battle yet ahead he said. I fretted about what I would do if he asked me for my ships to replace the pair he had lost.

The weeks languishing on the muddy waters of the Johor River in the heat and humidity passed by slowly. Tedium set in. Efendi kept the men busy with menial tasks while every so often I made them scrub the ship and themselves down clean with chunks of coarse soap.

And then in late September, with Malacca secure, Castro surprised us. Incredulously, he split his fleet in two while facing a dangerous opponent. He took half his ships and sailed south, leaving the rest behind to protect Malacca, the precious key to Indonesia. Matelieff could hardly believe his good fortune. He promptly called his senior officers, along with Dijksma and me, over to *Oranje* for a council of war.

"You've all heard the gossip," Matelieff said as he stood on the quarterdeck gleefully rubbing his hands together. He had assembled us out on the quarterdeck to enjoy a cool, ocean breeze. He offered no wine or beer or ale or stronger spirits - all symptoms of his diminishing supplies.

A few days earlier I had turned his quartermaster away when the fool had the gall to come aboard my ship and demanded as much flour, beans, rice and other staples as I could spare. It was no secret that amongst Matelieff's men there was growing discord brewing. Men were slowly starving and longed to return to their homes. Though the sultan had made good on his promise to supply the Dutch with gunpowder, he had failed to deliver any victuals. The admiral was all too aware of the whispers of mutiny amongst his men, whispers he needed to quell and quickly.

"Castro has sailed off," he continued, "leaving behind only ten ships to defend Malacca. Five galleons accompanied by four inferior ships lay anchored just outside the harbor in a crescent-moon formation."

"Do we know Castro's destination sir?" Dijksma asked.

"Don't have a clue. For the moment I don't care. The man has provided us with a splendid opportunity and we must not squander it."

"And what of the city Admiral?" Klaasz, *Mauritius'* captain and the hero of Rachado asked.

"The sultan has sent word that six thousand souls have perished from disease and starvation, half the population. A great tragedy. Had Castro not arrived in the nick of time the city would have certainly fallen to us by now."

"What is this "nick of time" Ewoud?" I asked in a whisper.

"A nick, a precise cut, so a precise time," Dijksma whispered back.

"What do you say there Ewoud?" the admiral asked gruffly, clearly annoyed by the interruption.

"Beg pardon sir. 'Tis nothing."

"Ahem, very well. The Portuguese have perhaps two hundred soldiers fit for duty. The Japanese have sailed off. Even so, Furtado still has his blacks and those damn heavy guns of his overlooking the harbor."

I braced myself for ugliness when the admiral turned to me.

"Your men Lady Mary have seen no action. They are fresh. I need you to land a strong force outside the city. I need you to take the redoubt overlooking the harbor and spike those damn guns."

"Beg pardon, Admiral?"

"Was I not clear?"

"With respect sir, I did not sail all this way to claim a patch of sand for king and county. My men are mariners not soldiers. I made no commitment to the Company to provide an army."

"I'm certain the Company would disagree with you there my lady. If you are unwilling to give the order you will leave me with no choice but to give the order for you."

"Even if I were inclined to agree with your interpretation of my contract Admiral, my men will not fight for you," I replied but immediately caught myself. I needed a stronger argument before Matelieff threatened to arrest me or worse. "Many of my lads have been stricken with the bloody flux, fever or have been laid low by scurvy. They're weak from lack of nourishment because I shared our precious supplies with you. I have barely enough able-bodied men to work my ships. I humbly beg you to reconsider Admiral."

My claim was a preposterous exaggeration, a blatant lie, and I did not know what Dijksma would do as he stood next to me knowing my lie. And though he turned to me with a troubled look in his eye, Dijksma showed his honor; he proved his friendship and said nothing.

The admiral stared at me perplexed for a moment, pursed his lips and nodded. "Very well, I am sympathetic. We Dutch too are suffering. You can watch our flanks as we attack. You can do this much, yes?"

"You can count on us, sir." I answered, relieved. "And I can do better than that. We have ample stores of ball and powder. My ships can bombard the redoubt to distract the Portuguese harbor guns whilst you attack their ships."

"Wonderful, Mary."

Dijksma discretely took my hand as the longboat crew rowed us back to *Nemesis*. "I didn't realize so many of your lads are suffering Mary."

"No, how could you? You've been stuck aboard my ship recovering from your wounds. Most of those afflicted are with Jacob and Maurice."

Dijksma shrugged his shoulders. "Mary, Mary, Mary, what I'm I to do with you?"

I grabbed the Dutchman by the privates when my men weren't looking and squeezed. "A resourceful man, a clever man such as yourself will think of something I'm certain. I am after all in your debt..."

The following day Matelieff led us into the Straits of Malacca to resume the battle with the Portuguese. His actions that day were sharp, precise and decisive. He won my admiration.

My men and I, lazily cruising up and down the shore while lobbing iron balls at the high ground overlooking the harbor, watched Matelieff drive his ships straight at the Portuguese line. The Portuguese no doubt thought themselves secure sitting underneath the shadow of Malacca's large guns.

Matelieff's fleet attacked head-on with relentless, unflinching resolve. In rapid succession his ships closed with *São Nicolau*, *Santa Cruz* and *Todos os Santos*. *São Nicolau's* crew managed to cut their cables and flee but the Dutch caught *Santa Cruz* and *Todos os Santos* at anchor. Dutch sailors snagged the galleons with grappling hooks and swarmed aboard both ships, easily overwhelming their crews. After the Dutch removed their prisoners, and anything of value, they put the galleons to the torch and when they found *São Simeão* adrift and abandoned the next morning, they torched her too.

Down to two galleons, manned by frail and sickly men, supported by four inferior ships that were no match for the Dutch, the Portuguese chose to run their ships aground to deprive the Dutch of any prizes. And after the Portuguese removed their guns, their powder and ammunition and burned their ships, they withdrew into Malacca. At little cost to themselves, the Dutch had destroyed the entire

Portuguese squadron and had taken hundreds of prisoners, including senior officers.

Matelieff promptly sent a small delegation ashore under a flag of truce. In exchange for the release of all Dutch prisoners - plus a ransom of six thousand gold ducats - Matelieff offered to release his Portuguese prisoners. Furtado accepted. Matelieff wisely used the gold to quiet discontent spreading amongst his men.

Matelieff's impressive victory though was all for naught. With Malacca's defenses strengthened by hundreds of shipwrecked Portuguese and their cannon, with winter fast approaching and his supplies severely depleted, Matelieff's army was too weak to take the fortress city. He surprised me when, mimicking Castro, he split his own fleet in two and then surprised me again when he released my ships. He led six galleons south for Java to hunt Castro down while he sent de Vivere north with the other three for the Coromandel Coast of India, for what purpose I did not know or care. I was at last free from war.

My men and I accompanied Matelieff as far as to the Java Sea and there we parted ways. While Matelieff headed west for Banten, we turned east, hugging the coast of Borneo, for Ambon. Once we returned Dijksma to Fort Victoria, we'd sail on to Banda for our spices and then return to Banten for the pepper before sailing back to Europe. I was delighted to see the excitement building amongst my men at the prospect of returning home.

"You'll acquire six hundred tons of nutmeg and mace in Banda and one hundred tons of pepper in Banten." Dijksma said as we stood together on the quarterdeck, watching Matelieff's ships slip over the horizon.

"How is the pepper packed?"

"The Bantenese pack their pepper into burlap bags. Each bag of pepper weighs fifty-six pounds, Amsterdam pounds, not English."

"And how much is an Amsterdam pound?"

"A Dutch pound is a bit lighter than an English pound, by about one tenth of one percent. I know not why."

"And the value of all this cargo?"

"There is presently a glut of spices on the market. Prices were higher back when Elizabeth sailed for the Company. The current value of pepper in the European markets is fourteen silver reales-of-eight per bahar of three pikul - these are Indonesian weight measurements which fluctuate from island to island. In Banten this amount has been set at roughly the equivalent of thirty-six and three tenths of a Dutch pound. Let us call this amount of weight a unit. One hundred tons is equivalent two hundred thousand pounds. Divide two hundred thousand pounds by thirty-six - the weight of one unit - and you have, in round numbers, five thousand five hundred fifty-five units. Multiply five thousand five hundred fifty-five by fourteen silver reals-of-eight - the price per unit - and that my lady gives you a value of seventy-seven thousand seven hundred seventy silver reales-of-eight for one hundred tons of pepper."

"Impressive, though you are making my head spin. How many bags to load?"

"Well, let's see. Two hundred thousand divided by fifty-six pounds per bag equals three thousand five hundred seventy-one bags."

"If I may ask, what is the Company's profit?"

"Oh, it can be an obscene amount. Sometimes north of ten thousand."

"Ten thousand what?"

"Percent."

"Good God! And the value of six hundred tons of nutmeg and mace?"

Dijksma scratched the stubble on his chin as he made some quick calculations. "Hmm. Roughly four hundred thousand silver reales-of-eight I'd say. This is why pepper is the king of spices."

I scanned the deck looking for Lololi but saw only Ashaki resting against the main mast holding a book in her hand. "Ashaki," I called out, "could you please find your sister?"

Ashaki smiled sweetly and pointed to a spot underneath my feet.

I went over to the forward quarterdeck rail and saw Ling sitting with Lololi on the steps of the quarterdeck ladder below me, teaching her how to play the fiddle. A Jesuit priest had once told me that if you are naturally good at mathematics you are most likely good at music too and vice versa. This seemed sensible to me though I did not really know as I had no aptitude for either discipline.

"Ling, may I borrow Lololi for a moment?" I asked in my pitiful Portuguese. After Ling nodded politely, Lololi raced up the ladder to stand with Dijksma and me.

"Lololi, Ewoud is giving me a headache reciting a bunch of silly numbers to me. I will ask Ewoud to repeat what he told me to you and I want you to validate his calculations and then tell me what our take on all of it will be."

"You may wish," Ewoud interjected with a friendly smile, "to grab a pencil and a sheet of paper first young lady."

"No need," she replied, smiling sweetly back at the Dutchman with a hint of hubris in her eyes. "When you are ready sir."

"Very well," Dijksma said and raised an eyebrow. Then, purposely speaking rapidly and without pausing, he repeated everything he had just told me to Lololi.

Lololi turned to face me once Ewoud had finished. "I agree mostly with Meester Dijksma's math Mary, though he rounded-off. By his calculations one hundred tons of pepper has a value of seven-seven thousand, seven hundred, seventy silver reales-of-eight."

Dijksma frowned. "Yes? Is this not correct?"

"Forgive me sir, but no."

"Explain."

"You took two hundred thousand pounds of pepper and divided by thirty-six Dutch pounds giving you five thousand five hundred fifty-five. You should have divided two hundred thousand by thirty-six and three tenths. The correct unit weight is five thousand five hundred nine and six tenths. The correct value of one hundred tons of pepper is therefore only seventy-seven thousand one hundred thirty-four and four tenths silver reales-of-eight."

Beaming with delight, Dijksma pushed his hat back off his

forehead and whistled. "Have you read Simon Stevin's work *De Thiende* on decimals?"

"No Meester Dijksma. Please sir, what is the value of one silver real-of-eight to an English pound sterling?"

"The currencies of different nations fluctuate here and there but one silver real-of-eight will presently - to the best of my knowledge - buy you two and a half Dutch guilders. A Dutch guilder and an English pound sterling can be exchanged one-for-one."

I placed my hand on Lololi's shoulder. "Lololi, for the sake of my poor, pounding head, simple numbers only please."

"Mary, ten percent of four hundred seventy-seven thousand one hundred thirty-four and four tenths is forty-seven thousand seven hundred thirteen and forty-four hundredths in silver reals or nineteen thousand eighty-five and thirty-seven hundredths in pounds sterling if you prefer."

Dijksma reached out to shake Lololi's hand. "Quite a spectacle young lady. You are a prodigy with numbers! Perhaps you'd like to work for me someday!"

"And what," I asked, "is that last number divided by four hundred?"

"Almost forty-seven pounds sterling," Lololi answered.

"And what would that be in gold ducats?"

Lololi turned to Dijksma.

"Almost four," Dijksma answered.

I frowned, depressed. Less than forty-eight thousand English pounds sterling I thought to myself - a fortune to most but little more than a pittance to me. I had four hundred men or their widows to pay, provisions to purchase and ships to maintain. If I took nothing for myself and divided the profits equally amongst my men, ignoring the greater shares I would normally pay my officers and to those with special skills like Stachel and BB, the men would receive less than a year's wages as an ordinary seaman. I needed more, much more.

I went below to my cabin to study my charts. My thoughts turned to the question of sailing east or west once we had our spices. Though I longed to free Aminatu and her people, sailing west was plainly the wiser choice.

And then I remembered something Testu, my partner and lover until his death, had once told me while we stood within the walls of the Cimarron stronghold of Ronconcholan at the mouth of the Chepo River. The Cimarron he had said liked to bury the treasure they had taken from the Spanish in the muddy waters of the river. I had thought nothing of it at the time as this wealth belonged to my friends and allies. But Ronconcholan was no more and the Cimarron had scattered. God only knew if any of it still laid buried in the riverbed. And even if there was treasure, finding it would be difficult, nay perhaps impossible. The challenge though intrigued me - and I had found lost treasure in Panama before.

Later that morning, with my ships scudding gracefully across the rolling waves, Dijksma returned to the quarterdeck with two tins of hot coffee. He handed one tin to me and I was grateful for there was a chill in the air.

"Thank you, Ewoud. Lovely day if a tad cool."

"It is," he replied and added a generous splash of Dutch *genever* to my coffee.

"What's this? 'Tis a bit early for strong spirits."

"To ease the pain," he said while handing me a letter. "A parting gift from the admiral. We need to turn about and make a brief stop in Batavia as I'll need more men."

"What in God's name for?"

"You are to return me to Macau. Matelieff believes that with one swift kick at the door, the whole putrid edifice of Macau might fall. I am to muster three hundred men and test the city's defenses whilst you support me from the harbor with your artillery."

"That's it? That's the admiral's plan? And who do I fire upon? Innocent men, woman, and children? I will not."

"No, no, you will protect my men from any warships in the harbor that attempt to interfere and you'll protect my route of escape."

"This is madness Ewoud. You cannot take Macau with three hundred men!"

"True and yet I am duty-bound to try."

Seized with rage that blinds good judgment, I was sorely tempted rip Matelieff's orders in half and quit the expedition. But well I knew that insulting the Company a second time would have dire consequences. Dutch power and influence were on the rise not only in the East Indies, but in the West Indies too and I needed access to one or the other to survive. The Company might even declare me an outlaw and put a bounty on my head if I declined to obey Matelieff's orders. And I knew that if I abandoned Dijksma, he would attempt his mission even without my battlecruisers to support him, which could well mean his death.

Dijksma saw the sudden flush in my cheeks and caught the fire in my eyes. "Please Mary," he pleaded, "do not be cross. You need not risk yourself or your men. If there are too many warships in the harbor, I'll abort the mission."

"Sail with me to the Americas Ewoud," I blurted out. "I'll make you a captain of your own ship. A life unfilled is tragic. You were born for more."

Taken by surprise, Dijksma took a moment before responding; he held my gaze and smiled. "A tantalizing offer - for several reasons - the best I've ever had. But I owe the Company my fealty for two more years."

"The Company holds some debt over you? I will pay it."

"No, not a debt. An obligation I must honor. I agreed to serve the Company for seven years. I've given the Company nearly five already. After two more years I am my own man again. By then, if I'm still alive, I'll also hold a princely sum of Company stock."

"What are these other reasons?"

Dijksma leaned close to my ear. "You've captured my heart dear lady," he whispered.

I looked away to hide my silly tears.

Chapter Thirty-Two

could see the disappointment in the faces of my men when I gathered them on deck, when I told them what we needed to do. There was some grumbling amongst the newer lads but my veterans soon took care of that.

I was on the main deck training with Efendi when Dijksma approached us with three tins of fresh coffee. "Mustafa, Mary, good morning," he said as he handed one tin to me and another to Efendi.

"The last time you brought me coffee," I said, "it came with a heavy price."

"Perhaps you'd let me train with you," he said with a friendly grin. "I've been watching you both from up on the quarterdeck. I've never witnessed such skills."

Efendi raised his tin. "Mary was one of my best students. After breakfast if you like I invite you to show me what you can do with a weapon of your choosing, any weapon."

I patted Dijksma on the chest. "You best eat a hardy meal my friend, might be your last."

And then, high up in the masthead, the lookout cried out. He pointed to a strip of land off our port bow. We had reached the sleepy port of Jayakarta, or what the Dutch call Batavia, where the Dutch keep a goodly number of men. I went ashore with Dijksma, along with Atwood, Efendi and twenty men. Dijksma led us to the Dutch settlement, which was little more than a cluster of crude plank houses, small storehouses and patches of grass surrounded by a thin, wooden fence where I met Koopman, the other Company man Houtman had mentioned to me, for the first time.

I took an instant dislike to the fellow. He struck me as a

humorless, ill-tempered administrator, a clumsy ox with no imagination. He had an unpleasant smile and bad breath. Koopman was reluctant to release any of his men to Dijksma at first but relented after Dijksma produced Matelieff's letter. He agreed to part with one hundred fifty men, along with a seventy-foot yacht to transport them. In a hurry to see us go, he sent us on our way the very next morning and I for one was glad.

"You and Gerrit don't seem to like each other much," I whispered in Dijksma's ear as we walked towards the beach with a cluster of Dutchmen lugging backpacks and heavily armed with muskets, swords, daggers and bandoliers stuffed with cartridges and ammunition.

"We were cordial to one another until last year, about the time when Elizabeth and your men left for Amsterdam," Dijksma replied. "He has changed and not for the better. I cannot say why. No matter, you need not trouble yourself with him again."

"He's an odious, disagreeable fellow," Efendi offered. "Do you have one hundred fifty men Ewoud you can pull away from Ambon?"

"Not in Dutchmen. The fort's garrison commandant, a likeable German fellow, will need to keep a strong garrison to protect the island. But he has recruited a full company of Tanimbar and Ambonese auxiliaries. The Ambonese are untested but have heart. I'll take them with us, see what they can do."

As we set off for Ambon in heavy rains with our new passengers, I asked Ling and her young brother Jian to join me in my great cabin. Even though Ling's Portuguese and English were improving daily, Jian still struggled and so I invited Egbert to translate. An hour later I asked Dijksma, Efendi and Shaw to join us.

"Ah, gentlemen, come in, sit and rest yourselves," I said. "Have a glass of sherry, a small glass if you please for there is not much left."

"Jacob never had that problem whenever I sailed with him," Dijksma quipped.

"No," I replied. "I'll wager that dour, old Scot has bottles stashed away against the keel hidden underneath the bilge water. Since departing Macau, I've had several conversations with Ling and Jian.

As Ling promised, Jian has been most helpful. You gentlemen may ask them anything you like. The short and the long of it is thus: though this fellow Arslan's part, if any, remains unclear Wú, according to Jian, did indeed betray us and I'm of a mind to believe the boy. Wú wanted our ships and cargo but as you know he badly miscalculated the sturdiness of our vessels and the quality of our men and consequently his plan failed spectacularly. Jian claims Wú and a Javanese man, probably Prince Ratu's nephew, were also plotting with two other men, one of whom was a foreigner. Jian saw this foreigner just once at Wú's warehouse. The other fellow was Chinese."

"Does he know this foreigner's name or nationality?" Dijksma asked.

"Unfortunately, no. I also learned that Wú lives in a room above his warehouse. He is surrounded by dozens of men working in the warehouse day and night and rarely leaves but when he does, Wú is always accompanied by three or four personal guards. One of these men tastes his food and drink. Wú is also the proprietor of a place known as the *House of a Thousand Pleasures*, an establishment outside the city, an establishment that caters to the rich and powerful. Michael, Elizabeth, Ling and this Arslan fellow visited the *House* one evening as Wú's guests."

"None of this is particularly enlightening or surprising Mary," Efendi said and sniffed the air. "But I smell a plan brewing. Why else would we be sitting here?"

"Aye, I have the makings of a plan rattling around in my head and each of you will have a part to play. I will only proceed if we are all agreed and then I'll need to put my plan to a vote before Jacob and the others. I've already spoken to Jacob whilst ashore in Jayakarta and his response was, well, predictable. He was in a foul mood that day. He'll come around. We do this for Michael and for all our fallen, or not."

"Why do you need my consent, Mary?" Dijksma asked.

"Before you go running amok through the streets of Macau, I wish to go in a day or two before you, or perhaps it is best if we go in on the same day. I am not yet sure."

"What?"

"I saw many Chinese junks in Ambon sitting in your harbor Ewoud. I'll need to borrow one."

"What? Why?"

"All shall be made clear soon enough. I'm still sorting through the particulars of my plan. Lord only knows if I'll produce a gem or a turd. Ling, I'll need an apothecary skilled in the black arts, in poisons. Do you know of such a man, a man we can trust?"

Ling smiled demurely. "A man, no. A woman perhaps, yes."

The journey from Jayakarta to Ambon was short and uneventful. I gave my men two week's liberty while Dijksma gathered provisions, more men and tweaked the particulars of his own plan. A few days before we were to sail for Macau, I assembled my officers in the officers' mess at Fort Victoria. I invited Dijksma of course and Ling. Dijksma introduced us to the fort's commandant, a lanky, dark-haired fellow with sharp features and astute eyes, a German mercenary named Julius Shultz, and then spread a large map of Macau across a long table.

"This work is very fine Ewoud," I said as I considered the carefully drawn streets, waterways and buildings of note depicted on the map.

"The team I brought with me into Macau put this together," Dijksma replied.

"Perhaps we should start with your plan Ewoud."

"Thank you, Mary. We've discussed broad bits and pieces of these plans over the past few days. Several of you have contributed something to improve the plans and I'm grateful. We considered executing one plan at a time but after much thought, I think we are all agreed it best if we execute both plans simultaneously. We go in together at dawn, make our preparations during the day and strike at night. We return to our ships before the following sunrise. We have twenty-four hours to get in and get out, unless the Portuguese wish to surrender. Then we'll stay."

As men chuckled around the table, Dijksma grabbed a wooden rod leaning against the wall and pointed to the center of the map. "There's not much to the Dutch plan. The buildings drawn in brown are made of wood, the grey buildings are stone, such as the governor's house here and these two churches. The emperor has forbidden the Portuguese from fortifying Macau as he may wish to take his island back someday without bloodshed blood. The Portuguese have no stone walls, no artillery or redoubts. But note the locations of the stone buildings. They form a defensive perimeter around the island. I suspect the governor's house and the churches near the center of the city are each meant to serve as a kind of castle keep, as a last line of defense. The Portuguese have been very clever. They've fortified the island somewhat with the Chinese none the wiser. These stone buildings caught the attention of my team because of the subtle embrasures cut into the walls, suitable for muskets and crossbows. Even if Matelieff attacked Macau with his entire squadron and landed the army, I'm not certain he would prevail against these defenses and we are only three warships and three hundred men. As for the Dutch plan, the Portuguese use this wood building close to the governor's house as an armory and to store powder and these wood buildings here are barracks. Our objective is to destroy the armory and the barracks. We Dutch will sail into Macau with three Chinese junks. We'll beach our ships inside this remote lagoon to the southwest, wait for nightfall and then quietly make our way through these marshlands here and into the city. At midnight we'll blow-up the armory first and then we'll strike the barracks. Simple. Jacob, Maurice and Kinkae, when you hear the explosions within the city, this will be your signal to start blowing-up things along the waterfront to create a diversion whilst we Dutch fall back to our ships in the lagoon. This is the plan Julius and I have concocted. Questions?"

Atwood grunted. "'Tis a fine plan Ewoud considering the circumstances. Even if all goes well, what does the Company hope to achieve? As you say, you can't take the city. You turn an armory into ash and perhaps kill a handful of poor devils whose luck has finally run out. You are risking the lives of your men and yourself for what? You are a gnat biting at the rump of an elephant."

The German took a step forward and made a grand sweep of his arm. "If I may, this raid I think is meant to stir the pot Jacob, to show the Portuguese they are vulnerable. This will force the Portuguese to strip companies of men from other islands around Indonesia to reinforce Macau, leaving the defenses of those islands weaker. The Dutch for example could turn their attention to the Spice Islands if they wished or to the Philippines. This is the grand stratagem we Germans would use."

Atwood nodded. "Maybe. I do appreciate the concept though. All hail Julius Caesar!"

Dijksma handed the rod to me. "Mary?"

I drew a deep breath and took a sip of wine. I pointed the rod at a building on the waterfront I had circled earlier in red and then at another building on an island to the north that I had also circled.

"My plan is to kidnap Wú but is, I fear, a bit more intricate. Wú lives in a room above this warehouse on the waterfront. He is surrounded by scores of men working there day and night. Wú never leaves his warehouse without the company of at least three warrior monks, Japanese Sohei of the Tendai. Mustafa, do you know anything about these monks?"

"Not much. Their weapon of choice is said to be the *naginata* and they are known to wear *o-yoroi* armor. I know more about the samurai. They're exceptional fighters with remarkable discipline and unwavering determination. I'd expect these monks to be as good or better."

"Well, we must assume these men are quite dangerous. One of them always tastes Wú's food and drink. Wú also owns an establishment called the *House of a Thousand Pleasures*. Michael, Elizabeth, Ling, and this mysterious Arslan fellow visited the *House* one evening as Wú's guests though Wú himself did not attend and rarely visits. The *House* is miles outside the city on this small, remote island located here in the middle of this narrow river. Wú will be too difficult to nab at his warehouse or in the city so I intend to lure him to the *House*. We do this by kidnapping his foreman, a man named Lu-Li, and spirit him away to the *House*. We'll plant a letter in the warehouse incriminating Lu-Li in a plot with foreigners to cheat Wú and we let Wú know that Lu-Li is on his way to the *House* to entertain the foreigners. Wú must find that letter and then he must decide to travel to the *House* with haste to confront Lu-Li. We take Wú at the *House* if he shows. *Voilà*. That's the gist of it.

"Now for those troublesome particulars. First, I've secured a Chinese junk for ourselves. Once we reach Macau, I'll take the junk and forty men with me into the harbor. Mustafa, Rob, Ling, and I will slip into the city to visit a certain boy who cleans and runs errands for Wú. He's a Tanaka and lives on the water with his mother and father. Jian and the boy are friends. Ling knows the boat and the boy's parents. We'll stop by the boat before sunrise, before the boy leaves to begin his day at the warehouse. I'll offer his parents gold for the boy's services. The boy only needs to do two things, neither of which should put him in jeopardy. I'll give him the letter of introduction to place on Lu-Li's desk after Lu-Li has left for his afternoon meal and then, when Lu-Li fails to return and Wú asks about Lu-Li, the boy will inform Wú that foreigners stopped him outside the warehouse earlier and gave him a piece of silver to deliver a letter to Lu-Li. He'll also inform Wú that these foreigners told him to tell Lu-Li that they are accepting Lu-Li's invitation to meet him at the *House* later in the evening. Everything the boy will disclose to Wú will be true."

"Christ!" Atwood bellowed. "You're only at the beginning of your plan and much can go wrong. What if the boy or his parents are too frightened to help you? What if you fail to kidnap Lu-Li? What if the boy succeeds and you take this Lu-Li fellow to this *House* but Wú doesn't take the bait? What if Wú takes the bait but decides to stay put at his warehouse and sends his henchmen up to this *House* to grab Lu-Li instead?"

"True, any of these things could happen Jacob. But the mere possibility of failure will never dissuade me from trying."

"You're right of course. I want to go with you into Macau."

"As you wish. A one-eyed Scot the size of Goliath shouldn't attract any attention."

"Auck! Fine, fine, I'll remain with the ships."

"Good. Ewoud and I are entrusting our lives to you and Maurice. You must keep the harbor secure for us. Ohhh, forgive me Kinkae,

Henry, your roles are equally important. Kinkae, in Rob's absence you'll assume command of *Nemesis* and Henry, command of the junk is yours. Congratulations gentlemen on your promotions to captain."

As Kinkae answered me with a somber nod, and Henry thanked me with a wide grin, baring the teeth he had filed down into fangs years ago, Elizabeth jumped to her feet in obvious anger.

"And me Mary, what about me?" she asked indignantly.

"Why you are Maurice's second Elizabeth, nothing's changed."

"I intend no disrespect Kinkae," she said, ignoring me. "But command of *Nemesis* should be mine!"

"I've made my decision," I said flatly and ignored her childishness as she set her jaw and narrowed her eyes at me. "Next Ling will introduce us to a Chinese apothecary who happens to be skilled in the black arts."

"What is this black arts?" Schultz asked.

"Poisons."

"*Ach, sehr gut - das gift.*"

"Lu-Li takes his noon day meal every day at a nearby teahouse. Ling knows the proprietor well. Ling will pay the woman to slip a harmless drug from the apothecary into Lu-Li's tea, something to make him unsteady or nauseous. Mustafa, Rob and I will help the poor fellow out of the teahouse and into a cart parked nearby. Once we get him aboard the junk, we'll sail upriver to the *House* and wait for Wú. There are armed men at the *House* Ling tells me. She does not know how many or their quality and this is why I'm taking forty of our best fighters with me. Finally, when Wú arrives at the *House*, if he arrives, we'll overpower these monks of his and take him alive if we can. We'll kill him if we can't. We should hear the Dutch fireworks just about the time we are sailing downriver back to the harbor. That's it, that's the plan. Easy as making biscuits."

"The plan is audacious and smart Mary," Dijksma said with a hint of pride in his voice.

"What Mary," Maurice asked, do we do if things turn difficult in the harbor?"

"Wait for Ewoud and Julius and their lads for as long as you can.

I should think they'll reach you before I do. Do not wait for me. We have the junk. We can all rally at one of the islands off Macau. Just pick one. Ewoud and I are agreed, we'll abort this raid if the Portuguese have any powerful warships in the harbor."

"It's a slick plan Mary," Maurice replied. "Even so, it has many moving pieces and as Jacob said, much can go wrong."

"What you say is true Maurice. Taking Wú in the city would be far simpler. But storming into his warehouse may cost many lives and we might still fail and I have no wish of being caught in the city when the Dutch and you three captains start blowing-up things.

"But now listen to me my brothers and sister and listen well. Failing to avenge our brother Michael does not sit well with me. And yet, in truth, except for the satisfaction of killing the man who killed Michael, there is nothing to be gained by risking our lives on this dark quest. Aye, we took our revenge against the *Síol Faolcháin*. Is this not the same you might ask? No. Our great matter with the *Síol Faolcháin* was different. We were given no choice. We and the *Síol Faolcháin* lived in the same world together, locked in a struggle to the death. But Wú is no threat to us. We can leave this far end of the world and not worry about Wú one day sending his lackeys to the West Indies or to Europe to harm us or those we love. The sole purpose of this errand is murder, pure and simple. You must each reconcile this with your God or conscience. We can land Ewoud and his men in Macau and remain safely aboard our ships. Think on this long and hard before we vote."

Atwood shook his head at me in disbelief. "Are you feeling poorly Mary?"

"No, why?"

"The Mary I know would never allow Michael's death to go unavenged."

I cupped Atwood's cheek affectionately in my hand. "I swear on my honor that if we reject this plan, or if we proceed and fail, I will introduce myself to Wú someday at another time and place. He'll know my wrath."

"Good, rest assured the lads and I will be at your side you when you do Mary," Atwood said firmly.

"Please," Dijksma said and raised his arms. "As you consider all that Mary and I have said, I wish to invite you to the courtyard outside for a modest feast, to thank each of you for helping we Dutch in this last matter before you sail for home. And as Christmas is nearly upon us, we have good cause to celebrate!"

The Ambonese had prepared a fine meal for us. There were roasted meats, fish, fresh fruits and vegetables, music, dancing, song and plenty of Spanish wine and Portuguese ale. The moon was nearly full. The air was crisp and clean. In the midst of all the gaiety, Dijksma discreetly took my hand and spirited me away to his bedchambers. He kissed me tenderly on the lips. He kissed me softly on my neck and shoulders while he caressed my skin and teased me, while he undressed me slowly. He soon had me cooing with anticipation. Something about his gentleness touched me. We took our time indulging and pleasing one another. We moved gracefully as one and when we had finished, I felt warm and safe and happy in Dijksma's arms.

"A favor for a favor," Dijksma said as we laid together, spent and glistening in sweat.

"What is this favor?"

Dijksma smiled. "I do not yet know."

"How can I agree to such a thing? This sounds like a pact with the devil."

Dijksma roared with laughter. "No, I'm simply the Dutchman. I promise whatever I ask of you will not compromise your conscience, fair enough?"

"Fair enough. Tell me though, why do you owe the Company seven years?"

"You recall my story about betrayal?"

"Aye."

"The traitor was my brother. My service to the Company is my penance."

"Dear God! But why does the Company hold you accountable for the actions of your brother? You're not to blame."

"Oh, but I am. I was sloppy in who I trusted. My brother was able to do what he did because I said too much about things I shouldn't have spoken about - to anyone."

Chapter Thirty-Three

rom the helm of our Chinese junk, with Captain Henry deftly working the tiller, I watched my three battlecruisers slip into the still waters of Macau's sleepy harbor in the dead of night. I had Henry ease our vessel, she was a slow, clumsy thing, up against a lonely wharf close to where the Tanka keep their boats, not far from Wú's warehouse.

The day before, only one of the scores of unremarkable boats sailing in and out of port, we had traversed Macau's waters to have a look around. We saw only one Portuguese war carrack and a handful of lightly-armed vessels of modest tonnage. The second war carrack and the large galleon Dijksma's men had spotted during our first visit to Macau were nowhere in sight.

Ling led Efendi, Shaw and me, with Dijksma's blessing Egbert accompanied us too, to the floating Tanka village to find the boy. We had dressed ourselves in black tunics, black trousers, sandals and turbans and used dark scarves to conceal our faces. Earlier I had sheared-off Ling's luxurious, long black hair to make her a little less conspicuous.

The family was understandably terrified when we stepped aboard their boat just before sunrise. But when they recognized Ling, and after I showed them a purse fat with silver and gold, they relaxed a little and listened to what I had to say. Zhàn, about the age, size and build of Jian, was all too eager to help us when Ling explained what we needed him to do. I felt a rush of hope when Zhàn informed us that Wú was in Macau and at his warehouse. We left Zhàn to dress and make ready for the day ahead. I left the purse with his parents.

And then Ling led us to the apothecary near the center of the city. A wizened woman of ancient years with a crooked spine and long, stringy hair, hair as white as the whitest linen, answered the door to her shop holding a single candle in her hand. I caught the sparkle in her eyes when she saw Ling. She quickly waved us inside.

"Mary, this Mei," Ling said in her newly acquired English. "She widow of Kang, son of Heng. Heng serve emperor's imperial army alongside my father's father many year ago. She speak only Chinese. I translate with Egbert's help."

"I am Mary," I said and bowed my head respectfully. "These two men with me are Mustafa and Rob."

"You need different poisons?" The woman asked after she and Ling had exchanged many words.

"Yes, and I have gold. Will you help us?"

"Who is the poison for?"

"Ling, what do I tell her?"

"Mei despises man we seek. The truth."

"Very well. Tell her we want Wú."

The old woman grinned and nodded when she heard me utter Wú's name. "For what purpose?"

"I need one potion to incapacitate and one to kill."

"You'll need three potions not two. Twelve gold ducats. Twelve gold ducats is my price."

"Agreed. I'll give you six now and six upon our return. We need the fruits of you labor before midday."

"Keep your gold for now. Come back before the sun is at its zenith."

"My man Mustafa here will remain with you. Beware, he has expertise in the black arts."

She looked hard into Efendi's eyes. "Ah, a dark traveler, an Ottoman I think," she said and reached over to brush Efendi's cheek with the back of her hand. "Yes, yes, an Ottoman from the mountains is what we have here."

In a blur of motion Efendi caught the old woman's wrist before she could touch his face. "Touch me not woman!" he commanded.

"Ohhh quick you are my mysterious friend. Very quick you are indeed. Quicker than the cobra I see and thrice as deadly I'll wager."

"You've heard of the Hashshashin?" I asked. "The Hashshashin of the Nizari Ismailis?"

"Ahhh, you speak of the Old Man in the Mountain!" she exclaimed with a hideous cackle. "This one knows the Old Man, the Old Man in the Mountain. As foretold the pale, foreign woman from across the sea with her dark, Ottoman assassin has come. The world turns upside down."

"Is this woman mad in the head Ling?" I asked.

"She always been ... different ... Mary."

The old crone turned away and hobbled over to a paneled wall. She waved for us to follow. She led us though a hidden door and into a secret backroom with many shelves and bottles stored along the walls. A crude workbench stood in the middle of the room with candles and bowls and beakers of different sizes, with weights and measures and measuring cups of glass, of tin and steel. Off in one corner sat a stack of well-worn books.

"I can offer," Mei explained as she lit several candles around the bench, "arsenic - colorless, odorless, tasteless and difficult to detect, but death is slow. I have hemlock, an herb that ruptures the intestines. The victim feels a burning in the throat then vomits with excruciating pain in the abdomen. A favorite of the ancients, hemlock is quick and reliable. I have crane's red crown liquid and three-laugh death powder, named so because the victim grins scornfully three times before he dies. I can brew a batch of *jiànxuěfēnghóu* for you, an elegant poison found in the provinces of Yunnan and Hainan if you like. Very rare, very rare. When the poison touches an open wound, death is nearly instant. The victim can take seven steps forward or eight steps backward before he drops. I don't have any flesh-melting powder but I could concoct a batch if I had more time to purchase the necessary ingredients."

"*Jiànxuěfēnghóu?*" I asked Ling.

"I sorry Mary," Ling said. "How I say? Hmmm, meets blood seals throat, best I know."

"That's fine Ling. You're doing just fine. Tell Mei what we intend to do. Mustafa, are you certain you wish to stay?"

"There is much to learn here Mary. If the old hag doesn't deliver as promised, I suspect I can find what I need to make what we need. I'll see you before noon."

I took Ling, Egbert and Shaw with me to find our new friend Zhàn. The boy had agreed to meet us around the corner from the warehouse before Lu-Li left for the teahouse and his afternoon meal. We waited in the shadows for some time for Zhàn and I began to fret when the boy didn't show. Things had been too easy so far. But just as we were about to head back to Mei's shop the boy appeared, all smiles. He told us that Wú was in his office looking over his books and said that Lu-Li intended to leave soon for the teahouse. After I handed him the letter, and pressed a large, silver coin into his hand, he proudly told Ling before scampering off that he was ready to do whatever we required.

Next, we went to the teahouse to speak with the proprietor, whose name I never could pronounce, and after she and Ling embraced and spoke, she readily agreed to slip a potion into Lu-Li's tea to make him nauseous. She gladly took my gold. The affection Zhàn, his parents, Mei and this woman all seemed to have for Ling did not escape my notice. Accepting my gold made their affections no less sincere.

"I've used," Mei explained when we returned to her shop, "separate colors for each vial as you can see, soft to cruel so you won't forget the vial's purpose. In this light blue vile is a potion to paralyze. Once administered the person will feel stabbing pains in his bowels. He'll have difficulty using his legs and arms. But he will remain conscience and he will be able to speak and once the poison wears off, he will recover. This green bottle with the red band around the center is also used to incapacitate but this potion will render its victim unconscious for many hours. It is good for moving a man quietly from one place to another. A spoonful or two is all you need. For a big man like Wú use half the bottle, no more. A full dose will kill him or send him into a deep sleep from whence he'll never wake. Ah, and the liquid in this lovely black vial is death. Use it sparingly if you wish to

keep your victim alive for a bit. Only a drop or two on an open wound
is needed. A man like our Ottoman here might take a few minutes to
perish. A bigger man will die more slowly but death is no less certain.
If you wish to return tomorrow, I can mix an antidote for the potion
in the black vial."

"We are short on time grandmother and must go," I said and
handed the woman a leather pouch with twelve gold ducats. When
she refused to take the pouch, I turned to Ling, perplexed.

"Mary, Mei insists you give me gold and you must swear you take
Jian and me away from China. I explain your kindness to Jian and me.
I tell Mei you already agree to these things, yet she not accept gold.
She content to help you succeed in your task."

After I thanked Mei, I discretely pocketed two empty vials as we
were leaving the backroom and left two gold ducats on the workbench
for her comfort. Then Efendi, Shaw and I, after changing into more
common attire, hurried back to the teahouse to execute the next part
of my plan while Ling and Egbert walked back to a cart we had parked
earlier in a nearby alley.

Lu-Li arrived at the teahouse shortly after high noon just as Ling
had predicted. Halfway through his meal we watched him stand,
stumble and fall. Efendi and Shaw rushed over to help the Chinaman.
They carried him outside to the cart and once we were all back aboard
the junk, we raised our sails, circled around Macau and headed north
for the *House*.

I did not know if Wú would find the letter of introduction Zhàn
was to plant on Lu-Li's desk. I did not know if Wú would take the bait
even if he read the letter and queried Zhàn. But we had Lu-Li. We had
momentum. We had to press on.

With Ling as our pilot, we reached the *House* without difficulty
just as the sun began dipping below the treetops. I wanted to glide past
the island and land upriver to get a better look at the *House* but when
I saw a footbridge connecting the island to the mainland, a footbridge
we could not clear, I had Henry drop anchor a little ways downriver.

I dressed Ling in men's clothing and wrapped her bosom tight. I
applied soot and dark ointments to her face and then she did the same

to me. She looked like a boy in the candlelight and I looked like a man. Then Efendi and Shaw, now wearing fashionable European attire, undid Lu-Li's bindings and lifted him to his feet.

I could see Mei's potion wearing off as I stood before him on the main deck. "I'm the one who took you," I told him as Egbert translated. "Whether you live or die this night is entirely up to you. Nod if you understand."

He stared at me with a bewildered look but nodded. I removed his gag and pulled the two vials I had taken from Mei's shop from my pocket.

"Good," I said and handed him one of the vials, vials I had filled earlier with water mixed with a little sugar and a splash of cheap whiskey.

"Drink," I commanded. When he hesitated, I drew my knife and pressed the blade against his throat until I drew blood. He took the vial and drank.

"You have just consumed," I said as I squeezed his mouth open to make sure he had swallowed the liquid, "an interesting blend of *jiànxuěfēnghóu* and crane's red crown. Do you know these poisons?"

The Chinaman stared at me in horror and wet himself. Shaw bit his lip to stop himself from laughing while Efendi rolled his eyes.

"Yes, or no?"

"Ye, ye, yes."

"Good. Now listen very carefully to what I'm about to say if you value your life. The dose of poison you've just consumed is not strong. You'll most certainly die without the antidote, but you have time. In this other vial is the antidote. If you do as I say the antidote is yours. If not, well... Nod if you understand."

The Chinaman nodded vigorously. "How, how do I know you'll keep your word?" he asked.

"Do you know me?"

"No."

"And I do not know you. I am interested in another, not you. You have my word this vial is yours if you do exactly as I say. You really have no choice."

I called two of Kinkae's Blackamoors, a pair of hulking monsters wrapped in thick, hard muscle - terrors to behold in the night - to my side. "David, Sampson, are you ready to play your parts?"

The two men grinned and nodded.

"Very well then. Lu-Li, we are a short walk away from the *House of a Thousand Pleasures*. You shall be our host. You will get us inside. Mustafa, the man on your right, is a rich merchant from Turkey. You have brought him to the *House* tonight to dine and entertain him. The man to your left is Robert. He's from Ireland and he is Mustafa's junior partner. The boy in the dark over there and I are their apprentices. These two black fellows are manservants, slaves. Egbert is our translator and speaks Chinese. Now look at each man and repeat what I have just told you."

Lu-Li hesitated. "What you ask is impossible. I am no one. You have the wrong man. The *House* is a place for nobles and the rich. The *House* will not let a lowly laborer like me inside."

I slapped the Chinaman hard across the face. "We have no time for games. You are Lu-Li, a man of great power. You work at the warehouse close to the teahouse where we found you. You serve Master Féng Wú. You are his most trusted lieutenant and are feared by all. Lie to me again and I'll cut you."

"I, I remember you now," Lu-Li said with a more confident tone. "You aren't a man, you're the Irish woman, the wife of that Spaniard who was looking for Master Wú a few months back. This costume of yours fooled me, but your eyes and soft voice have betrayed you." Lu-Li paused to shake his head. "No, no, you have no understanding of Master Wú's power. Harm me and Master Wú will find you and when he does, he will kill you. He will kill your family. He will kill your friends and their families. The master is not a merciful man."

"False bravado from a dying fool or have you forgotten already what I told you about the poison?" I asked, untroubled by the Chinaman's threats. I removed the cork from the second vial and held the small bottle over the ship's rail. "You are running out of time. If I let this vial perish in the river you'll perish with it, most painfully as the poison slowly eats away at your stomach."

With bulging eyes and beads of sweat forming across his brow, Lu-Li took in the faces around him and then repeated all that I had said. He understood what he needed to do. I warned Lu-Li to choose his words carefully as Egbert spoke both the emperor's Chinese and Guangzhou Chinese and would translate every word, every tone, every inflection of his voice that was spoken for me.

We dropped a rope ladder over the side and stepped onto the riverbank. With Henry and thirty of his men following us at a distance - we left ten men behind to guard the junk - Ling led us through the trees to the footbridge a quarter mile away where five armed Chinamen stopped us midway across the bridge.

I held my breath, waiting to see what Lu-Li would do and say. He did not disappoint.

"I am Lu-Li," he declared as Egbert whispered his words into my ear in English. "These two men are merchants from the west. They are my guests tonight. Let us pass."

The man in charge, a scar-faced, colossal brute grunted. "I don't know you. You look like a street beggar. Return from whence you came old man."

Lu-Li surprised me when he backhanded the man, a man several heads taller than himself, hard across the face. "How dare you address me so you ignorant, shit-eating dog! I'll have you tied to wild horses and dragged off for your insolence. I'll make your whore a widow and turn your brats into street beggars. I am Lu-Li, counselor to Master Féng Wú! You are hereby relieved of your duties. Have your men bring the manager of the *House* to me at once! I wish to see Cheng. *Now!*"

When one of the brute's men stepped forward and whispered something into his ear, the brute suddenly took a step back in fear and promptly dropped to one knee. He obediently bowed his head and placed a fist against his heart.

"Forgive me my lord. I did not recognize you."

"A harmless mistake Captain, but you'd be wise to curb that unfortunate tongue of yours in the future."

"Yes, master. You and your guests may pass. You may leave the others in my care."

"I've agreed to allow the African slaves and the others to accompany their masters. We must honor the wishes of these vile foreigners. We must make these unclean barbarians feel comfortable before we fleece them of their wealth."

"Your will my lord," the captain said and waved us across.

As we stepped onto the island, Egbert told me that he was confident Lu-Li hadn't tipped-off the guards and I agreed. Lu-Li was a man who valued his life too much and desperately wanted the antidote. We left Henry and his men behind hidden in the woods. He was to storm the bridge and hold it if trouble found us.

The *House*, a massive four-story building of white clapboard, less than a palace but larger than any dwelling I'd ever seen before, was lit by more candles, lanterns, and torches than I could count. I saw a half-dozen armed men patrolling the grounds, though I knew there had to be more, and saw many small boats beached along the island, or anchored in the river close by. I took note of the island's only pier. If Wú came Ling had told me, he would come by barge, a large, extravagant barge and his crew would dock his barge up against the pier.

We climbed a wide, brick staircase flanked by two enormous stone monkeys, looking down and laughing at all who walked by, and passed through a pair of massive double doors decorated with carvings of dragons and other strange beasts. We stepped into a well-lit foyer and were greeted by a line of attractive male and female attendants, all smiles, dressed in simple robes of white linen.

Then a short, thin man with an air of authority suddenly came racing down the hallway. I knew he had to be the manager named Cheng. I told Lu-Li to dispense with the baths and I wanted a private room. After Lu-Li and Cheng exchanged a few brief pleasantries, Cheng led us through a pair of sliding doors and into a small room where he promised we wouldn't be disturbed.

The room was paneled in fine wood with eight stunning tapestries depicting mountain ranges, woodlands, fields and streams in silver changeant silk hanging along the walls. Ling explained the tapestries were a collection of well-known poems, of famous ballads and proverbs from ancient times as expressed in both the artwork and in the *hanzi* characters delicately drawn in calligraphy along the borders. In the center of the room, underneath three elegant chandeliers, Venetian crystal I think, stood an oval table surrounded by many silk cushions. Four beautifully painted vases of glazed porcelain filled with a variety of colorful silk flowers had been placed in each corner of the room.

"We are here," Lu-Li said curtly as we took our places around the table. "What happens next? You are waiting for someone, yes? Who is this person? Perhaps I can be of value?"

I stared coldly at the Chinaman. "You ask a lot of silly questions for a man who's slowly dying," I said harshly to shut him up. The man had a fetor of evil about him that made me uneasy.

An hour passed and then two. We finally asked for drinks and our suppers so as not to arouse suspicion. More time passed before we heard a commotion in the main hallway. Then Cheng stepped into our room. The master's barge had pulled up to the pier he said excitedly. Wú himself had come he said. A rare visit, a great honor. He hoped everything was to our liking. We must be very important persons indeed he proclaimed and he was deeply humbled to be of service. After he bowed and wished us a prosperous evening, he hurried off to welcome the master.

Lu-Li began sweating profusely. I could see by the look in his eye that at last he understood. Weasels like Lu-Li are always shrewd. Cunning is the weapon of choice his kind need to survive.

"You are here for Wú!" he blurted out and tried to stand. "Are you mad?"

"Sit before you fall," I said. "Feeling woozy? I added a few drops of another potion to your drink when Cheng informed us that Wú had arrived. The drug I've given you will make you sleep. You'll not die, not yet."

As Lu-Li plopped back down on his cushion and closed his eyes, David and Sampson moved over to the sliding doors while Efendi and Shaw pushed away from the table to give themselves room. I did the same, drew my pistols and then pulled Ling and Egbert behind me.

I was unprepared for the sheer immensity of the grotesque creature who burst through the doorway. Four warrior monks dressed in black leather facemasks and black armor, each man wielding a *katana* sword in one hand and a *tanto* short swords in the other, rushed into the room ahead of Wú. I had my pistols trained on Wú when Efendi, with ungodly speed, brought the first man down with the flick of his wrist. The blade found a sliver of exposed flesh between the man's facemask and his breastplate and severed his windpipe. Then in a whirl of motion Efendi launched himself over the table and plunged his dagger into the eye of a second man while Shaw shot a third warrior in the head. David and Sampson wrestled the fourth man down to the floor and strangled him.

The huge Chinaman stared at his four dead companions with indifference. He glanced around the table with disdain. No doubt he thought he was untouchable. I saw Wú clutching my letter of introduction in his hand and smiled. Young Zhàn had played his part brilliantly and I'd not soon forget the boy's eagerness and bravery.

"Rob, take David and Sampson," I said in English. "Go to the bridge, dispose of the guards and bring Henry and the others over. We'll use this big fellow's barge and any boats we need to return to the junk. Quickly now."

I turned to face Wú. "I have questions for you," I said and waited for Egbert to translate. "I'll take you back to the city where we can talk."

I had no intention of taking Wú back to the city of course. But we couldn't drug Wú and carry him out. He was far too large. Trying to walk him back to the junk through the woods would take too long and I had my doubts whether the man could even climb a rope ladder. I considered just killing him.

"Questions?" Wú asked casually as Shaw disappeared with David and Sampson. "I am always delighted to talk. This is most unfortunate. I came for that man slumped over the table, not you. Is he dead?"

"No, he has felt poorly since we arrived here. Angry bowels I think."

"Ahhh. And who might you be?"

"I'm Mary," I said and removed my hat to let my hair fall out.

"A woman. I see you haven't eaten your supper yet Mary. Why don't we retire to another room away from all this untidiness where we can eat, drink and enjoy good conversation without being disturbed."

"I prefer the city."

"I understand. I own a modest trading house near the water. Perhaps we can talk there? We can take my barge."

"You hold no grudge against us for the loss of your men?"

"Grudge? No, not at all. I have more men, many more. My retainers surprised you and you defended yourselves. I would have done the same. The warriors your men so easily dispatched were Japanese Sohei, martial fanatics to the core. Most impressive. I'll need to replace them with more serious fighters like your Arab over there."

"He's a Turk not an Arab. But I like your suggestion of retiring to your trading house. As soon as my colleagues return, we shall go there."

Ling then startled me when she suddenly stepped in front of me, when she removed her hat and wiped the smudge off her face. "You abomination!" she screamed and pointed an accusing finger at Wú. "Your day has come!"

Wú stared at her confused for a moment and then he roared with laughter, a laugh so sinister I felt a chill cut deep into the marrow of my bones. He took a menacing step towards us.

"Your poor mother, your poor father," he said as he perversely ran his forefinger slowly across his throat. "I sent killers to the caravan they traveled with after you and Jian deserted me. Foolish girl. I see all. I know all. At least your parents died quickly. Fortune will be less kind to you.

Ling stumbled backwards and buried her head in my chest. I held her as she wept.

"Well, well," Wú said as he turned to walk back into the hallway. "It would appear there is some mischief afoot here. It would appear we do have much to discuss. We shall remain here Mary and have a pleasant chat in my *House*."

Efendi whipped another one of his throwing knives across the room. The blade buried itself in the doorframe an inch away from the Chinaman's head.

"I think not," I said.

Wú slowly turned to face me. "With a snap of my fingers, dozens of armed men will come rushing to my side. You sad, pathetic fools are trapped."

"I brought more men with me than you did," I said and stood. "You've had a taste of their quality already. The three men I sent off are bringing the rest of my crew across the footbridge as we speak. You can go with us willingly or -." I paused when we heard the report of heavy cannon some distance away, followed by one explosion after another. "There is indeed mischief afoot this night Master Wú. Those are my guns you hear. The Dutch have come to take Macau! If you want to live to see the dawn, you'll come with us willingly."

And then Shaw returned with Henry and his men. "We must hurry Mary," he said anxiously.

"Aye," I replied. "We heard the commotion in the city. Henry, get us down to the pier. Kill anyone who tries to stop us."

While my men dragged Lu-Li out of the room by the arms, I grabbed four tapestries I fancied off the walls and had Egbert grab two vases. We marched out of the *House* in a cluster with Wú in the center. Scores of guests standing along a long, outside balcony on the second floor, watching the muzzle flashes reflecting off the clouds, looked down at us, at a large party of armed foreigners hustling Wú to his barge. No one tried to stop us, not even the *House* guards. I think the Chinese assumed we were escorting Wú to safety.

With thirty muskets pointing at them, with more explosions rocking the city, the crew on Wú's barge panicked and ran. Half my men piled into the barge and the others grabbed boats nearby. We rowed fast and hard.

Once we reached the junk, my men used rope and tackle to hoist Wú up. We brought him aboard like cargo. We cut the anchor cable, we wouldn't need it, turned the ship around and coasted with the currents back to the city. Once we reached the harbor, we saw small fires raging up and down the docks illuminating the waterfront and I could see the silhouettes of my three ships slowly making their way to the west - but I saw no sign of Dijksma. I had Shaw hoist a green pennant up the junk's main mast, the signal that all was well, and had Henry steer us towards our ships.

"Do you have the prize?" Atwood called out.

"Aye, we do," I said. "Where are the Dutch?"

"Haven't seen Dijksma yet. But we had unexpected company. That galleon Dijksma thought had sailed to Japan - she's here and she's fucking big. We've traded shots."

"Kinkae," I called out. "Come take us off this stinking boat. Jacob, Maurice, follow me. We sail for the lagoon."

After I was back aboard *Nemesis* with all my men and our prisoners, we took the junk in tow and raced towards the lagoon with all speed. We didn't need to sail far. Near the southwest corner of the lagoon, we saw muzzle flashes streaking across the water. We heard the boom of heavy cannon. We rushed towards the light, we hurried towards the sound of the guns and when we reached the lagoon we found the galleon, a portly sixty-gunner of about one thousand tons, sitting outside the lagoon with Dijksma and his men trapped inside. The galleon had already obliterated Dijksma's three flimsy junks beached along the shore, the boats were burning brightly, and her guns had started lobbing cannon balls at Dijksma and his men hidding behind the dunes.

One-on-one, my ships were no match for the galleon but together, the galleon was no match for us - or so I told myself. Mercifully, I did not need to put my bravado to the test. When the galleon's captain saw three impressive battlecruisers closing in on him, he didn't like the odds and fled. I immediately returned to the junk we had in tow with a skeleton crew and led six longboats into shore. I could see Dijksma lining his men up along the water's edge against the flames of his burning boats as we drew near.

"Ewoud," I called out. "How goes your evening?"

"Thank God you're here," he said wearily. "The Portuguese army won't be far behind. We should move like demons and depart these waters with haste."

We had to make three trips ferrying Dijksma's men back to the ships. The entire affair took us an hour and then some. Dijksma was the last man to step off the beach and won my admiration for it.

I cut the junk loose to gain speed and led us south-by-southeast away from the lagoon in ships awash in men. And as the first rays of light of a new day burst over the ocean, Dijksma and I glanced over *Nemesis'* stern rail for one last peek and caught the dark forms of Portuguese soldiers swarming around the three smoldering wrecks as they combed the beach for stragglers.

I had Lu-Li taken below to my cabin and told Dijksma to join me there after he looked in on his men. Too big to take below, my lads chained Wú to the main mast.

When Dijksma approached my cabin, I stopped him outside the door, looked him over for any wounds, saw none, and kissed him on the cheek. He ignored my peck, seized me in his arms and kissed me passionately on the mouth.

"You're a bawdy fellow sir," I said smiling and pushed him away before someone caught us. "You look no worse for wear. Did you lose any men?"

"Yes, thirteen are missing. Either killed or poor souls who lost their way in the dark, I know not. 'Twas a hard thing leaving men behind."

"Aye. Could have been much worse. That galleon could have been real trouble had her captain any stones."

"A catastrophe in the making to be sure. Perhaps the Portuguese would have spared the Ambonese and Tanimbar. But for the bravery of you and your lads, we Dutch certainly would have been massacred."

"Did you accomplish what you set out to do?"

"I suppose though the Portuguese will see our raid as nothing more than a nuisance. We did little more than interrupt their supper. You had a good night I see. Rob tells me that huge tower of flesh secured against the main mast is Wú."

"Aye and I have Lu-Li sitting in my cabin. I thought perhaps you two might like to become better acquainted."

Chapter Thirty-Four

After fleeing from Macau in haste, we raced towards the lovely island of Mindoro to reprovision and stretch our legs. The ships were terribly overcrowded. Men had to take turns sleeping in the hammocks or slept on deck and we had to drastically ration our food and water during the voyage. I worried about the cleanliness and the good health of the men.

After we landed on Mindoro's peaceful shores, we pitched our tents against the sea and sent foraging parties across the island to look for food and water. We used one of the rafts Kinkae's lads had built months before to ferry Wú over as none of the longboats could hold him. After a fine supper of venison, wild boar and oranges, I called my brothers to my side. I invited Ling, Dijksma and Egbert to join us though I cautioned them that they were merely guests and had no say in our proceedings. This was strictly a clan matter.

The evening was pleasant enough with a delightfully frisky breeze rolling off the water. The stars were bright and clear. The Pacific was at peace with the world. Earlier my men had built an enormous bonfire on the beach for the evening's spectacle. As the Dutch had graciously volunteered to assume the night watch aboard our ships, most of my lads were able to come ashore and had gathered around the great bonfire. I took a seat on the only chair.

Six men dragged Wú and Lu-Li out in chains before me. To his credit, Wú had refused to speak since leaving Macau. Lu-Li had sung like a bird, confirming most of what Jian had told us already.

Wú smiled when he saw Elizabeth. "Why Elizabeth my dear, what a lovely surprise. I'm honored we meet again, though I'm truly sorry you must see me like this."

Elizabeth offered no reply.

I cleared my throat. "Masters Féng Wú and Lu-Li, we've brought you to this place," I said, pausing to give Egbert a moment to translate for all to hear, "to stand -."

"A moment please madam," Wú interrupted. The huge Chinaman casually reached down, wrapped his massive hands around Lu-Li's throat and snapped his neck in two as if he were breaking a twig.

I jumped to my feet and drew my sword in anger. "Why?" I demanded.

Wú answered me with a haughty smile. I instantly regretted my intemperance, took a deep breath and eased my sword back into the scabbard.

"No matter," I said calmly and took my seat. "Lu-Li has already spoken. We shall proceed with your trial."

"Trial? What may I ask are the charges against me my good lady?"

"Piracy and murder."

"Oh? I've committed no such wrongs against you or any of your people."

"Lu-Li told a different story."

Wú glanced down at Lu-Li's corpse. "From this abominable cockroach? All Macau knows this filthy wretch was a thief and a liar. His words meant nothing."

"Who is Arslan?"

"Arslan? Why I know the man well. He and I do some trading together from time-to-time, here and there."

"Where is Arslan?"

Wú shrugged his shoulders. "Who can say? Arslan is and has always been a restless soul. He's a free man. He comes and goes as he pleases. That is the Mongol way."

"Do you admit or deny attacking our ships?"

"Ships? What ships do you speak of? When and where did I do these things?"

"Within hours after departing your warehouse in Macau nearly four years ago, thirty ships attacked my ships."

"I know nothing of these matters. I own no ships. 'Tis true I did business with Elizabeth and an Irishman named Michael Flannigan back then. We struck a good bargain benefitting us all. I had high hopes of doing more profitable business with them in the future. I considered them honest traders, good folk. Why would I do them harm? You say ships? Elizabeth and the Irishman left Macau in one ship. I saw but one ship. This is what I know." Wú paused to kick Lu-Li's body. "If this maggot did you wrong, I know nothing of it."

The man's sincerety, his composure and his logic caught me by surprise. But I had come prepared.

"Jian!" I cried out.

Ling's brother pushed through the crowd and hurried to my side.

"Jian, do you know this man?" I asked and pointed to Wú.

"Yes, Lady Mary. He Master Wú."

Wú peered down on Jian with vacant, cruel eyes, eyes devoid of any expression or compassion.

"Jian, how do you know this man?" I asked loudly for the benefit of my men who had not yet heard the boy's story.

"I do work for Master Wú. He most important man in all Macau."

"What work did you do for Master Wú?"

"I sweep floors at warehouse. I empty privy buckets. I run errands. I deliver messages. I do whatever master tells me. Always I do good work. I never cheat master."

"Are there other boys working for Master Wú?"

"Yes."

"Did he treat you well?"

"Yes. He like my sister's songs. He no beat me. He never take me to the *House*."

I did not press Jian to say anything more about the other boys in front of my men for I knew the unspeakable truth already.

"Did you ever see Elizabeth in Macau?"

"Yes."

"At Master Wú's warehouse?"

"Yes."

"Who was Elizabeth with?"

"Arslan and white man."

"Was this white man European, a man named Michael Flannagan?"

"He red hair man. I not hear his name."

"Did Master Wú, Elizabeth and this man do any business together?"

"Yes, yes. Elizabeth and her friend trade spices for Chinese cargo with Master Wú. I watch master's men load big ship. Master Wú most happy."

"And then Elizabeth and her friend sailed away?"

"Yes."

"Did anything happen before that? Did Master Wú ever speak to anyone about Elizabeth or her friend before they left Macau?"

"Yes."

"Who?"

"Master Wú and Master Lu-Li speak to Master Zhou Buwei in Master Wú's office."

"His office at the warehouse?"

"Yes."

"You were there?"

"Yes."

"Where?"

"I sit under table."

"Why?"

"I eating apple."

"Why were you under the table eating an apple?"

"I, I..."

"'Tis alright Jian. You are not in any trouble."

"I, I take apple from Master Wú's desk when he not see me."

I smiled and rubbed Jian's head. "Who is Zhou Buwei?"

"He has ships, many ships with big muskets."

"Chinese ships?"

"Yes and Portuguese ships."

"Was there anyone else there that night?"

"Yes, two men."

"Do you know these men?"

"No. I see them one time."

"Were they Chinese?"

"No."

"Portuguese or Spanish?"

"No."

"Irish perhaps like the man Elizabeth was with?"

"What is Irish?"

"Never mind. Tell me what you can about the other two men."

"One man say he from Java. Other man had foreign voice like soldiers on ships."

"You mean like the Ambonese or Tanimbar?"

"No."

"The Dutch?"

"Yes, I think, maybe. He white man."

"Can you describe this man?"

"No, he very plain."

"What did you hear?"

Jian suddenly went quiet and glanced down at the sand. Ling hugged him and after she whispered something in his ear, he reached out to take my hand.

"You are safe with me Jian," I said and squeezed his hand reassuringly. "We wish to know what you heard that night in the warehouse whilst you were eating your apple. We only wish to hear the truth."

"Perhaps Jian," Wú interrupted, "we should bring your friend Zhàn here and ask him about these matters before you say more. He's a good boy, an honest boy."

I watched Jian turn pale. After Egbert finished translating Wú's words, I lifted Jian onto my lap, held him tight and promised him that Wú would never have the chance to hurt Zhàn or anyone else again. Jian nodded.

"Master Wú," Jian continued, "tell Master Buwei and Java man to find Elizabeth, bring her back to Macau. Master Wú and Master

Buwei, Java man and white man all agree to share in good business."

My men began to stir once Egbert finished translating Jian's words. Many had heard enough. There were murmurs of pushing Wú into the bonfire. I stood and held my hands up for quiet.

"Was Arslan there?"

"I no see Arslan."

"Did you ever see a man named Mohamed Ratu?"

"I not know this man."

"Could the Java man be Ratu?"

"I, I don't know."

"Did you see Zhou Buwei again?"

"No, people say he die in big storm on ocean."

"Did you see his ship return?"

"He take many ships. Some come back, not all."

"Where any of his ships damaged?"

"Oh, yes, yes. All ships damaged in big storm, some very bad."

"Were any of Buwei's damaged by cannon balls?"

"I not sure Lady Mary."

"By fire?"

"Oh yes, many."

"Jian, is there anything else you can tell us, anything at all you wish to say?"

"No."

"Then you have our thanks Jian for sharing your story with us. You are a very courageous lad. You may run along now. Go find James if you like and play. You boys are not leave the camp, understood?"

"Yes, Lady Mary."

I looked up at Wú. "Does the prisoner wish to speak?"

"You accuse me of a vile crime?" Wú bellowed for all to hear. "But for the word of a mere boy, by his own corrupt tongue a dishonorable thief and a liar, where is your proof? You have none. Today is a farce, a mockery. No judge would find guilt in me. I dare you to bring me before the Governor of Macau, or before Pangeran Ratu if your destination is Java. Are you afraid to do this? I demand you treat me with dignity. I demand you treat me fairly in accordance with the law. And beware: I enjoy the favor of the Emperor of China. I do what I do under his supreme majesty's protection."

There was a day when I would have simply drawn my sword, parted Wú's head from his shoulders and been done with it. But the hunger to kill was not in me that night. I had my men bury a heavy stake deep into the ground. I had them chain Wú to it. I would let my brothers decide what to do with the Chinaman in the morning. After my men dispersed, I summoned Elizabeth to my tent.

I was sharing a beer with Atwood and Efendi when she entered. I took her hand in mine in a gesture of peace and goodwill, though she seemed to sense that something was afoot and flinched at my touch.

"'Tis time to make amends Elizabeth," I said. "'Tis time for you to atone for your sins."

"What?"

"This terrible tragedy could have been avoided had you not sailed to Macau on some silly notion of adventure. You made poor choices. You ignored your obligations to the Company. You trusted the wrong people. Out of pride, you attacked when you should have run and many a good man has perished for it."

"I am not to blame! How dare you speak to me of poor choices! What of you and the *Síol Faolcháin*? How much innocent blood is on your hands? Gilley? Hunter? The rest?"

Atwood jumped to his feet. "Elizabeth," he roared, "that's enough!"

I gently grabbed Atwood by the wrist and pulled him back to his chair. "There is truth in what she says Jacob. Elizabeth, I live with my past mistakes each day. For you to grow, for you to become the woman you are meant to be, you must atone."

"Atone? Atone how?"

"This is not for me to say. You alone must decide. Did you know Wú had Ling's parents murdered?"

"What? No. I didn't know. Why didn't you accuse him of this?"

"He confessed his crimes to me back in Macau, even boasted about them to hurt Ling. But these crimes, even if true, were not relevant to his treachery against us and so I said nothing. We all love you, Elizabeth. But you must face the consequences of your actions. You must accept responsibly for the mistakes you've made. If you are not to blame, then who?"

"'Tis obvious! Wú and Arslan and this Zhou Buwei scoundrel, they're to blame, they're responsible!"

"And what of your failure to inform us about Ling and the *House*? A lie by omission is still a lie and that's a betrayal against me."

"Betrayal? Ridiculous! Ling and the *House* were not relevant to your questions about pirates!"

"Ugh, you've learned nothing," I said wearily and shook my head. "You may leave us."

Efendi took my hand as Elizabeth stormed out of my tent, cursing a flurry of vulgar words under her breath in Spanish "What," he asked, "did you hope to accomplish Mary?"

"Damned if I know Mustafa. Of late, I've been most weary. My thoughts are often muddled. I long to be done with this expedition and far away from Asia."

"I will go and speak with her, Mary. In her heart she knows."

"I'm sorry to say it Mustafa," Atwood interjected, "but I'm not so sure. She is and will always be her father's daughter. She is a proud, obstinate, hot-blooded Spaniard."

"And yet," I noted, "she has many admirable gifts."

Atwood yawned and stretched his arms. "True, though sadly common sense is not one of them."

In the morning, I awoke with a fever and the shakes. I called my officers together to discuss what to do with Wú. The vote of course was quick, predictable and unanimous. We'd muster the men and let Wú choose between Chinese poison or the sea. But when a small group of us reached the spot where we had left Wú for the night, we found him already dead with a knife buried in his chest and with Ling, splattered in blood, sitting next to him. Ling looked up at me in tears. I knelt beside her and held her. She had the right and I told her so.

I told my men to disperse and enjoy a hardy breakfast. I returned to my tent with Ling and fell into my cot. I did not leave my bed for the next three days, taking only sips of water and cinchona, a gift from our good doctor Stachel.

"I'm told," Dijksma said with a gleam in his eye as he stepped inside my tent, "you are feeling better."

"Much better Ewoud, thank you," I replied as I struggled to sit up in my damp, smelly clothing.

"I've brought you a pot of good, strong, Dutch tea. A gift from one of my lads for you."

"Dutch tea?"

"Yes, have some. 'Tis soothing and very good. The Company will soon start shipping large quantities of tea back to Europe. I expect tea will become quite popular back home."

"How thoughtful."

"My men are grateful for what you did for us in Macau. You saved many lives. May I get you anything?"

"I'd pay gold for a hot bath, but no. I'll enjoy my tea and will try to eat something later. I suppose you Dutch are anxious to get back to Ambon."

"On the contrary. With plenty of good water and ample game on this island, my lads have very much enjoyed the past few days."

"I best put on fresh clothing and make the rounds amongst my own men. Perhaps later if I feel strong enough, we could take a stroll."

"That is a wonderful suggestion but first... Ashaki, Lololi, our noble commander is yours. I shall take my leave now."

"Beg pardon?" I asked.

Dijksma grinned as the twins entered my tent with towels and soap. "This is their idea. A bath, a hot bath, has already been prepared for you madam. Rest assured, you can count on me, I shall do my very best to protect your privacy whilst you bathe. I shall stand guard nearby and do my utmost to keep seven hundred lonely, hungry wolves from ogling you."

I managed a weak smile, my first in many days. "I know of but one wolf on this island who frightens me..."

Chapter Thirty-Five

After gliding past the chalk cliffs of Ambon Bay, with flying jibs and billowing tops'ls following an easy journey from Mindoro, we eased our way into Ambon's crowded harbor, furled sail and dropped our anchors under the shadow of the Dutch fort. Having fully recovered from whatever ailment had struck me low, I was in high spirits again. Against the odds my plan in Macau had succeeded without the loss of a single man and Dijksma could rightfully claim a Dutch victory.

"That fellow standing on the jetty," I asked Dijksma as my men rowed us into shore in the first longboat, "that looks like - Koopman?"

"Why so it is," Dijksma replied, squinting his eyes against the sun.

After my crew tied our boat against a piling next to the jetty where Koopman was standing, I stepped off with Dijksma behind me and nodded politely to Koopman. He did not nod back.

"This is a surprise Gerrit," Dijksma said.

"Ewoud, Mary, welcome back. What news Ewoud?"

"We gave the Portuguese a bloody nose, but we'll need more ships and men if we want to take Macau. We lost some good lads without accomplishing much. What brings you to Ambon?"

"I've come for nutmeg and mace. Three Dutch merchantmen from Rotterdam sailed into Banten two weeks ago. The crews are presently overhauling their ships. I want to have the spices ready for shipment before they reach Banda."

"The books are in my office at the fort. We can see what quantities are available."

"I've already taken the liberty of looking over your books Ewoud.

The Banda are holding six hundred tons. I've already prepared the necessary bills of lading."

"That's true," Dijksma replied. "But the Dutch will need to wait for the next harvest. I've earmarked those spices to Mary already. She'd be halfway to Amsterdam by now but for the mission Admiral Matelieff tasked us with."

"The Irish will need to wait. The Company's ships have priority."

"What nonsense is this?" I asked indignantly. "My ships are under contract with the Company therefore we are the Company's ships. That cargo is mine."

Koopman ignored me. "Ewoud, it is done."

"It is not done!" I protested loudly.

"What is this?" Atwood asked as he walked up behind me with the rest of our longboats floating in, crowded with Dutch, Ambonese and Tanimbar soldiers.

"Koopman," I said testily, "has a mind to take the spices which have been allocated to us and give them over to three Dutch ships that recently sailed into Banten."

Atwood turned to Dijksma. "How long will it take to harvest another six hundred tons Ewoud?"

"Two, perhaps three months. With Tidore and Ternate in Spanish hands, we no longer have access to cloves. And if the Bantenese could supply enough pepper, Gerrit wouldn't be here for nutmeg and mace."

"I'll not sit on my arse watching nutmeg grow for three months," I said defiantly.

"Come, let's return to my office," Dijksma offered in a conciliatory tone, "where we can discuss this matter further out of this hot sun. We're all friends here. There may be another solution, but I need to see my books."

I nodded and started following Koopman and Dijksma to the fort with Atwood at my side when Jian suddenly ran up to me and tugged on my arm. "Jian, not now," I said. "I have work to do. Where's your sister?"

Jian pulled harder.

"Stop!" I said sharply and yanked my arm away. My mood had turned foul because of Koopman. "Run along now!"

But when poor Jian flinched and glanced at me wide-eyed, I instantly regretted my callous tone. I had no right to be cross with the boy, with a boy who had been so brave in helping me, who had only recently lost his parents. I admonished myself for my lack of sympathy. I knelt down beside Jian while Koopman and Dijksma kept walking and wrapped him up in my arms.

"I'm so sorry Jian," I said and kissed his forehead. "Forgive me. What troubles you my little man?"

When I couldn't understand a single word gushing from Jian's mouth, I called Ling to my side.

"That man," Ling said, translating her brother's words as he whispered them into her ear, "he the foreign man Jian see with Wú, Lu-Li and Zhou Buwei."

I followed the length of Jian's arm. "Are you sure?" I asked while I quickly pulled his arm down.

"Yes."

"Are you very, very sure?"

"Yes, Lady Mary," Jian said slowly. "He plain face man I see."

I glanced up at Atwood and he nodded. I kissed Jian on the check and sent him back to the longboats with Ling and told them to wait for me there.

Efendi joined us just as Atwood and I stepped into Dijksma's office. We found Dijksma sitting behind his writing table, flipping through the pages of a book while Koopman sat across from him, casually sipping wine from a crystal goblet.

"Ah, Mary, there you are," Dijksma said. "Jacob, Mustafa, welcome, please sit. Have some wine. I've found two-hundred tons of nutmeg we can have stored in warehouses on two islands nearby. I'm still looking for more."

"I'd love some wine," I said in a friendlier tone and poured one glass for Atwood, one for Efendi and one for myself. I took a seat across from Koopman and smiled sweetly at the man.

We sat quietly while Dijksma continued thumbing through the

pages of two more books. He found another fifty tons, no more.

"That's it then," Koopman said briskly. "I must return to Batavia and I'm taking my men back with me Ewoud. I wish you all a good day. Congratulations Ewoud on your actions in Macau. I won't sail until morning. If you have written your report about the raid, I'd be delighted to deliver the document to one of the three masters from Rotterdam to take back to the Company for you. Captain Mary, gentlemen, I bid you safe travels."

"Two hundred fifty tons is not enough Ewoud," I said after Koopman left. "I'm already losing money on this venture."

"Though I do not answer to Koopman, he is senior to me Mary. I cannot undo what he has done. We can sail for Banten and look for Admiral Matelieff. Matelieff's got himself embroiled in some feud Koopman told me between Prince Ratu and the Sultan of Palembang in Sumatra, most likely over who controls the pepper markets. We can ask the good admiral to intervene."

"But the admiral may no longer be in Banten."

"This is true."

"And even if Matelieff is in Banten, he may choose to do nothing for me."

"This is also true. But Matelieff is a fair man and he respects you. He'll see the injustice of what Koopman has done. I'm certain of it."

"Perhaps. Perhaps we should simply ignore Koopman."

"Mary, as I've said, I do not have the authority."

"It is," Atwood interrupted, "at times like this Ewoud that a man must step forward, that he must show his quality - or not."

Dijksma stood and leaned forward with his fists resting against the tabletop. After a brief moment of reflection, he shook his head and turned to me.

"Damn Jacob, you're right. Mary, I'm sorry. I've not been a good friend. It may cost me my head, but let's go get your spices before Koopman does."

"I'd like you to keep your head," I said. "'Tis such a pretty head. There is a better way."

"Oh?"

"Koopman."

"Yes?"

"He's the man Jian saw in Macau with Wú and the others."

I watched Dijksma's jaw drop as he stared at me dumbstruck. But in his eyes, I could see as he thought things through that he believed the boy.

"Is the boy," Efendi asked, "absolutely certain of this Mary?"

"He is Mustafa. Jian told me this just before you joined us."

"The Company," Dijksma said soberly, "expects, even tolerates a certain amount of thievery and self-dealing out here. Half my men trade on the side for themselves. With what the Company pays them who can blame them? I turn a blind eye. I've suspected for some time Gerrit is crooked, but not this. No, not this."

Efendi clenched teeth. "Ewoud, I've watched you over these many months. You're a good and decent man, a moral man. Step aside if you like. Koopman must not leave this island alive."

"We need hard proof Mustafa," Dijksma replied. "The Company will never accept the word of a Chinese peasant boy over that of Koopman. The directors will think the boy is lying or simply badly mistaken."

"Jian has told no lies so far," Efendi said. "He has no reason to lie about Koopman now."

"I don't," I interrupted as I placed a comforting hand on Efendi's shoulder, "disagree with what you say Ewoud. "Hmmm. What to do, what to do I wonder?"

"I can file charges against Koopman," Dijksma offered. "There would be a hearing, a trial."

I finished the last of my wine and stood. "Too risky. Too messy, too much time lost. Let us try to get you this hard proof you need first Ewoud."

"How?"

"That's my problem. You simply need to stand aside and observe."

Atwood and Efendi waited for nightfall before they broke into Koopman's room. They slipped a hood over the Dutchman's head and pulled him from his bed. They bound his hands behind his back and dragged him kicking and cursing to a skiff nearby. They rowed him over to Nemesis where I, along with Elizabeth and the rest of my brothers, stood waiting on the main deck.

"Good evening Gerrit," I said after Atwood removed the hood from the Dutchman's head, as Efendi forced him to his knees.

Koopman snarled at me. "What's this? You think you can kidnap me, an officer of the Company? You think you can hold me ransom for the spices? You stupid, stupid woman."

"You are a piece to a puzzle," I said evenly. "I suppose you are here because of the spices in a way, but not as you suppose. Let us speak plainly with one another, shall we? I understand you know Féng Wú of Macau?"

When I saw the color draining from the Dutchman's face after uttering Wú's name, I knew Koopman was dirty. That was the moment I had no doubts.

"Well?"

"No."

"Huh. Strange. He knows you. I recently met with Masters Wú and Lu-Li in Macau whilst Dijksma was off playing soldier. We dined together at The House of a Thousand Pleasures. Do you know this place?"

"Of course not. I've never been to Macau."

"Are you certain? Master Wú told me to give you his warm regards. He told me you've been to his warehouse. I simply assumed he invited you to his private dining room at the House as he invited me."

"What do you want?"

"I'm finished with the Company. Now that I'm free, I want a percentage of the trade."

"What trade?"

"And you call me stupid? The trade between you and Wú of course. And in exchange for that percentage, you shall have the exclusive use of my ships to transport your illicit cargo between the islands."

"I don't know what you're talking about but even if I did why would I agree to such a thing?"

"Because Wú has already agreed - though he insisted I negotiate my percentage directly with you. He was most adamant about that. I understand a wealthy merchant named Zhou Buwei and many of his ships vanished in a great storm awhile back. You and Wú need ships, good ships, ships with teeth and reliable crews. You know what my ships and men can do against pirates like Mohamed Ratu."

"Just for amusement, assuming I did know something - why would I trust you?"

"Rob, Kinkae, the chest please."

Shaw and Kinkae disappeared below to retrieve a chest filled with Dutch guilders, money I didn't have, money that Dijksma kept at the fort and let me borrow for the evening. When Shaw and Kinkae returned, they set the chest down in front of Koopman and raised the lid.

"There are ten thousand Dutch guilders there," I said. "Good faith money. You can count it later. If we can agree on terms, you can hold that money to guarantee I perform my end of the bargain."

"And what if we cannot come to terms?"

"Then tonight I sail for Banda and take what is rightful mine and you can explain the loss of six hundred tons of spices to your masters back in Amsterdam. And whist you are doing that, I'll be negotiating my own arrangement with Wú. I understand I'll be sailing under the protection of the Chinese emperor. The choice is yours."

Koopman took a moment to consider my offer. "Very well, we do need to replace Buwei's ships. Subject to Wú's consent, five percent, five percent of what we net will be your share."

"Ha! I think not. I want twenty percent of what you gross. I have expensive ships to maintain and crews to feed."

"Twenty? Gross? No, no, no. Impossible. We have expenses too. Bribes are not cheap. Shall we say seven percent, net?"

"Who must you bribe?"

"The less you know the better."

"Fair enough. Fifteen percent, gross."

"Ten."

"Done. What of Arslan?"

"I do not know this man Arslan."

"No?"

"No."

"What of Ewoud? Does he need to approve of our arrangement?"

"Dijksma? No."

"I thought perhaps you were partners?"

"No! Dijksma cannot be trusted. He has given seven years of his life to the Company to live in this bunghole of the world and for what? Measly wages, insects and some scraps of Company paper that have no value? The man's a fool. Pity he didn't accommodate us all and die in Macau."

"Bunghole?"

"A new word I learned for the hole in your ass."

"Ah. I enjoy learning new words even when they are vulgar. Well, if Dijksma is not involved, I wonder if he has become suspicious of you. He has said some rather curious things about you. You may need to attend to this matter and soon."

"Men disappear on these islands all the time, never to be seen or heard from again. An accident, a dispute over money or a woman, a blood vendetta settled deep in the jungle or at sea, one can never be certain of the truth. If we have a deal, I trust this matter is something you could handle for me - as a sign of good faith."

"Just to be clear Gerrit, it would be better for us if Dijksma disappeared?"

"Yes."

"Perhaps we should ask Ewoud what his opinion is?"

"What?" Koopman asked confused.

I savored the moment when Dijksma stepped out of the shadows to stand by my side. Koopman stared up at Dijksma in horror.

"Gerrit, what the devil are doing down there on your knees?" Dijksma asked.

"Ewoud, thank God you're here! Help me. These scoundrels have kidnapped me. Look at the chest. They're trying to bribe me for the spices! They're brigands!"

I took a step forward. "Wú and Lu-Li are both dead you miserable abomination. You're finished."

"I know nothing of these things!" Koopman cried out. "I was merely playing along with you for my life. You're brigands and enemies of the Company!"

I drew my sword.

"Mercy!" he pleaded, whimpering like a child. "I beg you, please mercy!"

"Few have ever survived my mercy. Perhaps you should ask me for something else? Stop your pitiful yammering coward. Your sniveling hurts my ears. I should gut you from your privates to your naval and watch you flop around on my deck like a fish. Ewoud?"

"This problem is mine to deal with Mary," Dijksma replied. "May I?"

"By all means, I yield," I said and sheathed my sword.

"Why Gerrit?" Dijksma asked.

"Why what? I've done nothing wrong."

"We have witnesses who saw you in Macau with Wú, Lu-Li, Zhou Buwei and Mohamed Ratu. We have witnesses who heard you plotting with these wicked men against Elizabeth."

"Liars, all of them! You let this bitch kill me and 'tis murder. You're not my judge or jury. You cannot be my executioner. This matter must be referred to the Company. This is the law!"

"How odd. Wú made a similar plea before his death. You've betrayed the Company's trust. You've disgraced yourself as a man. Mary, how many fathoms under her keel?"

I looked over to Henry. "Henry?"

"About four fathoms Mary."

Dijksma nodded. "Mary, may I borrow a length of rope, say about six feet long? I shall require something heavy too. Something about the weight of a bag of Bantenese pepper will do."

"Gladly, Ewoud. You may keep these things for as long as you need them."

We watched Dijksma tie one end of a rope around Koopman's ankles and the other end around an iron fitting. With Atwood's help,

Dijksma lifted Koopman and the iron fitting up on the rail.

"Men disappear on these islands all the time Gerrit," Dijksma said, "never to be seen or heard from again. Wú is waiting for you on the other side in hell."

A soft push, a quiet splash and the deed was done.

Nearly two years had passed since I had left Amsterdam with Matelieff. I had sailed with two purposes in mind. First to settle my accounts with the Company and second to find those responsible for killing MacGyver and my men. I had, at least in part, achieved my second purpose though I found little satisfaction in it and now the time had come to fulfill the first - and then I had promises to keep in the New World.

"Do you still have the black vile Mei gave us?" I asked as I finished my breakfast with Efendi up on the quarterdeck.

"Of course."

"Good. Keep it safe. The old sorceress spoke true. I may have a use for it. I think I'll go ashore for a walk to stretch my legs."

"Should I accompany you Mary, or would you prefer I send some of the lads ashore with you? They can follow at a discrete distance."

I placed my hand on Efendi's cheek. "I'll be fine Mustafa."

"The Dutch are certainly scouring the taverns and whorehouses looking for Koopman by now. He was supposed to sail this morning. Might be some commotion in town."

"I shall keep my wits about me, I promise."

"Should you ever choose to settle down Mary, Ewoud would not be a bad fellow to have around."

"What the devil are you implying Mustafa?" I asked with false indignation, smiling despite my best effort not to.

"I always speak plainly Mary. I imply nothing."

"Well, I suppose I should visit Ewoud to discuss our spices."

Efendi grinned. "I suppose you should."

"Before I do, you and Rob will need to travel soon I suspect?"

"We do."

"Men and their silly secret societies."

"We returned with fine gifts last time as I recall. Do you still have it?"

I smiled as I thought of the stunning crucifix of solid gold studded with rubies, sapphires and emeralds Shaw had found years ago buried in the sands of the Syrian Desert outside the ruins of a medieval, Christian stronghold. "Aye, I keep it safely tucked away in Westport. Can your pilgrimage to the lands of the Ottoman wait until after I finish my business in the Americas? I'll want you by my side."

"Never would I let you make such a dangerous journey alone."

I kissed Mustafa on the cheek, then went ashore to look for Dijksma and found the Dutchman in the officers' mess eating breakfast with Shultz. "May I join you gentlemen?" I asked.

Shultz stood and offered me his chair. "Please Mary, sit. I must be off for morning inspections. Koopman has yet to show his face. I should start making inquiries."

"Thank you, Julius."

"I hope to see you before you depart Ambon. Should my duties keep me from this, allow me to say it has been a privilege. I bid you farewell Mary and wish you a safe, easy passage home."

"Thank you, Julius. I pray you are blessed with good fortune. I pray you are reunited with your family soon."

"I'm curious," Dijksma asked after Shultz walked off. "When you asked Koopman if I had a part in any of this sordid business, did you truly wonder if I was somehow involved? Do you think I could betray good men?"

"I thought I saw something in your eyes when I stepped into the room just now Ewoud. You did not seem altogether pleased to see me. Good God no my dearheart, not in the least. You think I would give myself to a man like that? I knew what Koopman's answer would be but wanted you to hear it for yourself, from Koopman's own mouth."

"I see. You think me a fool as Koopman said?"

"No. I think you are a man of principles and I admire you for it. But there are more men within the Company I suspect who think like Koopman. They view principled men as weak."

"Well, sometimes I think I'm a fool. 'Tis only two more years and then I'm done. Actually, my remaining obligation is closer to eighteen months as the Company is obligated to return me to Amsterdam before my term expires."

"And you tell me this why?"

"I, well, I thought you might like to know."

"Why?"

Dijksma reached across the table and took my hand. "Because I'm in love with you, Mary."

I felt my pulse quicken. I squeezed Dijksma's hand reassuringly. But I could not bring myself to reply in kind.

"Love?" I asked. "I once thought I knew what love was but no more. Be not offended. The years can corrupt the heart, numb the senses. Loss, betrayal, and hurt can take a heavy toll. Love is a plaything for the young and innocent. I respect, even admire you Ewoud. I'm fond of you and I relish the moments we share together. These qualities are far more enduring than love I think and perhaps worth more. Oh, I see I've offended you. I am sorry."

"The world is filled with pain and loss Mary. What you're describing is friendship, not love. I hope, in time, you can find love again. Life has little meaning without it."

I took a pencil out of Dijksma's hand and a scrap of paper off the table. "Should you wish to find me, you may send your letter to this tavern in Westport, Ireland," I said and handed the paper to Dijksma.

"*Banshee's Lament?*"

"Aye. 'Tis a long story. Remember Westport, a port on the west coast of Ireland, and *Banshee's Lament*. Come, walk with me. I'd like to know this Dutchman named Ewoud Dijksma a little better."

We took a long stroll outside of the town walking hand-in-hand. We walked and talked about silly things as couples are wont to do until we stumbled upon an unattended stable where I ripped Dijksma's shirt open and pushed him down on a pile of fresh hay. I slipped out of my trousers, unbuckled his belt and mounted him. There was nothing gentle in our movements.

"I will miss these moments," I said as we dressed.

"'Tis always a good day when a man can breach a woman's maidenhead, especially when she's pretty."

"I've heard many a lewd word spoken when the subject turns to fucking, but that description I must confess is new. My maidenhead I fear was breached long ago."

"Silly me. I meant to say Alter of Venus."

"And what do you say love is?"

"Huh, well... Ah, love, love is the sublime joy one feels from the heart for another. Love is when that person is more important to you than you are to yourself."

"I like this answer, though I would say love is the offspring of the brain, not the heart."

"Either way."

"If what you say is love, then I can say I have love for you. Shhh, say nothing. Let us part ways with this wonderful memory between us. The future will take care of itself. With all my heart, I hope we find each other again Ewoud Dijksma."

With our bills of lading in hand and our ships in prime condition, we sailed for Banda next where we took on six hundred tons of nutmeg and mace, in addition to the two-hundred fifty tons Dijksma had found for me. And then we sailed on to Banten for the pepper. Atwood, Maurice and Shaw all agreed we could squeeze nearly two hundred tons of pepper into the ships and still have room for provisions for the long journey home. Once in Banten, we stuffed nearly six thousand bags of pepper into every last nook and cranny. Some men slept alongside a bag of pepper in their hammocks. I had bags of pepper stacked against the walls of my great cabin. After much thought and discussion with my brothers and Elizabeth, we finally agreed to sail west instead of east. Though driving our ships across the Pacific was tempting, I knew in my heart returning to Amsterdam first was the better, wiser choice.

We pushed our ships hard and made the journey from Banten to Amsterdam, through storms, sickness, spoiled food and mishaps common to all mariners, in eight months. The Fates took five good men along the way.

We entered Amsterdam's harbor flying the bold colors of the VOC and were given priority by the harbormaster to ease our ships up alongside the Company's docks. We wasted no time offloading our cargo. Houtman came out to greet us. And after his men completed their inspections, after they tallied the final inventory totals, Houtman handed me a bank note for our commission and I handed him Dijksma's report on Macau. Though the leather pouch was sealed, I knew the contents of the report already. Dijksma offered his observations of Matelieff's actions at Malacca, provided details of his own raid on Macau and reported the peculiar disappearance of Koopman. He was generous in his praise of our contributions.

I parted with Houtman as a friend. I parted with the Company on good terms. And as we put to sea again, Atwood for Scotland, Maurice for Boulogne and me for Ireland, we all agreed to meet back in Westport in two months' time, give or take.

Once I reached Westport with *Nemesis*, I paid my men a disappointing sum. I promised them there would be more from our next journey and wished them all Godspeed.

I called out to BB from the quarterdeck rail as I watched him climb into one of the longboats. "Master BB, will you look for better prospects or will you return to us?"

Our chief cook and victualler smiled back and waved. "Never been to the Americas my Lady. I shall see you at the appointed time."

I waved back and looked over at Henry and Kinkae, who were standing next to each other on the main deck. "Two months here and then on to Guadeloupe. I can only imagine how hard it has been on you and your men being away from home and family for this long. Truly I am sorry."

"Our homecoming will be all the sweeter," Kinkae replied with a chuckle. "Though a few of the lads I suspect are perhaps in no great hurry."

And then I turned to my own growing family, Shaw, Elizabeth, Ashaki, Lololi, Ling, young Jian and James, waiting patiently for me in the last longboat. I grabbed my gear, climbed over the side and into the boat, happy to be back in Ireland again.

Chapter Thirty-Six

For the next two months I contented myself with doing very little. Once a week I'd ride to the top of Cruach Phádraig. I went to the mountain for solitude, for contemplation and to breathe in the rugged, stirring beauty that is Ireland. When I took them with me, my James, Jian and Lololi couldn't hear the call of the mountain. They didn't understand its magic. But Ashaki and Ling both understood. As for Shaw and Elizabeth, we rarely saw them. They disappeared out into the countryside together more often than not and I was happy for them.

Early fall soon turned into late fall and the weather turned too. Ling and Jian were awestruck when the rains gave way to snow. I was less enthused when the dampness cut through me and caught myself longing to embrace the warmth of the Caribbean again. Before my men began trickling back into town, I gathered my odd, little family - each one of us a castaway in one way or another - to Shaw's splendid tavern for supper.

"I'd like to hear from each of you," I said in English as we ate our meals in my private room. I had worked hard teaching English to the twins, Ling and Jian since leaving the East Indies.

"We'll go around the table. Rob, you're the eldest, I'll start with you. Winter's fast approaching. Jacob, Maurice and all the others should be on their way and soon we'll be sailing west for the Americas. Are you content to join me or is there something else you wish to do? I would hear the truth from each of you now. Take heart, whatever your answer, I'll not be insulted or offended."

I had placed Shaw in command of a fine warship after he had proven his skills at sea. He had the spirit of a true warrior adventurer.

I knew what his answer would be already but thought it best to ask. Elizabeth had not changed. She continued keeping her distance from me and yet she too chose to sail with me again. Brave, beautiful Ashaki, a fearless fighter in the making, a seasoned mariner with wonderful intuitive sense along with her brilliant, spirited sister Lololi, were both staunchly with me. They had the most to lose and yet the twins had become devoted to me. Young James only knew the sea and there was no keeping him from it. Shy, polite Ling, a striking beauty with a voice from beyond this world, but a delicate flower too, thought she had no choice but to sail with me. I was determined to show her otherwise. And Jian, a fireball of vitality and vigor, a carefree, happy spirit, an endearing boy curious about the world around him like some puppy and unafraid of mischief, was game for anything.

"Wonderful," I said after Jian finished speaking. "I thank each of you for your candor. I'm grateful for your trust, for your loyalty and friendship. Let us eat, drink and be merry and after supper I have small gifts for each of you, just trinkets, as Christmas is nearly upon us."

A week later I returned to the tavern for supper with all my officers present. After a fine, hardy meal of rabbit stew, clams, carrots and potatoes, a new food imported from the New World, I passed a bottle of good Scottish whiskey around and convened a council of war.

"I hear Mary," Atwood said smiling, "you've been handing out presents for Christmas. I've yet to see mine."

"I thought perhaps a patch for your other eye," I replied sweetly.

"Then again," Atwood replied to the chuckles around the table, "I've never been very fond of gifts."

I walked around the room to refill each glass with more whiskey. "Mustafa, how many men have we?"

"With the men Jacob and Maurice returned with, two hundred sixty-eight souls in all Mary."

"A better showing than I dared hope for considering what I paid them last."

"Do you have any money left Mary?" Atwood asked.

"No. I sent Master BB out for provisions and have spent every penny. He has had to purchase a good amount of what we need on credit and I had no choice but to pledge *Nemesis* as collateral. At least we have fewer mouths to feed. Mustafa, Rob, Kinkae and Henry have kept the lads busy keeping *Nemesis* in good repair. Jacob, Maurice, what of your ships?"

"*Spitfire* could use a splash of paint and a touch of varnish, but she's is in excellent condition overall."

Maurice nodded. "As is *Cerberus*, Mary."

"Do you still intend," Atwood asked, "to go after this Salamanca fellow Mary?"

"Aye. I made promises I'm honor-bound to keep."

"He must be a wealthy man."

"True enough Jacob, though most of his wealth is in the land. As for gold and silver, I suspect he keeps his money in banks."

Atwood chuckled. "Well, when it comes to gifts Mary, you have the gift of persuasion. I have no doubt you'll loosen his tongue. He'll have something of value hidden somewhere on his property."

"Perhaps. My brothers, my sister, a voyage to New Spain is indeed the plan. Whatever Salamanca has in wealth we can take with us, I'll need to give a goodly portion to Ashaki's and Lololi's people and to the Cimarron who helped me. Why the sudden glum faces I see around the table? That's only part of my plan. Maurice, what say you to a trip to Ronconcholan?"

Maurice looked at me perplexed. "Ronconcholan? What for Mary? There's nothing there."

"I recall Guillaume once telling me whilst we were in Ronconcholan - you, Mustafa and Zekowtah were there when Testu said this to me - that the Cimarron hid the treasure they had taken from the Spanish in the muddy waters of the Chepo."

"Yes, this is true Mary, but only the elders knew where. I don't know where any of it is buried. Neither will Zekowtah. The Chepo is not a small river Mary. Looking for anything buried in the riverbed would, I fear, be an impossible task."

"The treasure," Atwood said, "if it was ever there, may be long gone."

"What you both say is true. And yet, it will cost us nothing to

M. McMillin

have a look around."

"What if the Spanish have settled there?"

Elizabeth surprised me when she came to my defense. "When," she asked, "have we ever walked away from a thing simply because it is difficult, simply because it comes with risks and challenges?"

"How," Shaw asked with skepticism, "do you propose we search the waters of a river?"

Others started voicing their doubts too.

"Gentlemen, my lady," I said and raised my hands. "We need not return to Panama. Tell me what you think we should do. As concerns the how of it Rob, I do have a thought. Should I share this thought with you now, or should we move on to discuss other opportunities? We can always find ourselves a good war to fight, hire ourselves out as mercenaries or we can ferry cargo for the Dutch VOC again or for the English EIC. Perhaps we should sell our ships and guns off and learn how to become shopkeepers, tradesmen, farmers or fishermen. Over the years we've considered many options."

"I wish to hear more about this treasure Mary," Efendi said.

Kinkae and Henry both quickly nodded their approval too.

I stood to walk around the room again. Never shy about using a touch of theater, I went from chair-to-chair massaging shoulders and refilling glasses as I spoke.

"The obvious, easy part is we search both sides of the riverbank. We walk up and down the river looking for markers or clues. But there is another way that might help us. The young men of Margarita are renowned for their skills in pearl diving. These boys can remain underwater for long minutes at a time I've heard. Why not employ a number of these fine fellows to search the riverbed for us?"

After we finished discussing my plan and all had agreed, Efendi joined me for a walk down the streets of Westport. The air smelled of snow. We fought against biting winds whipping all around us. Efendi insisted I take his woolen scarf when my teeth started clattering.

"And how does young James' training go Mustafa?"

"He is a clever lad Mary, a sweet, young man."

"He's indeed a good lad," I said. "Smart too. You have more to say though I think?"

"There are many things in this life he can do well. Soldiering isn't one of them."

"Is he not strong and brave?"

"He has heart. But at heart he is a gentle soul."

"And his training?"

"James has a carefree nature. He admires beauty and the pleasures that follow beauty above all else. I say it bluntly, he is more lover than fighter. He lacks discipline and steadfastness."

"I see. This is not what I wanted to hear but I trust your judgment. Can you toughen him up?"

"Certainly. But unlike you and me, he'll never have the soul or the instincts of a killer."

"We keep trying. And what of Ashaki and Lololi?"

Efendi smiled. "The twins are smart and brave and staunchly loyal to you. Both girls are fine athletes. I suspect Ashaki is capable of commanding her own ship someday. She was born to lead. Lololi is no less impressive."

"What of Ling and Jian?"

"Jian shows great promise. Ling is a sensitive, enchanting woman, an artist. She is more like James, more so."

"And yet she had the fortitude to dispatch Wú."

"She had the hate to kill Wú. There is a difference, Mary."

After departing Westport on Christmas Day, we dropped anchor twenty-three days later off the lovely island of Guadeloupe. For Kinkae, Henry and their men, we were at long last home. I had my men raise my battle flag to the masthead - a flag of yellow-gold with a coiled, red sea serpent poised to strike in the center, colors well-known by the Carib - and as we lowered away the longboats villagers in droves poured out of their huts and hurried down to the water's edge to greet us.

I saw the King of Guadeloupe, once one of my lieutenants we

knew as Fish because of the pair of sharks tattooed around his neck, standing amidst his people wielding the king's spear. He wore a simple loincloth and his magnificent headdress decorated with colorful feathers and dripping with pearls. And standing alongside the king I saw a tall Cuachicqueh warrior, an angry bumblebee, and my heart sang with joy. Like Efendi and me, Zekowtah and I shared an inexplicable bond of the spirit.

After the king laid his hand upon my head as I knelt before him, after he welcomed me with words of friendship and lifted me to my feet, scores of women and children bolted down to the longboats to find their men. Then Zekowtah reached out to embrace me. We held each other and wept.

"I have," I told the king after I dried my tears, "trinkets for the children. But I have no gold or silver for your Majesty. We suffered a reversal of fortunes on our last voyage."

"You are our friend and ally Mary," King Joseph replied. "You have always been generous to the Carib. Let us go to the great council lodge. I would like to hear your stories and then we can celebrate this joyful reunion with food and drink, with music, dance and song. Bring your officers. Zekowtah will join us."

Elizabeth and my brothers followed me into the village. I brought Ashaki, Lololi and Ling too. The king listened thoughtfully as we each told our story. And when I told King Joseph of my intentions to land in Veracruz to free Salamanca's slaves with the help of Gaspar Yanga, and then sail on to Panama to search for Cimarron treasure, Zekowtah insisted I take him and his warriors with me. I could think of no reason to refuse him and welcomed the additional muscle. I pledged one portion of whatever we found to the king and another portion to Zekowtah and his people.

With a crimson sun melting into the dark waters of an empty sea and a sliver of moon rising into the heavens, I made my way down to the shore where the Carib were preparing a great feast. Our ships sat quietly in the bay close by and I could see the night watch moving about the decks lighting the lanterns. And though the world around us was at peace, we had primed and loaded the great guns before coming ashore - hard lessons learned.

I plopped down on a blanket near one of the campfires to warm myself, even in the islands the air can feel cool at times, and waved Ling to my side. "Sit with me Ling," I said. "Jian appears to be enjoying himself with the other boys."

"He is a happy child Mary."

"Good, I'm glad. And what of you?"

She bowed her head respectfully. "I am most fortunate."

"And I am fortunate to have you as my friend. But I worry. I don't think you were meant for the hardships of the sea and the dangers we face day-to-day. Perhaps we can find a more suitable place for you and Jian, something more to your liking?"

Ling looked at me with sudden apprehension. "You wish to send us away? Please, I beg you Mary, no!"

I grabbed Ling's hand reassuringly. "No, no, no. I would never abandon you or your brother. We are family now. But what if we could put your skills to better use?"

"What does this mean?"

"I'm not yet sure. I wonder if you'd like to learn more about what I do? Perhaps you could represent me here in the West Indies? You might even enjoy managing your own hostel with a tavern? You could entertain your guests with that sublime voice of yours. You would be the mistress of your own establishment. Just thoughts to ponder on. You need not answer now."

"You are most kind."

"There are many who would disagree," I said. "Wú for one and Lu-Li for another. Do not suppose I am unselfish. By helping others, I help myself."

"No Mary, you are most kind."

"As are you Ling. Well, we'll remain on this island for a time. But I have a mind to visit another island not far from here in a day or two. The voyage is very short. Will you join me? There is a woman I would have you meet. Her name is Esmeralda. She lives in a beautiful city named Santo Domingo. Guadeloupe is a wonderful island, but the West Indies has more to offer, especially to one with your talents."

When I saw Kinkae and his family walking by, I waved him over.

"Sit with us for a moment Kinkae," I said. "I'll not keep you from your family long. They are well?"

Kinkae laughed. "My boys are tall and strong. Jacinta welcomed me back waving a club in my face. She said if I ever disappeared for so long again, she'd take another for a husband."

"She is a beautiful woman. I wouldn't blame her."

"She's a woman of strong opinions."

"I have no intention of returning to the East Indies. We'll rebuild our prospects here in the West Indies if we can. Will your boys want to become mariners like their father?"

"I believe so. They're nearly of age. Life is good on the islands I tell them. The sea is a cruel mistress I say. Soon they must choose for themselves."

"Ling and I were just now having a similar conversation. Do you recall the part you and your lads played at La Asunción?"

Kinkae grinned. "I do. That was a good day, Mary."

"Would you care to reprise your role again?"

"I'm turning old and grey but I still know how to be a slave."

"Excellent," I said and patted Kinkae's shoulder. "Ling, what's your pleasure?"

"Yes Mary, I travel with you."

"Wonderful. I *will* travel with you."

I took fifty of my Irish veterans and set out for Hispaniola with *Nemesis*. I went ashore with Ling and Jian and Efendi insisted upon coming too. We spent the better part of a day exploring Santo Domingo. The city fascinated Ling. And when we saw a shop with musical instruments for sale, I purchased a Spanish guitar for her to commemorate the occasion. In the evening we walked to Esmeralda's modest house. She greeted us with warm hugs and kisses. It saddened me to see her growing thin and frail. She led us back into a small kitchen to make us a simple supper and we talked well into the night. Esmeralda surprised me. I had expected her to live out the rest of her days as a free woman in quiet. Instead, she had kept herself busy carefully rebuilding my network of spies and had found several promising business prospects for me. One potential opportunity was with a prosperous trader named Bomboussa, a former slave who owned a goodly number of small coasters and liked to dabble in smuggling. Another happened to be a wealthy Dutchman. Before we said our goodbyes, with spies again in my employ, I tasked Esmeralda with finding the whereabouts of one German ship's master named Conrad Schmidt and his repugnant lieutenant Nuno Amrriquez, two barbarians who owed me blood.

After returning to Guadaloupe, with my men well-rested and our ships in fighting trim and fully reprovisioned - a king's gift to me - we promptly set out for the port of Porlamar on the island of Margarita next some four hundred miles to the south, a place where I had caused some mischief years ago. Zekowtah and twenty of his warriors sailed with us while Ling and Jian remained behind with a good Carib family to look after them.

With Spanish colors whipping around the mizzen gaff, I took *Nemesis* into Porlamar while *Spitfire* and *Cerberus* remained at sea. I went into town with Efendi, now dressed in Turkish attire, together with Elizabeth, Ashaki, Kinkae and six of his Blackamoors carrying a chest filled with a handful of reales of silver and gold sprinkled over fifty pounds of sand.

"I wish to see your best Señor Salvador Mojarro," I said in a respectful tone. Mojarro was the richest pearl trader on Margarita we had learned from various Porlamar merchants. But for the impressive black pearl dangling from a long strand of gold on one ear, there seemed nothing particularly remarkable about the man.

"My dear lady, my divers are not for purchase," the Spaniard replied gruffly. "I agreed to meet you here at the market because I understood you were interested in acquiring pearls in bulk. I offer the finest."

I smoothed out the creases of my dress, a flattering Chinese gown Ling had made for me, and took a seat across from Mojarro at a table outside on the veranda of a quaint tavern. The day was bright and hot. Mercifully we sat in the shade.

"At the right price, everything is for purchase," I said, pausing to pour Mojarro a glass of wine and then I turned to Kinkae and his Blackamoors standing against a brick wall out in the sun. "You there Tomas, open the chest. I wish to show Señor Mojarro my sincerety. And send Rodriguez over with a fan. I'm hot."

"Yes mistress," Kinkae dutifully replied and opened the chest.

Mojarro smiled despite himself when he saw the silver and gold inside. "Who are these good people in your cortège my dear?" he asked as one of Kinkae's men rushed over to fan me.

I glanced over at the table next to us where the others were seated. "The Ottoman, his name is Mohamed Ratu, is my business adviser. The Spaniard is Lady Maria de Menendez from Barcelona, my good friend and traveling companion. The beautiful black is Isabella, my maid-in-waiting."

Mojarro stroked his goatee as he looked Ashaki up and down appreciatively. "She is a free woman or a slave?"

"A slave."

"Perhaps we could make a trade, two of my best divers for the girl?"

"No, no. Isabella is much too valuable to me. She is a cultured Castilian, a refined rare gem, and has been with me for many years."

"Did you not say everything is for purchase?"

"Ah, so I did. But I wish to purchase twenty of your strongest pearl divers, not two."

"Twenty?"

"Yes."

"No, no. I'll not part with twenty divers."

"You fear I'll compete against you in the Caribbean?"

"Yes, most certainly."

"You need not be. I recently returned from the East Indies. Several islands in that part of the world are known for their pearls but the natives there do not have pearl divers. This is why I am here. We can enter into a legal contract between us, a binding contract that forbids me from competing with you anywhere in the West Indies if you will agree to stay away from the East Indies. Show me your stock and name your price. No need to by shy. I'm in a generous mood."

Mojarro took a sip of wine before he stole another quick glance at Ashaki when he thought I wouldn't notice, then looked over at the chest again and his eyes sparkled as he smiled. "Very well. My pearl factory is not far. It is within walking distance. Shall we?"

We followed Mojarro on foot for about a quarter mile down to the beach until we reached a long, rectangular pavilion with a wooden roof supported by dozens of wood posts. A number of boys, without a stich of clothing, stood around tables underneath the roof prying open piles of oysters. They pushed the meat aside into buckets and tossed any pearls they found into glass bowls placed at the center of each table. Other boys dressed in short braies sat in the sand while they rested against the posts. One man with a machete on one hip and a whip on the other stood watch. Along the beach I saw a dozen boats parked side-by-side and several hundred yards offshore I saw another dozen boats riding anchor with boys diving in or coming out of the water. I discretely sent one of Kinkae's men, a strong runner, back to *Nemesis* to alert the crew.

Mojarro had his overseer assemble the boys. I counted about thirty boys in all.

"I will sell you ten divers for the chest and the girl," Mojarro said. "You can pick the boys you favor. I'll have my lawyer draw up the necessary papers regarding territory."

"Your price is too steep Señor Mojarro," I said, stalling for time. "Half the gold and silver in the chest is far more than generous considering you'll only part with ten divers."

Mojarro shrugged his shoulders. "These are my terms."

"Your slaves," Efendi interjected, "must be very obedient. I see no one watching over them except for your man there."

"My boys are good boys. I treat them well. Miguel needs to do little more than supervise. Oh, on occasion some discipline is required but as for runaways, Margarita is a small island, there is nowhere to run, and theft is rare."

When I saw *Nemesis* moving away from the pier, I turned to Kinkae and Efendi. "Tomas, Mohamed, it is time."

Kinkae reached over and snatched the machete off the overseer's hip.

"What is this?" Mojarro demanded.

"We must run," I said. "Tomas, tie Señor Mojarro and his man to one of the posts in the shade. If they complain, tie them to a post out in the sun where they can bake. You boys, freedom is yours if you want it. I suggest you come with me, but you may remain behind if you prefer. Mohamed, let's get all those who wish to follow us into the boats."

About half the boys went with us. We piled into the boats sitting along the beach, launched them into the surf and rowed, freeing other boys out on the water as we passed them by.

"How old are you?" I asked the smallest boy after Kinkae had assembled the boys in a line on *Nemesis'* main deck.

"Eleven, mistress."

"You may call me Lady Mary," I said with a comforting smile. "And your name sir?"

"Juan."

"Thank you, Juan," I said and stepped over to the next boy. "And what is your age and name young man?"

"I am Phillipe. I am fifteen or sixteen I think."

As I went down the line asking each boy the same question, I shook hands and patted shoulders. We had twenty-one divers in all from ages eleven to nineteen.

"I have work for you if you want it," I told them. "Work for which you will be paid fair wages. But you are free men now, you can choose to sail with me or not. That big fellow over there is Kinkae. He was once a slave like you but now he is a free man, one of my officers, a boss man. He'll take you below where our ship's cook has prepared a hot meal for you and answer any questions you may have. After you've filled your bellies, you'll all return here and each of you will tell me what you have decided."

Chapter Thirty-Seven

ose ends. México. Veracruz had occupied my thoughts as much as anything since the day I had escaped with Ashaki and Lololi from Salamanca.

With twenty-one new souls on board, we sailed west from Margarita under full sail and made good speed, stopping briefly at Aruba, a small island I'd never stepped foot on before, to take on fresh water. Aruba, the name men say comes from either the Spanish words oro hubo, meaning there was gold, or from the Carib word *oruba*, meaning well-placed, is inhabited by the Caquetíos, a congenial race of exceedingly tall men and equally tall women of exceptional strength and beauty. From Aruba we headed straight for México.

The closer we came to the great port of Veracruz the more ships we passed, ships of all types flying flags from many nations, and once we sailed past Veracruz, we hugged the coast for another thirty miles or so until we reached a lagoon to the north, a quiet spot of water familiar to the twins and me where we furled sail and dropped anchor.

I laid a map of México across the table in my great cabin and waved my officers inside. "I've asked Ashaki and Lololi to join us for obvious reasons," I said. "I've invited our brother Zekowtah too of course."

"No one," Atwood said as he glanced over at the twins, "will think less of you ladies if you choose to remain behind with the ships. We all know how very brave you both are. This undertaking will be no picnic. Men will certainly die."

"What," Ashaki asked, "would you do Captain Atwood if someone held your family as property, if someone worked and whipped them like dogs?"

Atwood turned to me for help, but I ignored him. "We are here," I said, placing my forefinger on the map. "We'll take one hundred men ashore, Kinkae's Blackamoors, Zekowtah's warriors, Henry's Carib warriors and the rest from Maurice's crew. No need to be traipsing through Veracruz's countryside with a bunch of white Europeans. Gaspar Yanga moves his camp frequently. He controls this area to the northeast. It is mostly uninhabited, rugged land of hills, ravines and forests."

"That's a vast tract of territory to search Mary," Shaw observed.

"It is Rob, but we don't need to find Yanga. He'll find us."

"And the Spanish army?" Atwood asked.

"Everywhere," I replied.

"And where might Salamanca's lands be?" Atwood asked.

"A little bit north of these two towns, Córdoba and Orizaba."

"God's blood, between and within spitting distance of the Spanish strongholds at Veracruz and the City of México. A rather unpleasant circumstance. You do know I am coming with you."

"Jacob, I need -."

"I know, you need me to stay with the ships," Atwood interrupted. "I've heard it all before but no, not this time. I'm coming with you and that's the end of it."

"Fine. We all know what the consequences will be if we're caught. Maurice, you'll assume command."

"And *Spitfire*?" Atwood asked.

"Elizabeth, can I entrust you with *Spitfire*?" I asked as a peace offering, still desperately hoping to restore our friendship. I was pleased when I caught the twinkle in her eyes.

"But of course," she replied cheerfully.

"Good. You and Rob will both answer to Maurice. Understood?"

"Yes."

"Very well then. Maurice, should we fail to return within, let's say thirty days, make your way to this small village to the north called Tampico. We can rendezvous there."

The following day I went ashore with Atwood, Efendi, Kinkae, Henry, Zekowtah, the twins and one hundred men. We looked first to see if Matosa's lugger was buried in the sand but there was no boat to be found and so we formed a single file and began our journey inland. We marched due west and then north and then west again, moving deeper and deeper into México's wildlands. It did not take long for one of Yanga's patrols to spot us. The lead man recognized the twins and me. He agreed to take us to Yanga and sent a runner on ahead.

Yanga's new war camp, with tents, campfires, stacks of weapons, and two split-rail fences, one to hold horses and another to hold cattle and oxen, sprawled across many acres of open field atop a plateau with good visibility in all directions. Yanga's men could see any approaching danger from miles away. Parked in the center of the camp stood dozens of two and four-wheeled carts loaded down with provisions next to six pieces of Spanish field artillery.

"Ashaki, Lololi!" Yanga called out excitedly as the twins raced ahead. The Cimarron chieftain embraced and kissed the girls with obvious affection. "Hallelujah! You survived! You both look heathy and strong!"

"What news of our mother and father?" Lololi asked anxiously.

"I'm sorry to be the bearer of sad tidings. Your mother is well. Quaco has passed."

"How?" Ashaki asked. "How did he die?"

"Old age. Nothing sinister. He died peacefully whilst resting against a shade tree."

I placed one hand on Ashaki's shoulder and the other on Lololi's. "Quaco was a good man," I said softly. "Without his kindness, I'd be dead. Go now and sit by the fire as you quietly lament."

Yanga offered me a friendly nod as the twins did as I instructed. "I did not know if you'd return Mary."

"I keep my promises and I've brought some friends."

Yanga grinned. "So, you have. Do I see Cimarron and perhaps a few Aztecs amongst your crew?"

"You do Gaspar. Allow me to introduce my officers first. This big fellow is Jacob Atwood from Scotland. The man with the impressive mustache is Mustafa Agah Efendi from Turkey. I found Kinkae here in Trinidad bound in chains some years ago. This fine fellow with the many earrings is Henry, a Carib from Guadaloupe. And this tall tree of a man is Zekowtah, a prince of the Aztec."

After Yanga shook hands with Atwood, Efendi and Henry, he embraced Kinkae and called him brother, then rested his hands on Zekowtah's shoulders. "Xicohtencatl? Zekowtah of Ronconcholan?"

"Yes," Zekowtah replied.

"I've heard stories about you. I'm honored. By God, you are all most welcome in my camp. Mary Yanga, may I embrace you as my sister?"

"I'm so very glad we meet again," I said as I wrapped my arms around Yanga's broad shoulders. "We landed at the lagoon where Francisco keeps his boat. We didn't see the boat."

"Francisco left for Cartagena nearly two months ago. He has yet to return. I fear the worst."

"I pray he's only delayed."

"This is possible. Come, let us fill our bellies and then you can tell me your plan. You are here for Salamanca?"

"Aye, I have debts to settle."

"You've brought many men. By the looks of them, they're good fighters too. But you'll need more."

"More?"

"Yes. Salamanca has struggled these past few years. Drought, blight, his crops have suffered. He provides lodgings to the Spanish army for gold these days. The Spanish quarter anywhere between one to two hundred men at his hacienda, an excellent position between the City of México and Veracruz to respond to attacks by rovers and bandits."

I nodded to Atwood to acknowledge his earlier wisdom. "Well, this is a fine pickle we find ourselves in. We cannot take on such a large force without spilling buckets of blood."

Ashaki jumped to her feet. "I'll return to the ships Mary," she volunteered. "I'll bring back more men if Gaspar will give me a guide to show me the way."

"No, my dearheart," I said. "I won't risk the ships. We left less than sixty sailors aboard each ship, barely enough men to work the rigging and half the great guns if there is trouble."

"Come my friends," Yanga said. "Let us eat, talk and rest. Perhaps I can offer a solution to your dilemma."

Yanga's people treated us like royalty. Women and children doted on us, bringing us blankets, cool water and healing salves for sore feet. We ate fresh ham and chicken roasted on the spit. We ate fresh vegetables and fruits and drank good, mellow wine, wine liberated from the homes of wealthy Spaniards.

Yanga plopped down next to me as I ate my supper alongside the twins and my brothers. "If your plan is to free Salamanca's slaves," he said, "I will help you."

"The Spanish," Atwood interjected, "have always stationed their best soldiers in New Spain to protect their gold and silver. You risk a great deal by taking on two hundred seasoned, Spanish regulars."

"The haughty, empire-crazed Spanish can be practical when they wish to be," Yanga replied thoughtfully. "The viceroy tolerates a certain amount of theft and bloodshed as a cost of keeping the greater peace. Though I have the men and arms, I'll not march against two hundred Spanish soldiers and kill them. Discretion is how my people have survived all these years. We take only what the Spanish will tolerate. What I will do is match your one hundred men Mary with one hundred of my own. I propose fifty of my men raid Salamanca's lands and the lands of his neighbors to the north and west to lure a good number of the Spanish garrison away from Salamanca's hacienda. As the Spanish chase after my men, you and your men can move up from the south and east towards the house. I'll send word to Aminatu to be ready."

"How," I asked, "do we get Aminatu and her people back to my ships? Not all the Spanish will chase your men Gaspar. The children and older folks will slow us down considerably."

"Fifty of my men will travel with you. They'll serve as your rear guard. My men are very adept at this tactic as you will recall. But you'll return here, not to your ships. The Spanish will not follow you into the wilderness. After a few days have passed, the Spanish will lose interest in Salamanca's problems. Many who leave Salamanca may wish to join me. Aminatu and any of her people who want to sail with you will be free to do so."

"This is a fine, fine plan Gaspar," I said and turned to my brothers. "Are we all agreed?"

We were all agreed.

Yanga sent a pair of his swiftest riders that very night to inform Aminatu to be ready. A few days later the riders returned with Aminatu's own message. Salamanca was at the hacienda she said but intended to leave for Veracruz within two weeks with a good number of his slaves to sell at auction for the cash he needed. She implored us to move quickly.

Salamanca's hacienda was a grueling seven-day march over difficult ground under a relentless, unforgiving sun. We carried muskets, swords, daggers, pistols and bandoliers aplenty filled with ball and powder. We had stuffed our backpacks to bursting with food and we brought five pack-mules carrying even more supplies for those we hoped to free.

When we came within sight of Salamanca's big house, I broke my men down into three companies. I took the center with Zekowtah and his warriors and brought the twins and Efendi with me. Atwood took the left wing with forty Cimarron from Maurice's crew while Kinkae and Henry took the right with their men. We crawled across a dusty cornfield ravaged by drought in the early twilight. We slipped into a bone-dry gully fifty yards away from the big house and waited there for darkness to settle in around us. Yanga's fifty men remained behind to watch our flanks and rear.

I could see women moving about the house lighting the window candles and the outdoor lanterns around the front porch. And though I could not see him clearly, not even with my Spanish glass, I could hear Salamanca's distinctive voice. The loathsome pig who had enslaved me, who had refused to consider my innocence, who had humiliated me and savagely scarred my flesh, was sitting on the porch casually smoking a cigar while playing cards with six other men. Two of his guests were dressed in officers' uniforms. Perhaps a bit of good luck for us I thought.

An hour passed before we heard the crackle of musket fire to the north and west. We waited patiently in the gully until we heard the fighting fading off in the distance as Yanga's men lured a good number of Spanish soldiers away. Salamanca and the others appeared untroubled by the excitement and continued with their game.

"Breathe," I whispered when Lololi appeared uneasy - she had begged me to let her fire the first shot. "Relax, take your time. Remember to squeeze the trigger back gently when you are ready. 'Tis a hard thing to take a life. Are you certain you wish to do this? There is no shame if you choose not to."

She answered me by slowing her breathing down. She held her musket steady. She took her time and then - with a simple *click-boom* and a puff of smoke - she robbed the life of a man sitting across the table from Salamanca.

"How do you feel?" I asked as I took her musket from her to reload.

She looked at me without emotion. "I feel no joy in what I've done Mary. But I feel no guilt either."

After I finished reloading, I handed her musket back and started massaging her shoulders. "Good, good," I said, "why that man Lololi?"

"Even in the dusk I recognized his face. Salamanca once gave my friend to this man for his pleasure. She was a cheerful, sweet girl. After that night she was never quite the same. One day she walked down to the lake by the old bridge and kept walking until she drowned."

I kissed Lololi lightly on the cheek, lifted my musket and stood. "Buckle on your courage boys," I shouted, "we're going in!"

Ashaki needed no instruction or inspiration from me. She was the first to climb out of the gully. She was the first to reach the house. I bolted up the front porch steps a stride or two behind her - Salamanca and the others had already fled inside - with Efendi, Lololi, Zekowtah and the rest of his men following close behind me. And as we charged the house, Atwood swept around the left side of the house with his men while Kinkae and Henry swept around to the right with their men.

Not that it mattered but no one had thought to lock the front door. We burst into the house shoulder-to-shoulder and came face-to-face with Salamanca, two Spanish officers and three handsomely-dressed gentlemen huddled together in the front parlor. The officers had drawn their swords but quickly lowered them when they saw our numbers. And then we heard musket fire in the backyard and in the fields nearby.

"Quick Zekowtah," I said in Spanish, "go tell Jacob and Kinkae to hold their fire. We have two officers we can use to bargain with. Perhaps we can avoid further bloodshed. Have your men search the other rooms, the upstairs and the cellar too."

"You're Irish!" one of the Spanish officers exclaimed with surprise.

"Aye," I answered. "No matter how hard I try, I can't seem to lose this irritating accent." I saw Salamanca stiffen when he recognized me. "How have you been Señor Esteban Francisco de Salamanca?" I asked with an unpleasant smile.

"I'll not be as merciful this time," he replied sharply with a hoarse voice, then started coughing violently into a handkerchief stained with splotches of blood.

I'd seen such symptoms before. The yellow tint around the eyes and in the hair, the pallor of the skin, the raspy voice and the persistent cough with phlegm and sometimes blood - all signs of the affliction that attacks many who partake in tobacco.

"Well I remember your last words to me," I replied. ""No need to be gentle," you said. "I wish to hear my lady scream," you said. Should I now return the favor? Should I strip you naked before your guests and whip the flesh off your bones?"

"You've made a grave miscalculation," the senior Spanish officer proclaimed boldly and took a menacing step towards me. "I have two full companies under my command."

"And I have you," I replied.

"Piracy!" he exclaimed. "I'll see you dance the gallows' jig before the rising sun."

"Careful, Captain. My mercy has limits. It is captain I assume?"

"I am Captain Marcos Segura of His Majesty's First Provisional Tercios."

"The First you say? I happen to know a Dutchman who fought the First at Nieuwpoort in 1600."

"I was there. Not a happy day for Spain. And you are?"

"Her name is Mary," Salamanca sneered, "a runaway slave."

"This man," Efendi asked threateningly as he turned his musket on Salamanca, "whipped you, Mary?"

Before I could answer Efendi, Zekowtah returned with a dozen blacks in tow. I saw Catalina and Felipe, and Carlos amongst them.

"Mary, we found these folks in the house," Zekowtah said. "Jacob and Kinkae have the Spanish pinned down inside the barracas. They await your instructions."

"Why Catalina, Felipe and Juan Carlos," I said, "how good to see you all again. I have grudges to settle with each of you. Go stand by your wretched master whilst I decide what to do with you."

Ashaki leaned close to my ear. "May I kill Salamanca now Mary?"

I ignored Ashaki for the moment and turned to Zekowtah. "Zekowtah, please watch our prisoners. Mustafa, Ashaki, Lololi, follow me."

I led Efendi, the twins and the nine other blacks through the house and into the backyard where a cluster of men and women with lanterns in hand had gathered, curious to see what all the fuss was about. As the twins and many in the crowd exchanged hugs, tears and kisses, I listened to the sporadic musket fire off in the distance. The skirmishes to the north and west were drawing to a close. We needed to move out smartly before the Spanish soldiers returned.

"Ashaki, Lololi," I called out. "Time is short. We must find your mother and gather all those who wish to follow us."

"And what about Salamanca, Catalina, Juan and Felipe?" Ashaki asked.

"Leave Salamanca to me," Efendi said.

"Salamanca is already dead," I said. "He has the tobacco sickness. His end will be slow and painful. But I'll let Aminatu decide what to do with him and the others. Girls, remember, the Spanish officers must not be harmed. I promised Gaspar. Go now and find your mother. Mustafa, find Jacob, Kinkae and Henry. We'll all meet back here. Quickly now!"

When the twins returned locked arm-in-arm with their mother, together with a large crowd of men, women and children, and with Efendi, Atwood, Kinkae and Henry already at my side, I rushed over to Aminatu. "Grandmother!" I cried out and embraced her.

"Mary, Mary, Mary..." she blurted out and kissed me on both cheeks. "Despite the years, I never lost faith."

"We must hurry Grandmother before the Spanish soldiers return. We've taken Segura and another officer. We'll bring them with us as hostages until we're safe. What do we do with Salamanca and the others?"

"Let God judge them. Let us leave this wicked place of tears and sorrow and not look back."

"I'll tell Zekowtah we're leaving," Ashaki offered and raced back into the house.

Moments later we heard a single shot inside the house. I rushed to the front parlor with Atwood and Efendi and found Ashaki, so very much like me when I had been her age, standing over Felipe's body with a smoking pistol in her hand. She had decided Salamanca could live out the rest of his days in agony, but that Felipe had to die.

"Ashaki, go help your mother," I said softly. "Jacob, the two officers will be coming with us. Go tell the senior man in the barracas that we have his officers, that we'll set them free along the road unharmed provided we're not followed. Mustafa, help me with this man."

Efendi grabbed Salamanca by one arm as I grabbed him by the other and we dragged him down into the root cellar. I stood him up against the very wall where Carlos had whipped me. I drew my knife and pressed the blade against his throat.

"Your gold for your life Esteban. If you refuse, I'll hand you over to my Turk here - oh what gruesome wounds he can carve into flesh with his sharp blades, turns my stomach to think about it - and then I'll torch this place with you in it. Ashaki has a mind to nail you to a cross as you Spanish are fond of doing to the Cimarron. Crucifixion is a horrible way to die I hear."

Salamanca stared at me in terror, then pointed to the cot that had once been my bed.

"Mustafa," I said and jerked my head at the cot.

Efendi flipped the cot over and removed several loose bricks from the floor. "We have," he declared, "three modest chests of gold Mary."

"Good Mustafa," I said. "Now where is the rest, Esteban?"

"That's all of it," he replied meekly.

"Mustafa, the name of the woman upstairs is Catalina and the man standing next to her is Carlos. Take them aside and ask them separately where Salamanca keeps his flight cash. I'm certain one of them will tell you if you ask them nicely. Esteban, if you're lying to me by Christ, you'll suffer..."

"Wait, wait, there's a strongbox behind the bookcase in the library with money and jewelry. This is all I have in the house. I swear it. I keep the rest in a bank in Veracruz."

With torches and lanterns in hand, we took all those who wished to leave with us, together with two Spanish officers, three chests of gold and one strongbox, and slipped away into the night. We marched north into the highlands and once we were confident the Spanish army was not pursuing us, I handed the captain his sword and a waterskin and left him and his lieutenant alongside a dirt trail unharmed as I had promised. When we reached Yanga's camp ten days later, I spotted the notorious African rebel lying in the grass with his head resting against a log and hurried to him.

"Greetings Mary," he called out casually when he saw me and stood.

"Good morning, Gaspar. Have your men returned safely?"

"Yes," he said with open arms. "I hear you lost no one."

"We were most fortunate," I replied as Yanga and I embraced. "We killed no soldiers. One hundred fifty-four souls chose to travel with us and we have some treasure to share."

"Aminatu?"

"She's at the tail end of the column riding one of the pack mules."

"Good, good. My men returned with some of Salamanca's livestock. They spilt no Spanish blood. Did you leave Salamanca dead or alive?"

"We left him alive. He's very sick. He's dying. Filipe did not have as good a day."

"Filipe will not be missed. When Viceroy Mendoza hears of our raid, he'll be annoyed but nothing will come of it. The price of peace. Come, let us sit by the fire. Tell me your story before Grandmother comes to replace me as the leader of our small nation."

"She has become old and frail I fear Gaspar. With one blow to the face, I once saw her lay a man low. Not the biggest man I've ever seen but even so. Those days are behind her."

Yanga threw his head back and laughed. "Only a fool would cross that woman."

Yanga ordered a celebration feast as the column snaked its way into camp. From Salamanca's livestock he had his men butcher the choicest cows, the youngest, tenderest sheep and the plumpest pigs. He had kegs of new ale tapped. We all ate well around the campfires that night.

At first light the next day, after we had finished our stories, filled our bellies and said our farewells, my men and I prepared to march. I left a portion of the booty I had taken from Salamanca with Yanga and I would give another portion to King Joseph and Zekowtah to share upon our return to Guadeloupe. It wasn't a great fortune but I had come to Veracruz to fulfill a promise, not for plunder. Freeing Aminatu and the others was satisfying but exacting my vengeance on Salamanca - unlike the day I had purged the *Síol Faolcháin* from the world - had left me strangely hollow.

Loaded down with all their gear, the twins surprised me when they stepped into the line with the rest of my men. We had hugged and kissed and cried earlier at breakfast. I thought we had said goodbye.

"Ashaki, Lololi, what's this?"

"We've decided to return to the ships with you," Lololi replied.

"But what of your mother and all the others? This is your home."

"My daughters are free to choose their own path," Aminatu said as she walked up behind me. When I spun around, she cupped my face in her hands. "A great gift Mary. Their destiny is entwined with yours. I see this clearly now. May God light your way and keep you safe child."

I looked over at Yanga for help. "Gaspar?"

The grizzled Cimarron with piercing eyes simply laughed and walked off, waving blindly back at me as he made his way towards the mess tent.

I turned and kissed Aminatu on the cheek. "Fare thee well Grandmother. I shall watch over your daughters as if they were my own."

"Imagine such a thing," she said smiling to herself, then turned to follow Yanga.

With a dozen of Yanga's men to guide us, I lifted my musket and a knapsack over my shoulder, a heavy burden, and with sixty newly liberated souls who wished to follow us, I waved my men forward. Yanga had already sent a pair of riders out to alert Maurice that we were coming. And though the women and children traveling with us slowed us down considerably, we finished the journey back to the coast in fair time and without incident. But as we approached the lagoon, my heart skipped a beat when I saw only two ships. *Spitfire* was missing. I quickly shook hands with Yanga's men and thanked them before they set out and then waited anxiously at the water's edge for our longboats floating in.

"Where's *Spitfire*?" I called out to Maurice as he jumped down from the lead boat.

"A war carrack with a damaged zabra in tow sailed by two days ago," Maurice replied warily as he knew I'd be displeased. "Elizabeth gave chase."

"What the devil for?" Atwood asked.

"She did not say."

"Why did you not stop her?" I demanded, but instantly regretted the harsh words thoughtlessly spilling out of my mouth.

"Her crew," Shaw interjected as he stepped off his boat, "weighed anchor Mary and set sail - what could we have done? Be not angry. Maurice and I weren't about to follow her and leave you stranded here."

"No, no, of course not," I said apologetically. "Please, forgive me for lashing out. That woman confounds and exasperates me. How large was this carrack and in which direction did she travel?"

"She was a twelve-gunner heading south," Maurice replied. "I'll wager she was making for Veracruz, the nearest port."

I shook my head in disgust. "Let's get everyone aboard the ships. Quickly now."

"What do you intend to do Mary?" Atwood asked.

"I intend to get your ship back Jacob. Beyond this, I do not know."

When the winds abruptly freshened, whipping the lagoon into a frenzy, we lost nearly two hours ferrying everyone back to the ships. I grew more frustrated when we lost even more time recovering our longboats in the tricky seas. We were lucky none of the boats capsized.

Keeping close to shore, with lookouts scanning the horizon in all directions, our two ships sailed south for Veracruz with a mile of water between us. There wasn't much traffic and just before we lost the light, one of my men spotted *Spitfire* heading north for the lagoon.

We swung our ships around. We raised the distinctive red, white and blue flags of the VOC and gave chase. After *Spitfire's* crew recognized us and heaved to, Maurice and I eased our ships up alongside her and our three ships came to rest bobbing up and down on an empty sea. I spotted Atwood's first officer, a serious, young Scot named Samuel Bishop, standing at the helm with Elizabeth nowhere in sight. A man from Ayr like Atwood, Bishop had impressed me as a bright, eager young man, an up-and-comer who showed promise.

"Samuel, where's Elizabeth?" I called out.

"She went below my lady to fetch something. Ah, I see her climbing up the aft ladder now."

"Why are you smiling Elizabeth?" I asked testily when she stepped onto *Spitfire's* quarterdeck holding a wicker basket in her hands. When she set the basket on the ship's rail and did not answer, I called out to her again. "Elizabeth, have a boat lowered away. I would have words with you. Mr. Bishop, you will accompany Elizabeth."

With Atwood, Shaw and Efendi standing at my side, I met Elizabeth and Bishop on *Nemesis'* main deck as they stepped aboard. "For the love of Christ, Elizabeth, where have you been?" I demanded. "And why do you carry that silly basket? It has a godawful stink."

"A war carrack spied us," Elizabeth replied in a haughty tone and grinned. "I thought it best to run her down before she put in at Veracruz to report our position."

"You were concerned with one small twelve-gunner with a broken zabra in tow?"

"The carrack's master might have returned with more ships Mary had I simply let her go."

"Why would he do that? He saw three ships of no importance anchored off a desolate stretch of beach far from any town. Crews frequently go ashore to procure food and water. You know this."

"I did not think it wise to take the risk."

"What risk?"

"Well Mary, we shall never know for certain, will we?" she answered flippantly and then - with a broad, triumphant smile - she tipped the wicker basket over. "Meet her captain," she proclaimed boldly as a severed head tumbled out of the basket and struck the deck hard with a sickening thud.

I glared at Elizabeth, too stunned to speak.

"We sank both ships," Elizabeth declared proudly and handed me a purse. "The carrack fired upon us and killed two of my men with a lucky shot. We made short work of her guns after that and then boarded. I took the captain's head just as you took Dowlin's head all those years ago when he grievously offended you. I took his purse of silver too for our troubles."

"What," Atwood demanded, "in God's name possessed you to do such a thing? We're not a war with Spain."

I was far less charitable than Atwood. "Damn you, Elizabeth!" I lashed out and snatched the purse out of her hand. I took a peek at the coins inside and then pitched the purse over the side. The silver was no more than blood money to me.

Elizabeth watched the purse disappear in wide-eyed disbelief.

"You've risked all of our lives for this foolishness," I exclaimed loudly for all to hear, "to satisfy some absurd, juvenile bravado and good men have died! The Spanish were no threat. You were to wait for us in the lagoon. Nothing more."

With nostrils flaring and cheeks burning bright, she stared at me full of malevolence "*I... protected... the ships...*" she proclaimed defiantly, snarling at me.

I ignored her nonsense and turned to Bishop. "What do you have to say for yourself Mr. Bishop?"

"Beg pardon Mary? I was obliged to follow the orders of my captain."

"Who fired the first shot Samuel?"

Bishop exchanged glances with Elizabeth and hesitated.

"You'll direct your attention at me sir when I am addressing you," I demanded crossly.

"We, we did Mary," Bishop answered uneasily.

"How far from land was the crew when you put them into their boats?"

"Not far, but we left them with no oars. They won't reach shore anytime soon."

I threw my hands up in the air, exasperated. "Those poor souls who did us no injury might never make landfall. Jacob, return to your ship with Sam and make ready. We sail south for Guna Yala. If we happen upon the Spanish, we'll tow them into shore. Elizabeth, return to *Cerberus*. Maurice can deal with you. I have no more words for you. And someone get that fucking head off my deck!"

Atwood followed me as I stormed up to the quarterdeck. "You're angry," he said softly and handed me a flask of whiskey.

"Angry? I'm furious. I sometimes wonder if that woman has turned to opium again."

"Opium? No, I think not. Maurice would know of it. I don't blame you for your anger. And yet, in truth, there is some logic in her thinking."

"Surely you jest Jacob? You would have done the same?"

"Certainly not. She has shown poor judgment."

"Aye, to put it kindly. I don't understand her."

"She seems compelled to prove herself to you Mary."

"I think she has a mind to prove herself my better."

"Perhaps. Perhaps jealousy is what drives her."

"Jealousy? What drivel. She's free at any time to leave and strike out on her own. Let her find her own ships and men, make her own fortune and eclipse me if such is her desire. Well my friend, shall we? We have over two thousand miles of sailing ahead of us. I pray the winds are with us. I pray we need not do much tacking. I weary of this journey."

Chapter Thirty-Eight

Lost treasure, plunder, the spoils of war. Gold, silver, pearls and precious gems. Men, so easily seduced by wealth's allure, will kill without hesitation, without remorse or shame for the glittering metal, for the pretty stones and baubles. I've never understood the perverse obsession. But I understood the need to provide for myself and my men. This is what drove me now to return to the savage, unforgiving jungles of Panama.

I left Atwood in command with our ships anchored in the still waters of Guna Yala. I left Shaw with *Nemesis* and I had handed *Cerberus* over to Kinkae with Maurice's blessing. Elizabeth was furious at the snub of course, though she had no right to be after her foolishness, her misadventures off Veracruz and I told her so for what little good it did me.

Guna Yala, little more than white sand with palm trees and thick foliage, is an uninhabited, peaceful spot. But the bay is a mere twenty miles from Nombre de Diós - the Name of God - the primary port from whence the Spanish load their great wealth from the New World onto their enormous treasure galleons destined for the old one. Many ships from many nations transit those waters. Pirates too swarm to the western Caribbean like flies, looking for any easy pickings. Atwood and I agreed we'd rendezvous in Bahía Sapzurro, Port Pheasant, Drake's old hide-a-way near Columbia, if anyone took too much interest in our ships.

I brought Maurice, Efendi and Zekowtah ashore with me along with one hundred men, a mix of Cimarron, Aztecs, my Irish and our divers from Margarita of course. Zekowtah and his warriors knew every trail, footpath, swamp, cave, gorge, body of water and hill in Panama and brought us to the lake and marshlands feeding the Chepo in a single day.

The Chepo begins life as a small brook in the heart of Panama then snakes her way through rugged country swathed in dense jungle, gathering strength along her journey from rains and numerous tributaries before she is swallowed up by the Pacific. Though the great ocean was only ten miles due south of us, our meandering path along the Chepo would take us many more miles over difficult, dangerous ground, across territory patrolled regularly by Spanish soldiers, by grizzled veterans forged in war and hardened by the hostile lands over which they held absolute dominion.

"What's this?" I asked as I stood with Efendi and Maurice at the murky headwaters of the Chepo planning our day. Something seemed amiss about the man. I reached over and pulled the broad brimmed hat off his head.

"Ashaki!" I blurted out surprised.

"Please do not be angry Mary," Ashaki pleaded. "My place is here with you."

"Where's Lololi? Is she with us too?"

"No, Lololi stayed behind on the ship with James as you instructed."

"I'm glad one of you understands the meaning of obedience," I said annoyed and turned to Maurice and Efendi. "Did either of you rascals know about this?"

When Maurice answered me with a blank stare and Efendi shrugged his shoulders, I could only sigh and shake my head. "This," I said as I turned to Ashaki, "isn't Veracruz, Panama is a cruel land. You've heard this all before, but exposing you to such dangers is not what I promised your mother."

"You were not so different Mary," Efendi quipped, obviously amused, "from Ashaki at her age as I recall. The word headstrong comes to mind."

"Fine Mustafa," I replied in a huff, "you can watch over her. Ashaki's your responsibility now."

Efendi chuckled good-naturedly. "It would seem I've been cursed with watching over young damsels who are rebellious of authority and long for adventure for the better part of my years."

I rolled my eyes as I gathered my men. I divided my modest expedition into two teams. Zekowtah and Maurice took forty men and ten divers down the right bank of the river while Efendi and I took forty men and the rest of the divers with us down the left bank. Zekowtah sent his twenty warriors out ahead and around our flanks to scout for any trouble.

We scoured the riverbank for clues, markers or signs. We sent the divers into the river, which was barely more than a stream, every few yards or so to haphazardly poke their way around the riverbed. The river was narrow, the water was shallow, clear and easy to ford. The work went smoothly enough at first. But the farther south we travelled the wider and deeper the river became and our progress suffered. Our hunt for treasure soon deteriorated into a slow and tedious crawl.

To add to our privations, I had taken us into Panama during the height of the rainy season. We were traveling light, carrying only our weapons, ammunition, food, some tools and rope. We had no tents or foul-weather gear. We slogged through mud and slept, ate cold food and emptied our bowels and bladders in the rain while we watched the river rise.

On the third day a great wave of elation swept over our expedition when one of the divers found a gold doubloon buried in the riverbed. Spirits soared. The other divers immediately converged on the spot to look for more, but after several hours of searching there was nothing more to be found. Efendi and I waded out to a sandbar in the middle of the river to meet with Maurice and Zekowtah. I held the doubloon up for all to see.

"Perhaps this coin was carried downriver?" I asked. "Are we looking in the wrong place? Perhaps the elders of Ronconcholan hid their wealth upstream in the lake?"

Maurice took the coin from my hand to take a closer look. "What you say is possible Mary. But I think this doubloon is nothing more than a stray that fell out of somebody's pocket. I suspect the Cimarron of Ronconcholan kept their wealth closer to home. Even so, beginning our search at the river's headwaters made good sense."

"Keep to your plan Mary," Efendi advised. "We're covering about six to eight miles a day by my reckoning. At this pace, we should reach the Pacific in another five to six days."

Zekowtah nodded. "I'll send one of my men back to the ships, let Jacob know all is well but we'll need more time."

"Very well," I replied. "I'll reward the boy who found this doubloon by letting him keep it. Let's press on."

The days passed by slowly and with no lack of hardships. We suffered in relentless rains and boot-sucking mud. We had no change of clothing. We struggled trying to keep our powder cartridges dry. And though Zekowtah's warriors, each man an accomplished hunter, kept us fed with raw fish, roots, bananas and berries after we had devoured the last of our victuals, hungry gnawed at us still. There was plenty of wild game around to fill our bellies but Zekowtah wisely forbid any fires. And then on the seventh day, tragedy struck. We lost one of Maurice's men to the white plague and soon thereafter we lost one of the boys to a deadly terciopelo snake hanging from a tree. The poor lad did not last long after the hideous creature sank its fangs into his neck. We buried our dead the next morning in a pretty spot near the riverbank before resuming our march to the sea.

Nine days after leaving our ships, with only a single Spanish doubloon, a crate of empty beer bottles and one discarded shoe to show for our efforts, we at long last reached the mouth of the Chepo where her dark waters feed the blue waters of the calm Pacific. Not far off we could see the last vestiges of Ronconcholan's broken wooden wall. Vines, like tentacles, had wrapped themselves around charred timbers, vegetation had sprouted up in cracks and seams as the jungle went about reclaiming what had always been hers.

The delta of the Chepo is at least five hundred yards wide and perhaps as much as one thousand yards long, though the water didn't look particular deep nor did the currents appear terribly strong. After finishing our search along the river's left bank, Efendi and I doubled back with our men to a place where we could ford the river to rejoin

Zekowtah and Maurice on the other side. As I stood next to my brothers, I waved the oldest, most experienced diver over to us.

"Jerónimo," I asked the handsome, light-skinned pearler with a fine physique and pointed to the estuary, "what do you think? Can you and your friends dive in those waters?"

"Yes, my lady. Could we build a few rafts first? We can make more dives each day with something floating over our heads."

"If this will ease your burdens some, certainly," I replied. "What else do you require?"

"Rope to anchor the rafts in place and leather straps or strips of vine will do. Most divers wear stone belts around their waists or wrists to give them weight."

"Very well," I said and turned to the others. "Gentlemen?"

"I'll see it done Mary," Maurice offered. "Come Jerónimo, let's construct a mighty squadron of rafts any admiral would envy!"

"And I," Zekowtah said as he wiped the rain out of his eyes, "will see if there is anything in the old town we can use as shelter. I've seen enough rain. I've sent patrols out in every direction. We'll not be surprised by any unwelcomed intruders."

"Excellent," I said, then turned to Efendi. "And pray tell what you will be doing maestro?"

My Turk cracked one of his rare, thin smiles. "All seems in order here Mary. You can find me by that large boulder over there enjoying a well-deserved nap."

For three days we watched the boys of Margarita dive to the bottom of the riverbed. I marveled at their stamina. The length of time the boys could stay below the water's surface astounded us all. They went about their labors cheerfully for long hours with little rest and I think they took pleasure in flaunting their prowess for us. For three days we watched the boys dive and rise to the surface emptyhanded. Despite all their extraordinary efforts the Chepo gave them nothing, not a single discarded tool, not a broken sword or lost penny.

"What do you want to do Mary?" Efendi asked as he and Zekowtah approached my campfire, a small fire Zekowtah had allowed me to build earlier within Ronconcholan's crumbling walls. I was sitting with Ashaki and Maurice, chewing on a piece of roasted wild boar.

"I know not Mustafa," I mumbled as he and Zekowtah wearily plopped down next to us. "The night watch is set?" I asked in a dejected, exhausted tone.

"Yes," Efendi answered.

I glanced around the campfire. "Any ideas? Anyone? Where might you hide treasure if it was yours to hide?"

"We were always told," Maurice said absently, lost in thought, "the town's riches were buried deep within the riverbed. I wonder. There's a creek nearby on this side of the river. There was once a storage shed back there for keeping tools and such. Do you remember the old shed Zekowtah?"

"Yes," Zekowtah replied, "I remember. I remember the pits the elders had us dig in the earth close by for shitting too."

"Yes, nasty place," Maurice mused. "Can't imagine anyone looking for treasure there."

My eyes must have popped as I jumped to my feet. We all jumped to our feet together. Infused with renewed vigor, we grabbed our torches and our tools and made our way in the fading light to take a peek at Maurice's creek. To my astonishment the shed was still standing and we found the latrines not far off. The pits had eroded away but the wooden frames for squatting over were still intact.

In the morning, with better light, our men started digging out the old privies while the boys crawled along the shallow creek bed, turning over rocks, roots and stones. We soon found a chest filled with jewelry hidden deep within one of the privies and then another. Men, who earlier I'm certain had been wondering why I had dragged them into this misery for nothing, were now congratulating one another, shaking hands and slapping each other on the back. One of the boys uncovered a chest in the creek hidden underneath the steel breastplate of some unfortunate conquistador and another boy found a box of gold coins stuffed inside the hollow of a tree trunk well below the water. By late afternoon we had dug up treasure enough to ransom a king. The chests, boxes and casks we found were filled to the brim with gold and silver bars, with gold coins and pieces of silver, precious gems and pearls. By nightfall we had uncovered sterling silver bowls, chalices and cutlery, assorted jewelry, finely crafted neck watches and even a large, jewel-encrusted crucifix of solid gold, all mixed in with other trinkets of great value. The wealth of a nation of runaway slaves lay at our feet and we marveled at the sight for some time before we bedded down for the night.

In the morning we grabbed our axes and our saws and built more rafts. I decided we'd pull our heavy booty over the water rather than drag it all across the narrow, rugged footpaths. Maurice and Zekowtah were both certain there was more treasure to find, but we had been very lucky so far and I had no wish to overstay our welcome, to press our luck too far. I had always taken care over the years not to insult good fortune with gluttony.

The next day in drizzle and stifling humidity, we stacked our chests, boxes and barrels by twos and threes on top of our rafts. We lashed them down with sturdy rope, with straps of leather and vines. And when all was ready - we did not rest or linger - with half my men on the left bank of the river and half of us on the right, we began the laborious task of pulling our clumsy, blunt vessels against the river's currents using rope and tackle. When we reached a sandbar or came across rapids or a fallen tree, we had to unload our cargo and carry our rafts over or around each obstacle. We endured our hardships in silence and trudged on. The rains never stopped.

Chafing against my wet clothing, my skin turned raw around my shoulders and inside my thighs. I walked gingerly because of the blisters on my feet. I was bone-weary, filthy and every muscle ached, even muscles I had long ago forgotten. And yet I managed to smile when my thoughts turned to Hunter and to my first excursion into the wilds of Panama to look for lost, Aztec gold. Hunter's love for me, his belief in me, had never wavered. My first adventure into Panama had been far more grueling and yet I survived. Inspired by my past, I summoned up my strength and willed my legs forward.

We were met by thick fog when we reached the lake. I could barely see Ashaki an arm's length away. We had been on the move since well before midnight. My stomach had started grumbling and thoughts of breakfast and a little rest consumed me. And then I heard a voice cry out *piratas*. I heard someone discharge his musket followed by a scream. More shots rang out. I could hear steel scraping against steel as men fought each other with swords and long daggers.

I grabbed Ashaki by the belt and pulled her down to the ground next to me. "Mustafa!" I called out. "Maurice, Zekowtah!"

I could see nothing in the fog.

"Over here," Maurice whispered.

"Stay low!" Efendi cried out. "Spanish regulars."

"Ambush?" I asked.

"Only a patrol I think," Maurice replied.

I crawled over to the sound of Maurice's voice, taking Ashaki with me, as he was closest to the head of our column and the action. "Can you tell what is happening Maurice?" I asked.

"No but listen. The sounds of battle are fading. The Spanish must be withdrawing."

Then Efendi plopped down next to us. We let a moment pass before we carefully picked our way forward, keeping our heads low to the ground. Maurice had guessed rightly. Our advance guard and the Spanish had unwittingly blundered into each other in the fog. Just bad luck. We found six bodies crumpled over one another, three of Maurice's men and three Spaniards. And then we saw one of Maurice's men leaning against a tree holding a bloody arm with another man sitting on the ground next to him with his back against the tree, moaning and trying to keep his guts tucked inside his belly.

Maurice knelt beside the dying man. "Francois," he said softly and laid a hand on the man's shoulder.

"Last journey, Capt'n," the man replied weakly.

"Water?"

"Please."

But before Maurice could uncork his waterskin, Francois' eyes fluttered for a bit and then he was gone. Maurice gently laid the dead man's head on the ground. After he reverently made the sign of the cross, he turned to the other man.

"Pedro, what happened?"

"We stumbled into them Capt'n. Spanish were as surprised to see us as we were to see them."

"How many?"

"Don't know sir. At least a dozen. They weren't lookin' for a fight. They scattered down that deer trail to the left and disappeared."

"Looks like you used your arm to spar with a man wielding a sword."

"Aye, Capt'n. 'Twas my arm or my neck."

"Well, let's tend to that wound Pedro before you bleed to death."

And then one of Zekowtah's warriors, a young man named Xipil, appeared. "Mary, the Spanish have taken Zekowtah and Zuma is missing."

"Zekowtah was shot?"

"No, I saw a Spaniard club him from behind with the butt of his musket."

"And Zuma?"

"I do not know."

"Can we track the Spanish in this fog?"

"If we hurry, yes. They have wounded. There's an easy trail to follow. But I saw one auxiliar indio with the Spanish, a scout, a Totonac warrior. There may be more. This man will know his way around these lands. He'll know the tricks and tactics of the Aztec."

"This patrol is out of Viejo?"

"Most likely Viejo, yes. Maybe Nombre de Diós. It is possible they came up from Columbia but they have no pack animals or horses. God be praised, this is not a large caravan accompanied by many soldiers."

"Take three men Xipil," Maurice commanded, "and find which way the Spanish are traveling. Send a runner back when you know. You and the other man keep tracking them. We'll follow. Go."

Maurice turned to me after Xipil slipped into the swirling mist. "Mary, I can't leave Zekowtah or Zuma behind."

I grabbed Maurice by the arm. "Never," I said and turned to Efendi. "Mustafa, I'll go with Maurice and Zekowtah's men. You return to the ships with the boys and the rest. Take whatever treasure you can carry."

"No," Efendi said.

"No what?"

"No, I'll not leave you," Efendi said defiantly while he inspected Pedro's wound. "The jungle has rotted your brains. You'll need more than twenty men. Let's hide the treasure by the lake and send the boys back to the ships with one of Maurice's men to guide them. We have a few sick lads too who will only slow us down. We can send them back with the boys along with Pedro here. That's a nasty gash Pedro. I can see bone. You could lose that arm if we don't get you to Stachel."

"Aye, you're right of course Mustafa," I said. "See it done. We'll take one chest of silver with us. Perhaps we can negotiate a trade to avoid more killing."

When one of Xipil's warriors returned a short while later, we sent the boys back to the ships with the sick and wounded while the rest of us grabbed our weapons and followed Xipil's man down a narrow footpath heading south towards Viejo, an important stronghold on the Pacific and not far from where Ronconcholan once stood. Every few weeks long mule trains make their way to Viejo carrying unimaginable amounts of Columbian silver and Venezuelan gold. The Spanish store their piles of treasure in Viejo, away from the Caribbean and her marauding pirates, until it is time to move their hoard overland to Nombre de Diós to load aboard the treasure ships heading back to Spain.

Ten years earlier I had been with the English army when Drake sent us into Panama to seize Viejo's treasures. The Spanish had thwarted Drake's plans with a spirited defense in the woods just outside the town. The Spanish fought well that day and forced the English and my men back with heavy losses, forever killing Drake's dreams of winning new glory. Viejo is where Atwood lost an eye.

While Xipil's man was leading my men and I through woods and jungle, Maurice took Zekowtah's warriors and raced ahead of us to cut the Spaniards off. Zekowtah's men could run all day and all night with great speed across difficult, rugged ground without stopping.

Just as the sun began burning through the fog a few miles later, a short, wiry Aztec named Coyotl found us. Maurice had sent him back to guide my men and I to a spot where he and Zekowtah's warriors had caught up to the Spanish. The Spanish, not knowing our numbers, had decided to retreat up to the top of a rocky promontory to defend themselves Coyotl told us. With Viejo not far off, the senior officer in charge no doubt thought he was safe.

"How many men have they?" I asked Maurice when he stepped out of the woods as we approached the hill. The Spanish had hastily built themselves a wall of decaying branches, dead brush, rocks and dirt around the hilltop. I couldn't see any faces.

"We counted twenty men. Could be more. We found one straggler and intercepted one runner on his way to Viejo. They now dwell in the land of the dead blind, deaf and dumb."

"When can we expect Viejo's garrison commander to send out a patrol to look for his men?"

"A day or two perhaps. If there is shooting the men in Viejo will hear the shots and..."

"Aye," I said absently as I considered matters. Efendi walked over to stand by my side as Coyotl led my men into positions around the hill.

"How many soldiers do you think are garrisoned in Viejo?" Efendi asked.

"Hard to say Mustafa," Maurice replied. "Two, perhaps three hundred is my guess. Could be less, could be more. If there's a fight, Viejo will send out a relief column supported by horse and small calibre artillery. If we wait for nightfall, we can crawl up to the hilltop. We can get close. Plenty of rocks and brush to use as cover. We can attack at first light. With or without surprise - it won't matter - we have the men we need to kill every Spaniard."

"Let me try talking to the Spanish first," I said.

"I'll accompany you," Efendi insisted while rubbing the bridge of his nose.

"As will I," Ashaki declared as she walked up behind me.

Too tired to argue, I nodded. Following Efendi's example, Ashaki had become more and more protective of me.

The sky had turned sapphire blue without a cloud in sight. The noonday sun was uncomfortably hot. I began sweating heavily as I scaled the side of the hill with Efendi and Ashaki at my side, as I waved a soiled handkerchief in my hand, a handkerchief that had once been white. I struggled to gain purchase against steep ground made slippery by the rains.

"That's far enough," a deep, unfriendly voice commanded when we were halfway up the hill. "What do you want?"

"You have two of my men," I replied after I caught my breath. "I want them back."

"Huh, something different. A woman, an Irishwoman in the middle of the wilderness making demands of the Spanish army. You're worlds away from home my lovely. You must be lost. We execute your kind in Panama, even pirates with no cocks dangling between their legs."

"We're not pirates or outlaws. What's your name soldier, your rank?"

"I'm Sergeant Major Rodrigo Sanchez of the King's Columbian Musketeers if you must know," the voice answered with a touch of predictable Spanish arrogance. And then a darkly tanned fellow with a thick beard, with a red plume attached to his steel capacete and a red sash running diagonally across his leather doublet, stood to face me. "Who are you?" he demanded.

"Mary."

"Mary?"

"Just Mary."

"Well just Mary, you and your villainous scum murdered three of my men and grievously wounded three others."

"Murder? No, not murder. I know not who fired first, your men or mine. I'll wager you don't know either. You surprised us in the fog as we surprised you. Someone panicked. A most regrettable, unfortunate incident to be sure. You lost men and I lost men."

"It makes no difference who fired the first shot. You killed the king's men on the king's highway. Your words mean nothing. His Majesty King Phillip shows your depraved kind no leniency. You'll reap the painful consequences of your high crimes soon enough."

"Your threats carry no power out here Sergeant Major Sanchez. You can release my men, or you can die atop this fucking hill."

"By God you're a feisty slut! I have fifty men and hold the high ground. Viejo is nearby. I've already dispatched a messenger to the fort. Reinforcements will be here soon."

"You only have about twenty men and the messenger you sent to Viejo has been, well, detained. I have five times your number and we have you surrounded. My lads are quite adept at killing. Many are Cimarron and ohhh how the Cimarron loath you Spanish. They'll show you no quarter."

"Come closer and I'll show you how good we Spanish are at killing. We've vanquished whole empires. You cannot have my prisoners. They're only filthy Aztecs. No one will miss these murderous rogues. Begone, I say!"

"Then you're a fool."

"If you're here in the morning woman, this putrid shithole of the world will become your grave."

I lost my patience; I grit my teeth, drew my sword and pointed the tip at the Spaniard. "Whether I live or die today I promise you this: we'll slaughter you and all your men before anyone from Viejo can reach you. I have ships at Guna Yala. I have more men coming to join us, more men than you can expect from Viejo and my lads will bring swivels and canister shot. They're be here before nightfall. Do not test me, Spaniard."

"You're bluffing."

"Am I? You and your men are running out of time. But, before you say anything more with your misplaced hubris, before you do something stupid, I'm willing to spare the lives of you and your men, let bygones be bygones as they say. To avoid further bloodshed, I'm willing to sweeten my offer. I'm willing to purchase my men from you. What say you? Do you wish to live and prosper or die?"

After a long and agonizing silence, I turned to my men below. "Lads," I cried out loud enough for all to hear. "Prepare to charge the hill!"

"Wait," Sanchez called out. "How do you intend to purchase my prisoners?"

"We have silver, a chest full of silver."

"A chest full of silver you say? How interesting. Spanish silver?"

"Silver is silver."

"Let me see this silver."

When I turned and nodded to Maurice, he sent Xipil and Coyotl up the hill carrying the chest of coins between them. After they left the chest at the top of the hill and started back down, I waved them over to me.

"Xipil, did you see Zekowtah and Zuma?" I asked. "Are they alive?"

"Yes, Mary, they live," Xipil answered. "Coyotl and I counted twenty-seven Spanish regulars and the Indian. They've taken up positions within a hollow. If it comes to a fight, they'll fire one volley, only one, before we overrun their position and kill every man."

While I listened to Xipil, I watched two soldiers grab the chest and disappear behind their makeshift wall. A moment later Sanchez and another Spaniard pushed Zekowtah and Zuma up onto a rock ledge. I smiled and waved them towards me. I should have felt joy but sensed only dread. Something was amiss. Both men had their hands tied behind their backs. Neither man returned my smile.

"Thank you for the silver my lady," Sanchez called down to me and laughed. "Most generous!"

I watched in horror, in utter disbelief and shock, as the sergeant major savagely jerked his knife across Zekowtah's throat. The soldier next to him did the same to Zuma. Their limp bodies tumbled over the ledge and started rolling down the hill.

Before I could utter another word, Ashaki raised her musket and shot Sanchez dead. Efendi fired his musket too and dropped the second Spaniard. Below us the woods erupted in smoke and flame.

Xipil and Coyotl did not wait for the others and sprinted past me, wildly swinging their battle axes above their heads, shouting words I did not understand. Without thought or care, I chased after them with Efendi and Ashaki a step or two behind me. Maurice led the rest - men ravenous for the kill - up the slope behind us, howling a thunderous war cry the devil himself would dread.

At the top of the hill, I came face-to-face with death. Standing down in the hollow, his face smeared with streaks of black and red warpaint, the Totonac warrior had his musket pointed at my chest. A soldier on his right and another on his left turned their muskets on me too.

So, this was the end I thought to myself. There would be no shifting to the right or to the left, no parrying or thrusting or falling back. For the briefest of moments, the world around me stopped. Do we turn to dust and sleep forever or do we move on to heaven or hell or something else? Interesting questions to ponder I suppose, though pointless to ponder just the same. My death, long overdue, had come for me at last.

But as I braced myself for pain I could see, out of the corner of my eye, my brave, fearless Ashaki offer her life for mine. She ignored the Spaniard standing in front of her. She stepped in front of me and fired her pistol at one of the soldiers pointing his musket at me. The man stumbled backwards and fell.

In that same instant the Totonac Indian offered me a grim smile but he turned his musket on the other soldier. "For noble Xicohtencatl, the best of all the Aztecs!" he shouted and shot the Spaniard dead.

Then he dropped his musket and drew his hatchet. He turned to strike a soldier standing behind him. But the Spaniard had seen the Indian's treachery and shot him first. I'd never know the warrior's name. I'd never know his story. I only know that but for Ashaki's willingness to trade her life for mine, and the righteousness of a stranger, I would have surely perished that day.

Then the Spaniard with his musket pointed at Ashaki pulled the trigger. I saw the hammer strike the flint, but nothing happened. Wet powder, a bad flint, a broken frizzen spring, I cannot say. With a flick of his wrist Efendi ended the Spaniard's life with one of his sharp blades.

Next a horde of angry men with old and new grudges to settle then ran past me. They descended into the hollow and the day's savagery quickly turned to slaughter. Stunned by our numbers and by the ferocity of our assault, many Spaniards tossed their muskets aside and tried climbing out of the hollow to escape. Others raised their hands to surrender. I saw one man holding a crucifix in his hands drop to his knees and pray. Only a few soldiers fought back. With Maurice leading the charge, Aztecs and Cimmaron ripped through the Spanish like a whirlwind. No one was spared, not even the man who had fallen to his knees to ask God for mercy.

When the screams and wailing faded into to quiet, when the smoke cleared and every Spaniard lay dead, we had little time to squander. The garrison at Viejo would have heard the sounds of battle. The Spanish commander would dispatch a large force to hunt us down. But before we could bury our dead and leave, I watched Efendi and Ashaki dragging a pig of a man by the arms towards me. I saw a musket ball lodged in his temple. I saw a red sash draped diagonally across his chest.

"I only wounded him Mary," Ashaki explained.

I took a moment to study the loathsome abomination standing before me. "You murdered a great man with a noble heart, a prince. I wish to know why?"

When the Spaniard offered me an incomprehensible, senseless grin I slapped him across the face. "You have no honor," I scolded. "Your stupidity and barbarity Sergeant Major Rodrigo Sanchez of the King's Columbian Musketeers have killed yourself and all your men. Any last words?"

When the man refused to answer, I undid the frog fasteners to his doublet. I pulled my dagger from my belt. I took my time pushing the blade through the red sash, through his shirt and in-between his ribs. I savored the moment when he took his last breath, when his eyes went dark forever.

We had lost Zekowtah and Zuma and four of Maurice's men had fallen too during the battle. When I told Maurice and Xipil how the Totonac Indian had traded his life for mine, how he had honored Zekowtah with his own death, they helped me place his body alongside Zekowtah.

From father to son, from mother to daughter, the Aztec pass down the history and the brilliance of their people and will do so until they are no more Zekowtah had once told me. Zekowtah's father's father had been a Cuachicqueh, one of the Shorn Ones, the greatest of all the Aztec warriors, greater than the Cuauhtli, the Eagle Warriors, or the Ocelotl, the Jaguar Warriors. The Cuachicqueh were the bravest of the brave and Zekowtah was every bit his grandfather. With Zekowtah's only child Iztli cruelly cut down in his prime by a spear, it was left to me to retell Zekowtah's story, what I knew of it at least, to any who would listen. I'd keep his name and good deeds alive.

After we hastily placed stones over our dead and offered up our prayers - I had no wine to sprinkle over the hallowed ground, I could make no libation and this, strangely, troubled me - we returned to the lake to retrieve our treasure and then hurried back to our ships as best we could, carrying our heavy metal, our pretty stones and trinkets, with a large company of angry Spaniards out of Viejo only a few strides behind us. We did not pause to rest. We pissed our trousers on the run. And when the Spanish finally caught up to us with our backs against the sea, the outcome might have been disastrous for us but for the six longboats packed with armed men floating into shore and the great guns on my battlecruisers primed and ready. The Spanish wisely turned around and walked away.

We were sailing close-hauled near the coast just off Cartagena on our way back to Guadeloupe when a monstrous storm overtook us. Fearsome winds out of the east whipped-up huge rollers and sent them crashing down into our path. Stinging rains pelted us hard. We set the storm jibs and reefed the main sails. We tossed our sea anchors out. With the blessing of Captain Shaw, I had our best man take the helm.

I had him sail us straight into the angry swells.

I was standing on the quarterdeck with Lololi recounting Ashaki's selfless act of valor at *The Battle for the Hill* for the second or third time in as many days when I saw Efendi sprinting down the main deck towards us. He bolted up the quarterdeck ladder and grabbed me by the arm.

"Mary, Elizabeth is at the bow babbling nonsense," he shouted against the wind. "She's threatening any who try to approach her with her sword."

Before departing the waters of Guna Yala, Kinkae had brought Elizabeth over from *Cerberus* to *Nemesis*. Suffering from severe stomach cramps, coupled with a high fever, vomiting and diarrhea, Kinkae thought it best for Stachel to examine her. After our ship's physician gave Elizabeth a concoction to calm her bowels, he pulled me aside and told me that he strongly suspected Elizabeth had turned to opium again. I decided to keep her close.

I rushed forward to the bow with Efendi and found Elizabeth standing atop a barrel lashed against the bulwarks. Holding a line in one hand for balance and a sword in the other, she was slashing at the air to keep Henry and Kinkae away.

"Elizabeth, do not move!" I commanded as I reached out for her with both arms and offered a comforting smile.

"You're a charlatan, a deceiver Mary," she shouted. "Stay away. You treat me like a servant girl. You think I am simpleton. You think me unworthy of command."

Whatever smile I had vanished. "What?" I asked incredulously. "Have I not always shown you love? Have I not always treated you with respect and kindness - as if we were blood sisters? Did I not make you one of my officers and give you a command?"

"Respect?" Elizabeth scoffed while she stepped up onto the ship's rail just as tremendous wave crashed over the bow, drenching us all in seawater.

I lost my footing when *Nemesis* crested the massive wave and plummeted down into the trough. I had to grab Efendi.

"*Whoa!*" Elizabeth shrieked with a hideous laugh.

How she managed to keep her balance on that rail I shall never know. When I took a step closer, she turned her sword on me.

"That's rich," she said sharply. "Respect from a woman who makes us all grovel at her feet like dogs, who doles out scraps to her serfs whenever it pleases her to do so. Always flaunting your power, always disparaging those around you. Never a kind word to say. Stay back I tell you!"

I began to cry. "Please, please, Elizabeth, step down from there. Let us talk. We can find a way to make amends. We can find peace between us."

"Talk?" she asked as she pulled herself higher up onto the bowsprit just as a bolt of lightning flashed overhead, followed instantly by a deafening clap of thunder. "I don't need to hear you talk your high and mighty majesty. I need you to listen!"

"Have you lost your senses? What are you saying? Please, I beg you, step down from there before you harm yourself. This is the opium talking, not you. If not for me, come down for your brothers. Let them wrap their arms around you - feel their love. We all want to help you."

She turned to look at Henry and Kinkae next. "Ha! Even as I bid you farewell Mary is still barking out orders. Well, I'll show you what I can do! You survived the test, Mary. You cheated the sea. You returned to the world reborn, stronger and wealthier than before and I shall do the same!"

I watched in horror as Elizabeth leapt off the bowsprit. With supernatural quickness Efendi reached out and miraculously caught her by the arm, but only for a second. He had to let her go when she tried to slash his wrist with her sword. In an instant she was gone.

When morning came, with the last remnants of the tempest fading off to the west, we launched our longboats and scoured the waters around Cartagena for hours hoping to find Elizabeth. And then we went ashore. We searched the streets and alleys. We searched the hospital, the taverns and shops, the churches, inns and schools. We combed the beaches too. But we never did find Elizabeth or any hint of her.

Elizabeth is the daughter of Rodriguez Miguel de Cortés y

Ovando. She is a proud, formidable and clever woman. She is a beautiful, resourceful woman. I like to think she somehow made it to shore. I like to think she is alive and well and will find her way back into the world reborn, stronger and wealthier than before.

I kept to my great cabin as our ships scudded across the dark and barren sea for Guadaloupe. I could not eat. I could not sleep. I could not focus my thoughts on much of anything. Shaw and Efendi stood nearby as I wallowed in my misery, as I grieved for Zekowtah and the loss of my poor, tormented Elizabeth.

My mood improved once we reached Guadeloupe and I saw Ling and Jian holding hands, waving happily at us from the beach. I gave our men fifteen days to rest and heal. I gave King Joseph his fair portion of the booty we had taken during our journey west and left another share with Xipil and his people. I would divvy-up the remainder amongst my crews upon our return to Ireland. Each man's take would more than make up for all the lean years they had struggled through. I released my divers from Margarita and paid them too, good lads all. King Joseph invited the boys and Aminatu's people to remain on his island, a place of charm and peace, and they accepted.

When it was time to say our farewells, Ling wanted to sail with me, as did Jian. And though I had grown very fond of both of them, Ling was too frail for the sea and Jian was too young. I worried how the Irish might treat my Chinese family if I left them in Westport and so I took them to Hispaniola with me where I purchased a better than modest inn with a tavern and surplus rooms for Ling and Jian. I hired Ling to manage the establishment and then I had to promise Jian that he could sail with me in one year's time if he obeyed his sister and proved himself a good boy. I left the four exquisite tapestries and the two lovely vases I had pilfered from the *House* - interesting mementos with a story to tell - with Ling to decorate the tavern.

Esmeralda, nearing the end of her days, happily agreed to watch over Ling and Jian for me. She promised to teach Ling - now Madam

Ling - everything she knew about our business and my Chinese sister eagerly accepted her new role as my representative in the New World.

Esmeralda also handed me a thoughtful gift. She had learned the whereabouts of the vile creatures known as Schmidt and Amrrique. They had lost their ship and were stranded in San Juan, an easy day's sail away. I immediately dispatched Efendi and Shaw to find them.

"Welcome to Santo Domingo gentlemen," I said as I stood before the two men a few days later.

Efendi and Shaw had stripped both men naked and had tied them to chairs in the middle of an old, abandoned storehouse outside the city. The wretched pair both stared up at me in disbelief.

"I did warn you," I continued. "Had you not betrayed me, we would not be here now. Mustafa, did you bring it?"

Efendi handed me Mei's black vial of death.

"You have both already been tried and convicted," I said evenly. "As much as I'd enjoy a duel, I'm short on time. Truth is I'm curious to see what the liquid in this bottle does."

"What do you want?" Schmidt asked. "I lost my ship. I have no money."

"Ah, right to the point. I respect that. What can you offer for your freedom?"

"Nothing."

"Nothing? No, you have your life and that will do just fine."

Schmidt smiled contemptuously at me. "Coward," he said and spit.

"What's that you say?" I asked.

"You heard me. You may have taken my man Chang down with a lucky blow, but I'm not Chang. Are you afraid to fight me?"

"Mary," Efendi said, "let's end this now and leave. The ships are ready, the men are waiting."

But I had been in a peculiar mood for days. My thoughts were clear and focused. I had found myself, my true self, and had found my purpose again.

"Mustafa, Rob, untie this man," I said. I raised my hand to cut Efendi off before he could say more.

"Do it," I commanded when Efendi and Shaw both hesitated.

"Might I have my clothes?" Schmidt asked after my brothers untied him. "Seems undignified to fight in the nude."

"Give this man his trousers!" I barked.

"Nuno and I are free once I kill you?" Schmidt asked as we circled around each other.

My answer was a swift, sharp punch to the face. The big German reeled backwards with a bloody nose but caught his balance and lunged at me. He threw several blows and missed. He retreated, removed his belt from his trousers and fiddled with the buckle, a curious thing to do I thought, and whipped the belt at my face. I easily blocked the blow. Even so, I felt something sting my hand.

Schmidt stepped backwards, roaring with laughter. "Ha-ha-ha! I've filed the prong of my buckle down into a needle. I've coated the needle with the venom of the Omdurman Scorpion from Sudan. You'll die without the antidote."

I thought Schmidt was bluffing until I felt a strange numbness spreading up my arm. I started feeling warm, light-headed and unsteady.

"Mustafa, the pig does not lie."

Efendi, two heads shorter than the German, brought the man down with one sharp kick to the shin. I heard the snap of bone.

"The antidote, give it to me now!" Efendi demanded as he put a knife against Schmidt's throat.

"Let me go and you shall have it," Schmidt replied, clenching his teeth in pain. "You can keep my man there as a hostage to guarantee my return."

"Nooo, don't leave me here to die Conrad!" Amrrique pleaded.

Efendi turned to me. "You're sweating Mary. We may not have much time if this coward is telling the truth. Rob and I will go with him to get the antidote."

"No Mustafa," I said. "He's lying about the antidote. Whatever happens next is fate."

I took my knife and pricked Schmidt's hand, just enough to draw a bead or two of blood, and poured a drop of Mei's potion into the wound. "What I do now is not for my own personal retribution as you might suppose Conrad, as sweet as that would be. In the name of unholy *Vengeance* this is my gift to all those who you would have done injury to in the future."

Then I walked over to Amrrique and did the same. We left the bodies in the storehouse to rot and God could judge me later.

Efendi and Shaw carried me on a makeshift litter to Ling's new establishment. I suffered with cramps, hallucinations and the sweats for several days. Ling and Efendi rarely left my side and when they slept, the twins stood watch over me while Stachel slept in a room close by and looked in on me every few hours. I did not die.

I had one last debt to settle before setting out for Ireland. I led us into the quiet waters of Bahía Vizcaína and to the Tequesta village called Chequescha where a holy man named Tayhoot, who against his will was still chief, and his people had once been kind to me. I gave the Tequesta gifts and when it was time for us to sail, we left behind new friends and promising allies.

Mindful of Efendi's concerns about young James, I was at first uncertain what to do. He was a fine lad with a genteel nature and a kind heart. I decided I'd toughen him up as best I could for the challenging days ahead. But not every man can be a killer and so I decided to introduce the boy to navigation and chart making, skills highly prized by all mariners. Upon our return to Ireland, I'd also need to let Efendi and Shaw make their pilgrimage east to the lands of the Ottoman, as much as it would distress me to do so.

And as for me, I've always detested loose ends. Not knowing whether Elizabeth was alive or dead weighed heavily on me. Having failed to find the mysterious half-breed Arslan troubled me too. And then there was the Dutchman. I hoped to find a letter from Dijksma waiting for me back in Westport. I was curious to know what favor I owed him. I was curious to know if I could settle down, if I could find love's joy again.

Despite the hardships and the dangers, I'd always been happiest, I was at my best, when sailing across a rolling sea seeking out adventure in some faraway land. With some notion of a plan rattling around in my head, with a sound ship under my feet and good men to lead, I was game for anything. Perhaps, I thought, the Dutchman would join me...

Afterword

On March 20, 1602 the Dutch government created the world's first publicly-traded company, the Dutch United East India Company, by merging several rival trading companies into a single powerhouse. The Dutch gave the Company, or the VOC, extraordinary powers to wage war, imprison and execute convicts, negotiate treaties, strike its own coins and to colonize territories around the globe.

In the 1600's sailing from the Netherlands to East Indies at seven knots (thirteen kilometers per hour) took roughly eight months. Between two to three fleets departed from the Netherlands each year carrying thousands of Europeans to the East Indies and returned with countless tons of nutmeg, mace, pepper, cloves, cinnamon, tea, and other commodities like silks, cottons (the finely decorated chintz cotton was especially popular in Europe), opium, gold, silver, copper and porcelains. The Company's profits, even by today's standards, were nothing less than astonishing (the Company sometimes even burned down whole warehouses full of spices to keep prices artificially high). The Company established settlements, trading posts and colonies in the Cape of Good Hope, Persia (Iran), Bengal (Bangladesh), Malacca (Malaysia), Siam (Thailand), China, Formosa (Taiwan), southern India (from Surat to Calcutta) and Jakarta. By 1669, with over 50,000 employees, 150 merchant ships, 40 warships, and a private army of 10,000 men, the VOC had evolved into the world's first international mega corporation.

Dutch expansion into the East however came with a heavy price. Generally known as the Spice Wars, the Dutch were dragged into one expensive conflict after another with the mighty (and jealous) empires of Spain, Portugal and England. In 1799, following the financially disastrous Fourth Anglo-Dutch War (1780 - 1784), the Dutch government nationalized and eventually dissolved the VOC. Still, it is truly remarkable - a testament to Dutch brilliance - that a small nation of only about a million and a half people at the beginning of the 17th Century, with little in land or natural resources and fighting a costly war for independence against Spain, the great super power of the age, achieved so much.

A quick note on style. As with *The Butcher's Daughter* and *Blood for Blood*, I've written in a contemporary voice because we live in contemporary times. Even so, I've tried using words and phrases the men and women of the 16th and 17th Centuries would have understood and used themselves and to this end the Online Etymology Dictionary has been a wonderful resource.

Odds & Ends

VOC Territories (shaded areas)

Vereenigde Oostindische Compagnie Flag & Logo

The Dutch galleon *Mauritus* by Hendrick Cornelisz Vroom (1600)

Return of Jacob van Neck in July 1599 by Cornelis Vroom

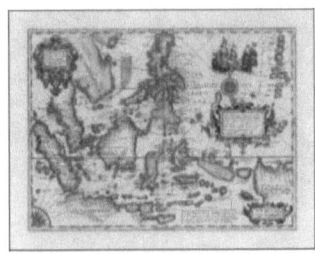

East Indies, 1604
by Jodocus Hondius, Flemish engraver and cartographer

Jayakarta (Batavia) 1605 - 1608

Ambon (early 1700's)

Macau in 1598 by Theodor de Bry

Japanese Red Seal ship (1634)

Araki ("Wild Tree")

Crest Oda Clan Crest

17th Century Kora-Kora by *Joan Blaeu - Atlas Major*
Published from 1662 to 1665, the *Blaeu Atlas Major* or *Cosmographia Blaviana*, with 594 stunning maps, exquisite illustrations and 3,368 pages of text, was one of the most expensive and extravagant multi-volume works of its time.

Spitfire may seem like a modern name. Built in 1534 by the Portuguese, the 1000-ton, 366-gun *São João Baptista* (nicknamed *Botafogo, Spitfire*) was the most powerful ship in the world.

Fort A Famosa at Malacca

M. McMillin

The Bourse d'Amsterdam (1611)

(复仇)

Fùchóu - Vengeance

He was a brilliant young man, cut down needlessly in his prime by
greed and stupidity;
She was the brightest of torches, extinguished too soon by a ruthless
disease.
Godspeed dear brother; Godspeed dear sister...

For

Robert G. McMillin and *Suzanne Grace Maiden*